MAXWELL'S MATCH

School can be murder...

On a two-week staff exchange, Peter 'Mad Max' Maxwell leaves behind his familiar comprehensive for the altogether more sophisticated charms of Grimond's, a private school steeped in tradition and money, but within a day of his arrival Maxwell has yet again stumbled upon a suspicious unnatural death. Two days later another teacher is dead, and this time it's definitely murder. With journalists besieging the school and parents in a panic, the Headmaster is scrambling to preserve Grimonds' reputation. When Maxwell's girlfriend, DS Jacquie Carpenter gets assigned to the case he soon finds himself involved in a complex investigation...

MAXWELL'S MATCH

MAXWELL'S MATCH

by

M. J. Trow

Magna Large Print Books
Long Preston, North Yorkshire,
BD23 4ND, England.

British Library Cataloguing in Publication Data.

Trow, M. J.
  Maxwell's match.

  A catalogue record of this book is
  available from the British Library

  ISBN   978-0-7505-2912-9

First published in Great Britain in 2003 by Allison & Busby Ltd.

Copyright © 2002 by M. J. Trow

Cover illustration © Brighton Studios by arrangement with
Allison & Busby Ltd.

The moral right of the author has been asserted

Published in Large Print 2008 by arrangement with
Allison & Busby Ltd.

Magna Large Print is an imprint of Library Magna Books Ltd.

Printed and bound in Great Britain by
T.J. (International) Ltd., Cornwall, PL28 8RW

Chapter One

He stood in the doorway for a while, shoulders heaving with exertion, then half-stumbled into the pool of light. His shadow grew long on the floor and his face was a mask of terror. He still held the doorframe with his left hand, the long blade flashing silver in his right, tilted down. For a moment he stood there, swaying in a silence that was deafening.

'For Christ's sake!' a voice boomed in the darkness, followed by the thud of a lib hitting the hall floor. 'This whole bloody play is about blood. It drips through every speech, it's smeared on every action. Macbeth is knee deep in the stuff. He actually says, does he not, Sanjit, "Blood will have blood"? Not that I've heard you say that since the read-through. The point is, I can't see any. Donna!'

A confused face appeared around a curtain and there were sniggers and whistles, while Sanjit, the Thane of Cawdor, took five.

'Are you or are you not Make-up?'

Donna blinked and grinned, the prerogative of make-up artists the world over. She who didn't want the limelight was now staring blindly into it.

'Did I or did I not specifically ask you to smear Macbeth's dagger with blood? Tanya!'

A second face appeared downstage left, as blank as the first. 'Shouldn't there be two daggers, dear?

You being Props and all. Macbeth's just dispatched the guards; careful to smear their weapons with Duncan's blood, right? So where's the other one gone? Two guards, two daggers. Can it really be so difficult?'

'Er ... that's my fault, Paul.' Another voice trilled, female this time and over the PA, more disembodied than Hamlet's father, but that was another story. 'I can't quite put my hand on... Oh, thank you, Benny.'

'Lights!' Paul Nicolson had always seen himself as a latter day Cecil B. DeMille and, as they flicked on, he blinked in the cold reality of Leighford High School Hall, with its rows of assembly seats clamped together for opening night. All he lacked really was the pair of jodhpurs, bullwhip and multi-million dollar budget.

'Tanya – two daggers. Donna – heavy on the ketchup, if you please. Take five everybody.' He ignored the fact that Sanjit already was and the Great Director swept from the scene.

'Fag, miss?' Benny was the most enterprising props assistant Sally Greenhow had ever worked with. He was the charmer of the Special Needs group, as cuddly as you could be with acne, terminal psychosis and a fetish for his willy hat.

Sally Greenhow loomed over the lad in the darkness of the wings. That was how Benny liked it, with Miss's tits at his eye-level, modelling smarties under the purple ribbed jumper. He could certainly have a roll in that neck, but Benny was far too fly to let his libido show in his day job.

'Get thee behind me, Satan,' Sally said, tapping the lad's outstretched hand, and taking the

Lord's name in vain at the same time. 'You'll get me the sack. Where was that knife?'

'Sticking in Mr Nicolson's back with a bit of luck,' Benny grunted. Sally peered around the curtain to see the first and second violins fencing with their bows. How true. How true.

There was only one other soul in the staffroom, that bastion of sanity from which knights valiant and ladies fair rode out to do battle daily with the dragons of indifference and the ogres of stupidity.

'Tell me, Max,' Nicolson threw himself down in the nearest soft chair, paid for by a lottery bid, 'why didn't I do *Hello Dolly* rather than the Scottish Play?'

'Because, dear boy, you couldn't have lived with yourself. Froth before the Bard, tat before pure gold... We'd have found you twirling from the rugger posts by now. Assuming, of course, that we had any rugger posts. Coffee?'

'Ah, you darling man.'

'Have a care,' Max twirled with a practised hand to the coffee machine behind him. 'In these politically correct days, the merest whiff of our torrid romance could spell Sunday serialisation for us both.'

Peter Maxwell already had his shapeless tweed hat perched on his barbed wire hair, ready for the off. Paul Nicolson didn't need to look down to know that his corduroy trouser bottoms were clipped for the pedals and he didn't need to see the bike sheds to know that Maxwell's bespoked steed, White Surrey, shone in the late afternoon sun, waiting for its master, champing at the padlock. 'No sugar, I'm afraid. I'd offer to run up to the second floor and get some from my office, but I can't be arsed.'

'Nectar.' Nicolson took the mug with both hands.

'Dress jitters?' Maxwell noticed the slight tremble in the fingers and the yellowing of the eyeballs. Tell-tale signs.

'Don't ask. Ever produced a show?'

'Christ, no.' Maxwell flicked open the Staff Suggestions Book, still, after all these years, dangling from its ancient string like some chained monastic tome, all part of a feeble ploy to make the staff believe that Leighford High was some sort of democracy where feelings were considered and opinions counted. 'I don't need the nightmares. Sam not cutting the mustard as he who is not of woman born?'

'Oh, Sam's all right, considering his dad's chairman of governors and all. Sanjit's fine as Macbeth – I knew he would be. And you were right, by the by, to advise not to do this as a modern dress Hindu-Muslim thing. And that juvenile bastard playing Duncan's grown up since I read him his future in a tarot pack after he chose to misquote in the Technical.'

'Misquote?' Maxwell was mentally elsewhere, lambasting the Deputy Head in the Suggestions Book with a suggestion that was unlikely, probably illegal and almost certainly, physically impossible.

'"What" – and I misquote – "fucking man is that?!"'

'Ah, adolescent wit at its finest,' the Head of

Sixth Form smiled, but he tucked it away for later, just in case. He was, after all, Mad Max and he and one-liners went hand in hand.

'Max,' a bespectacled head appeared round the staff room door. It was the Headmaster, as Maxwell still quaintly called him, James Diamond, B.Sc., M.A., T.W.A.T. 'Could I have a word?'

'Black Rod,' Maxwell beamed at Nicolson. 'A fine ancient tradition we'd do well to implement here.' Maxwell the historian knew perfectly well that the allusion was entirely lost on Diamond the biologist. And he hung the Suggestions Book back by the darts board. 'A word only, Headmaster, I fear. My 1,265 hours were up last week and this half of the term's only four days old.'

James Diamond – 'Legs' to Peter Maxwell in memory of the Prohibition gangster of the same name – never knew when to take his Head of Sixth Form seriously. Usually it was when he stood like an ox in the furrow, his mouth set firm, his head sunk onto his shoulders. Always, it was when he heard the dread words 'With respect, Headmaster...'

James Diamond was pushing forty-five, but he seemed a different generation from Peter Maxwell. He was of the managerial school of headteachers, all clipboards and mission statements. He had no rapport with kids whatsoever.

They stood in the draughty corridor of the mad March day, the Headmaster and his Head of Sixth Form. A slip of a girl from the front office slithered past, hoping to make a quiet exit.

'Good night, Thingee,' Maxwell's eagle gaze

had caught her, like a rabbit in his over-meta-phored headlights.

'Goodnight, Mr Maxwell. Goodnight, Mr Diamond.'

'Goodnight, Sophie.' Diamond's artificial smile broke, Blair-like, across his blank face.

'So that's her name,' Maxwell clicked his fingers. He'd only known the woman for three years. 'The word, Headmaster?'

'Oh, yes,' Diamond took his Head of Sixth Form gingerly by the arm and led him towards his office. 'You know I was on a course over half term?'

'Were you, Headmaster? Such devotion. I was in the pub.'

'Er ... yes,' Diamond grinned. 'Well, I got talking, like you do, to this chap from Grimond's...'

'Where?' the voice called from the kitchen.

'Grimond's. It's a private school in north Hampshire. Petersfield way.'

'Why you?' the voice wanted to know.

Peter Maxwell stretched his slippered feet out onto the pouffé, wondering how long it would be before his big toe finally worked its way through the plush. 'Legs said it was because I went to a school rather like it. Not sure anybody else on the staff could cope with the culture shock.'

'It's not you I feel sorry for, it's the poor bastard who's coming to Leighford.'

The voice appeared in the doorway, framed by the neon brightness behind her. Maxwell loved her most in those jeans, stone-washed and patched like those tatty, sad little teddy bears they sold nowadays, tufted and grey. Her head was on one side, her hair piled high on her head. He knew that face so well, even in the half light of his B&Q electrics, that warmth, that love.

'Policewoman Carpenter,' Maxwell arched an eyebrow. 'I hope you're not casting any kind of nasturtiums on that great centre of excellence, our local comprehensive school, whose sixth form, I might add, is led by a luminary of legendary legerdemain ... sorry, am I talking bollocks?'

'Coffee?' she passed him a mug and sat next to him, nuzzling her hair against his shoulder.

'That was mighty fine blueberry pie, ma'am.' It was pure Alan Ladd to Jean Arthur, the mysterious gunfighter Shane thanking the loyal pioneer wife Marian Starrat for his home-cooked meal. Policewoman Carpenter was just a *little* young to notice.

'But I still don't understand,' she nestled back into the strong arms that folded round her.

'Conferences,' Maxwell told her. 'They're all the same, especially residential ones. Some of those keynote speakers are bloody good and they enthuse their audiences. Away from the classroom, even the most jaded cynic gets carried away. Legs Diamond is, alas, not the most jaded cynic. In fact, he's nauseatingly gung-ho. Kind of idiot who says he's doing it all for the kids, you know.'

'And you're not, I suppose?' She looked up his nostrils, digging him in the ribs at the same time.

'You know I couldn't eat a whole one, Jacquie,' Maxwell said. 'Anyhow, the idea apparently cropped up about sharing colleagues' experiences

13

from other schools. Best practice, that kind of thing. Probably took the Secretary of State for Education's notion to heart about what we can learn from the Private Sector. Dear old Legs probably had his first drink during the week, got talking over the snowballs and crème de menthe and before you know it, wham, an exchange is on between Grimond's and us. Talk about chalk and cheese...'

'So who's coming here?'

'Here to Columbine, no one,' Maxwell assured her. 'I've had a word with Nursie...'

'Max,' Jacquie Carpenter sat upright, her head catching Maxwell a sharp one on his nose. 'Oh, sorry. You're not imposing on Sylvia Matthews...'

'Sylvia Matthews's middle names are Imposed Upon,' Maxwell said. 'We talked long and hard and she said she'd be delighted. Guy's doing supply in Portsmouth at the moment and he can't get back easily, so it's perfect. Bit of company and pocket-money for her. And my swap-mate won't have the chore of going out for his own take-aways.'

'Men!' Jacquie shook her head and reached forward for her mug. 'Talking of which ... hello, Count.'

The large black and white Tom known as Metternich sidled around the lounge door. Named after the coachman of Europe who kicked ass in the Congress of Vienna when Maxwell was a boy, his feline namesake took no prisoners. Hunting was slow tonight. And he wasn't about to tell these two he'd lost a field mouse up at the Rec. He merely twitched his iron-grey whiskers and

14

shrugged his heavy shoulders. One little mistake. He knew he'd done it. And why. The third toss in the air, that's always the one. He'd flipped too high and the terrified little bugger had bounced on the hedge and done a scamper. Well, the night was young. He'd get him on the way back. But now, time to bury his nose in some of the tinned stuff. Okay, it had E-numbers, but at least it stayed still in the bowl and didn't give you fur balls.

Metternich still wasn't sure about Jacquie Carpenter. It had been six months since she and the old Duffer had cemented their relationship – whatever, to a neutered Tom, that meant. The smell of her was everywhere. She hadn't exactly moved in to Metternich's demesne at 38, Columbine, but things had appeared in Maxwell's bedroom that Metternich had only ever seen dangling on other people's washing lines. And after all those years of solitary bachelor life, Metternich shook his head. The writing, had he been literate, was definitely on the wall.

Maxwell threw the arrival a cat nip mouse. The great piebald beast flicked an ear and padded upstairs for a quiet nap before resuming the hunt. He had no need of such artificial prophylactics. He'd call in to the kitchen for eats on the way out.

'And when is all this happening?' Jacquie settled back on Maxwell's chest again.

'Two weeks today. The Grimond bloke is coming down on the Sunday. I go up the same day. I imagine it'll be sub-le Carré at the end; me and him being swapped back like spies on some windswept bridge.'

15

'That's assuming they want you back,' she murmured and he pressed a cushion, lovingly, over her face.

Chapter Two

It had to be said that Peter Maxwell was not cock-a-hoop with the idea, going into his place of work on the Sabbath. In the old days, when his hair was still chestnut and that nice Mr Bonar Law was at Number Ten, he had his own key to the door of Leighford High and came and went as he pleased. Many was the UCAS reference he'd scribbled in the dead of a Leighford night, huddled in coat and scarf against the Autumn cold, cocooned by the over-glassed, leaky box that some sixties architect considered ultra-chic.

Now it was all alarms and pre-set buttons, CCTV cameras and electronics beyond his comprehension. The kids of Year Eleven had taken a deputation, stirred up by Peter Maxwell, to the Headmaster, on the suspicion that there were secret cameras in the loos.

'Not my idea, Betty,' the Head of Sixth Form said again to the long-suffering caretaker Bert Martin. Ever a stranger to others' susceptibilities, Maxwell called a spade a spade. Earlier generations of kids and most of the staff called Bert Martin 'Doc' after the boots. Maxwell called him 'Betty' after 'All My Eye of a Yarn and Betty Martin', but since he knew the Latin original *and* its meaning, everybody, including Bert Martin, thought it best to let it go.

'What time's he coming, then?' Martin asked.

'This whatsisface?'

'Graham,' Maxwell waited while the keeper rattled his keys. 'Anthony. Don't you hate people with Christian names for surnames? Causes endless confusion in my book. Thanks, Betty. I'll be in my office.'

'I'm not a bloody receptionist, you know,' Martin reminded him.

'Right,' Maxwell winked at his man, clicking his teeth. He bounced up the wide stairs that led to the mezzanine floor. Macbeth's posters still fluttered sadly in the post-production anti-climax. It hadn't been too bad in the end, apart from everybody sniggering at the witches and Lady MacB drying up completely while washing her damned spots. Most of the comments were flattering enough. *The Leighford Advertiser* seemed to like it, allowing for the pre-pubescence of its editor. In the awful cold turkey of the after-show experience, both Donna and Tanya could be seen weeping buckets in the Sixth Form Common Room, along with Sanjit. Maxwell had risked his reputation and his career by putting an avuncular arm around both girls and they had sniffed their way to their lessons. With Sanjit he'd merely nodded wisely. It was a man thing.

The Head of Sixth Form hauled off his hat in front of the photograph of the Secretary of State for Education with a nauseating Legs Diamond smiling over her left shoulder and genuflected as well as a middle-aged man in a hurry could, before rounding the corner to his own inner sanctum.

He unlocked, banged on the kettle switch and

threw his hat onto the desk.

'Memos, memos everywhere,' he murmured. 'Christ, I need a drink.' Around the walls of his magic den, the film posters that represented a quarter of his life stretched out in endless line. A tortured Victor McLaglen pointed a damning finger at him in *The Informer;* a distraught Vivien Leigh ran towards him from burning Atlanta in *Gone With the Wind;* Michael Caine stared blankly at him from behind his scenic shades in *The Ipcress File* almost mouthing the words 'Hello, I'm an espionage expert' and four terrified actors, wet and still hysterical, prayed to him in the roaring rapids in *Deliverance.*

The Spring Term. Maxwell stretched out on the low chair and closed his eyes. Why didn't they stop all this nonsense of the wandering Easter, the moveable feast? It played merry Hamlet with his revision schedules and for the first time since the introduction of pay for teachers, he actually approved of a government initiative – the six term year. Well, he was a funny age.

'Mr Maxwell?' The Head of Sixth Form jerked his eyes open. God. Had he dropped off? The years clinging perilously to the chalk face had clearly taken their toll. 'Your caretaker showed me up. Anthony Graham.'

'Ah,' Maxwell took the man's hand. He was a rather cadaverous young man, like the corpse in the *Death and the Lady* painting by Baldung, only with more hair. 'My friends call me Max.'

'Max. I'm Tony.'

'This brown stuff is what passes for coffee at Leighford, Tony. Join me?'

19

'Why not? It's good of you to give up your Sunday.'

'I live here anyway,' Maxwell said. 'How was the journey?'

'Fine.'

'You drove?'

'Yes. I'm parked by the steps. Is that all right?'

'Perfect.' Maxwell rattled the mugs in his hunt for the school spoon. 'Especially if you're in the space marked "Head". Tell me ... Tony, are you happy about this? The exchange, I mean?'

'Well ... er...'

Both men laughed. 'No,' Maxwell broke the ice. 'Me neither. Your Head a particularly deranged sort, is he?'

'Off the wall. Yours?'

'As a wagon-load of monkeys. Still, I suspect I'm getting the better deal.'

'Oh?'

'Well, the food can't be worse than Leighford, believe me. Word to the wise,' he patted the side of his nose, 'real people don't eat quiche.'

Graham laughed again, taking Maxwell's proffered seat. 'That's Jesus,' he pointed to the Head of Sixth Form's scarf, dangling from the door handle.

'I'm impressed. Don't tell me you're a Cambridge man?'

'Peterhouse.'

Maxwell's face fell. 'Ah, not quite, then. What did you read? Legs said you were a Housemaster.'

'Legs?'

'Diamond. You know, the gangster. Actually, anyone less like a smooth psychotic killing

20

machine I can't imagine.'

'Well, I'm a linguist at heart. French with German. I'm not quite sure how I drifted into the pastoral bit.'

'Ah, indeed. Drift is the right word for it. The Geographers use it a lot, don't they? Tectonics or something. Seems to go with the vagueness of the subject. How's the coffee?'

'Fine,' Graham smiled.

'Liar,' Maxwell growled.

Graham was taking in the room. 'Now, don't tell me you're a film buff?'

'I dabble.' Maxwell was modesty itself.

'Me too,' Graham enthused. 'You know, they ought to re-release *The Informer*. Wonderful stuff. We've got a film society at Grimond's. You must go to one of their screenings. I never miss.'

'Excellent,' Maxwell said. 'I will. Now, come on. Let me show you round the zenith of flat-topped sixties kitsch, over a school built for four hundred that now houses three times that. A learned institution where our Maths GCSE results have been known to reach double figures.'

Graham looked oddly at him.

'Just kidding,' Maxwell slapped the cadaver on the back and led him out to the harsh light of the mezzanine day. 'They never have.'

The lights along the Shingle twinkled in the black-purple that stretched away from 38 Columbine. Maxwell was sitting in his swivel, the modelling chair in which he escaped from the cares of the 21st century. He'd cracked Eleven Zed's explanation for British appeasement in the

21

'30s, resisting the urge to consign the lot to his wastebasket having smothered their books in red ink. Unable to face yet another explanation of the outbreak of plague in 1665 from Year Seven, he pushed their pile of books out of sight and trundled up to his attic, that Holy of Holies on top of the world where another quarter of his life stretched out under the lamplight.

Three-hundred-and-twenty-three plastic horsemen, immaculately modelled and painted, sat on their troop-horses patiently, waiting for word from the Sapouné Heights. On the desk in front of him, under the fixed magnifying lens, lay William Perkins, number three-hundred-and-twenty-four.

'Trumpeter to you, Count,' Maxwell said, although to be fair, the cat hadn't asked.

The great beast was dozing, dreaming of the rat-haunted night and the crack of bones in his jaws. Why the idiot who provided the tinned stuff should closet himself up here with those weird bits of white he proceeded to stick together and change their colour, Metternich couldn't imagine.

'Hence, oh, bugger...' the tiny bugle slipped from Maxwell's fingers and vanished somewhere in the darkness of the carpet. Why, oh why had he bought a brown one? He joined the piece of plastic on the floor, patting the tufts in the blackness until he found it. 'Oh, shit. Sharp, aren't they,' his crimson head bobbed up again. 'Plastic bugles? As Perkins was in the 11th, he'd have spent most of his time playing *Coburg* on this instrument. *Coburg*, Count, it's the slow march of the 11th

22

Hussars, in honour of their Colonel, Prince Albert. Of *Coburg*. Get it? What do we know of Trumpeter Perkins, I hear you ask? Not a lot, really.'

Maxwell concentrated, frowning as he stuck the plastic bugle onto the plastic back. 'He enlisted in 1846. Rode the Charge of course, hence his inclusion in the Diorama of Fame. Became a Trumpet-Major eventually. Lived in Forest Gate, Essex – well, I suppose somebody had to. Do you know...'

That black plastic thing shattered Metternich's peace. The sharp, metallic ring it made always evoked the same response in his Master. Sure enough, as Metternich watched, Maxwell reached across and started talking into it. At least that made the ringing stop.

'...he was a bog attendant at an underground lavvy somewhere in the City? Fancy that. War Office?'

'Max. Sylv.'

'Nursie, darling.'

'Is this a good time?'

Maxwell laid Trumpeter Perkins down on his face to let his bugle dry. 'Always a good time for you, Sylv.'

There had been a time when Sylvia Matthews's heart would have leapt at those words. Now, it just gave her a warm glow. She'd loved Peter Maxwell once and loved him still in a way. But there was her Guy and his Jacquie and an ocean of ifs in between. It had been time for them both to move on. They had. But Sylvia was still Matron at Leighford High, the Florence Nightingale of the comprehensive system, patrolling the corridors with her lamp and Morning After pills.

'Thought I'd fill you in on your swap-mate.'

'Tony? You bitch, I'd thought you'd never ring. Do tell.'

'Well, he seems very nice. Not at all the snob I thought he'd be. Into films, just like you.'

'Now, Sylvia Matthews, wash your mouth out. Snob, indeed. There but for the grace of a careless job application thirty odd years ago...'

'You've never taught in the Private Sector, have you, Max?'

'Amazingly, no. The nearest I've come is a Grammar School. I'm looking forward to Grimond's. The staff there will all be Oxbridge by way of MGS.'

'MGS?'

'Mighty great shitheads. You know the type.'

'Well, Tony's not like that.'

'I'm sure he's not,' Maxwell reached across for his nightly tumbler of Southern Comfort, the amber nectar glowing in the half light. 'Will he cope, do you think? At Leighford?'

'Will he be doing any teaching?'

'That's up to Legs, I suppose. Can he, d'you think?'

'Ten Bee Four might have him for elevenses,' Sylvia was surmising, knowing her charges as well, if not better, than Maxwell. 'Incidentally, while I remember, you won't be seeing Michelle Whitmore for a while.'

'Termination?'

'Septic piercings.'

'Ah, the curse of the artistically challenged. And

24

don't tell me where on her person; I haven't long eaten. What of Private Tony?'

'Bit of a mummy's boy, I'd say. Daddy was a civil servant.'

'Retired?'

'Dead, I believe.'

'Well, that's the Civil Service for you.'

'He's got a way with him, though.'

Maxwell felt rather than heard the silence. 'Oh?' Sylvia could hear his eyebrow rising.

'Oh, it's nothing. Just a way he has of ... oh, focussing, I suppose.'

'Focussing?' Maxwell repeated. 'Come on, Sylv. I invented body language, remember? What are you talking about?'

'Well, he *looks* at you. *Listens*. Really listens. You know Legs, how his eyes are always glancing everywhere else in case somebody more important is passing...'

'You're being unkind, Nurse Matthews,' Maxwell scolded. 'He's put his personality down somewhere and can't find it, that's all.'

'And Maurice Bell,' Sylvia went on. 'He's always just staring at my cleavage.'

'Oh, thank God,' Maxwell patted his chest. 'I thought it was just mine.'

'Well, Tony really cares. Or if he doesn't, he's a bloody good actor. And ideas. He's really full of them. I must admit, I'm a fan. He was very taken with you.'

'Aw shucks!' Maxwell rolled his head in the best Slim-Pickens-deep-South anyone was likely to see East of the Pecos. 'I jest bet he says that to all the good ol' boys.'

'No, seriously. He said you'd fit like a hand in a glove at Grimond's. Said you were larger than life. The sort of master he'd had at school.'

'Ah, yes,' Maxwell chuckled. He'd heard that before. 'The vanishing breed.'

'I told him the kids call you Mad Max.'

'As well they might. Here I am, fifty-something, in the prime of my life, with another desperate round of GCSE and A-levels imminent and I'm going to waste my time doing ... what? Buggered if I know.'

'You're going to enjoy yourself, Max,' Sylvia told him. 'Relax for a bit. You owe it to yourself.'

'Sylv,' he said. 'I am feeling guilty.'

'What about?'

'Foisting Tony on you.'

'Oh, don't be silly,' she blustered. 'It's not so bad. It's only for a fortnight.'

'Keep me posted,' Maxwell smiled and hung up, shaking his head. 'Methinks, Count,' he looked wryly at the cat, 'the lady doth not protest nearly half enough.'

Maxwell said his farewells as dawn climbed behind Leighford abattoir, as it normally did about that time each Monday morning.

'Well, I think that's the lot, Count.' He glanced across the hall at the piebald beast who sat in the way that cats do, his left hind leg upright behind his ear, his nose up his bum. Rather there than somebody else's, Maxwell always supposed.

'Now, it's not for long.'

No sound but the slap of fur on fur.

'Look, this is a man thing, Count. When two

26

old chums say goodbye, well,' he shrugged, 'they don't get all girlie and dewy eyed. They just say "Sayonara". That's if they're two old Japanese chums, of course. Otherwise, they just say "Ciao". But of course, that makes them Italian … oh, bollocks, Count, you know my views. Jacquie'll be in with the goodies tonight. And, yes, Mrs B. is still coming to clean on Wednesdays, as per usual. Now, you behave yourself. And remember…' he wagged a warning finger, 'any lady friends in and you make sure you've got protection, okay?' And Maxwell left.

Metternich had barely time to lift the other leg behind his ear when his master reappeared. 'Oh, but I forgot. *That's* why I had you done all those years ago, wasn't it? So that we wouldn't hear the scamper of tiny little pads? No, no,' he gushed. 'Don't thank me now.' And the front door clicked behind him.

He was on the train. Along with a few hundred others, wondering if they'd ever get to work that day, next day, sometime never. He'd done his homework, he reflected, as the Hampshire fields flew by, already a pale green with the Spring sowing. Jedediah Grimond had been a nabob, one of those scions of the none too honourable East India Company who had sailed to the sub-continent two centuries ago with not much more than the clothes he stood up in and a writing slope full of unbridled optimism. When he came back, he had somehow acquired a small fortune and become carriage folk. Grimond's was his country pad, a modest little thousand hectares or so with grooms, under-butlers and tweenies without number. But death and taxes caught up with Jedediah Grimond and his descendants, as they do with us all, and the house sold to pay death duties. It was a convalescent home for officers during the Great War and had become a school during the '30s.

'Coffee, sir?'

Maxwell turned from the window to peruse the cornucopia of delights available on the Southern Train trolley. It didn't take him long.

'Mr Maxwell?' He turned at the sound of his name, glad to be off the train with its mobile-phone users and terminal coughers and on the windy platform at Petersfield. A tall, sandy-haired young man stood there, hand extended.

'David Gallow. I'm Head of History at Grimond's.'

'Mr Gallow.' Maxwell shook it.

'David, please. I gather from Dr Sheffield you've come to do a spot of observation.'

'Observation?' Maxwell followed the younger man through the station concourse. 'I had hoped for a spot of teaching, even. Who knows?'

'You're familiar with AQA courses?' Gallow checked, flicking his electronic remote as they reached the car park.

'My dear boy,' Maxwell smiled. 'I *wrote* most of them.'

Gallow's laugh was brittle. 'Well, we'll see. How was your journey?'

'Please,' Maxwell scowled. 'There are some things that are just too painful. You have a Head of Sixth Form?'

Gallow looked sideways at him, helping him load his bags into the car boot. 'After a fashion.'

'Ah.'

'No, no,' Gallow laughed again. 'I'm not being Machiavellian; it's just that, as you may know, Grimond's has not too distantly joined forces with a girls' school, St Hilda's.'

'I read your prospectus,' Maxwell clicked into his seatbelt.

'Two different systems – our Houses versus their Years – vertical and horizontal. It hasn't been easy. Noses can so easily be put out of joint, can't they?'

'Tell me about it,' Maxwell grunted. 'Do you live in?'

'Yes, I'm an Assistant House Master. I used to have a little place here in Petersfield. Not far from Churchers, as a matter of fact, so there was not much respite from the sound of leather on willow. Are you a cricket man?'

'Not since the Don,' Maxwell shook his head. 'But isn't it ... what? The Cross Country season still?'

'Till Easter, yes,' Gallow crunched his way through the gears of his Audi, 'Then it's back to flannels.'

'Oafs at the wicket, eh?' he smiled at the Head of History, who didn't seem to take the misquotation at all well.

It was a pleasant drive, as a pale sun at last climbed its way above the morning mist. The road snaked out before them and they purred north-west under the rising ground of Butser Hill with its Iron Age ghosts, past East Meon with its half-timbered cosiness and the wraith of Izaak Walton, the Great Fisherman, dozing by the river bank.

'Over there,' Gallow was providing the running commentary, 'is West Meon, burial place of Thomas Lord.' He noted Maxwell's blank expression. 'As in Lords,' the Head of History patronized. 'You know, the cricket ground.'

Maxwell nodded. 'As my memory serves,' he said, 'he's rubbing shoulders – and let's hope nothing else – with dear old Guy Burgess, friendly neighbourhood defector and spy.'

The running commentary came to an end.

It was much as Maxwell expected; a smallish Palladian red-brick pile, Jedediah's old house, dwarfed by a plate-glass add-on not unlike his own Leighford High. He knew at once, though, that here, things were different. There was no patronizing County sign "Learning to make a difference"; no burnished-spray graffito telling the world what it already knew, that "Diamond is a wanker"; no crèche for unmarried Year Eleven girls by the school gate. Instead, there were ancient gateposts and an elegant coat of arms emblazoned on both, where wrought iron lions roared defiance in the sun. That would be right. Maxwell's homework told him that old Jedediah Grimond had bought his K along with every-thing else that wasn't his birthright. And the College of Arms wasn't above adding to its coffers by drafting the odd heraldic design in exchange for a little folding stuff.

Gallow's car crunched on the Grimond gravel and he unhooked the boot. 'Mr Maxwell,' he said before he opened his door, 'You'll enjoy yourself here, won't you?'

There was something odd in his delivery, a tone that Maxwell couldn't place for the moment. 'I'll do my best,' he told him. Then the younger man was out of the car and on the steps, worn and cracked, that led to the glazed double doors.

'Parker!'

A middle-aged man, rather thick-set, with horn-rimmed glasses and extensive white hair appeared from nowhere.

'This is Parker,' Gallow said. 'Our steward. Parker, take Mr Maxwell's things to Tennyson, would you? And see that Mrs Oakes sets a place for lunch with Dr Sheffield.'

'High table?' Parker checked.

'Of course. Mr Maxwell, just in time for coffee.'

The staff room at Grimond's could not have been in greater contrast to Leighford. There was no sign of the TES anywhere. But then, presumably there weren't eighty odd people – and at Leighford they didn't come much odder – looking for job vacancies as an escape route from Grimond's. The furniture was elderly and there was more than a hint of pipe smoke wreathing around the pigeon holes where everybody's letters were addressed to people with letters after their names and the words 'Cantab' and 'Oxon'.

Gallow introduced Maxwell to a dozen or so, the men outnumbering the women. Alan Somebody was Head of Chemistry; Colin was Languages

31

overlord; Bruce dabbled in Politics. At the mention of the word 'comprehensive' he noticed all of them shift a little and one or two edged away, eyeing him with curiosity or disdain. He read their minds; what was this oik doing here? What was he – some pinko-liberal? It wasn't catching, was it? Had he heard of Oxbridge at all? He smiled benignly at it all.

'Well,' Dr Sheffield sat back in the opulence of his study a little before lunch. 'What do you make of Grimond's, Mr Maxwell?'

'Very civilized, Dr Sheffield,' Maxwell told him. 'A little of a culture shock already and I haven't met the kids yet.'

The Headmaster was probably just the wrong side of forty, but he'd clearly founded the Young Fogeys' Club. His tweed jacket looked like an old one of Jack Hawkins' and his gown hung like an old one of Bela Lugosi's on the back of his door. Maxwell's office would have vanished without trace in Sheffield's Inner Sanctum. He recognized it for what it had once been – Jedediah Grimond's drawing room, in which the old East Indiaman had toasted his nuts against the unaccustomed cold of English Hanoverian winters. Its walls were a dark English oak and the volumes that lined them of faded leather and clearly bought by the yard.

'James thought you might fit in quite well.'

'James?'

'Mr Diamond.'

'Oh, Legs.' It had been three days since Maxwell had seen his own beloved Lord and master. That was a lifetime in teaching. 'Well, sort of. I went to Halliards.'

'Really?' Sheffield lit his pipe, an act of bestiality Maxwell hadn't seen since he was a green probationer in the year the Germans had shot Edith Cavell. 'They closed last year, didn't they?'

'They did,' Maxwell nodded. 'End of an era, in some ways.'

'Sad,' Sheffield nodded. 'We can't afford to lose schools like these. You'll be staying in Tennyson House. Bill Pardoe's the Housemaster there. I think you'll be all right.'

'I'm sure I will, Headmaster. Tell me, will I be doing any teaching?'

'Teaching?' Sheffield chuckled. 'No, I don't think so, Mr Maxwell. James thought you'd be able to...'

'Pick up a few tips?' Maxwell smiled.

'That sounds patronizing,' Sheffield said. 'It isn't meant to.'

'That's all right,' Maxwell said. 'I'm sure your Mr Graham will come back a changed man too.'

'Ah,' Sheffield smiled. 'Tony can look after himself. Strictly between you and me, there are other colleagues at Grimond's who could learn a great deal more from this exchange than he.'

A bell rang in the corridor of power. 'Lunch, Mr Maxwell. Shall we join the staff for a sherry?'

The last time Peter Maxwell had seen sherry on school premises was when Eight Eff had discovered Sharon Claverhouse reeling around the bike sheds at Leighford High, off her face on Croft Original. Maxwell had carried her to Sylvia Matthews and Sylvia Matthews had force-fed her black coffee, hosed her down in sick bay and driven her home. Just as well Sharon Claver-house was Head of Food Technology; if a kid had got hold of the bottle, God knows what the up-shot would have been.

'Charming!' Maxwell beamed.

Sherry was delightful. Old Peculiar if Maxwell was any judge. Lunch was food; hot and edible. Maxwell even found himself joining in the Latin grace, roared in stentorian tones by a colleague pointed out to him as the Head of Physics. The oik from the comprehensive sat elbow to elbow with Dr George Sheffield and watched the kids. He was pleased to see that they *were* kids, for all they wore blazers, ties, polished shoes and atti-tudes; they were kids for all that. Laughing and joking in the last careless rapture before the mortgage and the kitchen sink and the rat race took hold. Perhaps, however, Maxwell might have had the foresight to bring his gown. But then, he wasn't really having to blend.

On his right, Bill Pardoe, Head of Tennyson House, was a giant of a man with a full beard, curling grey. He was Maxwell's age, perhaps a year or two younger, with kind grey eyes and a gentle smile.

'I used to teach in a comprehensive, Mr Max-well.' He was wrestling with a recalcitrant piece of bread and butter pudding.

'Really?' Maxwell was impressed.

'There were people back then who said I sold out.'

Maxwell looked at his man. 'Did you?'

'I used to think so,' Pardoe said, his gaze somewhere in the middle distance. 'Swapped problem kids for boys with cellos and IQs off the scale. Now, I'm not so sure. You're staying in Tennyson, I believe.'

'So I understand,' Maxwell accepted the extra custard from the white-coated girl hovering at his elbow. 'Thank you.'

Pardoe paused. 'There's an inter-house Cross Country this afternoon. If you'd like to freshen up first, I'll take you over. Rather a lot of standing around, I'm afraid.'

'Goes with the territory,' Maxwell remembered from his school days. 'I'd be delighted.'

They crossed the Quad under the awning of the new chapel with its sandstone facings and its arty-farty cross, no doubt something by Basil Spence on a bad day. Boys in rugger shirts clattered past them in their studded boots.

'Jenkins,' Pardoe stopped one of them. 'Twentieth man, eh?'

'Yes, sir.' Jenkins pulled up short.

'Twentieth man is just as important as the first. Understand?'

'Yes, sir,' the boy smiled and Pardoe ruffled his hair.

'I wouldn't dare do that,' Maxwell said as the lad dashed off to join the others. 'I'd be struck off.'

'Nonsense!' Pardoe's comeback was too fast, too abrupt.

'Just an observation,' Maxwell smiled. 'One of those little differences that divide our worlds, yours and mine.'

'Your loss,' Pardoe held open an oak-panelled door.

'Yes,' Maxwell agreed. 'I think you're right.'

The Head of Tennyson swept into his study, as oak-panelled as the Headmaster's and the door they'd entered by. The walls were hung with old photographs, the ones Maxwell remembered from his own schooldays, unsmiling young men with arms folded, sitting on their dignity, all tasselled caps, long shorts and incipient moustaches. Where have all the young men gone, long time passing? But it wasn't the décor that caught Maxwell's eye first; it was the full colour magazine open on Pardoe's desk where two blond boys, of uncertain age, writhed naked on a wrestling mat. Pardoe saw it too and swept it quickly into the sleeve of his gown before turning to Maxwell.

The Head of Sixth Form had never seen a man age so fast. Pardoe was the colour of parchment. 'Mr Maxwell, I... Could you wait here, please? I'll have my Captain of House show you to your rooms. Excuse me.'

And there was no sound but the click of his heels reheating along the corridor.

Chapter Three

That night, Maxwell perched under the eaves like a rather puzzled bat. The room must have belonged to the tweeniest of Jedediah Grimond's servants, up a tight spiral twist of stairs. It had been tastefully done out, Maxwell guessed, in about 1958. Since then, it had probably doubled as a storeroom, where old Latin Primers had mildewed against the day that the Secretary of State for Education should see the light and reintroduce real Classics in schools.

Dinner was good, rather more substantial than lunch but with the same grace. The Day Boys and Girls had gone home, of course, so that the ranks over the evening meal tables were thinner. Courtesy of the Headmaster, the Boarders were allowed to wear mufti, although most of them seemed to be modelling for Next or else in mourning for Gianni Versace. After nearly three hours of standing on the touch-line as over a hundred grunting, gasping teenagers staggered back from the agonies of Cross Country, Maxwell was more than ready for the vat of Mrs Oates' minestrone soup that lay waiting on High Table. Maxwell empathized with the runners, like Pheidippides dragging back from Marathon. He remembered it well, the torture in the lungs, the feet of clay. Somewhere in a Warwickshire field, his gymshoe still lay after all these years, sucked from his foot by the clawing mud. And his shin still carried the scar of the barbed wire that he hadn't seen until it was too late.

He hob-nobbed with the Headmaster and David Gallow as the evening shadows lengthened and the chandeliers sparkled in the dining hall. He became engrossed after dinner in a post-prandial chat in the Senior Common Room with Michael Hemsley, the Head of Watered-Down-Classics, on the merits of Hancock's Half Hour and its role in Fifties Ultra-Realism.

Of Bill Pardoe, there was no sign.

'Takes me back, really,' Maxwell said, lolling on his bed and staring at the swirls on the artex ceiling. 'Even the smell of the place. Polish and cabbage. You never lose it.'

'I don't think we had either of those at my school,' Jacquie told him from her end of the mobile super-highway. 'Are you bored yet?'

'To sobs,' Maxwell chuckled. 'You lady detectives don't miss much, do you? Still, I think I'm allowed into the library tomorrow, so I'll see how much half-inching I can do for my own dear History Department. Ah, how I miss it; Paul Moss screaming at Year Seven, Sally Greenhow blowing Joe Plumley's nose for him one lesson, me knocking his block off the next. The essential rhythm of life.'

'I gather Grimond's is not like that.'

'You gather right, Woman Policeman. Our kids at Leighford have only just realized they can walk on water, courtesy of Political Correctness and the Court of Human Rights. The kids here have always had power; the sort that comes with money and birth and privilege. It might not be Eton or Harrow, but it'll do. The Captain of House calls me "Mr Maxwell" but he'd clearly like his fag to polish his boots with me. I'm some sort of nasty smell under his nose.'

'Oh, Max...'

'I kid you not, dearly beloved. The lad's eighteen going on fifty with all the bonhomie of Osama bin Laden.'

'Darling,' he heard her say. 'I've got to go now. Early shift in the morning.'

'Of course.' He sat up on the bed. 'Give my love to that humourless bastard you work for.'

'Henry sends you his best wishes, too,' Jacquie laughed. 'Love you, Peter Maxwell.'

'Love you too, Woman Policeman,' and he heard the line go dead. He held the mobile out under the bedside lamp, wondering again which button you had to use to switch the thing off. Did people really get mugged for this irritating piece of plastic, he asked himself as the midnight lamps burned. Why, oh why? There again, he now had hard evidence that using one dims the little grey cells; he'd known how to switch it off when the call began.

He couldn't tell the time in his moment of waking. And it was a while before he remembered where he was. Something had woken him. One thump or two? It seemed to be overhead at first. But there was nothing overhead. Except the roof. Outside, then, on the spiral? There it was again, a single thump. Then scurrying. Rats in the wainscoting? Cockroaches? The people who live under the stairs? He was wide awake now, his digital alarm winking at him. Two-thirty-eight. Was there such an hour? He'd heard the sounds all evening: comings and goings below, footsteps, laughter. At ten, a solemn bell had sounded across the quad and the House began to settle. At ten-thirty, a voice he recognised as that of John Selwyn, the Captain of Tennyson, echoed through the corridors. 'Lights out in the House. All's well.'

How quaint, Maxwell thought; every man his own town-crier. Unless the Lord keepeth the city, the wakeman waketh in vain. Perhaps this was standard. Perhaps at two-thirty-eight every morning there was a series of thumps and a scratching. Perhaps it was an old Grimond custom. Or the long-gone ghosts of mob-capped servants carrying steaming bowls of hot water. But he was suddenly on his feet anyway, fumbling his way to the window, agonizing cramp freezing his toes as he hobbled around trying to end it. Below, frozen in the moonlight, old Jedediah Grimond's courtyard stretched away into darkness. Here the horses had once whinnied and clashed, steel on cobbles and the post-chaise had creaked on its housings as the master came home. The birch next to the chapel spread its shadow arms across the tarmac, dappling silver on the ground and the roofs shone in the fullness of the moon.

At first he saw nothing moving, just the odd set of headlights on the horizon, on the far A3, a long-distance tanker making the hard miles. Then a shadow flitted across the moment and Maxwell's eyes were drawn down to the ground. A figure – no, two – hovered in the angle of the old house, dipping in and out of the darkness. They seemed to be waiting for something, glancing backwards and forwards, left and right. One, Maxwell could make out, was female, her hair long and dark under the moon, swaying as she rocked in, then out of the shadow. The other was taller, more solid, clearly male and dressed in black. Surely, that couldn't be a gown? Then, as suddenly as they'd appeared, the pair had gone, their shapes melding with the shadow of the chapel and the stand of birches. Nothing more. No thumps now. No scratching. No lights and shadows. Maxwell let the curtain fall, wrestling with it all on his way back to bed. Comings and goings between the dorms. He couldn't get his bearings yet. Austen House, the girls' dorm, he'd only seen briefly in the harsh light of a Grimond day. The dark and the moonlight threw it all into confusion and he couldn't be sure where it was in relation to Tennyson. The other boys' Houses, Dickens and Kipling, were only names to him as yet. Forget it, he told himself as his head hit the pillow. Whatever it was, it couldn't hold a candle to the nocturnal prowlings of his Leighford Highenas along the sea front of a Friday night. Suffice it to say that the sex education programme provided by the Social and Religious department was one huge waste of time; and after all, wasn't that what bus shelters were made for? Sleep knit up the unravelled sleeve of Maxwell's care.

Most of them had never seen a corpse before. Not one with a broken neck, anyway. Bill Pardoe lay in the quad in the chill of that Tuesday morning, sprawled at an impossible angle. He was wearing his pyjamas and, bizarrely, his gown. His right leg was twisted under him and his head lay against the chapel wall. Beneath it, like a dark pillow, his blood had congealed, running down the slight gradient into the drain nearby. His beard was matted with it and the kind, grey eyes stared intently at the clouds.

In the silent, motionless crowd, most of them still in pyjamas and dressing gowns, one girl started to cry. Like an infection, it spread along the rows, mounting hysteria, until the Captain of Tennyson forced his way through.

'Get them away, Splinter!' he barked. 'All of you, back to your dorms. Somebody get Dr Sheffield.'

An ambulance arrived first, clanging and flashing through the Hampshire lanes, but far too late to be of much use. It would do duty as a hearse later. Then the squad cars, three, four, five and a police Landrover for good measure, all flashing lights and wailing sirens. Pale, eager faces pressed to the windows – the wide-eyed ingénues of the Lower Fourth and the sophisticates of the Sixth, as one in their sense of shock and bewilderment. Their harassed teachers, desperate to make sense of the madness, shooed them away to their desks and made some attempt at normality.

'Please sir, what's happened to Mr Pardoe?'

Out of the one unmarked car stepped a tall, square detective in a three piece suit. Aliens in white zip-ups and hoods were already erecting a flimsy marquee over the body.

'Nothing to see here, children,' a junior housemaster was hurrying his charges past. 'Nothing to see. Come on, now. We've places to be.'

The suit waited with an oppo until the marquee showed some degree of permanence, hammered into the tarmac with steel guy pegs.

'Jesus!' It was the wailing sirens that had woken Peter Maxwell. He'd overslept. He knew when breakfast was and where it was. But the bloody alarm hadn't gone off. Now, he was standing in his pyjamas staring down at the mayhem below him. Dr Sheffield was in the thick of it all, pointing up to his corner of the building. And he was talking to someone Maxwell knew.

'Jesus,' he said again and turned to fight his way into some day clothes.

'Inspector…' Sheffield had never looked at a dead colleague before.

'Hall,' the suit told him, kneeling over all that was left of Bill Pardoe. 'And that's Chief Inspector, Mr … er…?'

'Sheffield,' the Headmaster said, 'and if we're being meticulous with our titles, that's Doctor.'

'Touché,' Hall said. It was the nearest to drollery you got with Henry Hall. 'What do you make of this, sir?'

Sheffield was at a loss. He stood in the eerie lighting of the marquee while SOCOs traipsed round him setting up cameras and wires, taking measurements with metallic tape measures. 'I don't know what to say, Chief Inspector.'

'You could start with his name,' Hall said,

running a latex gloved finger under the man's hairline behind his ear.

'Pardoe,' a voice behind him made the Chief Inspector turn. 'He was a housemaster here.'

Hall was on his feet, staring intently at the arrival. 'Thompson!' he snapped, his face pale, his jaw-ridge flexed.

'Guv?' a uniformed face appeared around the marquee flap.

'Would you escort this gentleman outside, please?'

Thompson's face fell. 'Sorry, guv, he said...'

'I'm sure he did,' Hall cut in. 'Outside. Now.'

The arrival left, followed by Henry Hall. 'Mr Maxwell,' the DCI gave himself a moment. 'How many schools do you teach at in this great country of ours?'

'I was about to ask you a very similar question, Chief Inspector,' Maxwell smiled. 'In purely jurisdictional terms, you're a long way from West Sussex. Still, manors maketh man, I suppose.'

'Secondment,' Hall snapped, in no mood for Maxwell's wit at this hour of the morning. 'You?'

'Observation,' Maxwell replied. 'I hadn't expected to observe anything like this.'

'Thompson,' Hall turned to the uniform. 'The next time you let an unauthorized civilian cross a ribbon and invade a scene of crime, I'm going to have your warrant card. Do we understand each other?'

'Yes, sir.' Thompson stood there, under his peaked cap, like a kid with his hand in the cookie jar.

'God, this is awful.' Dr Sheffield had joined the

two. 'I just had to get some air. I feel sick. Is that usual?'

Hall looked at him, then at Maxwell. 'Dr Sheffield, I will need to talk to you. And your staff...'

'Of course.' Sheffield consciously tried to pull himself together. 'Look, the children... I mean, we can keep all this quiet, can't we?'

'A man is dead, Headmaster,' Hall said, ever the master of the cliché.

'Of course. Yes. I see. It's just that ... well, suicide has a certain ... stigma, doesn't it?'

Hall looked at Maxwell again. 'Oh, yes, Dr Sheffield. It does.'

Like a torrent in the trees, like a deluge on the dykes, Mark West hurtled up the granite steps into his boss's office, Headquarters Building of the Hampshire Constabulary.

'What the fuck is going on?'

It wasn't the best way to address a Chief Superintendent with toothache. 'Do you want to pass that by me again, Chief Inspector?' The Chief Superintendent was keeping his cool admirably, all things considered.

'DCI Hall,' West snapped, leaning towards his superior and swaying with fury.

'What about him?' the Chief Super, ever the Deflator of Situations, sat down. Going head to head with Mark West was always counter-productive.

'He's trampling all over my patch. There's been a death at Grimond's.'

'So I believe,' the Super nodded, resting his

45

elbows on his desk and his lips against his raised fingers, trying not to feel the throbbing in his lower jaw.

West sat down unbidden. 'Look, Dave…'

Dave did and West didn't like what he saw. He stood up again. 'Shall we try this one again, Mark?' he asked, plugging the raging molar with his tongue. 'Do, please, have a seat.' The DCI did. 'Now, what seems to be the trouble?' It was the sort of ice-breaker you heard in any doctor's surgery in the country on any day of the week (except Sundays when they shut).

West's jaw flexed in the mid-day light. The glare of the March sun was in his eyes and patience was one virtue the DCI did not possess. 'I think you know, Mr Mason,' he growled.

When David Mason heard his surname, he knew he was in for a bitch of a day. 'You're tied up with the bank job in Petworth – or you damned well should be. Hall was at a loose end…'

'But what's he doing here?' West wanted to know.

Mason looked at his man. Mark West was knocking forty, solid with a close-cropped head that would not look out of place on the football terraces. He was short on charm and short on fuse, but he got results. 'You're a man down.'

'Yes,' West leaned back in his chair for the first time. 'Ben Pollard's broken his collar bone, so I'm a *sergeant* down. Another DCI I don't need. What are we, Castor and bloody Pollux?'

David Mason, like Peter Maxwell, had been to a good school. He was impressed by the classical allusion. 'I won't bore you with the Chief Constable's initiative details, Mark,' he said. 'Caring, sharing – it's all part of his mission statement.'

West's hands were in the air. 'When I was a beat copper, we caught villains, we didn't have mission statements.'

'That's why you're a DCI,' Mason told him disarmingly, 'why I'm a Chief Super and the Chief Constable is a Chief Constable. He's paid to have the big picture. You and me, well…'

'We're in the frame,' Mark West could out-analogy his Chief Super any day.

'Quip while you're ahead,' Mason winked at him and felt his tooth throb anew.

'Where does that leave Henry Hall?'

'On our patch,' Mason said, 'sharing experience, good practice. Don't you read your inter-departmental memos?'

'Is the Pope a Shi'ite?' West wanted to know, reaching for the ciggies metaphorically burning a hole in his pocket.

'Just think, Mark,' Mason patronized, 'You could be going back to West Sussex with him in a week or so.'

'Joy,' West growled.

'In the meantime,' the Chief Super leaned forward in the way that Chief Supers do when they're no longer being Mr Nice Guy, 'Henry Hall is observing how we do things here in Hampshire. He has my full authority to co-ordinate and to lead on any case that naturally comes his way. You will give him every co-operation, Detective Chief Inspector; is that clear?'

'Crystal,' West growled again.

'Good,' Mason leaned back in his swivel. 'Now,

put that bloody cigarette out.' West fumed, but did as he was told. 'That translates as keeping out of Hall's face as far as the Grimond's thing's concerned. Right?'

West shrugged. 'Fine,' he said.

'I think that about wraps it up then, Mark,' the Chief Super said. 'You'll keep me posted on Petworth?'

'Yeah, sure,' West sighed and saw himself out.

'Marcia,' Mason pressed his intercom, desperate to alleviate his problem, 'Do we have such a thing as oil of cloves in this man's police force?'

'Did you know,' Dr Robert Firmin was at his most expansive over the hospital's cottage pie, 'that the New York Medical Examiner's Office carries out seven thousand post mortems a year?' A blob of mince fell off his fork and he had to retrieve it. 'Of course, they call them autopsies over there, but a rose by any other name.

'Riveting,' Henry Hall stuck to coffee. If truth were told, he'd never really been happy around corpses – he who had seen so many. He'd lingered for as long as he'd had to in Firmin's basement mortuary, but the bright lights and moving people of the hospital canteen were altogether more comforting. Even so, the memory of the dead man on the stainless steel kept him away from the culinary delights across the counter.

The ritual of English law had begun. The police had contacted the coroner; the coroner had contacted the pathologist; and the pathologist, he'd gone to work. Firmin's findings were neatly labelled on the pink form alongside his trifle, all of it surprisingly legible for a medical man. Identification of William Francis Pardoe had come from DCI Henry Hall, via Dr George Sheffield, there being no known relatives to do those particular honours for the dead man. On the slab, Bill Pardoe had been photographed again, as he had been on the tarmac at Grimond's, his pale, dead eyes immune to the camera flash, his pupils dilating no longer. Piece by piece, Firmin and his assistant had peeled off the dead man's clothes – his black gown, stiff with his blood around the nape and shoulder, then his pyjama jacket and trousers, a sickly green and white stripe under the arc lights. There was a small, three-cornered tear on the jacket sleeve and he was wearing no underwear.

Bill Pardoe dead weighed ninety-nine kilos, about right for a man of his height and age. Slowly, the magnifying lens attached to his forehead, Firmin had covered every inch of the Housemaster's body, from the blood-matted thatch of silver-grey hair to the broken toe-nail on his left foot. He mechanically noted on the pink form every mole, scar and blemish. Appendicitis. Three teeth extracted. Four fillings. Numerous old lacerations to both knees – the scrapes of boyhood or the clashes of lusty youth. There was a thickening of the skin on the middle finger of the right hand – that trade mark of teachers, the writer's ridge, born of years of marking. Bill Pardoe was a smoker. His tongue, his teeth, his fingers all bore testimony to that long before Firmin got to his lungs.

Firmin noted it all on the body outline diagram

on his form, paying particular attention to the angle of the neck where the impact of the fall had snapped his third vertebrae and to the ghastly crush fracture that had caved in the occipital plate of his skull.

Then, as rigor was fading and Pardoe's limbs hung loose and flabby at his sides, the good doctor had gone to work with those instruments of ingenuity that Henry Hall would rather not think about, but that Peter Maxwell would have recognized as being appropriate to the Holy Inquisition. Not that Bill Pardoe would have cared – he was way beyond torture now. Firmin sliced a 'Y' into his body, lifting the neck and thorax with a skill that often astounded his guests over the Sunday roast.

One by one he filled the canoptic jars of modern pathological science – samples of Bill Pardoe's skin, bone, blood, muscle, urine and stool tissue, brain and spinal cord.

'Hmm,' Firmin scooped his trifle, 'just like dear old Mum used to make.' He waved a cheery hand to the floozy beyond the counter, who smiled ingratiatingly back; she still harboured secret hopes of marrying a doctor, even one who was up to his elbows in dead people all the time.

'So, the cause of death?' Hall had to hurry his man along. There were questions waiting to be asked at Grimond's and no one but he to ask them.

'Broken neck, my dear chap; in layman's terms, that is. I suppose that's what you're after.'

'And the damage to the head?'

Firmin flicked a walnut fragment out of the gap

in the front of his teeth. 'You told me he fell from a building, Chief Inspector,' he said. 'What are we talking? Thirty feet?'

'Forty,' Hall reckoned.

Firmin shrugged. 'That'll do it. I haven't done much pure velocity since A-level Physics, but it'd be rather like being hit by a train. In falls, the body pivots forward, head and upper torso leading. Depending on the weight, side winds and so on, it twists, arms and legs flailing. No matter how determined you are, or how inevitable the descent once it's underway, it's instinct. You fight it. It's involuntary. Your hands claw the air, looking blindly for a ledge, your feet for a footing, however flimsy; something to break the fall. And if you've changed your mind, I don't even want to think about what's going on inside your brain.'

He reached for his coffee. 'Shite,' he hissed, 'cold again.' He looked at Hall, hiding, as he always did, behind his gold-rimmed glasses. 'You turn, once, perhaps twice in a forty foot drop. It was evens that Pardoe would hit the ground on his front or his back. Never on your feet. It just doesn't happen. He fractured his left arm, too, but it was the snapping of the spinal cord that killed him.'

Hall waited. Nothing. 'All right,' he said, tapping a spoon gently on the formica surface of the table. 'Let me ask you a question you've probably heard before: did he fall or was he pushed?'

The sun was gilding the arms of old Jedediah Grimond on the cupola and the breeze that blows between the worlds slapped the rope against the flagpole. The Grimond crest flew at half mast and there was a funereal stillness about the place.

Peter Maxwell stood out on the leads of the old house, watching a straggling line of cross country runners winding its way over the darkening fields. It would be dusk soon, the new buds of spring shrinking in against the threat of the still-chilly night. From where he stood, Maxwell could see the wooded slopes of Selborne Hanger, the beeches silent sentinels above the granite called the Wishing Stone on its summit. Two hundred years ago Gilbert White had sat there, noting the nature around him in all its summer glory. The patchwork of fields showed a dull green with the spring sowing and a lonely tractor rattled its way across Wheatham Hill. To the south, Maxwell could make out the pretty wooden tower of the perpendicular church at Steep and the dark tunnel of yews that shielded coffin bearers with their heavy loads. Someone was ringing the peal of bells, a mournful sound that echoed the solemnity of the time, the place. 'My name is Mary, I ring to the Glory of God.' One the pall bearers had not carried there, though his cottage still stands nearby, was Edward Thomas, who slogged up to Arras with rifle and pack and the Royal Garrison Artillery until a bullet found him on 9th of April 1917.

'"No one cares less than I,"' Maxwell found himself murmuring, remembering, '"Nobody knows, but God, whether I am destined to lie under a foreign clod." You are, Edward,' he sighed, his voice dying on the wind.

Below him in the quad, the police marquee was a living reminder of a newer death, as pointless as the poet's perhaps, and the blue and white tape fluttering around it in the afternoon breeze. What was the drop from here? Thirty-five feet? Forty? It couldn't be less. From somewhere, he heard a sound not often heard in the Rother valley on a spring day in the 21st century. It was halting and under-rehearsed, but it was unmistakable. It was the Last Post. "'But laughing, storming, scorning,'" Maxwell recited to himself, "'Only the bugles know what the bugles say in the morning, and they do not care, when they blow...'"

Forty feet. He ran his hands over the smoothness of Jedediah Grimond's stone, mellow in the fading light. The knot of runners cursed and slipped their muddy way below the limes, past the curve of the Astro-turf and on out to the cricket pavilion for the last, lung-tearing lap. He looked over the edge, at the certainty of the drop. Was it gravity that pulled him forward, willing him to jump? To feel, for a moment, the air rush through his veins in the exhilaration of flight? Is that what Bill Pardoe had felt? Before he leapt into eternity by way of Grimond's quad? Before the ground had come up to hit him like a sledgehammer and All Things Ceased?

Peter Maxwell shook himself free of it – the pull of freefall. He was Mad Max, for Christ's sake. He'd stood on the sites of men's deaths before. They don't really come back. Dead men don't tell tales. All that is Hammer and Hollywood. All there is is emptiness and pointlessness. A sad,

disturbed man had taken his own life. It happened every day. But what kind of man was it
that did it so publicly? What kind of teacher killed
himself in a place where he knew his kids would
see him, all dignity gone, all life spent?

He was glad to be inside, on the stairs again,
the brightness of the evening sky behind and
above him, going down the slow way. He'd just
reached the corridor that led to his twist of the
stairs when he saw a boy framed in the last shaft
of the dying sun. He was carrying rugger boots in
his hand and the laces dangled to the floor. His
yellow shirt was splattered with mud and his legs
caked the colour of his socks. It was Jenkins, Bill
Pardoe's twentieth man, the eternal runner.

'Sir.' The boy couldn't have been more than
twelve.

'Yes?' Maxwell faced him.

'Mr Pardoe, sir...' Jenkins' voice trailed away
and Maxwell saw the chin quiver, the eyes large
with tears the boy was willing not to fall.

'What about him, Jenkins?' The voice was soft
and strong and safe.

'He didn't do it, sir.' Jenkins' chest was heaving
and not because of the run. 'He didn't kill himself, sir. Not Mr Pardoe.'

Then he was gone, his stockinged feet sliding
on the polished floor, the tears streaming down
his grimy cheeks, his sobs bursting from him in a
pain he'd never known.

'Do you know, Jenkins,' Maxwell whispered to
himself, 'I'm beginning to think you may be
right.'

Chapter Four

'The sixty-four thousand dollar question is, heart of hearts, what is Henry Hall doing here?' Peter Maxwell had asked himself the question all day. Now he was asking somebody who might conceivably know the answer – Jacquie Carpenter.

'Secondment,' she said. Jacquie had put off that mess under the stairs for too long. Now, at last, she was putting the cleaning into spring, the phone tucked under her angled neck in the way that everyone except Peter Maxwell could do. She hauled a box of dead *Cosmos* out from the dark, wondering privately how long it would be before they were *Women's Weeklies* or even *People's Friends*.

'Is that usual?' she heard Maxwell ask.

She felt her back go just a little as she straightened up. 'It'll be some initiative,' she told him, 'at Chief Constable level. Well, they've got to earn their obscene salary somehow, when they're not banding together against the Home Secretary. Is he on his own?'

'Er...' Maxwell had to think about that one. 'Seemed to have another suit with him. Nobody I knew.'

'It'll be a DI,' Jacquie was sure. 'Local bloke, somebody who knows the form. How's everybody taking it? The kids, I mean?'

Maxwell shrugged. Cradled in his hands was the

Grimond's prospectus, all gloss and achievement, with the Combined Cadet Force doing hearty Outward Bound things and the First Fifteen grinning alongside a rather confused looking Martin Johnson. 'Don't know. The Captain of House was magnificent, apparently, when they found the body. He took charge, shooed everybody away, just like a public schoolboy in a shipwreck, really. They're holding a service in the chapel tomorrow.'

'Anything like this ever happen in a school of yours, Max?' Jacquie was sifting through her mags.

'Not exactly. Oh, a couple of nervous breakdowns, tears, tantrums. I believe it's called CWS – class war syndrome. But suicide, no. There again...'

Jacquie Carpenter sat upright, transferring the cordless to her left ear. 'What?' she wanted to know.

'Sorry,' Maxwell chuckled, crossing his feet at the ankles like some crusader knight on a memorial slab. 'Do I detect a change in tone, Woman Policeman?'

'There's that word "detect" again,' she said, getting to her feet and slopping on her mules into the kitchen, staggering just a little as the blood trickled back into her ankles. 'What are you up to, Peter Maxwell?'

'Twelve-year-olds,' Maxwell murmured.

'Really?' she arched an eyebrow. 'I don't remember your name from our files and does West Sussex Education Authority know?'

'No,' he laughed. 'I'm not talking about the Sex Offenders Register, I'm talking about the sagacity

56

of the age.'

'You what?'

'Kids are queer cattle, Jacquie,' he sighed, beginning to itch at this witching hour for a pint or two
of Southern Comfort. 'Until they're eleven,
they're appalling – juvenile, smelly, with no
common-sense at all. Somebody farts and they
think it's the funniest thing in the world. The word
alone brings on paroxysms. At thirteen, it starts all
over again. Friend Shakespeare got it wrong; there
are eight ages of man, not seven. No sooner have
they stopped mewling and puking than they're
farting and smoking – not to mention the Act That
Makes You Blind.'

'What are you talking about, Max?' Jacquie was
looking for her kettle under the debris of J-cloths.

'Puberty, dear heart. Hormones whizzing
around like there's no tomorrow... Of course, for
Bill Pardoe, there isn't a tomorrow, is there?'

'Max...'

'Sorry,' he said. 'I'm rambling and it's late. No,
the age of twelve, Jacquie – that tiny window of
perspicacity and clear thinking as the age of
innocence ebbs and the age of GCSE Guilt
begins. I met a little boy yesterday – and again
today. His name's Jenkins.'

'And he's twelve?'

'I'd say so,' Maxwell nodded at his end of the
mobile. 'And he doesn't think Pardoe jumped.'

'Oh, come on, Max...'

'I know,' he said. 'We've been down this road
before, haven't we, you and I?'

'You and I, kemosabe?' she said.

Maxwell laughed. He loved it when Jacquie

came out with phrases she only knew from him. *The Lone Ranger and Tonto* had been his Saturday morning viewing, not hers.

'What does Hall think?' she asked him.

'Do you know,' he smiled. 'I was just going to ask you that very question.'

There was a pause. Maxwell knew what that meant. 'Oh, no.' Yep, that was the response he'd expected. 'Out of the question.'

'Why?' It was a whining, wheedling tone Peter Maxwell had learned from Years Eight and Nine. His answer to them was invariably *because I said so, sunshine. Any problem with that, kiss your arse goodbye.*

'Because.' Jacquie was emphatic, rummaging in her cupboard for the cocoa.

'Go on,' he lapsed into his Private Pike. 'Go on, Captain Mainwaring, why? Why?'

'Stupid boy,' she growled dutifully. 'Because Hall is there with you. And I'm here ... without you. I mind about that, by the way...'

'Me too,' he smiled. 'Join me, then.'

'You what?'

'Hop in the car tomorrow. Tell Hall he forgot his thermos flask or something and you've kindly brought it for him.'

'That's believable.' She switched on the kettle.

'I need someone on the inside, Jacquie,' he told her, knowing she was already shaking her head.

'I can't, Max.' It was a well-worn track in their mutual CD. 'And it's nothing to do with ethics this time. Hall's on secondment on his own. He's got all the back up he needs your end from the local nick. If I turned up, he'd just turn me round

58

again. Result? No help to you and a double bollocking for me; one from Hall and another from my DI.'

'Doesn't promotion give you any power?' But he already knew the answer to that one. A man doesn't get to be Head of Sixth Form for a thousand years and not realize where the corridors of power are. Peter Maxwell would never make the Senior Management Team – he'd trodden on too many toes and ruffled too many feathers and used too many metaphors over the years.

'I'm a DS, for Christ's sake,' she chuckled. 'Not Commissioner of the Met.'

'Ah,' he smiled. 'It's early days.'

'Why don't you ask him?'

'What?'

'Hall. He knows you're there. He's bound to want to talk to you. Get some information back.'

'Like who killed Bill Pardoe, Chief Inspector?'

'If that's the information you want. Rest assured, the Fourth Estate will be asking.'

'Ah, yes,' Maxwell nodded. 'The paparazzi.'

'Have they been around, yet?'

'I haven't seen them. I expect George Sheffield has gun emplacements on the gates and searchlights on the cricket pavvy. Private schools are always paranoid about their reputations.'

There was a silence between them, one that even at either end of a phone call they were comfortable with. 'There's one more thing, Jacquie,' he said, reaching a page in the Grimond's glossy where lads were enthusiastically climbing wall bars. 'How up are you on the gay porn scene?'

'Not my favourite bedtime reading,' she told

him. 'Why?'

'There was a mag I caught a brief sight of in Bill Pardoe's office ... oops, study.'

'What was it?'

'Well, that's just it,' Maxwell said. 'I didn't see the title. It was open at a page with what appeared to be two naked lads wrestling.'

'Colour?'

'Yes.'

'Did you see any text?'

'Don't think so.' He frowned, trying to remember. 'Is it important?'

'Not necessarily. But lack of text implies, foreign import. It'll be Dutch or Swedish. I'll have a discreet word with our Dirty Squad, if you like.'

'Thanks, darling,' he said. 'I appreciate it. You take care, now. I'll call you tomorrow.'

'Why?' she asked, wide-eyed, 'when my name's Jacquie?'

Maxwell's groan said it all, but he was already dialling another number. 'Sylv?' The matron's voice had sounded odd.

'Jesus, Max. Do you know what time it is?' She'd rolled over, peering from under the duvet, trying to sound coherent and to focus on her bedside clock at the same time.

'Damn,' he snapped his fingers. 'It's probably quarter-past-twelve there. I keep forgetting the time zone thing. It's only half-past-three here. Soz.'

'You utter shit,' she yawned. 'What's the matter? I do have eighty Heaf tests to sort out in the morning.'

'I know, sweetheart,' he cooed. 'I'm out of order,

I know that, but I really need to talk to your Mr Graham.'

'He's not exactly *mine*, Max,' she scolded him. 'He's probably asleep.'

'Ah, not coping, eh?'

'Would you?' Sylvia Matthews was not at her best in the wee-wee hours of the morning. 'I tell you, talking to Tony has opened my eyes about Leighford High School, and no mistake.'

'That be mutiny, Nurse Matthews,' he rasped out his best Robert Newton. '"Them's that die'll be the lucky ones." Wake him up, will you, Sylv? It's important.'

He waited while she tutted off into the middle distance. There was the rattle of a door and a thud, followed by a 'bugger' as the school nurse collided with something on her landing. Maxwell heard muffled voices and lighter feet dancing on the stairs.

'Hello?' A male voice had picked up.

'Tony?'

'Max? What's up?'

'You haven't heard ... from Grimond's, I mean?'

'No. Should I? What's the problem?'

'Look, Tony. Sit down, will you?'

'Max,' he could almost hear the frown in the man's voice. 'I'm standing in the bedroom of my landlady wearing not a great deal and although she is a perfect lady, I cannot vouch for the propriety of the situation. What's happened?'

'There isn't an easy way of doing this, Tony. It's Bill Pardoe.'

'Bill? What about him?'

'He's dead.'

For a moment, so was the line. 'Oh, my God.' Tony Graham was sitting down now, as Maxwell had suggested, perched on Sylvia's bed in the lamplight.

'I'm sorry. I thought Dr Sheffield would have been in touch.'

'Er … um … yes. Yes, so would I. What was it? Heart?'

'He jumped, Tony. From the roof of Tennyson.'

'Oh, Christ.'

'Look, I know this is a shock for you. I don't know yet how everybody's coping. Will you be coming back?'

'I suppose I'll have to. Somebody will have to run Tennyson. What about you?'

'I'm seeing Sheffield tomorrow. I'd like to stay on.'

'You would? Why?'

'Tony, you must have known Bill Pardoe pretty well.'

'Well, not really. Okay, I was his junior in Tennyson, but only for the last year. This is pretty unbelievable, actually. No,' he was talking to Sylvia now, partly covering the receiver with his hand, 'No, I'm fine. Just some bad news. Thanks, Sylvia.' Sylvia Matthews knew the signs. She'd been on bereavement counselling courses. But Tony Graham was public school. He seemed calm, collected; perhaps they took things like this differently there.

'Would you say,' Maxwell asked Graham, 'he was the suicidal type?'

'Max, I don't know what the suicidal type is.

62

There were rumours, of course.'

'Rumours?' Maxwell was all ears.

'No, look, I'm not going down that road. It's all just innuendo and I'm not even getting into it. I'll see Diamond in the morning and get to you by midday. All right? How's John taking it?'

'John?'

'John Selwyn, Captain of House. He and Bill were close.'

'I don't know,' Maxwell said. 'I'm not sure how I'd have coped when I was eighteen, not with something like this.'

'Christ, Max,' Graham muttered. 'Age has got nothing to do with it. I'm thirty next month and I'm shaking like a bloody leaf. Look, I've got to go. I'll see you tomorrow. Goodnight, Max.'

'Goodnight, Tony.'

He waited until Sylvia came on the line. 'Can you tell me, Max?' she asked, as quietly as she could.

'Tony's immediate supremo,' the Head of Sixth Form told her, 'apparently killed himself last night.'

'Oh, how awful.'

'Look after him, Sylv. There are a lot of Leighford colleagues I'd cheerfully strangle with their own underwear, but seeing them lying dead at the bottom of A-Block is a completely different story.'

It was that hour again; the one at which Maxwell had been jolted awake the night before. He forced his eyes to focus on the digital green: two forty-five. He lay on his back for a while, staring at the blackness of the ceiling. He'd got his bearings during the day. Bill Pardoe, Lord of Tennyson House, had left the parapet diagonally above the room in which Maxwell lay. His study and its accompanying flat occupied the floor below. On his way back after meeting Jenkins, he'd tried to gauge the direction of the noises he'd heard, twenty-four hours ago from now. His own stairs ended in his room, an L-shaped contrivance not unlike his rooms at Jesus all those years ago in the Granta days. For Bill Pardoe to have walked up to the roof, he would have had to have taken the next staircase, the one that led from the corridor. He would have passed the bottom of Maxwell's spiral and three, perhaps four doors before he reached them. He couldn't have come up the other way because the corridor ended in a solid wall.

There'd been nothing out of the ordinary up on the leads. No tell-tale marks of a scuffle. No obvious footprints. And anyway, Maxwell reflected as he lay there in his bed, Bill Pardoe was a large man and reasonably fit. Who could have dragged him all the way up to the roof in the dark? And how could they be sure they'd cleared up behind them? Drag a dead man, drag an unconscious man and you'd leave heel marks. Besides, the SOCO team had been up there already, their heads bobbing up and down on the parapet and glancing down to the quad like a latter day team of Isaac Newtons testing gravity. They would have found prints if there were any. All that day, when he wasn't bored to death in various classes, he'd watched Henry Hall's men going about their macabre business. The men in the white suits measured, photographed, bagged, talking in monotones and whispers.

Walls, especially in a school, have ears. Maxwell knew that. What he didn't know is why he got out of bed at that unusual hour at the dead of the night and why he didn't switch on his bedside lamp. Come to that, he didn't know why he twitched his curtain aside. But he did, nevertheless.

There was no moon tonight to lend a silvered unreality to the rooftops. He could make out the police marquee, a ghostly white virtually below. He found himself gripping the mullion stone at what he saw next. What appeared to be a funeral procession was winding its way across the quad, past the chapel and out across the First Eleven's hallowed turf. They were soldiers, ramrod straight in their khaki and berets, not unlike the melancholy troop that probably laid Edward Thomas in the Arras clay. Between the six, arms locked across each other's shoulders, they carried a coffin, draped with what looked even in the darkness, like the Grimond's flag, the gold lions on the sable field. Eeriest of all, they made no sound. Maxwell squinted to see their boots. Army issue ought to be clattering on that tarmac, but there was no sound at all. It was just as if someone had pressed the mute on their TV remote. He watched them until they'd vanished beyond the elms that ringed the fields, sloping down to the lake. Then he went back to bed. But not to sleep.

The chaplain did the honours the next morning,

saying a few words over the missing body of Bill Pardoe. He was a large, balding man with a silver tongue and a voluminous cassock. It was like a scene from Lyndsey Anderson's *If*. Maxwell half-expected the padre to emerge out of a desk drawer any minute and Malcolm McDowell to leap down the aisle spraying everybody with machine gun bullets. But a lunatic had done that already in a school. For real. At a place called Dunblane. The Headmaster was standing in the chaplain's place now, like God in a pulpit, staring down at the massed rows of his flock, immaculate in his gown and his dark suit and his black tie.

'We will all miss Mr Pardoe,' his voice rang out high and firm, with a power that belied his wiry stature, 'and that is right. But life must go on. We have all learned a lesson from what happened yesterday. None of us is invulnerable. None of us is here for ever. It's a lesson worth noting. It may be this is the hardest one you'll ever learn at Grimond's.'

His cold grey eyes raked them all. 'What happened must make us stronger,' he told them. 'Make us one. We are a good school, a proud school. In the days and weeks ahead, it may be that you will hear unkind things, cruel things. It may be you are asked difficult questions by the police. You must talk to no one else. Not the newspapers, not even your parents at this stage. Day pupils will have a harder time of it than boarders. But I remind you all of your loyalties, to yourselves, to Grimond's and to Mr Pardoe. For whom now, a moment's silence...' and he bowed his head.

Peter Maxwell felt like Charlton Heston's El Cid, in the film of the same name, standing alone against the guilty King Alfonso. All the other Castilians grovelled to their liege lord – the Cid, *sans peur* and *sans reproche*, could not. So now, Maxwell's head remained unbowed. He watched the blazered rows, the solemn, still uncomprehending faces. Here and there shoulders shook and arms furtively crept out for comfort.

'Show some respect, for God's sake,' a voice hissed next to him. 'You might not have known Bill Pardoe, but that's rather beside the point, isn't it?'

Maxwell turned to his accuser. She was mid-forties with a mass of wild, red hair and a Cambridge gown. Her head was down but her eyes were everywhere.

'Thank you.' Sheffield broke the silence. 'Mr Larson will dismiss you.' He paused on the top step of the chaplain's pulpit. 'Tuesday. Business as usual, please, everybody.' And there was an audible breath as he clattered down the aisle, gown flying in his wake and backed by the prefects of Tennyson and Dickens and Kipling and Austen, glittering in coloured ties and silver braid.

'I'm sorry, Mrs...' Maxwell turned to the redhead.

'Miss,' she snapped.

'Of course,' Maxwell smiled. He hadn't heard such a convincing Dick Emery in years. 'I meant no disrespect to Bill Pardoe, I assure you.'

'So why didn't you bow your head?'

'I've got this neck problem,' Maxwell smiled at her.

'No doubt this is not how you do things in Dropout Comprehensive or wherever you come from.'

'No,' Maxwell told her. 'Not exactly. And that's Leighford, by the way. Leighford High.' He held out a hand as the ranks began to file past. 'I'm Peter Maxwell.'

Her green eyes flickered in hesitation, then she managed an apology. 'I'm sorry,' she said. 'We're all a bit on edge. I'm Maggie Shaunessy. I'm Head of Austen House.'

'Miss Shaunessy.'

She turned to go as her girls trooped out. Then she stopped. 'Look, er ... Mr Maxwell. I feel ... oh dear, I'm not good at this. I've got a free now. Would you care for some coffee? I owe you that at least.'

Maxwell smiled. 'Coffee would be nice,' he said.

She laughed. 'I can't guarantee that. Cassandra.'

A beautiful girl with eyes a man could drown in swung to her side. 'Miss Shaunessy?' Cassandra was tall and elegant in her silver-braided Prefect's blazer and her neat, pleated skirt. Next to her, Maggie Shaunessy looked like an unmade bed.

'Mr Maxwell will be taking coffee with me in Northanger. Tell Dr Sheffield I'll be along later, will you?'

'Of course, Miss Shaunessy,' and the girl was gone.

'Is this some kind of fact-finding tour, Mr Maxwell?' the Housemistress asked. 'Your being at Grimond's?'

68

'Max,' he said. 'Call me Max. In a way. But it's all rather eclipsed now, isn't it?'

He walked with her across the quad and between the red brick buildings that housed the Art Department. 'I suppose it is,' she said. 'God, it's unbelievable. This way.'

Austen House was very definitely not part of old Jedediah Grimond's grand design. It looked very eighties, but the pale pink of the bricks showed a real attempt to make it blend with the original. Maggie Shaunessy led Maxwell up a broad open-plan staircase lined with vast oil canvasses of girlie subjects. Then they were in the rather pleasant suite of rooms she called Northanger, all plants and air and light. Rowing trophies lined the corridor and ancient shields and cups shone silver in glass-fronted cabinets.

'I know,' she smiled. 'Not exactly an abbey, is it? But it's in keeping with Jane Austen. The trophies are all from St Hilda's.'

'You teach English?'

'For my sins,' she trilled. The Killarney brogue was there still. Overlaid perhaps with Benenden and Girton, but there all the same. She busied herself with the coffee makings. Not for Austen House the clapped out kettles of Leighford. This was a rather suave espresso maker, puffing and bubbling as it went through its motions.

'You knew Bill Pardoe well?' Maxwell asked.

'Not really,' she said. 'I'm from St Hilda's you see. We only joined Grimond's two years ago. I was Head of Sixth there.'

'Dear lady,' Maxwell sat up on the soft, pastel chair she'd given him, saluting a kindred spirit when he saw one. 'There aren't many of us left.'

She laughed. 'You too? I miss it. I wasn't sure I'd be very good with the little ones. Eleven and so on. It's a terrible age. Look,' her eyes dropped as she fought for words, 'what I said about Drop-out Comprehensive... I didn't mean...'

He held up his hand, shaking his head. 'Forget it,' he said. 'If you went there, it would probably reinforce your view.'

'Sugar?'

'One. Thanks. Ah,' his eyes lighted on a poetry book on the Head of House's shelves. *Up the Line to Death*. Edward Thomas lived near here, didn't he?'

'Over at Steep, yes. Are you English Lit., Max?'

'No. God, no. History. English is my subsid, but I've never taught it for real. What was Bill?'

'Classics.'

'Ah,' Maxwell smiled. 'Now that really is the Great Divide between us, isn't it? Thanks.' He took the proffered cup.

'Not done at ... er ... Leighford?'

Maxwell shook his head. 'Although I do have several kids to whom every subject is Greek.'

'Mind you, it's dying here,' Maggie Shaunessy said and instantly regretted it. 'God, this is so difficult.'

'Soldiers,' Maxwell changed the subject. 'You have a Cadet Force?'

'Army, yes. It used to be combined, I believe, but that was before my time. Those things depend of staffing, don't they?'

'Indeed. Who runs that?'

'David Gallow, Head of History. He's a

Captain or something in the T.A. I'm afraid, coming from a girls' school, I don't know much about it. Coffee not too awful?'

'The coffee's fine,' Maxwell smiled.

There was a knock at the study door and the lovely girl popped her head around it.

'Cassandra?' Maggie Shaunessy was arranging herself on the chair opposite Maxwell's.

'Sorry to bother you, Miss, but Dr Sheffield would like to see Mr Maxwell. Now.'

'Oh?' the Head of House frowned. 'But...'

'No, no,' Maxwell was on his feet. 'His Master's Voice,' he swigged what was left in the cup. 'Thanks ... Maggie. Perhaps we can talk again.'

'I'd like that. Cassandra, take Mr Maxwell across, will you?'

He walked with the girl down the open staircase and out into the day. They passed the limes and made for the main buildings, old Jedediah's house.

'Cassandra,' he said. 'Old Priam's daughter.'

'Sir?' the girl arched an eyebrow, looking him up and down with vague disgust.

'In Greek mythology,' Maxwell explained. 'Cassandra was the daughter of the Trojan king. The God Apollo was transfixed by her beauty and gave her the gift of prophecy.'

'I was actually named after the Gulf of Cassandra,' she told him flatly, 'in Southern Greece. Where, apparently, I was conceived. That's fairly typical of my mother, to remember where, but not necessarily with whom.' They had reached the Headmaster's door and Cassandra rapped on it. 'You have a nice day, Mr Maxwell.' And she

71

was gone, her school skirt swinging to the sway of her hips.

'Agamemnon's plaything,' Maxwell was talking to himself now in the corridor at the end of the world.

'Ah, Maxwell.' The Headmaster had dropped the 'Mr' in the space of twenty-four hours. Maxwell had been to a school like this; he wasn't surprised. Surnames were de rigeur – that and silly, politically incorrect sobriquets. He stood in the opulence of Sheffield's study and wasn't asked to sit down.

'Leave?' Maxwell repeated. 'That's a shame, sir.'

'Yes, well, there it is. No one's going to be themselves for a while, not really.'

'All the more reason for me to stay,' Maxwell told him.

Sheffield looked up at his man. There was a steel about Maxwell he hadn't noticed before, an inner strength.

'I could tell you to go,' Sheffield reminded him.

'You could,' Maxwell nodded slowly. 'But I don't think that's the Grimond's way, is it?'

'Er...' Sheffield was rather flustered. One of his housemasters was dead. There were policemen in the quads, paparazzi at the gates in ever increasing numbers, nosing, poking about, photographing. And a stubborn stranger staring back at him across his own carpet. George Sheffield's world was becoming decidedly pear-shaped.

Chapter Five

The whispers began that afternoon, shortly after Mrs Oakes had done everybody proud with her baked cod. Maxwell tried to catch them as he wandered the library, drooling at the array of A-level texts for which he himself, given another throw of the psychopathological dice, might have killed Bill Pardoe.

'They say he was pushed,' was the sage comment of a Lower Fifth kid out of the corner of his mouth.

'Sheffield did it,' his ginger oppo told a little huddle who were supposed to be researching land forms for Geography.

'They never got on,' a fat girl from Austen House confided, but what did she know, the lads silently asked themselves.

'I heard it was Tubbsy.'

'Never!'

'He wouldn't have the nerve.'

'There's only one of 'em in the clear,' the ginger nut participated. 'Mr Graham. He was the only one not here.'

'What about ... him?' the fat girl's breasts were oozing out over the table as she leaned low to whisper. Her thumb shot out in Maxwell's direction.

'Who the fuck *is* he?' the sage hissed. And the question had barely left his lips when Maxwell

73

was hovering over them all. 'I'm your worst nightmare,' he smiled. 'A teacher with twenty-twenty hearing and eyes in my arse. Does that answer your question, young man?'

And suddenly, for the whole table, Geography landforms, open on their books before them, had never seemed so fascinating.

At Grimond's front gates, between the pillars with their stone gargoyle lions, the Horatius that was George Sheffield stood squarely in front of the invading hordes that were the Fourth Estate. To his right, Mervyn Larson, his Deputy, stood like Herminius. And to his left, the Lartius of the Grimond three was Anthony Graham, hot foot from Leighford to the sunny south-east. He had taken his leave of Sylvia over a grabbed breakfast, dashed in to Legs Diamond's office as a courtesy and had driven north-west.

'I'm sorry, gentlemen,' Sheffield raised both hands for quiet. All three had left their gowns on their hooks, lest they inflamed the more Leftie tabloids, their politics bristling with envy. All would have been well for the *Mail* and the *Telegraph*, but the *Guardian* was there and the *Independent*. Readers of the *Sun* and the *Mirror* would have assumed they were wearing fancy dress. The blokes from the *Daily Sport* were skirting the hedge, trying to get photos of the girlies in a netball match.

'I'm sorry, but I have no intention of letting you in,' the Headmaster was saying. 'There are over five hundred children in this school and they are all in my care.'

74

'What about the dead man, Dr Sheffield?' a journalist asked between the popping of the camera flashes.

'I have been instructed by the police to say nothing to you,' the Headmaster went on, clearly irritated by the lights and the booms pushed under his nose.

'Is Superintendent Mason calling a press conference?' another asked.

'I have no idea. This whole thing is a tragic accident. Can we please leave it at that?'

He turned away from another barrage of questions, then turned back. 'Just one thing more,' he bellowed, the veins in his neck standing out. 'I will not tolerate any of my staff or my pupils being pestered by you people. Rest assured, I shall be straight on to the Press Complaints Commission the instant I get wind of anything like that.'

And he marched off, leaving Larson and Graham to swing the iron gates to and lock them.

'How do they find out about these things, Meryn?' a bewildered Sheffield asked his Number Two as the man joined him, their feet crunching in time on the gravel.

'Blood.' From nowhere, Peter Maxwell was with them. No one had seen him striding out across the Grimond grass. 'They smell it, like sharks in the water. Hello, Tony.' He nodded at Graham.

'Have you some experience of this sort of thing, Maxwell?' Sheffield asked.

'Some,' Maxwell nodded, tilting back his tweed hat. 'Who's your newest recruit?'

'Staffwise?' Sheffield pondered. 'Tim Robinson. Games and Physical Education. Been with us since the start of term.'

'That's who they'll go for.'

'Mr Maxwell,' Larson smiled, unconvinced. 'You sound like an old pro.' The Deputy Head-master had met the Head of Sixth briefly at lunch the previous day. He was a tall man with chiselled features and iron grey hair, immaculately groomed.

'Earning my last five bob,' Maxwell winked at him. 'Trust me, gentlemen.' He turned to face them where the Science Block arched to the south. 'I've been in your position before. One of my sixth form was killed, some years back. At least,' he pointed to the gate, 'you've got some sort of security here. Our site is wide open.'

'But that's trespass, surely,' Graham said, 'if one of them comes onto Grimond's property.'

'This isn't the dark Ages, Tony,' Maxwell growled. 'What are you going to do? Set the dogs on them? The man-traps? They'll have every excuse under the sun for being somewhere they shouldn't. And if they can't wriggle out, they'll just stump up whatever fine the law throws at them. They can afford it, all of them. Christ, the sons of the heir to the throne can't get any privacy. What chance do you think you stand?'

'What's your advice?' Sheffield asked, hating himself for doing it.

'Talk to your new man – Robinson? Make sure he's sound. Send out a letter to parents, day kids and boarders. Explain the reason for "softly softly". Work with Hall.'

'I wanted to ask you about that,' Sheffield said, waiting until a brace of children had passed, saluting them with a frosty 'Good afternoon, whoever you are. How do you know him?'

Maxwell chuckled. 'We're old sparring partners,' he said. 'He's almost as cuddly as a barracuda – no station hugs for him. But he's shrewd as all get out and I'd go to the wire with him.' He looked at their faces. 'Sorry,' he smiled. 'A few too many clichés there, I'm afraid. I watch a lot of television.'

Sheffield closed to Maxwell. 'Can you talk to him?' he asked. 'I want the lid kept on this. And if you know the man...'

Maxwell raised his hands. 'I'm not sure that would work,' he said.

'Mr Maxwell,' politeness had returned. 'An hour ago I was all set to kick you off the premises. Now, well ... I may have been hasty. I'd like you to stay and I'd like you to work with Inspector Hall. Please?'

Maxwell looked at his man. George Sheffield had aged a thousand years in the last day and the straw he was clutching at was a crusty old Head of Sixth Form from Dropout Comprehensive. 'I'll give it a whirl, Headmaster,' he smiled.

'Thank you,' Sheffield shook his hand warmly. 'Mervyn, get hold of Robinson, will you?' He patted his Deputy's arm. 'Word to the wise and so on. Now, Tony,' he put his arm around Graham's shoulder, 'about running Tennyson...'

Incident Rooms are the same the world over. It doesn't matter whose patch they're on; whether they're in a state of the art nick or a village hall. This one was a village hall, in the heart of Selborne, with the dark-treed Hanger rising above it. The Ladies Bridge Club had put in an official complaint to the Chief Constable and the Ladies Aerobics Group (virtually the same ladies, in fact) had done a runner at the arrival of the fuzz. Only their Treasurer, a feisty old biddy addicted to reruns of the Golden Girls, had stood her ground, spitting blood in the face of a rather bemused sergeant about how she paid his inflated salary. It was just the pique of someone tragically losing life's eternal battle against cellulite.

The phone points moved in, the electricians and the computers. There were more miles of cable than crossed the Atlantic on a daily basis. And of course, it was raining. Henry Hall's anonymous specs were beaded with water as he ducked in under the Gothic porchway some Victorian Selbornians had lovingly arched over the door, providing a reading room all those years ago for the natives of Gilbert White's village.

'Here,' he pointed to the corner of the anteroom where he wanted his desk and a pair of long-suffering constables gratefully deposited the load. 'Afternoon, Mark.'

DCI West had arrived, unannounced, his hair plastered to his forehead and his raincoat steaming. 'Settling in all right, Henry?'

'It's early days, as you see.'

West did. It irked him all the same, that it was his officers bustling hither and yon, at the diktat of an outsider. His smile was pure cyanide. 'The Chief Super asked me to look in.'

'He did?' Hall had wiped his glasses now and his eyes behind them had resumed their lifelessness.

'In a manner of speaking.' West was mechanically taking stock, watching the whirl of activity around him. 'Not like that, Carter, you'll rupture yourself. Any chance of a coffee, Lynda?'

'Er ... Mark,' Hall clicked open the side door. 'A word?'

West followed his Sussex counterpart into the Inner Sanctum, where another desk, chair and computer were already set up. 'The Chief Super didn't send you, did he?' He looked his man squarely in the face. West's jaw flexed, then he relaxed and smiled. 'No,' he said. 'It's a fair cop. Look, you know how it is. My patch and all. You'll be the same when I return the compliment.'

'Sorry?'

'You know,' West was still smiling. 'When I come to your manor. Any date fixed for that, yet?'

Hall shook his head. 'I haven't heard,' he said. 'Now, if you don't mind, Mark.' He checked his watch.

'Yes,' West sighed. 'Of course. I've got a bank job in Petworth to sort out. You wouldn't credit what goes on behind locked doors in these sleepy little towns, eh? Well, keep in touch.' And he swept out, slamming the door just a *little* hard for Hall's liking and whisking a WPC away by the elbow as he made for the door. Hall let him go and gave his new team ten minutes. Then he called them to order.

'For those of you who don't know me,' he said, hands on hips to show off his three-piece, 'I'm DCI Hall, out of Leighford, West Sussex. I'm here because of politics – inter-force co-operation between top brass.' He raked them all with those unfathomable eyes, knowing the reaction of hard-nosed coppers to the very word 'brass'. 'I know there are those of you who would prefer to work with DCI West.' There was the odd shuffle and flicker of eyeballs. 'Well, that's understandable. But there's a man dead at Grimond's school and until I decide otherwise, we're treating the death as suspicious and you will take orders from me. Is that understood?'

There were murmurs and the odd, scraping cough.

'Half an hour,' he said. 'Then I want everybody back here in full reporting mode. Got it?'

More murmurs.

'Lynda?' He caught the eye of the pretty, dumpy WPC in the corner.

'Sir?'

'Any chance of a coffee?'

Henry Hall's new team didn't know much. William Francis Pardoe was fifty-one years old when he went off the Grimond's roof. He'd been educated at Charterhouse and Merton College, Oxford. After a brief spell in insurance, he'd gone into teaching, a state school somewhere in the North East. He'd joined Grimond's twenty-one years ago, as Assistant Classics teacher. He'd taken over Tennyson House eight years later. Nothing was known of his private life. The team had drawn a blank there. Henry Hall thanked them and told them all to carry on. He didn't like brick walls and dead ends; and that, in the life of Bill Pardoe, seemed to be all there was. If he killed himself, why? If someone else had done it, who?

As another spring dusk descended on sleepy Selborne, the Chief Inspector hung his jacket over the back of his chair and looked at the objects on his desk, lit with the radiance of his lamp. They were all the worldly goods of William Francis Pardoe, apart from the books that still lined his study at Grimond's. There was a Swiss Army knife, a glass paperweight with swirling bubbles, a letter opener and a pipe with a worn, gnawed stem.

'No tobacco pouch, Mr Pardoe?' Hall murmured to himself. 'Where's that, I wonder? And who...' Hall picked up the handsome silver-mounted photograph of a pretty blond boy, '...is this?'

The boy was sitting cross-legged on what appeared to be a tree stump. An alert-looking Border Collie sat with him.

He clicked the intercom. 'Lynda. Get me Leighford nick, will you. DS Jacquie Carpenter. I'll wait.'

Michael Helmseley served a mean brandy. Mean in the sense that Peter Maxwell could barely see the film of it covering the bottom of the glass. Clearly, 'three fingers' was a measurement lost on the head of Classics. He was a large man in a shapeless grey suit that looked like an old one of Patrick Moore's. His glasses were thick and he had the smallest mouth Maxwell had ever seen on a grown man.

'Domineering wives,' he murmured. 'That's what that lot need.'

'Sorry?' Maxwell was relaxing in the lamp-lit

81

corner of the Senior Common room, which the historian in him knew had been old Jedediah's master bedroom. Helmseley was lounging in what was clearly 'his' chair and probably had been since St Patrick had kicked all the snakes out of Ireland.

'Those arrogant buggers in Upper Five Bee. You know the sort, Maxwell, I'm sure; think they know it all because they learn a bit of Caesar. Caesar!' he downed his brandy. 'It's like reading *Noddy Goes To The Toilet*. You don't have Latin, I suppose, where you are?'

'No,' Maxwell smiled. 'When I first joined there was an elder statesman on the staff who hand-picked the Oxbridge types and took them through a bit of Virgil, I believe.' Maxwell smiled to himself. That was a long time ago and he *was* that elder statesman now.

'Even here, of course,' Helmseley ruminated, 'it's all watered down. Classical civilization. The language and literature element is only a minor part. Might as well pass it all over to Gallow's department. You're an historian, aren't you?'

'So rumour has it,' Maxwell nodded. 'Tell me, Michael, how are you going to manage without Bill Pardoe?'

'Lord knows,' Helmseley sighed. He was leaning back in the huge, leather armchair, his hands clasped across his chest, the brandy balloon stem cradled between his fingers. 'I expect George will place an advertisement after a suitable period. What possessed him?' He was shaking his head.

'You're surprised?'

Helmseley's eyes flickered behind the bottle-bottomed lenses. 'No,' he said. 'Not really. Would you care for another brandy, Maxwell?'

The Head of Sixth would, in that he'd barely had a first one, and he held out his balloon. Helmseley struggled over to the drinks cabinet and poured for them both. 'You know,' said the Head of Classics, 'I lived on this stuff at Oxford. Brandy and Mars Bars. No wonder I lost control of my waist years ago. Here's to happier times,' and they clinked glasses.

'You were telling me about Bill Pardoe,' Maxwell settled back on the Chesterfield.

'Was I?' Helmseley frowned. 'Oh, yes. Well, I've known Bill Pardoe for the best part of sixteen years, man and boy. He wasn't happy lately.'

'Oh?'

'Little things, you notice. He took to late night walks when the school had gone to bed, down by the lake mostly. Developed an obsession about mail.'

'Mail?'

'Yes.' Helmseley was still trying to puzzle it out. 'We get the conventional two deliveries a day here at Grimond's. He'd be there when he could, waiting for the postman, as if he were perpetually expecting some vital missive.'

'Did it ever come?' Maxwell asked.

'God knows!' Helmseley shrugged. 'Bill was never exactly the demonstrative type. In the life of a boarding school you get to know the House staff pretty well, really. David Gallow now, is an open book; cricket-mad with a nodding awareness of his subject. Tony Graham; keen as mustard and a nice chap to boot. Old Tubbsy ... well, enough

83

said, really. You know the names of their first pet hamsters and their invisible childhood friends, which rugger team they support and so on. But Bill ... well, he was a charming man and a bloody good Housemaster, but he'd only let you know what he wanted you to know. I think he might have been married once.'

'Really?'

'Oh, not in the time I knew him, obviously. I've never been tempted to tie the knot myself, but I remember one time he was looking at a photograph, thing in a frame. It was a woman and child if I remember rightly.'

'And?'

'Well, this was in his study at Tennyson. I'd gone to sort out a time-tabling glitch with him and there he was, just standing there, staring at it. He pushed it into a drawer as I arrived, saying it was an old photo of his mother and him as a boy.'

'And it wasn't?'

'Fashions were wrong. The boy in the photo was flaxen. Bill's hair was still brown then. Unless he'd become a slave in the intervening years to Grecian 2000 and his mother was the Nostradamus of the catwalk, it didn't make sense.'

'Would that explain his waiting for the post?' Maxwell asked. 'Some contact with his family?'

Helmseley shook his head. 'I don't know,' he said. 'In the last couple of weeks particularly, Bill became ... well, withdrawn, distant. I wish now I'd talked to him. You know, sat him down and talked him out of it. It's funny, I'd never have said Bill was the suicidal type. He always seemed so strong, somehow. Capable. I'm not sure Tony's got it.'

'What?' Maxwell asked.

'Whatever it takes,' Helmseley said. 'That indefinable something that makes a good Housemaster. He's a good listener though, I suppose, but all the same, a little too intense. You're a Head of Sixth, aren't you? It must be the same for you.'

Maxwell quaffed the last of his brandy. 'I'm not sure, Michael, that anything at Leighford is the same as here.'

'It's late, Max.' Tony Graham was already in a towelling bath robe and slippers, in the rooms down the stairs and along the corridor from Maxwell's landing.

'It is,' Maxwell checked his watch. The witching hour. 'I'll call back.'

'No, no,' the acting Housemaster opened the door more fully. 'Don't be silly. Come in. I'm trying to make sense of all this.' He waved around the interior of Bill Pardoe's study. 'To tell you the truth, I'm feeling bloody guilty about being here.'

'Guilty?'

Graham closed the door behind his visitor. 'Like standing in a dead man's shoes. What the hell happened?'

Maxwell shook his head. There were papers everywhere, piles of books and student files. 'Damned if I know,' he said. 'I've just come from Michael Helmseley.'

'Christ, then you'll need a drink.'

Maxwell laughed. It seemed almost sacrilegious

in Bill Pardoe's Sanctum. 'That infamous, is he? I did get two brandies.'

'No, you didn't. You barely got one.' Graham clinked glasses as he rummaged in Pardoe's cabinet. 'That won't have touched the sides. Doesn't have much of a giving nature, our revered Head of Classics. Sylvia Matthews tells me you're a Southern Comfort man. 'And he pulled out a bottle of the same.

'Manna!' Maxwell beamed. 'I didn't know Bill Pardoe but I'm warming to him already. Have you been able to talk to anybody yet?'

'Dr Sheffield had a word. Funny, suddenly it's "call me George". I remember it was the same when I made House Prefect all those years ago.' He whistled through his teeth.

'You're Head of Tennyson now?'

'Acting,' Graham told him. 'I won't take it, of course. Dead men's shoes. Not a good omen. The chaps are pretty cut up.'

'Jenkins especially.'

'Jenkins?' Graham passed Maxwell his glass.

'Lower Fourths or thereabouts. Jug-handle ears. Always twentieth man in the Cross Country team.'

'Oh, yes,' Graham placed him. 'Jenkins. Look at this place.' He slid a pile of files off a chair for Maxwell to sit down. 'It was turned upside down when I got here. Looked as though it had been ransacked.'

'That'll be the boys in blue.'

'The police?'

'It's routine. When a man dies, they go through his desks, his laundry basket, every orifice the

poor bastard's got. And they're not very particular about putting anything back afterwards,
either. My light o' love is a detective.'

'Ah, that'll be Jacquie,' Graham smiled, sitting
opposite his man and sipping his drink.

'I knew it was a mistake sending you to Sylvia's.
Is there anything you don't know about me?'

Graham laughed. 'You know that woman used
to be in love with you, don't you?'

'Sylv?' Maxwell's eyes widened. 'You're having
me on.'

'Just an observation,' Graham shrugged.

'You'll be telling me next Dierdre Lessing, our
beloved Senior Mistress, has the hots for me.'

'Ah,' Graham's face fell. 'No, I can't bullshit
you there, Max. Bit of a dragon, isn't she?'

'The original Drakul, dear boy. When the
boilers pack up, we get her to breathe on them.
Invaluable, really.'

'Something else I don't know about you,'
Graham said.

'Oh? What's that?' Maxwell quaffed the amber
nectar.

'Why you're still here.'

'It seems Dr Sheffield has need of me.'

'Oh yes. I was there, remember. From his point
of view you're a hero on a white horse and the
Seventh Cavalry all rolled into one. But what do
you get out of it? You didn't know Bill Pardoe.'

'No,' Maxwell nodded. 'That's true. But a little
boy called Jenkins did.'

Graham blinked. 'Jenkins asked you to stay?'

'Not in so many words,' Maxwell smiled. 'Now.
Let's see it we can't brainstorm a little, late as it

is. What can you tell me about Bill Pardoe?'

She felt goosebumps crawl over her shoulders and arms. All the same, she'd come this far. She'd go through with it now. She let her long hair cascade over her naked back, peeling the lacy bra down so that her large breasts jutted out pert under the fitful moon, sneaking furtive glances at her behind its cloud cover.

She held the velvet heart in both hands, kneeling on the cold, soft earth. She whispered her name over and over, the name of love. Then she stood up, shaking now with the cold of night and the emotion of the moment. She slid the tracksuit bottom and her panties down her solid thighs and kicked them off. Now she was skyclad, kneeling again with the little trowel flashing in her hand. She muttered the words she'd learned, the words of love, the forbidden words, driving the steel again and again into the dank moss, making the sacred hole.

She took the heart again, the one she'd made secretly in needlework with their initials embroidered with silver beads. And she buried it there, her hair enveloping the hole as she whispered into it, like King Midas of old. A few deft strokes and the soil was back and the hole gone and the heart covered.

She closed to the spot, her lips moving imperceptibly above the moss. 'Cassandra. Cassandra.'

Chapter Six

The school was still at chapel when DCI Hall arrived in his polished Volvo. There was a woman with him, DS Carpenter. They left the car under the limes, Hall carrying a briefcase, Jacquie a tape recorder.

Sheffield was waiting for them in his study. 'I've put you in here.' He led them into a side office. 'You shouldn't be disturbed and as you see, there's a door of your own, as it were. Tell me, Chief Inspector, do you intend to do anything about the gentlemen of the Press? They're besieging my gate.'

'I know,' Hall nodded. 'I just drove through them. Unfortunately, they're not breaking the law by being there.'

'I won't have them pestering my people.'

'There's no clear law against that, either.'

'Privacy, surely?' Sheffield insisted.

'It'll be a cold day in Hell when you can make that one stick. I'll get someone from the local force to talk to them; at least they might get somewhere with your local rag.'

'Er ... I'm sorry, you mean you're not Hampshire CID?' Sheffield was confused.

'No, sir.' Hall set up his briefcase on the desk in front of him. 'Neither is DS Carpenter. Jacquie, this is Dr Sheffield, Headmaster.'

She held out a hand. He took it absentmindedly. 'Sir Arthur is on his way over. He'll want to talk to you.'

'Sir Arthur?' Hall supervised as Jacquie set up the tape recorder, leads and wires, coiling the microphone flex on the side table.

'Sir Arthur Wilkins, our Chair of Governors. I got in touch with him in Bermuda. He's flown back.'

'Essential, is he?' Hall asked. 'Your Chair of Governors?'

'Vital,' Sheffield assured him. 'Especially now Grimond's seems to be open house to half Fleet Street or wherever they keep these people nowadays.'

'I'd like to talk to your teaching staff first, if that's all right.'

'Well, they all have full timetables, Chief Inspector,' Sheffield said.

'Not as full as mine, sir.' A more human policeman would have smiled at that point. Jacquie noticed that not a flicker crossed Hall's lips.

'I'll send Mervyn Larson, my Deputy,' Sheffield reached for his gown. 'I've set up a rota of prefects to act as runners. Will that do?'

'I'm sure it will,' Hall nodded.

'And coffee. You'd like some refreshments?'

'Thank you.'

'I'll get Parker, our steward, to set up a machine for you. I expect interviewing is thirsty work.' The Headmaster hauled on the gown, looked at the officers for a moment, then went about his business.

'That's a worried man,' Jacquie observed.

'Of course,' Hall nodded. 'He's got something

to hide.'

'What?' Jacquie was testing the equipment.

'That,' Hall was arranging his papers, 'remains to be seen.'

'Morning, Max. I may call you Max?' David Gallow was emerging from chapel before day and battle broke.

'Please,' Maxwell said. He'd been impressed by the kids this morning. After the solemn words of yesterday, there was a briskness about the chapel service, the chaplain more muscular in his Christianity. John Selwyn, the Captain of Tennyson, read the lesson in his impeccable Home Counties, an anonymous Music A-level type (you could tell them the wide world o'er) played a bit of Bach beautifully and everyone was reminded, via the hymn, that Christ was their cornerstone.

'We've got a debate next lesson,' Gallow said. 'The Lower Sixth arguing the toss over Charles I's responsibility for the Civil War. Care to sit in on that?'

'Very much. On the way over, though, you can tell me about the CCF.'

The Corps?' Gallow shrugged. 'Nothing much to tell.'

'You're a T.A captain, I understand?'

'Slow down, Wentworth!' the Head of History barked at a hapless child hurtling down the chapel steps. 'P.E.,' he tutted. 'He doesn't dash to his History with the same relish, I've noticed. Who told you about my rank?'

'Er ... Maggie Shaunessy, I think. Does it matter?'

'No,' Gallow said. 'Not at all.'

He led Maxwell up a flight of shallow steps into a low-ceilinged room with maps of Europe all over the walls, and posters extolling students to read History at Stirling, Aberystwyth and Belfast. Ethnomania and the Celtic Fringe had even reached Grimond's, Maxwell noted.

'They'll be a few minutes yet. House assemblies on Wednesdays.'

'You're not attached to a House?'

'Dickens, nominally, but the Corps duties get me out of most of that. What did you want to know about them?'

'Do they ever carry out night exercises?'

Gallow frowned, pausing as he stacked exercise books on his desk. 'We have,' he said slowly. 'There was a big joint operation with Churchers and Bedales last year. I'm not sure it's worth all the organizational trauma, though. Why do you ask?'

'Well,' Maxwell chuckled. 'It's funny, really. I may, in fact, have been dreaming, but I could have sworn I saw a group of them night before last.'

'Where?' Gallow wanted to know.

'In the quad,' Maxwell was looking at it now, staring out of the History Department's window. 'And the odd thing was, they were carrying a coffin.'

Gallow was suddenly at his side. 'A coffin? Max, are you serious?'

Maxwell turned to him. 'You mean, did I seriously dream it or seriously see it?' He smiled. 'I'm not sure.'

'Where would they get a coffin, for God's sake?' Gallow asked him. 'It's not exactly an everyday object at a school, is it?'

'I thought, perhaps, the woodwork shop?'

The door opened and a jumble of assorted sixth formers, male and female, tumbled in, mumbling inconsequentially about this and that.

'Shut up!' Gallow screamed at them, slamming a textbook on his desk. 'For God's sake!'

To Maxwell, it seemed a little overkill. Nobody, after all, was jumping off a table or gobbing out of a window.

'Psst!' Maxwell spun to the sound. He couldn't believe it. Tucked in behind the lowest branches of a large cedar tree was a face he knew. He checked that the coast was clear.

'Jacquie!' and they kissed, while he selected which cliché to choose. 'What are you doing here?' It had to be, really.

'Working with Hall.'

'You're seconded too?' he joined her the lake side of the ancient, gnarled trunk, away from the buildings.

'Got the call late yesterday.'

'Why?'

There'd been a time when Jacquie Carpenter had told Peter Maxwell nothing about a case she was working on. That was when she didn't know him. Ever since then, he'd wheedled things out of her. He'd flutter his long eyelashes and do his little-boy-lost look and she was his, butter in his mouth, putty in his hands, whatever metaphor came to mind. She'd hated herself, of course,

93

because she'd been unprofessional in a job she loved and because she knew he'd use the information on whatever amateur game he was playing. If only Peter Maxwell had joined the police all those years ago after Cambridge – the combination of his brain and her computerized street-cred would have been irresistible. As it was, he'd gone into teaching, casting his pearls before swine and he'd become Mad Max.

'I don't know.'

She knew the look. The arched eyebrow. Followed by the big, doe eyes and the downturned corners of the mouth. 'No,' she all but stamped her foot. 'I *really* don't know.'

Maxwell leaned back against the bark. 'Don't think he's after your body, do you?'

She ignored him. 'He's after somebody's.'

'He's interviewing?'

Jacquie nodded. 'Working his way through the staff. He's got through Larson so far – Deputy Head?'

'I know him,' Maxwell said. 'Strong silent type?'

'Now, Max...' her hand was already in the air.

'I know,' Maxwell interrupted her; they'd played this game before. 'You can't divulge, etcetera, etcetera. What did he tell you?'

A distant clanging of a bell saved Jacquie's professionalism.

'Lesson Two,' Maxwell said, turning to where, extraordinarily, uniformed children were on their way with amazing rapidity to classrooms. How utterly unlike life in his own dear school. 'They still call them periods here; quaint, isn't it? Who's he seeing next?'

'Graham.'

'On the grounds that Pardoe was his boss?'

'That's right.'

'What's he up to, Jacquie?' Maxwell was frowning, puzzling it out.

'What?' There were times when she couldn't keep up with this man.

'Who's interviewing?'

'I told you,' she said. 'Me and Hall.'

'Hall and I,' he couldn't help correcting her – it went with the territory. 'Nobody from the local force?'

'No.'

'And the tone in that "no" means...?'

'All right,' she conceded. 'It is a *little* unusual. I'll fish.'

'Good girl.' He reached across and kissed her forehead. 'You'll make someone a good wife, Woman Policeman Carpenter.'

'Thank you, kind sir,' and she curtseyed. Maxwell didn't know she knew how to do that. As he turned away from the tree, she caught his arm. 'What are you doing?'

He dug a piece of crumpled paper out of his jacket pocket; his timetable for the week. 'French. Lower Fifths. Pure joy.'

'No,' she said, hands on hips. 'What are you really doing?'

'Talking to the new bloke, Robinson of PE, about the death of Bill Pardoe. Where are you staying?'

'Same hotel as the DCI. Barcourt Lodge, out on the A-Something.'

'Ring me tonight,' he whispered. 'I'll watch for thee by moonlight, though Hell should bar the way.' And she watched as he lost himself in the surging sway making for the Languages Block.

'What's going on, George?' Sir Arthur Wilkins had just fought his way through an army of paparazzi at his own front gates. And even with a crystal of the Headmaster's best claret in his fist, he was not a happy bunny. Wilkins was the epitome of the country squire, eternally pissed off that Oxbridge had let the oiks in, his own family had been crippled by death duties and everything was New Labour and television presenters were called Ali G.

'Arthur,' Sheffield was at a loss. 'You know as much as I.'

'If you'll permit me, George, bollocks. You're the bloody Head, for Christ's sake. It's your job to know.' He closed to the shorter man, his silver moustache bristling. 'It's what we pay you for.'

Sheffield ran an exasperated hand through his sandy hair. His large, comfortable study was suddenly appallingly small. 'The bottom line is, Arthur, there were ... rumours ... about Bill Pardoe.'

'Rumours?' Wilkins had been a navy man all his life. He knew about rumours. It could seep into men's souls, sap the will, sink a ship. 'Bout what?'

'That he was...'

'Queer as a coot?'

Sheffield blinked, sighing. It was better now that it was out in the open. Someone had said it at last. Now he could make a stand. 'There is absolutely no evidence,' he said defiantly.

'No evidence?' Wilkins growled. 'Good God, man. We're trying to run a school here. Can you imagine what those bastards camped at the gates will do with a thing like this? They're the Press, for Christ's sake; they don't need evidence. The last newspaperman with any integrity was William Russell in the Crimea. Who's taking over as Housemaster?'

'Tony Graham. He's young, but he's the obvious choice as Pardoe's junior.'

'Oh, yes,' Wilkins remembered. 'Pushy little tick, but he'll do. Well, get him onto it.'

'What?'

'The evidence,' Wilkins snarled, quaffing half the glass. 'Get him talking to the boys. I want to know if Pardoe had touched any of them up.'

'Now, Arthur...'

'For fuck's sake, George, face reality, will you? The private sector, like the Catholic church, is crawling with perverts. Too many schools are so desperate to recruit, staff and boys, that they don't ask any questions. It's a pederasts' paradise out there. Well, it's not going to happen at Grimond's. Is that understood?'

'Of course, Arthur, but Bill...'

'There are no buts here, George,' Wilkins shouted his man down. 'None at all. If there's been any dinky finger in the dorm, I want to know about it. And get on to Howard.'

'Howard?'

'Gritchley, George, Gritchley. You know, Treasurer to the Governors. Balances the books and pays your wages.' He turned to the window, glowering at the grounds below and the smoking, skulking mob at the gates. 'If any boys are involved, we may need to get our chequebooks out.'

'Arthur...' Sheffield couldn't believe his ears.

'Realism, George,' Wilkins turned to him, barking sharply. '"Every man has his price" after all. It's quite astonishing how reasonable parents can be when the offer of waived fees is on the table.' He turned back to the window. 'Who's that?'

Sheffield joined him at the leaded panes. A man in a Cambridge scarf and a shapeless tweed hat was sauntering across the front lawn, glancing at the mellow brick of the building every now and again, and at the little crowd at the gates. 'Er ... Peter Maxwell. He's here for a couple of weeks, from a state school in Sussex.'

'State school?' Wilkins turned purple and almost swallowed his dentures.

'Someone I met on a course in London,' Sheffield reminded him. 'It seemed a good idea. I sent you a memo.'

'I hope you know what you're doing, George,' and he followed Peter Maxwell with his eyes along the drive that led to the gym. 'Now, where's the flatfoot in charge of the case?'

'I've put him in the planning office.'

Wilkins slammed down the glass. 'What are we going for here, George? Suicide or murder?'

The Headmaster blinked again, feeling himself railroaded as ever by his Chair of Governors. 'We're going for the truth, aren't we?' he asked.

Wilkins guffawed. 'It's obvious you weren't my appointment,' he growled. At the study door, he stopped. 'Suicide,' he said. 'That's what we're going for. "Balance of mind disturbed", that sort of thing. Nobody goes off a roof by accident, so we can't sell anybody that one. Suicide implies derangement of course, and therefore a certain lack of judgement on our part. But it's infinitely preferable to murder, don't you think? I don't even want to go there... Coming, George?'

They faced each other along the dull pink of the piste, the Captain of Tennyson and the Captain of Austen. Maxwell had clashed some steel in his time and he was enjoying this. The spring sunshine was streaming in through the reinforced windows high above the wall bars. Grimond's gym smelt like gyms the world over – rubber mats, feet, groin liniment. And it boomed with the thud of action.

'Who's your money on?' he whispered to Tim Robinson, sitting next to him on the excruciating gym bench.

'Selwyn's got the strength,' Robinson said, 'but he's not as fast as Cassandra.'

'Cassandra?'

'Yes. Have you met?'

'After a fashion,' Maxwell nodded, watching the girl's lithe body in front of him. 'I didn't recognize her under the mask. Bit of a cold fish.'

'Watch,' Robinson told him. 'Fence!'

The foils slid together as the bout began, Selwyn waiting, public schoolboy that he was, for Cassandra to make the first move. One step, two, she drove him gently back.

'You're the new kid on the block, then?' Maxwell asked Robinson.

'That's right. Keep your guard up, John.'

'How are you finding Grimond's?'

Tim Robinson was thirtyish, with a Zapata moustache that gave him a vague 'seventies look. His eyes were dark and flashing. Small wonder there was a coterie of white-suited Austen girls hanging near him, hoping he'd notice their parries-en-sixte. 'It's a learning curve,' Robinson smiled. A shout and a clash. 'First blood to Austen.' A whoop from the girls. 'Keep that guard up, John. I warned you.'

Cassandra bounced back to the starting position.

'You're not electric?' Maxwell asked, noting the lack of wires and circuit boxes.

'Not for practice bouts. This is a warm up. The inter-house is next week.'

'You're Head of Games?'

'God, no. Richard Ames has that distinction.'

'Where were you before?'

'Fence!' the blades scraped together again. 'Army originally,' Robinson said.

'Ah, so this is your first post?'

'No, I was at Haileybury.' Robinson looked away from the action for the first time. 'You ask a lot of questions, Mr Maxwell.'

'Just nosy, I guess,' the Head of Sixth Form shrugged. 'I just feel a little like a fish out of water here, to be honest. Comprehensive oik in a private school. I thought you might relate to that.'

'Did you? Nice one, Cassandra.' The thud and grunt told Maxwell that Cassandra had scored a second palpable hit. The Austen girls whooped and bounced again.

'Dr Sheffield's had a word?'

Robinson half-turned. 'Mr Maxwell, I really fail to see…'

There was a squeal and Selwyn retreated, blade by his side, point down. Cassandra was nursing a bruised rib. The Austen girls booed and hissed. 'Yes, all right,' Robinson signalled, his turn to be taken off guard. 'Two-one to Austen. Everybody all right? Fence!' He closed to Maxwell. 'Yes,' he said quietly. 'Dr Sheffield has spoken to me. The need to keep the lid on things, not to talk to the Press and so on. He really didn't have to.'

Steel rang as Selwyn tried the fleche, but he over-reached himself and came off the piste, steadying himself against the wall. There was a distinct 'Naa-naa-de-naanaa' from the Austen girls. 'Assume your positions!' Robinson told them and the bout recommenced. This time, Cassandra was ready for Selwyn. She crouched like a greyhound in the slips, her right arm locked forward, probing the boy's defences, the red button on her foil tip a blur in the shaft of light. Her feet were firmly grounded, her legs balanced as she came at him, sliding her blade along his, looking for a third opening.

'Tell me,' Maxwell whispered, 'As a relative outsider, do you notice anything odd at Grimond's?'

'Odd? Watch him, Cassandra. Watch your balance. In what way, odd?'

Maxwell shrugged. 'Undercurrents, shall we say? Moods? Every school has them.'

'I'm not all that used to schools, Mr Maxwell. I was only at Haileybury…'

'Hit!' the girls behind the bench roared, giving each other high fives. Selwyn turned away, clenching his fist is fury as the girl had given him a pummelling again. Cassandra bounced back on her agile feet, foil blade wobbling in the morning air.

'Three-one to Austen,' Robinson called out. 'Fence!'

Selwyn's parrying was faster, Cassandra's ripostes more desperate. Each hit was taking it out of her as the stronger fencer banged her blade aside. She winced behind the mask.

'All the more observant, then,' Maxwell persisted. 'You've got an outsider's slant. Bill Pardoe, for instance. What did you have to do with him?'

'Almost nothing. The PE staff aren't attached to Houses. Pardoe was a Housemaster. We'd nod in the corridor, that sort of thing. Easy, Selwyn. This is only a practice.'

The boy ignored him, driving his opponent back. Suddenly, his blade came up, too high and lashed the girl across the mask so that the steel rang out. Cassandra crashed sideways, off the piste. There was a scream from the spectators' gallery overhead and uproar from the girl fencers on the ground. Tim Robinson dashed across the floor to the fallen girl. He helped her to her knees. Cassandra had taken off the mask and knelt there, shaken but unhurt, her long dark hair across her face. Robinson turned to Selwyn who took off his mask and stood there, gnawing his lip in frustrated silence.

'The bout's over,' the gym master said. 'Selwyn, you will apologise to Miss James.'

'Sorry, Cassandra.' The boy saluted her with his sword, an over-the-top flourish if ever Maxwell had seen one, but Robinson hadn't finished. He closed to the lad. 'You're out of the competition next week,' he hissed.

'What?' Selwyn shouted.

'You heard me. Now, do you want to make even more of an exhibition of yourself than you've done already?'

Selwyn drew himself up to his full height, looming over Robinson. 'I shall have a word with Mr Graham,' he said, in that sarcastic way of his.

'You do that. And he'll tell you the same as I would. This sort of behaviour is not on. Epee strokes are not permitted in a foil bout.' Robinson helped Cassandra to her feet. 'Right. Showers. You've got ten minutes to the next lesson. All this gear to be put away. You girls, you're not doing anything.' He pointed to the gaggle who had been giggling near him by the bench. 'Put this lot away.' The Austen girls moaned and began to haul at the piste mat.

He crossed to the visiting Head of Sixth Form. 'Mr Maxwell, I'd be grateful if you didn't distract me again. You must, as a teacher, know how easily accidents happen.'

'Accidents?' Maxwell echoed. 'The Captain of Tennyson broke every rule in the book with that cut. Even for a sabre stroke, it was questionable, but for foil unforgivable.'

Robinson scowled at him. 'Thank you for your observation.' And he spun on his heels. As Cassandra slid past Maxwell, she bent her head a little and smiled, letting her hair fall free of the mask.

It was in the corridor outside that Maxwell waited. He'd hoped that Tim Robinson might be more amenable than the rest, a chink in the defensive wall that was the Grimond staff. As it was, he turned out to be more close-lipped than any of them. A dark-haired girl was coming down the stairs from the gallery, her face scarlet and her cheeks running with tears, dripping onto the starched white of her blouse.

'Are you all right?' Maxwell asked, a Head of Sixth Form in spite of himself.

She looked at him through tear-filled eyes. 'Yes,' she said. 'I'm all right.'

'I'm sure she'll be fine,' he said.

'Who?' the girl sniffed.

'Cassandra. It was you who screamed, wasn't it?'

'Oh, yes,' the girl swallowed, looking through into the gym where the clash of arms had happened. 'I'm sure she'll be fine,' and she spun on her heel and clattered off down the darkness of the outer corridor.

They lay in bed that night in her room at Barcourt Lodge. The green electronic figures read two-sixteen.

'I wonder what's going on at Grimond's tonight?' he asked.

Jacquie propped herself up on one arm. 'Thanks,' she snorted. 'Your mind elsewhere, as always!'

He tried to shove the duvet over her mouth and they giggled in the darkness.

'Are you sure you won't stay?' she asked,

suddenly still, suddenly serious.

'What?' he chuckled, 'and face Henry Hall over the breakfast kipper? "I understand you've been sleeping with one of my officers, Mr Maxwell."' It was a damned good DCI Hall. '"I have to caution you..."'

She cuffed him playfully round the head. 'I don't think I joined the SS,' she said. 'I am allowed to choose my sexual partners, you know.'

'Sexual partners!' he guffawed. 'Sounds like a rather bizarre square dance. Back to back and a dosy-doh!'

'Seriously, though, Max...' she smoothed the hair away from his temple.

'Seriously though, Jacquie,' he took her fingers and kissed them, one by one. 'I must get back. It's been...' and he clambered out of bed.

'Yes?' she said archly.

He turned to her in the darkness, then reached across the bed again, taking her face in both hands before kissing her deeply and slowly. 'More than I deserve and more than I could ask,' he told her and turned away as her eyes filled with the tears he knew were there. 'Now, why would you have hidden a pair of less-than-reputable boxers? And you such a normal-looking girl.' And he counted only to two until her pillow hit him on the back of the head.

She took him back through the moonlight-dappled lanes of Hampshire, the headlights flashing back on the cats' eyes as they drove. A hundred yards or so from Grimond's, he pulled in to the side of the road and cut the engine.

'I can't believe they're still there.' He peered into the darkness ahead where the road was silver under the moon in the absence of Jacquie's head-lights. A dark-headed hydra coiled and recoiled by the gate posts, its breath smoking on the night air. 'They must be frozen. Are the Fourth Estate so desperate these days?'

'Drugs, sex, rock 'n' roll and private schools,' Jacquie said. 'It sells newspapers. Can you find your way from here?'

'There's a little postern to the south-west,' Maxwell told her, unhooking his seat-belt, 'and a little marble cross below the town. I'll do better there than the Barbican at the front. Catch me tomorrow. Where will you be?'

'Same place,' she told him. 'The office off Shef-field's study. We're starting with Tim Robinson.'

'Well, good luck to you,' Maxwell smiled. 'You're bound to do better than I did,' and he kissed her before slipping into the night.

It was chilly as he skirted the hedgerows and the grass felt wet and cold against his trouser bottoms. In an hour or two all would be frost and magic in those hallowed grounds. He'd left the tell-tale scarf and hat in his room under the Grimond eaves and his dark clothes gave him a certain invisibility. Even so, he kept close to the wall that ringed the school and waited until Jacquie's Ka roared off into the night, taking the road to the south to avoid the night-watch of the paparazzi.

Somewhere in the darkness ahead the white ghost of a barn owl flew on silent wings, signify-ing death for some luckless creature of the predawn. Maxwell hurried along the grassy bank, careful not to let himself slip down onto the road and then he was out of sight of the main gates and looking for the chink in the wall.

The side-door he'd told Jacquie about was there all right, but it was locked. Luckily the stones jutted at crazy angles by the lintel and he was able to haul his way up. Gingerly negotiating the jagged glass on top, he lowered himself over the other side, steadying himself before getting his bearings. Grimond's lay black and unlit below him, a sleeping monster in the first tentative rays of pink that tinged the East. To his right the lake lay chill and chiselled with its windy ridges and there was a sighing of the rushes that ringed the water. It was there he saw it, a movement half in, half out of the shadows. And he froze.

Kneeling by the wall, his back against the stone, Maxwell listened. There were muffled voices, male and female, but they were fragmented, like snatches of prayer at vespers in some long-dead monastery. The teacher in him knew that whoever it was should not have been there, in that place, at that hour. The boatyards. That's where it was coming from and he still couldn't make it out. He moved nearer, crouching low and keeping his head down. Damn. There were no clouds overhead now, just the three-quarter brilliance of the moon. He stopped halfway, glancing back at the little, buried postern gate and the gothic blackness of old Jedediah Grimond's little piece of ostentation.

Then he was there, his fingers spread on the cold corrugated iron of the boating-shed wall. He could hear clearly now, a rhythmic grunting punctuated by a screeching sigh. The speed was erratic, but insistent.

'Oh, Christ,' he heard a male voice. 'Oh yes. Cassandra. Yes.'

It was a voice he thought he knew.

Chapter Seven

He heard the scratching again that night, softer this time and nearer to his door. The time was wrong too, not two something but nearer five and he hadn't long fallen asleep. He thought it was part of his dream at first, that Dierdre Lessing, the Fata Morgana of Leighford High School, was running her Nosferatu nails down his blackboard. He woke up sweating, a faint pounding in his head. Then he heard it again.

This time, he didn't bother with the view from the window, whatever that view may give him this time. This time he wrenched open the door and trod on something hard and sharp. 'Shit,' he hissed in the darkness, although the pain told him at once that his diagnosis was wrong. He grovelled on the carpet and stumbled back into his room, holding whatever it was up to the light under his lamp. A cassette, ninety minutes play and with nothing written on it. Surely not Tony Graham giving him a sneak-preview of tomorrow's French lesson with the Upper Sixth? If Peter Maxwell had been Batman, he'd have had a cassette player on his trusty Utility Belt. As it was he'd have to wait until morning.

'Actually, Mr Maxwell, at Grimond's we don't encourage staff to bring coffee into the classroom. It's dangerous and smacks of sloppiness.'

'*Quelle fromage,*' beamed Maxwell, but the bon mot was lost on Stella Cousins, the Head of Modern Languages, a steel-haired blue stocking who might actually have been older than Maxwell and he carried on drinking. 'I've come to have a look at Mr Graham's lesson,' he said.

'Ah, I see.' Stella Cousins was of the old, old school. A teacher from St Hilda's, she realized that women now had the vote and padded shoulders and so on, but her own dear Mama had told her that, deep down, Papa knew best, so, at the merest hint of an obstacle, she tended to defer to men. 'Well, you won't interrupt, will you? The Upper Sixth are off to Avignon week after next and Mr Graham's working on their dialect. It's all about *langue d'oeil* and *langue d'oc*, you know.'

Maxwell knew. He'd cut his teeth on the Albigensian crusade and was the only person still alive to have bought the single of almost the same name by Dominique, the Singing Nun. And anyone more likely to end up in the dock than this frosty old matron, the visiting Head of Sixth Form had yet to meet. It was with something of a relief that he caught sight of Tony Graham wrestling his way in with an armful of exercise books. 'Let me help you with those, Mr Graham.'

The acting head of Tennyson took in the situation at a glance. 'Stella driving you to drink already?' he whispered, smirking, passing a bundle of books to Maxwell.

'You might have warned me,' Maxwell hissed.

'Ah, she's Grimond's secret weapon,' Graham told him, leading the way into a classroom. 'I'm

110

surprised Dr Sheffield doesn't just unleash her on those people on the gate.'

Three or four sixth formers, in their braided prefects' blazers, were ambling into the room, positioning themselves at computers and adjusting headphones. One of them Maxwell knew. It was the plain, heavy girl he'd seen crying buckets the day before. He smiled at her. 'You okay now?' he asked. She ignored him.

'To work, *mes enfants*,' Graham commanded. 'Helen, let me have that Voltaire by week today, will you? Time and tide, you know.'

It was debatable whether Helen knew much at all by the expression on her bovine face, but the key difference, Maxwell had realized, between his kids and Grimond's is that the Grimond's people had the panache to *look* as if they knew. 'Wander round, Max, if you like. It won't be chalk and talk today. By the way, can you join us in Tennyson tonight? Film Club.'

'Delighted,' Maxwell beamed. 'What are you showing?'

'*Witchfinder General.*'

'Ah,' the Head of Sixth Form beamed. 'Dear old Mad Vince at his maddest.'

'John,' Graham caught the lad's eye. 'Can I have a word?' John Selwyn, the Captain of Tennyson, looked very different from Maxwell's previous sightings of him. He'd first seen him in his regulation Grimond pyjamas, directing his House away from the body of Bill Pardoe. Yesterday he'd seen him losing his temper behind his fencing mask and beating seven bells out of the lovely Cassandra. And last night? Well, Peter

111

Maxwell hadn't really seen John Selwyn last night, but he had a pretty good idea he'd heard him being altogether gentler with the girl. There again, in the dark, voices could be deceptive. And he wasn't absolutely sure.

'Hi,' Maxwell perched on the desk next to the PC of the plain girl. 'What are you doing?' he asked good-naturedly.

'Logging on,' said the girl, with undisguised contempt, wondering what sort of idiot this man was.

'Ah, yes, of course,' Maxwell beamed, the man to whom a spreadsheet was something you had on a picnic. He held out his hand. 'I'm Peter Maxwell, by the way.'

She looked at it as though Maxwell had just exposed himself and touched his fingers in the most cursory of ways.

'And you are?' It was like drawing teeth.

'Janet Boyce,' she told him.

'You're Cassandra's friend?'

He watched Janet turn the colours of the rainbow. Her eyes flashed fire, in any direction but his. Then her hand was in the air. 'Sir!'

Tony Graham drifted away from the far corner where he was talking House to his Captain. 'Yes, Janet. What?' Maxwell knew that tone well. Clearly Janet Boyce was someone who would try the patience of a saint.

'I can't work here, sir. I'm being distracted.' Her mouth was a sullen slit in her large, now pallid face.

'Janet...'

'That's all right,' Maxwell cut in. 'I'm being a

112

nuisance. Mr Graham, do you have a spare cassette player?'

'Of course, Mr Maxwell. Homework?'

Maxwell smiled. 'It is actually,' and he patted the tape in his jacket pocket. 'Something I forgot to check earlier.'

'John,' he beckoned the lad over. 'Show Mr Maxwell the studio, will you? Cassette players aplenty there, Mr Maxwell.'

'Thanks.'

John Selwyn was a head taller than Peter Maxwell with a thatch of curly brown hair he probably longed to be straight. He had that patrician disdain that is born of money and the careless assurance that comes with having a nose like Basil Rathbone's.

'In here, Mr Maxwell.' He switched on the light in a small windowless room. A fan hummed into life. 'We call this the hotel loo,' Selwyn confided, 'for obvious reasons.'

'Loo?' Maxwell raised both eyebrows.

Selwyn grinned. 'Well, bog, actually.'

'That's more like it,' Maxwell smiled, transported instantly to his own school days when no one wept except the willow. 'You've got quite a right arm on you there, young man.'

'Hmm? Oh, the bout. I lost my cool. That was unforgivable. It's not like me.'

'Still,' Maxwell smiled, 'You and Cassandra probably kissed and made up later, eh?'

Selwyn's smile seemed somehow less, but the answer was firm, the gaze still steady. 'We're the best of chums, yes.'

Chums, mused Maxwell. This post-pubescent

little shit was taking the piss, going all 'thirties on him. Still, enough boats were being rocked at Grimond's, especially last night in the boat-house. He'd bide his time before rocking any more.

'Cassette players aplenty,' Selwyn said and bowed out, closing the door behind him.

What he heard when he'd worked out the gadgetry made Peter Maxwell's skin crawl. He'd heard the tone before, mocking, taunting. Then, it had been the Geordie hoaxer claiming to be the Yorkshire Ripper – 'I'm Jack.' And he'd heard it on the radio, on the television, on specially recorded free-phone numbers. This accent was decidedly Home Counties, but it was weird, distorted, as though the words were delivered through a sock. 'We know about you, Bill,' the tape whirred. 'The little boys. We've got your number. The whole school knows about your dirty little habits. What with the books and the showers. I don't know how you can live with yourself. Why don't you do the decent thing? Why don't you end it all? After all, you're no use, are you?'

The hum continued, the mic still on, but no one speaking. Then there was heavy breathing, rapid, rhythmic and a stifled snigger. Silence. Maxwell rewound it, played it again and a third time. He knew what it was. But he needed a second opinion.

He was gratified to note that Grimond's had its knot of clandestine smokers too, just like Leighford. They were probably Gauloise or something even more ostentatiously exotic, but he had neither the time nor the interest to find out. The skulking culprits cupped their ciggies behind their hands in that sullen, guilty, hormonal teenage way as 'the enemy' loomed into view. Maxwell cut across the sloping ground that led to the cricket pavilion and found her waiting.

'God, Max, it's freezing out here.' Jacquie's breath snaked out on the lunchtime air. 'I feel like a schoolgirl again with all this pussyfooting around. What's going on?'

'You got my note, obviously,' he said, uncoiling a set of headphones from his pocket. 'Sorry about the melodrama, but I wanted you to hear this before Hall does. Put these on.'

She shrugged and did as she was told. He clicked on the battery operated cassette player and waited. Grimond's children wandered in the distance under the limes, stuffed with Mrs Oakes' ratatouille and spotted dick. The more studious huddled in windy corners swotting and sweating for a Physics test that the afternoon would bring. The studs swapped unlikely bonking stories, looking wistfully at the girls of Austen House, but always from a safe distance. Snatches of their universal dialogue reached Maxwell, leaning on the pavvy post as he was. Were it not for the cut-glass accents, he could have been back at Leighford.

'Gagging for it, she was ... right there, in the living room ... just as well her parents were away ... four times, yeah ... oh, yeah, nice girls swallow all right...'

'Jesus.' Jacquie was frowning, pulling off the headphones as Maxwell read the ancient graffiti carved into the woodwork. He'd never heard that

115

about Mr Chamberlain. 'Max, where did you get this?'

He turned to sit beside her on the hard wood of the seat worn smooth by the flannelled bums of First Elevens over the years. 'Outside my door in the wee-wee hours. A calling card.'

'Did you see who left it?'

He shook his head. Then nodded in the direction of the school. 'One of them,' he said.

'A kid?'

'Kid, member of staff, dinner lady, bedder,' he shrugged. 'Who knows. What do you make of it?'

'Distorted voice, obviously, but definitely male.'

'Age?'

It was Jacquie Carpenter's turn to shrug. 'Could be anything from fifteen to fifty.'

'Addressed to Pardoe,' Maxwell was thinking aloud.

'"We know about you, Bill",' Jacquie was quoting. 'Presumably. But where's this been? We didn't find anything like this in Pardoe's study.'

'Of course not,' Maxwell said. 'He wouldn't want it broadcast on the school radio, would he? An everyday story of paedophile folk. "The whole school knows",' Maxwell was quoting now. 'Do they? Anybody you've spoken to given you an inkling?'

'That Pardoe was not as other Housemasters?' Jacquie was shaking her head. 'No. Oh, wait. There was a photograph.'

'A photograph?' Maxwell turned to her.

'Hall's got it in the Incident Room.' Jacquie was trying to focus, to see it in her mind's eye. 'It was

116

of a boy.'

'A Grimond's boy?'

She shook her head. 'No uniform. Just a plain grey jumper, I think.'

'What colour was his hair?'

'His hair? Good God, Max, I don't know. Er ... blond, I think. Why?'

'Michael Helmseley, Head of Classics – have you talked to him yet?'

Jacquie hadn't.

'He told me about a photograph. It was of a woman and a boy. He'd seen Pardoe looking at it in his study. Evidently, Pardoe didn't want it noised abroad, whatever it was. Stashed it away as soon as Helmseley came in.'

'When was this?' Jacquie asked.

Maxwell didn't know.

'Pardoe was here long before the St Hilda's girls amalgamated.' Jacquie was trying to work it out. '"Books and showers". Max, you went to a school like this. Do Housemasters supervise showers?'

'Thorough ones do,' he told her.

She clicked her fingers. 'The mag you saw on his desk when you arrived.'

'Oh, yes. Any joy with that yet?' he asked. 'Your dirty squad?'

She shook her head. 'They don't give much away, that lot,' Jacquie told him. 'You know the expression tight as a vice?'

Maxwell smiled. 'So much for inter-departmental cooperation. "Why don't you end it all?"' He remembered the last words of the tape. 'Somebody knew about Pardoe's little secret and was suggesting he top himself. Is that a crime?'

'Suggestion to murder?' Jacquie shrugged. 'I doubt the CPS would entertain that for a moment. And suicide hasn't been on the statute books for a hell of a long time.'

'Until 1833,' Maxwell told her, 'they'd bury the poor bastard at a crossroads with a stake through his heart. Undeserving of Christian burial, with his soul forever pinned to the ground. Ah, the good old days. What'll you do with this?' He pointed to the tape.

'Give it to Hall, of course,' she said. 'It's evidence, Max. It might also be the first break we've had. Forensic will dust it for prints, eliminating yours and mine. They'll be able to do magic things with the sound quality, isolate the voice patterns, despite the distortion.'

'What do you do then?' Maxwell asked. 'Finger and voice print the whole school?'

Jacquie laughed. 'Ever heard of the Court of Human Rights, Max?'

'No,' he said, frowning in mock-fascination. 'That's a new one on me.'

She cuffed him on the arm. 'It's my guess any one of these little darlings has parents with enough clout to bring Strasbourg and Brussels down on our necks if we so much as look at their loops and whorls. You'd have no objection, I suppose? To a voice test, I mean?'

'Me?' Maxwell was aghast. 'Woman Policeman Carpenter, are you telling me *I* am a suspect?'

'Mervyn Larson thinks you are,' she smirked.

'The bastard!'

'And that's classified, by the way,' Jacquie was quick to warn him. 'I don't want you calling the

118

bloke out or whatever idiotic romantic thing you'd do. Pistols at dawn behind the bike sheds. Hall will have me back on the beat.'

'Hmm, not a bad idea,' Maxwell mused. 'You must look very fetching in a blue and white head-band. Then there's the blouse, the stockings, the handcuffs. Ooh, I'm getting all hot!'

'Behave yourself,' she growled at him. 'Gallow suspects you too.'

'What?' He gave her the full John McEnroe. 'You cannot be serious.'

'I'm not,' she said. 'But I think he was.'

'Great. Nice to know one can rely on a fellow historian. Bloody revisionist!'

'See it from their point of view, Max,' she urged. 'You arrive out of the blue on Monday – apparently Sheffield had neglected to tell any-body until the day before – and on Tuesday morning, they find the body of Bill Pardoe. The death of a colleague isn't an everyday occur-rence, you know.'

'So they *do* believe it's murder, then?'

'That seems to be the trend,' Jacquie nodded. 'Although the *official* line from George Sheffield who apparently got it from Arthur Wilkins, his Chairman of Governors, is that it's suicide.'

'What about Tim Robinson? He didn't care for me much either.'

'Don't know. Haven't seen him.'

'I'm sorry.' Maxwell was confused. 'I thought you were starting with him this morning – or so you told me last night.'

'Quite right,' she said, 'but he didn't show. We saw the chaplain instead. That man could bore for England. I bet he doesn't get many taking communion.'

'He's not much of a fencing instructor,' Maxwell volunteered.

'The chaplain?'

'Robinson. I watched him in the gym yesterday. Didn't know an epee stroke from a sabre cut.'

'Well, fan my flies,' Jacquie said. 'Haven't you always told me nobody in the private sector knows what they're doing? Isn't that why they're in the private sector? Hiding from the competence of the world? Isn't that the Gospel according to St Max?'

'Now, Policewoman,' he chided her. 'I do believe I'm being quoted out of context here. I think what I actually said...'

But Peter Maxwell never finished his sentence. It was punctuated by a scream from the direction of the lake and the thud of a dozen feet rushing uphill past the cedars with shouting and chaos.

'He's dead!' one shrill voice rang out above the pandemonium. 'It's Mr Robinson. Come quick, somebody. He's dead!'

'Here's to you, Mr Robinson,' Dr Firmin tilted his glasses on top of his head and leaned back in his swivel chair. He didn't mind the pressure via DCI Hall from Chief Superintendent Mason to get his arse in gear. He didn't even mind working late into the night. What he did object to was having to write up his own report. But then, he reflected in the chill glow of the computer screen, he did work for a Third World Health Service. How many hospital trolleys full of patients had he tripped over just getting here? They'd be stashing the poor sods in his own mortuary lockers next.

He'd read the report from the police surgeon and the one from DCI Hall. Firmin couldn't help smirking. The DCI must be feeling more than a little vexed with himself – a body found under his own nostrils. At least that tended to clarify the position vis-à-vis Bill Pardoe. A suicide followed by a murder, all in the space of a few days? It strained credulity. And whereas he still had forensic and professional doubts about Pardoe, he had none about Robinson. The Games master lay in a dark, cold drawer behind the pathologist, his viscera in assorted jars, carefully labelled.

Some kids had found the man floating face down in the lake at the school, his arms trailing ahead of him in the water, his legs slightly below the surface with the sheer weight of liquid in his tracksuit bottoms. The first copper on the scene was a woman, a DS Carpenter, accompanied by a civilian, Peter Maxwell. Together, they'd hauled the man out of the water in case there were still signs of life. There were none. All this was at twelve-forty-eight. The DCI had arrived four minutes later, but Carpenter had already raised the hue and cry and SOCO were on their way inside ten minutes. They'd been delayed by traffic and a newly galvanized gaggle of reporters at the school gates, suddenly aware that something was up but even so they were at the water's edge by one-thirty-two.

Firmin had removed the dead man's clothes, his tracksuit, sports vest, underpants and socks. He carried nothing but a handkerchief in his pocket and a whistle still dangling from a ribbon

121

round his neck. The wreck that was the back of his head told the story eloquently enough. Someone had caved in his skull with a blunt object, probably wood and very possibly an oar. He'd lost consciousness and his footing and had gone into the water where the shock of the cold revived him. Bleeding profusely, dazed and confused, Tim Robinson had floundered around. He had not gone into shock, the dry drowning of laryngeal spasm and cardiac arrest. Too weak to get himself out of the water and the weed at the lake's edge – it was trapped between his teeth and clung to his fingers – he'd struggled for perhaps a minute before sinking.

It was text-book stuff, really; a fine white froth coating his drooping moustache, the lungs ballooned to bursting with the contents of the lake. People drown more quickly in fresh water than salt, the water seeping with a frightening speed through the mucous membranes of the lungs by osmotic pressure. Analysis of Robinson's heart blood had confirmed this, thinned and diluted, with a sharp resultant drop in its chloride concentration.

The pretty little diatoms which Firmin had found under his microscope slide confirmed that the man had been alive when he hit the water. They floated invisibly in their millions in the waters of an inland lake, gulped into the lungs and passed into the bloodstream and the heart. Firmin's own heart had sagged when he realized what he'd got. There was no doubt where the body had been found, but what if he'd been killed elsewhere and his corpse dumped into Grimond's lake? Hall would want to know this for a fact; Firmin already knew the DCI was not a man to go on surmise. And there were over fifteen-thousand species of diatoms to check. Miracles Firmin could do now; that little job he might have to leave until later.

Time of death was tricky. Robinson's toes and fingers had not yet thickened and whitened with the immersion of water, so he'd been in the lake for less than twenty-four hours. Police reports confirmed this; Robinson's movements on Wednesday evening were well catalogued. No one except his killer had seen him after late afternoon, but Firmin was sticking his neck out that the man had died somewhere around four in the morning. The temperature of the water had fluctuated sharply – a cold snap developing during the morning and it played hell with his rectal thermometer readings.

Quite a waste, really. Firmin had rarely seen a corpse in this condition. Robinson clearly didn't smoke, drink or abuse substances. It took all the good doctor's restraint not to type into his report 'Must be boring as hell.'

The Film Society meeting went ahead that night. Tony Graham, as shaken as anyone by Tim Robinson's death, agonized long and hard and decided it was business as usual. So Peter Maxwell came into his own, courtesy of Tennyson's leading lights.

They stood up to a man as he and Graham walked in to the little theatre that doubled as a cinema. The seats were plush, but Maxwell saw no Mighty Wurlitzer and missed the popcorn girl enormously.

'Thank you, gentlemen,' Graham waved to them and to a man they sat down.

'Impressive!' Maxwell murmured. 'At Leighford they wouldn't have noticed anybody'd come in.'

'Oh, now,' Graham laughed. 'That may be true generally, but not of you, Max.'

'Would you care for a pint of beer, Mr Maxwell?' John Selwyn was barman for the evening and Graham caught the raised eyebrow of the visiting Head of Sixth.

'The sixth are each allowed one pint per showing,' he explained. 'Tradition, isn't it, John?'

'It is, sir.'

'Then, I'd be delighted.' Maxwell took the foaming tankard. Nothing as wussy as glass in Tennyson. He noticed the younger lads sitting in their seats, nattering together, but watching intently. 'No alcohol for the little ones, I assume?' he asked.

'Cocoa in the dorm later,' Graham said, 'is about as exciting as it gets, I'm afraid. John, do the honours, would you?'

'Of course,' Selwyn emerged from behind his makeshift bar. He looked even older in his civvies, like those gods of yesteryear, the prefects who had terrified Peter Maxwell when he was eleven and Mafeking was mightily relieved. 'I'd like to introduce you, Mr Maxwell, this is my Sub, Roger Harcross.'

'Known as Ape,' Graham raised his glass to the giant oaf who took Maxwell's hand. 'We don't know why.'

There were guffaws and whistles all round.

'And Tennyson's Secretary, Antonio Splinterino.'

'Splinter,' the dark eyed boy smiled, sounding about as Italian as a Domino's pizza.

'Secretary?' Maxwell frowned. 'What is it you do, Splinter?'

'Paperwork, sir,' came the obvious reply. 'I'm the recorder for the House, letter writer, front man and so on.'

'And you're all Prefects, I assume?'

'Yes, sir,' Ape and Splinter nodded.

'Gentlemen,' Graham had reached a desk at the front of the auditorium and called them to order. He chose his words carefully. 'So soon after the loss of Mr Pardoe,' he glanced across at young Jenkins, huddled with his mates a couple of rows back, 'which we all feel so keenly, we are today faced with another tragedy. Most of you will have been taught, albeit briefly, by Mr Robinson. We must mourn him too.'

A hand was in the air, four or five rows back.

'Andrews.' Graham pointed at him and the boy was on his feet,

'Sir, what's going on, sir? We don't understand this.'

There were murmurs around the auditorium. All eyes were on Graham. Graham's eyes were on Maxwell, the Housemaster looking as lost and confused as his charges.

'I don't know, Tom,' he said softly. 'I don't know if anybody does. But remember Dr Sheffield's words. And remember this,' he stilled them with a raised hand. 'We aren't just Grimond's, important though that is; we're Tennyson. What are we?'

'Tennyson!' Selwyn shouted back and alongside Maxwell, Ape and Splinter took up the chant, echoed back by row after row of post-pubescent voices. 'Tennyson! Tennyson!' It was the Sportspalatz in Berlin all over again – the mesmerized crowd roaring their adoration of the Fuhrer. This was as far from Leighford High as Peter Maxwell could imagine being. Then Tony Graham calmed it down with a wave of a hand as expert as Herr Hitler himself.

'Let us stand,' he said and there was a thud as the spring-loaded seats flipped upwards. 'And, in a moment's silence, pay our respects – Tennyson's respects – to Mr Robinson.'

Maxwell watched them again, as he had in the chapel when George Sheffield had announced the death of Pardoe. Maggie Shaunessy would no doubt have been appalled – he was still not bowing his head. Neither were Selwyn, Ape or Splinter, the Captains of the House. They stood ramrod-backed, unflinching, staring at the blank white screen ahead and Tony Graham just in front of it.

'Mr Maxwell,' Graham broke the silence at last. 'Are you familiar with this film?'

'I am,' Maxwell told him.

'Gentlemen,' Graham addressed his House. 'This is Mr Maxwell. He is an historian and the Head of Sixth Form at a school in West Sussex. Mr Maxwell, would you come on down and introduce it for us? As usual, gentlemen, there will be discussion afterwards. Mr Maxwell?'

The House erupted into applause as Maxwell reached the podium. Maxwell held up his hand.

'*Witchfinder General,*' he said. 'Known in the States, I believe, as *The Conqueror Worm*. It stars the late, great Vincent Price as Matthew Hopkins, a particularly nasty piece of work who made a lot of money denouncing witches in East Anglia a few years ago. Directed by a ludicrously young Michael Reeves and based on the novel by Ronald Bassett, it has rightly reached cult status and I'm delighted to be among you watching it tonight. By the way, I confess when I saw it first, long before any of you were twinkles in your various fathers' eyes, I fell madly in love with the leading lady, Hilary Dwyer.'

There were hoots and whistles from the Sixth Form.

'Sadly,' Maxwell went on, 'it was an unrequited love.'

'Aahs' broke from the back.

'But don't let my personal problems spoil your evening.'

'Perhaps you could tell us, Mr Maxwell,' Graham winked at him, 'who was key grip on the picture?'

'Of course,' Maxwell said. 'Nigel Benington.'

There were claps and whistles as Graham shook Maxwell's hand and the men took their seats side by side. They weren't to know he'd just made that up.

Peter Maxwell slept alone that night. All in all it had been quite a day. He'd helped the woman he loved drag a corpse out of a lake and shooed away a horde of children, at once horrified and fascinated by death. One by one the Grimond's

127

staff had come hurrying to the scene; Richard Ames, the Head of Games, sprinting appropriately ahead of the rest, Sheffield and Graham in their gowns, Larson in his. Behind them lay half-eaten lunches and a forgotten rubber of bridge as the cry had gone up – 'Master down!'

Maxwell had followed instructions to the letter as Jacquie had screamed orders at him. She pulled the choking weed from the dead man's mouth, closing her lips to his; dry and warm against wet and cold; living to dead. Gulping in lungs-full of air, she bobbed down again and again, then straddled the sodden body and bashed his chest with both fists, hammering on the tracksuit until Maxwell gently and firmly led her away.

She'd been all right at first, while the last of the kids were shepherded away by staff and prefects and the SOCO team arrived. Then, she'd suddenly lost it and buried her face in Maxwell's rough tweed.

'We'll talk,' DCI Hall said to him at the water's edge and turned to face the music of yet another scene of crime; more men in alien white suits, more fluttering tape; more *Do Not Cross*. It would mean a press conference, cries for heads. 'Get her out of here.'

They hadn't talked. Not then. Not later. Maxwell took Jacquie back to her car and she drove, still numb with shock, her coat and jeans still wringing wet, through the Hampshire lanes, back to Barcourt Lodge. He should have driven. But he'd forgotten how. In the dead space of years between now and the death on the road of his own wife, his own child, he'd lost first the will and now the ability. There, in the stillness of her room, they'd lain side by side on the double bed and Jacquie Carpenter had cried and cried.

'I'm sorry,' she said once she had no more tears left. 'I'm not usually so emotional.'

'Sshh,' he said and cradled her head, holding her to him as he had for the last hour. She pulled away slightly and looked into his steady dark eyes, smiling back at her. She'd give half her salary for those eyes on the cold night, on the lonely road, when her mouth was bricky-dry with fear or wet with salt-tears, as now.

'Have a shower,' he said. 'Get out of those wet things.'

'I must get back,' she said. 'Hall will need me.'

He put a finger to her lips. 'Hall has half of the Hampshire constabulary at his disposal,' he said. 'He can manage without you for a while longer.'

And he made her a strong, black coffee, lacing it with a little brandy from Room Service while she showered. Then she sat on the floor while he combed her long flame hair and kissed her forehead every now and then. She'd fallen asleep in his arms a little before dusk and he'd crept quietly away, leaving her a note and ringing for a taxi. Hall was now no doubt handling the official end of things with his usual taciturn aplomb. But there was no one to speak for Mad Max except Mad Max himself.

Then he'd watched a grim film in front of a hundred or so boys who were fast becoming men in the face of murder. He'd made his excuses as soon as Hilary Dwyer's screams died away across the bleak Suffolk landscape and he'd wandered the grounds under the all-seeing silver of the moon. He was still crossing and re-crossing the silent Grimond's quad a little before midnight.

Who goes home?

Chapter Eight

Friday, Friday. Hate that day. Every pair of eyes was on DCI Henry Hall in the old village hall at Selborne, doubling as an Incident Room. And the incidents were multiplying. The fourth day of one possible murder enquiry had become the second day of another. It clouded issues, muddied waters, tangled tales.

'Chief Superintendent Mason is holding a press conference this afternoon,' Hall told his team, 'in conjunction with Dr Sheffield from Grimond's. They both want some answers, people. What can we give them?'

'DI Berman, guv,' a keen looking detective began. He was a solid six-footer with forward-combed hair and the tenacity of a bulldog. 'My team are working on last movements.'

Hall nodded, sitting on the corner of his desk in the outer office.

'The deceased was a PE teacher. Had two lessons after the usual school assembly in the chapel.' He checked his notes. 'Er ... Upper Four Cee and Lower Four Bee. They were both in the gym. Third lesson he had a free.'

There were murmurs. Half the room would have killed Tim Robinson for his free period alone.

'Where was he then?' Hall wanted to know.

'He was seen in the staff room ... er ... Senior

Common Room ... by a Jeremy Tubbs, Geo-graphy teacher. At that point he seemed to be marking books.'

'What time was this?'

'Eleven-thirtyish. He was back in the gym by just after twelve, trampoline coaching.'

'This would be lunchtime?'

Berman nodded.

'What did he have?' Hall asked.

'Sandwich,' the DI told him, 'er...'

'Tuna,' somebody else piped up.

'You are...?' Hall frowned, trying, in the sea of faces, to locate the voice.

'Sorry, guv. DS Walters.' A prop-forward type was on his feet, shirt straining across his pecs. 'I've been working on the pathologist's report.'

'Christ,' somebody said from the far side of the room. 'They on overtime?'

There were guffaws and hubbub. Hall let it go. He knew the importance of a joke in a murder enquiry. But this was possibly a double murder – perhaps it needed twice the levity. 'After lunch?' he pressed Berman again.

'He taught another three lessons, all of them out on the fields. Rugger practice with the Second Fifteen, then Cross Country.'

'Was he on the school premises throughout?' Hall crosschecked.

'No, guv. He ran with the boys. Apparently, it's the usual circuit, round trip of a mile and a half. DC Gostelow's working on a plan of it.' An anonymous hand waved somewhere at the back. 'Robinson was back at Grimond's by three, quarter-past,' Berman went on. 'Robinson had a

132

shower – Richard Ames, his Department Head, will vouch for that.'

Eyebrows raised here and there, camp looks were exchanged. Sometimes, the only way to stay with their job at all was to be flippant and cynical in equal measure.

'Did Robinson live on site?' Hall asked.

'No, guv. DS Chappell.' If Walters was a prop-forward, Chappell was a fly-half, wiry and tough-looking. 'Checking out the background. I've drawn a bit of a blank one way and another.'

'Where does he live?' Hall wanted to know.

'Little semi on the edge of Petersfield. Rented. Not been there long.'

'He hasn't been in the job long,' Hall confirmed. 'So, Mr Berman ... Sandy, isn't it?'

'Yes, guv,' the DCI flicked over a page in his notebook. 'Robinson left Grimond's at about five, five-fifteen. Sometimes apparently he eats at the school. Last night he didn't.'

Hall eased his rapidly numbing right buttock. 'Who's been over the semi?'

Nothing. There were glances in various directions. Berman found his voice first. 'Word was we were to leave that alone, guv. That ... er ... you'd do it.'

Hall nodded. 'Good,' he said and risked the ghost of a smile. 'Relax, everybody. I'm on secondment, remember. This is all done to see how well you follow orders. Jacquie and I will get out there later.'

All eyes swivelled to the alien DS sitting alone at the other side of Hall's desk. She hadn't slept well and the circles around her grey eyes told their own story.

'SOCO?' Hall changed the subject.

'DS McGovern, sir,' a wraith-thin woman stood up, pencil-pleated with straw-coloured hair straight out of a bottle. 'The body was found by DS Carpenter and Mr Peter Maxwell in the lake at Grimond's at approximately one-oh-five yesterday. It was floating seven or eight feet out from the bank, the body fully clothed. Forensic reports a blow to the back of the head, probably with an oar...'

'Any weapon found?' Hall asked.

'No, guv,' McGovern shook her head, 'although Forensic are still checking all of them in the boathouse.'

'How many is that?'

'Twenty-four.'

Hall never let anyone know how impressed he was with an answer and the DS swept on. 'There were dozens of footprints around the bank. Forensic are still eliminating them. Kids, teachers, DS Carpenter, yourself.'

'So there may or may not be an alien set?' Hall was thinking aloud.

'That's right, guv.'

'All right. Keep at it, people. We want answers quickly on this one. DS Carpenter and I will...'

'Guv,' an Essex fly-half called from the corner where the cigarette smoke wreathed thickest.

'Yes ... er ... DS Chapell.'

'Well, there's something fishy about this Robinson, guv.'

'Oh?' Hall seemed bored by the whole topic. 'What?'

'Well, it's like a bloke with no fingerprints or no shadow. This one's got no past.' There were murmurs around the room.

'Explain.' Hall was at his curtest with two potential murders on his plate.

'He joined the staff at Grimond's in January, right? Three months ago.'

'So?'

'So where was he before that?'

Hall blinked. 'Don't you know? Haven't you checked with Sheffield?'

'Oh, yes, guv,' Chapell nodded. 'According to the Headteacher, he came from Haileybury.'

'Then, I don't see your problem, sergeant,' Hall shrugged.

'Well, it's just that Haileybury haven't heard of him.'

Silence.

'Yet here,' and Chapell held up a piece of fax paper, enjoying doing his Hercule Poirot bit, 'is the reference from that very school, duly signed by their Head.'

'Where's this going, Chapell?' Hall wanted to know.

'Well, I rang Haileybury first thing this morning, guv. Just as back-up, you know. Confirmation. I explained the situation and the Head was kind enough to fax me through a sample of his signature. This,' he waved the reference under Hall's nose, 'is a forgery and a bad one at that. The last Robinson they had taught Physics and Chemistry. His name wasn't Tim and he retired, according to the records, in 1948.'

There were whoops and whistles around the

room from impressed colleagues.

Hall's hand was in the air to shut them up. 'This is not a three-ring circus,' he snapped, 'and since when do officers applaud a problem? Can you explain this, Chapell?'

'No, guv,' the DS confessed. 'That's why I've drawn a bit of a blank.'

'Well, when you've found a solution,' Hall said quietly, standing now and looking his man squarely in the eye, 'when you've rubbed out the blank you've drawn, *that's* when we'll have a little in the way of congratulation. Until then,' he raked them all with his blank lenses, 'I believe there's work to be done. Jacquie.'

'Maxwell.' It was a name that had crossed Henry Hall's lips more than once before.

'Sir?' Jacquie, sitting beside him in the Volvo, was mentally miles away, kissing a dead man in her darkest dreams.

'Maxwell,' he repeated. 'What's he up to?'

'He's observing, sir,' she told him. 'Watching how they do things at Grimond's. Bit like you here, I suppose.'

'Nothing like me here,' Hall growled. Jacquie Carpenter had known Henry Hall, girl and woman, for six years. Most of what she'd learned she'd learned from him and whereas the bland bastard didn't exactly convince as the master, it was at his knee that the learning had been done. She couldn't remember a time when the guv'nor had been as tight-lipped and grouchy as this.

'Are you sleeping with him?' Hall asked.

She stared at him, then looked away, her neck

mottling with fury, her eyes flashing fire. 'I consider that an inappropriate question, sir,' she said.

'Do you? What if I say it's perfectly appropriate?' He rattled up through the gears as the hedges flashed by.

She looked at him levelly. 'I still wouldn't answer it,' she said.

They drove in silence for a few minutes. 'All right,' Hall tried a new tack. 'We'll let that go. What does he know?'

'About what?'

'Jacquie!' Hall shouted so that the DS jumped in her seat-belt. 'We are a long way from home, you and I, longer than you know. We need all the friends we can get.'

'Even Mad Max?' she asked and waited. A year ago, six months even, she wouldn't have dared ask a question like that. Now, it was different. She was sure of herself because she was so sure of the man she loved.

Hall's lips twitched. It was as close to a smile as she'd be likely to get this side of rigor mortis. 'Even Mad Max,' he nodded.

They snarled round the roundabout that led off the road below Butser Hill and on through sleepy Petersfield, past the Bear Museum and the Doll's Hospital and the green-sheened spelter of the Dutch William statue. Then they were growling down Spain Street and out towards the country again, the railings of Churchers flashing in the morning sun; Churchers who had faced Grimond's on many a bloody rugby field and hallowed cricket turf.

Tim Robinson's semi was very ordinary

137

indeed, one of countless '60s erections that had seen seriously better days. Hall ignored the curtains twitching to the right and the old boy tinkering with a lawn mower noisily to his left; two potential witnesses that Jacquie would have talked to, had she not been with the guv'nor; two potential witnesses that Peter Maxwell would have talked to had he been there; two potential witnesses that Henry Hall walked past.

His key clicked in the Yale and they were inside. Jacquie Carpenter had stood in dead men's houses before. They were all the same. Cold. As dead as their owners. There was an indefinable sadness about them. She'd known it first as a girl when her grandfather had died and she'd gone with her mother to sort his things out. She remembered the old man's pipe still lying by his bed, his hat and coat in the hall, his book half read and the crossword unfinished.

It was like that here. She hadn't known Tim Robinson. The first time she'd seen him he was lying face down in a brackish lake, cold as the grave and heavy with water. Their first introduction was the kiss she'd given him, a kiss which he'd returned with one of death. Then she'd done her best to break his ribs, to pound breath into the breathless, life into death. The remnants of cottage pie lay abandoned on an unwashed plate on the kitchen table and there was a bottle of cheap wine half-drunk on the top of the fridge.

'What are we looking for, sir?' she asked Hall, although she knew the answer already.

'Anything.' He didn't disappoint her. 'Anything that will tell us how the man who lived here

138

ended up dead in a lake.'

There was a pile of exercise books on the large coffee table. Hall was thudding upstairs, turning out drawers and rummaging in cupboards. It took Jacquie a while to work it out; what was odd about this little semi that was a dead man's last home. There were no photos. No wife. No kids. No family at all. Not even the ubiquitous Night Out With The Lads. She checked the sideboard, the drinks cabinet, the space under the stairs. Tim Robinson had drunk Stella in fairly copious quantities and had a secret stash of Malibu. No ciggies, although Jacquie, who had long since given them up, would kill for one about now. The dead man's wallet lay on the table. Credit cards. An old theatre ticket stub.

'No AA,' she found herself saying aloud. 'No phone card.' But there was his blood group. O Neg. Just like hers.

'Guv?'

Hall was already back on ground level. 'There's nothing here, Jacquie. We're wasting our time. Whatever we're looking for is back there, at Grimond's.'

'But, guv...'

'Jacquie,' he interrupted her. 'We're going to have to work double shifts from now on. Saturday and Sunday. Can you handle that?'

'Sure,' she nodded, trying to read that inscrutable face. 'But what about the local boys? Don't we need...?'

'No, Jacquie,' he cut in again. 'We don't need them. We just need us. Where will I find Peter Maxwell?'

Chief Superintendent David Mason was used to press conferences, those media circuses when cameras flashed and intelligent journalists like Duncan Kennedy asked questions that were just a shade too much to the point. He fielded them with his usual tangential skill, schooled as he was in the days of Thatcher and Major. Nobody'd invented the phrase 'spin policeman', but David Mason was one. Dr George Sheffield was less secure. Parents were his usual audience, governors and Old Boys, supportive, friendly, united in the cause of education-with-snobbery. And when he addressed them, he wasn't talking about murder.

Mason metaphorically held his hand, shoulders and lapels glittering silver. 'Ladies and Gentlemen, I want to thank you for coming along this afternoon. Dr Sheffield is, as you know, the headmaster of Grimond's School and he is as anxious as I to assure you all that there is no cause for alarm at the present time.'

A barrage of microphones probed forward and a forest of hands filled the air.

Mason selected his questioners carefully.

'Tom Simpson, *Guardian*,' the first one was on his feet. 'Dr Sheffield, how many pupils have left the school in the last few days?'

'Er ... none,' the Head shifted uneasily, suddenly hating the spotlight.

'But surely,' Simpson persisted amid the hubbub, 'with two murders in five days...'

'As I said a moment ago,' Mason cut in with that fixed smile of his, born of long hours in front of the cameras, 'we are keeping an open mind on

140

the death of Mr Pardoe.'

'Oh, come on, Chief Super,' the local hack, John Bennett, challenged him. 'I mean, what are the odds?'

'*News of the World*, Chief Super,' another cut in. 'We might get away with that on April 1; not at any other time.'

'Superintendent Mason,' another hand was straining forward. '*Daily Mail*. Surely you have a suspect? Is it sex? Drugs? Our readers have a right to know.'

'No, they don't,' Sheffield was shouting. 'These things are personal, private. You have no right to...'

Mason cut in again. 'Ladies and gentlemen. What we would both ask you, Dr Sheffield and I, is that you give the boys and girls the privacy to which they have a right. My officers are on the job and believe me, they will get results. Dr Sheffield's job is infinitely more difficult. He has to keep a sense of calm and order and to do his best to keep morale high during an intensely difficult time in the life of any school.'

'Who's leading the enquiry, Mr Mason?' the *Guardian* wanted to know.

'Er ... I cannot comment...'

'Come off it, Chief Super,' Bennett was there again. 'We at the *Chronicle* know the local boys. Is it Joe Nelson or Mark West?'

'Neither,' Mason snapped, getting to his feet and snatching up his cap and gloves. 'Thank you for your attention, ladies and gentlemen,' and he shepherded Sheffield away amid a cacophony of questions.

'God, that was awful!' Sheffield groaned, striding out of the room, still dazed by the lights and the whole experience.

Worse than that,' Mason grunted, closing the double doors behind him.

'Worse?' Sheffield turned to his man in the corridor outside. 'In what way?'

'Never mind. How many kids have you lost?'

'As of this morning, thirty-one. My Chair of Governors is on the point of closing us down.'

'No,' Mason frowned. 'Nobody leaves Grimond's. Not now. Not yet.'

'How exactly do you propose to stop them, Chief Superintendent? Throw an armed cordon around the Grimond walls and pick off stragglers with your SWAT snipers? I'm not sure that would do much for community relations initiatives.'

The Headmaster spun on his heel and stormed off to the waiting car. 'We need more men,' Sheffield shouted. 'One Inspector and a sergeant will hardly suffice.'

Mason reached the vehicle. 'I thought you'd appreciate the low-key approach,' he said, checking that no-one was within earshot.

'Low-key?' Sheffield snarled, stabbing the Superintendent with a rigid finger. 'Two of my staff are dead, Mr Mason. Tomorrow all this will be all over the front pages. Grimond's will be on television tonight. It's a little late, don't you think, for low-key?' And he bundled himself into Mervyn Larson's car.

'How many?' he asked his deputy, hauling the seat-belt into place.

'Eight since lunch-time,' Larson told him. 'The MacMister brothers, the Turtle girl. I've taken Miss Horsefield off the switchboard. She's been in tears all afternoon, poor soul.'

'Just drive, Mervyn,' Sheffield growled, sinking down in the seat to avoid the camera flashes popping beyond the windscreen.

David Mason reached into his limousine to grab the radio. 'Get me DCI West,' he barked. 'And move your arse.' He could feel his tooth bothering him again.

If there was one thing Detective Chief Inspector West liked, it was being proved right. He got the call from the Chief Super a little after four-thirty and by five was driving through the horizontal rain for Selborne and Henry Hall's Incident Room, ready to be brought up to speed. Mason, of course, was going to pay for this, West smiled, rolling his chewing gum around his tongue. Only time would tell how much. What had the stupid bastard been thinking of? *He* was the man on the ground, the insider. Foreign imports were okay, but they couldn't handle murder cases, not on their own. What was Mason on?

'It was just ... odd, Max,' Jacquie was only playing with her tagliatelle; she wasn't eating it.

'How, odd?' The candlelight shone on Maxwell's wine glass. The pair faced each other in the dining room at Barcourt Lodge. A particularly raucous Rotary dinner was happening in the annexe through the double doors, streamers flying, glasses clinking and cherry-nosed old farts

143

making spectacles of themselves.

'Well, usually a search like that would take two hours, perhaps more and that's with a full team. Hall went through the place like a bloody tornado. I reckon we were there less than twenty minutes.'

'What did you find?'

'Questions,' Jacquie pushed her plate away.

'Ah,' Maxwell waggled his fork at her. 'Now, what did your Mummy say about eating your greens?'

Jacquie twisted her lips. 'You haven't met my mummy yet, have you, Max?'

The Head of Sixth Form grabbed a spoon and held it in the air in the form of a cross with his fork, eyes wide with terror.

'Well, then, shut it,' Jacquie advised, doing a fairly bad John Thaw in *The Sweeney*, 'or I'll arrange it.'

'"Questions" you said,' Maxwell knew the moment to change a subject.

'That's right,' Jacquie held her wine glass in both hands. 'No answers.'

'For instance?' He sipped his wine.

'There wasn't a single photograph in the house, at least not on the ground floor. I didn't see upstairs.'

'So he's not a photo person,' Maxwell shrugged.

'One of the DSs, a bloke named Chapell, has been assigned background. He can't find any. Seems Robinson forged his references. The odd thing is that having been to his house we're none the wiser now. Hall just didn't seem interested.'

'Perhaps he thought somebody else should have combed the joint,' Maxwell suggested.

Jacquie shook her head. 'No, it wasn't pique. He chose it, apparently. Specifically told the team that he and I would handle that end of things.'

'I see.'

'He didn't talk to neighbours, check phone messages. Nothing. You don't think he's losing it, do you?'

'Henry?' Maxwell shrugged. 'Not a bit of it. How old is he?'

'The big five-o next month.'

'A mere stripling,' Maxwell chuckled. 'Probably hasn't lost all his milk teeth yet.'

'There's something else.'

'Oh?'

'The forensics report said that Tim Robinson was a teetotaller.'

'And?'

'I saw lager and spirits in his drinks cabinet. Half-drunk bottle of wine in the kitchen.'

Maxwell flared his nostrils. 'From which you deduce, Watson?'

Jacquie closed to him. 'From which I deduce there's something bloody peculiar about this case, Max. And I mean *bloody* peculiar. By the way, Hall hasn't spoken to you yet, has he?'

'No, should he have?'

Jacquie shrugged. 'He implied he was going to.'

'Is he here now?' Maxwell asked. 'In the hotel, I mean?'

Jacquie shook her head. 'Out. Said he'd be back later.'

He looked into her steady, grey eyes, burning into his with the intensity he loved. He reached out and held her fingers around the glass. 'You haven't by any chance got a key to Mr Robinson's abode?' he asked.

She suddenly dangled one in front of him. 'I thought you'd never suggest it,' she said.

It was a little after ten that Henry Hall drove into the car park at Selborne. The rain had eased, but it was still spraying onto his windscreen from passing traffic and the street lights threw diamond wetness onto the tarmac. The skeleton night shift were there, ready to burn the midnight oil, coffee steaming in cardboard cups and tired eyes straining at VDUs.

He was halfway across the outer offices when he realised. His inner office was occupied. More, it was occupied by DCI Mark West, sitting in his swivel, jacket sprawled over its back, shirt sleeves rolled, eyes squinting against his cigarette smoke, crumpled coffee cup at his elbow.

'Ah, Henry,' West looked up. 'Welcome aboard.'

Hall looked at the trio of officers with West. DS Chappell he knew, and Sandy Berman. He'd never seen the third man, a thick-set copper with a shaved head who might have been a bouncer in a previous existence.

'Could I have a word, Mark?' Hall said.

'Not just at the moment,' West lolled back, smiling. 'I'm conducting a double murder enquiry, and have quite a bit of time to make up. Any problems with that, perhaps you could talk to Chief Superintendent Mason, could you?' He pressed the intercom button. 'Lynda, bring us a cup of coffee through, could you, love? DCI Hall will see himself out.'

'Can't you stay a bit longer?' Janet lay in the shadows in the corner of her little hideaway.

'You know I can't,' Cassandra swayed upright, silhouetted against the curtains.

'Yes,' Janet said, fighting back the tears. 'I know.' She watched the lithe girl clip on her front-fastening bra and pull the lacy panties up her bare thighs, smoothing the thong around her bum.

'Look,' Cassandra faced her, hands on hips. 'We're going to have to be careful from now on,' she said. 'With all this ... whatever ... going on. There are eyes everywhere.' And she pulled her tracksuit bottoms on.

'I don't care,' Janet said defiantly. 'I don't care who sees us.'

'Yes,' Cassandra snatched up her top and pulled it and the hood over her head. 'Well, I do, dear. We're all out of here in June and some of us are off to Cambridge. Oh, I'm sorry, you're Reading-bound, aren't you? Never mind.' And she bent down, steeling herself as she felt the heavier girl's hand roving over her breasts, then stroking her cheek.

'You do love me, Cassie?' Janet whispered.

'Of course I do,' the taller girl sighed. 'But please, Janet, don't call me that. Now, I really have to go. Oh ... got any stuff?'

He sat alone behind the steering wheel, face darkened under the street lamp. His headlights were out and he wasn't moving, just watching the house across the road with an intensity he'd acquired over the years.

147

'Ten-thirty-four,' he whispered into a hand-held cassette recorder. 'He's reaching his front door now. Age about fifteen, possibly younger. Blond. Nice looking lad.' He watched as the boy fumbled with the lock. 'He seems pissed. This is quite promising. I'll keep you posted on this one ... I think he's a natural.'

And he clicked off the machine, watching and waiting in the darkness.

Chapter Nine

This time they'd do the job for real. Jacquie parked the Ka around the corner in the average-looking estate on the edge of Petersfield. They linked arms and marched off purposefully, an average-looking couple out for a stroll. Except that it was well past midnight and the pair's eyes were everywhere except on each other.

There were lights on in the right hand house that provided the other half of Tim Robinson's last known address. Squealing from somewhere down the road told them that the Petersfield youth were on their way home, lurching from bus-shelter lager-fest to quick gang-grope in the shrubbery. Ah, the youth of today.

Jacquie clicked the key in the lock and they were in, drawing curtains before switching on lights.

'What are we looking for?' Maxwell asked. Like Jacquie he'd done this before, combed through the debris of a dead-man's life. But he was an amateur, what crime writers call an amateur's amateur. Jacquie was the professional. He was happy to defer.

'Something.' She was getting her bearings in the lounge. 'Anything. I'm going to start upstairs. Check the answerphone, Max.'

She hadn't had time to do it last time, before the DCI had unceremoniously whisked her away.

149

Nothing. Just Tim Robinson's voice. 'Hi, you've reached Tim Robinson. I can't come to the phone right now, but leave a message after the tone and I'll get back to you.'

'No, you won't, Tim,' Maxwell said softly and began to rummage in the sideboard. The furniture was extraordinarily standard, MFI flat pack and it looked as if it had been delivered all together, as a job lot. There was a pile of exercise books on the table; GCSE PE. Maxwell riffled through them. Clearly, Tim Robinson was of the new school – ignore spelling and grammar problems.

'That's odd.' He was still talking to himself.

'What is?' Jacquie was back on the ground floor, making for the kitchen.

'What's a synapse?'

'You what?'

'Synapse. According to this, it's where two nerves meet and it resembles an arboretum.'

'Max, what are you talking about?'

He checked the front cover of the book. 'The gospel according to Jamie Atkins, Upper Four Bee. He thinks a synapse is like an arboretum.'

'Which tells us what?'

'Probably nothing,' Maxwell shrugged. 'Except that Tim Robinson wasn't a very careful marker. The kid means dendrite – the branch-like description of nerves; not a bush collection.'

'Does this have any significance?' Jacquie was combing the magazine rack.

'No,' Maxwell told her. 'It's the Leighford High school of marking too. Skim read and slap a level on every fourth page, with a merit sticker on

150

every fifth just to keep morale up. Sure beats intellectual rigour.'

'No PC,' Jacquie said, checking cupboards and alcoves.

'Not all bad, then, Tim Robinson,' the velociraptor of Leighford High commented.

'He was thirty-two, Max,' Jacquie countered. 'Most thirtysomethings surf the Net.'

'Do you?' Maxwell put the book back into the pile. 'Ah but it was my generation that put a man on the moon.'

'I can't help thinking that's who we're looking for,' Jacquie sighed. 'Looks like Hall was right. There's nothing here.'

'*The Man Who Fell to Earth,*' Maxwell said. 'Like David Bowie in the film of the same name, as if he didn't exist outside of Grimond's School.'

'Isn't that how you feel most of the time?' she smiled, putting an arm round his shoulder. 'That the world doesn't exist beyond Leighford?'

He was still laughing at that when the loud click made them both turn. Peter Maxwell had never stared down the twin muzzle of a twelve-bore before. That wasn't as unnerving, however, as the deranged eyes along the sight, blinking at them both.

'Don't move.' The gunman was the wrong side of sixty, wild grey hair dangling over his right ear, the mother of all combovers. He was wearing a plaid dressing gown and matching slippers.

'Now, look...' Maxwell's hand was in the air in a gesture of conciliation, but the barrels came up level.

'Don't you talk to him like that.' A second face

popped up near the first, a fierce-looking woman without teeth, curlers clamped into the dyed russet of her hair.

'What are you doing here?' the gunman snapped. 'Glenda, call the police.'

Jacquie eased her hand into her bag. 'I am the police,' she said quietly. It was the cliché to end clichés and the gunman wasn't buying it. 'Bollocks!' he snorted. 'You keep your hands where I can see 'em.'

Jacquie lifted her warrant card out and held it up like a crucifix before the undead, which is rather what the gunman resembled.

'Oh.'

The barrels wavered and Jacquie seized the initiative. 'Mr ... um?'

'Blundell,' the old man said. 'This is my wife.'

The curlered, toothless woman scowled at them.

'I'm DS Carpenter,' Jacquie said. 'Could you uncock that, Mr Blundell?'

'Oh, yeah. Right,' and he lowered the shotgun.

'Ask 'em what they're doing here, Harold,' Glenda blurted.

'I have,' Harold reminded her.

'We're conducting enquiries into the death of Timothy Robinson,' Jacquie said. 'He used to live here.'

'Who's she looking for, Harold?' Glenda still hadn't moved from her position behind her husband's gun-arm.

'Robinson,' the old man said. 'Lives here. Well, he used to.'

'Do you have a licence for that, Mr Blundell?'

152

Jacquie was establishing the moral high ground.

'Oh, yes,' he assured her.

'But it's not a licence to point it at people, is it?' Unlike Maxwell, Jacquie Carpenter had faced down shotguns before. It was always hairy. And you always came off, if you came off at all, slightly wiser. 'Well,' she was softer now, 'perhaps you could tell us what you know about Mr Robinson.'

The old man looked at his wife. 'Nothing, really. He kept himself to himself.'

'Tell her about the blokes, Harold,' Glenda nudged him.

'What blokes?' Jacquie wanted to know.

'Oh, that wasn't anything,' Harold muttered.

'You don't know what it was,' Glenda asserted. 'You tell her.'

'Perhaps if you tell me, Mrs Blundell,' Jacquie tried to ease Harold aside.

'Tell her, Harold,' the old girl shuffled further behind him. 'Tell her I don't talk to the police.'

'My wife had an unfortunate experience with a Special towards the end of the war, officer,' Harold felt obliged to explain. 'It's left her scarred.'

Maxwell and Jacquie could see that.

'There were some blokes come round,' Harold went on. 'Three of 'em.'

'When was this?'

'Ooh, they've been around a couple of times.'

'Tell her when, Harold,' Glenda muttered. 'It was last Monday and again the previous Thursday.'

'Would either of you know these men again?' Jacquie asked.

'It was dark,' Harold remembered. 'They come in the evening both times.'

'How many cars?' Maxwell asked.

'Just the one,' Harold told him.

'You don't remember the make, I suppose?' Jacquie was clutching at straws.

Harold didn't. Glenda however, 'Tell her she'll find it was a silver Audi Gti, licence number had a T and 48.'

Jacquie looked at Maxwell.

'My wife used to be a secretary in a garage,' Harold explained. 'Got a thing about cars.'

Glenda tugged on his dressing gown sleeve, looking up into the man's rheumy eyes. 'It's got special alloy wheels, racing trim. The first bloke was thick-set, about thirty, with a crew cut. The second was taller, sort of skinny, in a bomber jacket with a logo on the back – a pair of wings. The third had a moey, like Mr Robinson and dark glasses. I remember thinking why's he wearing dark glasses at night? That's all I remember.'

'Don't tell us,' Maxwell smiled. 'Your wife also used to work in the e-fit section of a police incident room.'

'Ask him if he's taking the piss, Harold,' Glenda urged, not taking to Peter Maxwell at all.

'You've been very helpful, Mr and Mrs Blundell,' Jacquie assured the couple. 'I may need to call on you again. Would you be prepared to make a statement?'

Glenda visibly jumped.

'It could be done here,' Jacquie said quickly. 'And I promise there'll be no uniforms.'

Harold took the DS aside. 'I'll have to work on

her,' he mumbled. 'She's not as sharp as she used to be,' and he nodded at Maxwell and led his wife out into the Petersfield night.

They waited until the front door clicked behind them. 'Ever felt as though you've just wandered into a parallel universe, darling heart?' Maxwell asked.

'Whoever these guys are, they're the only link we have between our Mr Robinson and the outside world.'

'You know what they say about teachers,' Maxwell sucked his teeth. 'They don't have homes or lives outside their classroom cupboards. When that damn bell *sans merci* sounds, they just climb into their dark coffins and wait for dawn.'

Jacquie threw herself down on Robinson's settee. 'Why didn't Hall talk to those two?' she was asking herself again. 'We've lost half a day.'

'Perhaps he didn't fancy getting his head blown off. It would have been particularly unfortunate for me had Harold opened fire – my heart was in my mouth at the time. What happens now?'

Jacquie checked her watch. 'Business as usual tomorrow at Grimond's, nine o'clock. That's the beauty of a boarding school – life just goes on at the weekend.'

'So,' Maxwell said grimly, 'does death.' He turned to face Jacquie, sitting next to her on the settee. 'How are you feeling now, about Robinson, I mean?'

She nodded and smiled at him. 'I'm fine,' she sighed. 'Busy, busy, busy. That's the way to be.' She stood up, anxious to be on the move. 'Coming back to the hotel?'

'Not tonight,' he shook his head. 'Most of what happens at Grimond's happens after dark. It's what we in the business call the hidden curriculum.' He got up and kissed her. 'Drive me away from all this, Woman Policeman.'

'You know why I've sent for you, of course?' Sir Arthur Wilkins already had a substantial Scotch in his hand though the sun was nowhere near the yard-arm. He hadn't bothered to offer the DCI one on the grounds that he assumed the man would decline by virtue of being on duty etcetera. He stood with his back to the door in Sheffield's study, silhouetted against the window.

'Perhaps you could be specific.' Hall was on the carpet.

The Chair of Governors turned with a back that was ramrod straight, his silver moustache bristling. 'Very well. Specifically, what the fuck are you doing?'

'My job.' Hall could be infuriatingly inscrutable when the mood took him.

'Your job,' Wilkins growled. 'Why are you, a West Sussex CID officer, heading an enquiry on Hampshire territory?'

'You'll have to ask the Chief Superintendent,' Hall told him.

'I have.'

'And?'

'David Mason and I go back a long way. He passed me upstairs to the Chief Constable.'

'Who told you?'

'Precisely nothing!' Wilkins slammed down his glass. 'Andrew Mulliner and I go back a long way

156

too. I'm not used to being cold-shouldered by friends.'

'Sir...'

'This school is falling apart, Chief Inspector.' Wilkins came round from his side of Sheffield's desk. 'I've got a Headmaster who's just about as effective as a wet shit, a staff who are dying in droves ... and you. By the way, who's this Maxwell fella?'

'Peter Maxwell? He's a teacher, on secondment of some kind. Surely, Dr Sheffield has explained...'

'Of course he has,' Wilkins stood nose to nose with the DCI. 'But it's rather like the airy-fairy explanations I've been getting from the Chief Superintendent and the Chief Constable. Nothing is quite as it seems. All I know is that this Maxwell shows up, like some damn plague bacillus and my staff start dying.' He lowered his voice. 'There's a rumour going round that you know him.'

'That's right,' Hall nodded. 'I do. He's the Head of Sixth Form at Leighford High School – that's on my patch.'

'So the two of you end up on mine, by the merest coincidence?'

Hall nodded again. 'That's about the size of it.'

Wilkins turned away, collecting himself for a moment, then he drained his glass. 'Well, I don't buy coincidences, Chief Inspector.'

For a moment the two men looked at each other. Then Hall broke the silence. 'Of course, we could co-operate,' he said.

Wilkins lowered his eyes and his lip curled. 'This is me co-operating,' he growled. 'I've told Mason I'll try and keep Grimond's open for another forty-eight hours – assuming we still have any parents who haven't pulled their children out. After that,' he slammed the glass down, 'I can't guarantee a damn thing.'

The papers that Saturday had a field day. The *Mail*'s circulation was up again and they were offering another dream cottage somewhere in stockbroker belt. In less encouraging news, there was a double page spread on the strange affair at Grimond's, as though it were something Miss Marple should look into. The *Daily Sport* was less euphemistic – 'Bent Sir Goes Off Roof' had been replaced by 'Double Whammy At Posh School'. All local news bulletins showed sundry footage taken at the school gates and the odd car going in and out. The salient fact was that none of the comers and goers was talking to the media and shots of anonymous car drivers who could have been anything from cleaners to publishers' reps were not terribly dramatic or helpful.

At Grimond's everybody tried to carry on as usual. There was no chapel service that day, but then, that was often the case on Saturdays. There was a big rugger fixture that afternoon against Lancing and Richard Ames, the Head of Games, was determined that that should go on. He stood on the touch line now, jumping up and down occasionally, in his Grimond track suit, roaring encouragement to the First Fifteen pack.

Maxwell joined him. 'How's it going?'

'Oh, fine.' Ames had once played for England himself and sported a Jonny Wilkinson haircut as a mark of solidarity. 'You're Maxwell, aren't you?'

158

'Max.' He shook the man's hand.

'I wanted to thank you for what you did for Tim yesterday. Groves, you girl! Tackle him!' The whistle blasted for an infringement and Ames trotted off to the pack forming up for a scrum. Amid the steam and sobbing grunts, Ames had a quiet word and trotted back.

'It wasn't enough, I'm afraid,' Maxwell said.

'Well, there we are,' Ames said, clapping his hands at the ref's decision on what happened next. 'Do that this afternoon, Johnson, and you'll be sin-binned. That,' he turned to Maxwell, 'would have taken a miracle. Which is precisely what this little lot will need against Lancing later.'

'Do they usually play a match before a fixture?' Maxwell asked, remembering how knackered he used to feel after eighty minutes pounding the hard yards.

'Oh, this is only a twenty-minute short. There's no substitute for the real thing in my experience. For God's sake, Selwyn, what sort of pass was that?' He cantered down the touch line, Maxwell ambling after him. 'Do you play?'

'I used to,' Maxwell said, flattered that Ames thought he still could. 'Second Row.'

'Ah,' Ames grinned. 'So you'll know all about what goes on in there, then?' He pointed to another sweating scrum forming back on the ref's mark, several stone of English private schoolboy getting down and dirty.

'Earnest, if brief, discussions on Impressionist Art?' Maxwell smiled. 'Oh, yes.'

'Go on,' Ames laughed. 'I bet you learned your choicest language in there.'

'Made me the man I am today,' Maxwell conceded. 'Tell me about Tim Robinson.'

'Tim?' Ames continued to watch the practice, the quality of the passing, the momentum of second phase ball. 'This sounds a little uncaring, but I barely knew him.'

'You appointed him,' Maxwell observed.

Ames looked at him. 'In a manner of speaking,' he said. 'Technically of course, it's the Headmaster who appoints.'

'On your recommendation.'

'Well, yes... Come on, keep up. You're walking, Thorpe! Yes, but there wasn't much choice, as it happened.'

'Oh?'

'Well, we short-listed in the usual way. Got down to three. But come the day only Tim showed up.'

'Really?'

'It happens, doesn't it?' Ames clapped his hands again to rally the troops. 'Get him low, Grimond's! You're in the business. You must know it.'

Maxwell did. One might drop out because they'd changed their mind or already got a job. Two ... that seemed like carelessness. 'Didn't they apologise?'

'Er ... no, actually, they didn't. Bad form, that. That's more like it, Selwyn.' A crunching tackle had brought the Head of Tennyson down but he rolled clear and was back in the attack immediately. 'That's it! That's it!' Ames roared, cheering on the drive. 'Don't you remember? We built this city on ruck and maul!' Complete with a tune of sorts and fist punching the sky, it was the Head of Games' idea of being hip, bonding with his back row.

'He seemed okay, though,' Ames was back with Maxwell, eyes still following the play. 'Keen enough.'

'Except he forged his references.'

Ames stood stock still for the first time since Maxwell had joined him. 'What? What are you talking about?'

'He was never at Haileybury. The police don't know who he is.'

'Good God... Crap, Johnson! One more mistackle like that and you're out of the game this afternoon. Now, bloody well wake up!' Ames closed to his man. 'How do you know what the police know? You're not one, are you? Cop, I mean?'

'Heaven forbid,' Maxwell held up both hands. 'I just don't like having to haul dead men out of lakes, that's all.'

'Look,' Ames had forgotten the action on the field behind him for the moment. 'Come over tonight, will you? That's my place, over there,' he pointed to an elegant house, half hidden by rhododendrons far more ancient. 'Gaynor usually does a mean curry on Saturdays. Around seven?'

'It's a date,' said Maxwell, leaping aside in time to avoid a hearty tackle over the touchline.

Henry Hall had never been so grateful for a cup of coffee in his life. 'Thanks, Jacquie.' He sat in the annexe of Sheffield's study, his Interview Room since last Tuesday. These five days had felt like years. 'How many have we seen?'

She checked the ledger on the desk in front of

her. 'Twenty-three,' she said. 'Another eight to go.'

'And then the kids.'

He leaned back in his chair, tilting the glasses back on his head. His eyes looked red-rimmed and tired. 'I don't even want to think about that,' he said. 'Still,' he swung the swivel in the direction of the window. 'There aren't as many as there were.' Outside on the gravel drive, yet another Range Rover was being loaded up with trunks and suitcases and a pair of irate parents were cold-shouldering Mervyn Larson, standing limply in his gown to see off another three sibling charges. Rumour had it that the Bursar would hang himself if it got much worse, fees fluttering out of the window like confetti.

'Sir,' Jacquie leaned forward across the desk littered with depositions. 'We need back up. Two of us just can't...'

He held up his hand. 'DCI West has got his beloved Incident Room back,' he told her.

'West?' Jacquie frowned. 'He's the local DCI?'

Hall nodded. 'Of course, you haven't met him, have you? One of nature's gentlefolk. Your Max would love him.'

Jacquie's face gave nothing away. For more years than she cared to remember, she'd been wedged between these two – the man she worked for and the man she loved. Sometimes she couldn't breathe; sometimes she couldn't sleep. But sometimes, she wouldn't have it any other way. 'So West's handling the Incident Room? Can't he spare any of his people here at Grimond's?'

'No,' Hall said flatly. 'No, that's not going to

162

happen. I talked to Chief Superintendent Mason on the phone this morning. Officially, West and I are giving each other every co-operation. Unofficially, we're giving each other a wide berth.'

'Politics!' moaned Jacquie, shaking her head. 'It always comes down to that.'

Hall let his glasses drop back into place. 'We could debate the need for a national police force,' he said, 'Or we could talk to Teacher Number Twenty-Four. Who is he?'

She checked. 'Jeremy Tubbs, Geography.'

Hall opened his file, moving the coffee to one side. 'Wheel him in, Jacquie.'

Richard Ames's house had once been the stables at Jedediah Grimond's country pad. Now it was a tasteful and extended four bedroom house and he acknowledged he'd been lucky to get it – one of the perks, arguably the only perk, of being Head of Games at Grimond's.

Gaynor Ames was a strikingly attractive blonde, whose curves filled her clothes and whose photographs appeared everywhere in the living room, posed with three adorable children, all now safely tucked up in their beds. Had Maxwell listened carefully, he'd have heard the gentle whiffling of the youngest over the intercom in the corner. As it was, he merely stumbled over their Bob the Builder toys, a testimony to the 21st century god, merchandizing, every parent's dread.

Richard Ames had not been exaggerating about his wife's curry; the smell of it from the kitchen was mouth-watering. Ames and Maxwell sat in the den, an Americanism Maxwell could frankly have done without. He had, after all, yet to forgive that great nation for Yorktown. All this and Southern Comfort too. (Maxwell could put aside his prejudices for a cup of the warm South). Sporting trophies littered the surfaces and Richard Ames stood smiling alongside Will Carling on several photos.

'Christ, Richard, cats and dogs out there!' a dripping Tony Graham called from the hall, letting his coat dangle on the pegs. 'Max,' he shook the man's hand. 'Haven't seen you since yesterday.'

'How's everybody taking the Tim Robinson business?' Maxwell asked.

'How d'you think? Ah, bless you, Richard Ames,' and he gratefully accepted a large Scotch. 'Here's to crime! Oh, sorry, bad taste,' and he took a swig. 'You know the Ratcliffes took their three away today?'

'God,' Ames muttered, freshening Maxwell's glass, 'that's a future fly-half gone west.'

'Well done this afternoon, by the way. Twenty-four-six. Quite a trouncing.'

'The wind was with us,' Ames said modestly.

'Young John's on form, though.'

'Indeed,' Ames sat himself back down. 'John Selwyn has all the hallmarks of a first class player. Maybe even international. All credit to the Housemaster,' and he raised his glass to Graham.

'That was Bill, wasn't it?' Gaynor Ames had joined the trio, bringing her glass of red wine with her from the kitchen.

'Gaynor.' Graham was on his feet, planting a not-altogether-solicited peck on the woman's cheek. 'Good of you to have me.'

'Yes.' She looked at him with a stoniness Maxwell couldn't fathom. 'Mr Maxwell, how are you at salad tossing?'

'Marginally worse than caber tossing,' he confessed. 'But if I can be of any assistance.'

'Gaynor,' Ames protested. 'You can't take Max away. He's a guest. I wanted a chat.'

'He's my guest as well as yours,' she pointed out. 'You boys will be talking rugger into the wee smalls, long after I've gone to bed. Let me see how domesticated they are in comprehensives these days,' and she dragged him into the brightly neon-lit kitchen.

'There you go,' she said, pointing out the basics. 'Vinaigrette to your left, balsamic to the right. I was going to ask you, Mr Maxwell, how you were enjoying Grimond's, but that's rather like that old joke about Mrs Lincoln and the play now, isn't it?'

'I'm afraid it is,' he nodded, hacking lettuce with a will. 'And that's Max, by the way.'

'Oh,' she said archly, leaning over his shoulder. 'You're a pro. Is there a Mrs Max?'

Maxwell smiled. There had been. A lovely girl with dark eyes that sparkled on a summer's day. She was dead now, her body broken as her car rolled over and over on a stretch of wet road far to the north. He shook himself free of the thought. 'No,' he said. 'No Mrs Max. You have a lovely home, Gaynor.'

'Thank you,' she busied herself at the cooker. 'I used to think so. Now ... well, it's all turned a bit sour somehow.' She turned to him. 'Max, this is not a happy school. Even before poor old Bill,

165

there were ... shall we say undercurrents?'

'Undercurrents?' Maxwell continued chopping. Had he found, and purely by accident, the chink in Grimond's armour?

She stopped and put her spatula down. 'Richard is a good man, Max,' she said. 'Oh, I know; I'd be bound to say that, wouldn't I? But he is, honestly. He wanted to talk to you about ... things. But now Tony's here, I don't suppose he will. Yes, Richard's a good man, but those others ... well...'

It was Maxwell's turn to stop. 'Do you think Bill Pardoe killed himself, Gaynor?'

She looked steadily into his eyes. They were smiling eyes; it was a face to trust. She closed to him, almost whispering. 'Never in a million years,' she said. Then she straightened, 'but he was old school. He played things by the book.' She turned back to her dishes. 'He had enemies.'

'Enemies,' Maxwell followed her, 'who would push him off a roof?'

Her hazel eyes flickered for the first time. 'Have you met Tubbsy?' she asked. 'Geography?'

'No,' Maxwell told her. 'I don't believe I have.'

'Talk to him.' She heard the others coming through to take their places at the candle-lit dining table. 'He'll tell you nothing sober. But after three G 'n' T's, he's anybody's. Good luck, Max!' And she whisked away with a hot tureen in her oven-mitted hands. 'Starters, everybody!'

Chapter Ten

'What the fuck do you mean, nothing?' DCI West was scowling at his sergeant.

'It's true, guv,' Steve Chapell shrugged. 'He stepped fully formed from somewhere. I've even been back to forensic, looking for old scars, operations, bridgework. Nothing. At least nothing that helps. Where's his wife, mum, dad, the bloke who repaired his car?'

'He hasn't got a car,' Sandy Berman was ever the dotter of i's and the crosser of tees. 'Travelled everywhere by bike. It's back in the sheds at Grimond's on the grounds that we didn't know where else to put it.'

'Clean?' West asked.

'As a whistle. His prints only.'

It was a Sunday morning, wet and wild after a torrential night. The wind had built a little after three, driving through the cedars that ringed Grimond's lake, chiselling its cold, dead surface. It had torn down the rickety picket fence that separated Tim Robinson's ex-Council house from Harold Blundell's next door. It was rattling now around the Victorian locks on the Incident Room at Selborne that was once again Mark West's.

'All right,' the DCI had his team's full attention. They all knew where they were with Mark West. He was a hard bastard, tight as arseholes and he didn't take prisoners. At least, though, you could read his eyes. Not like that bland bastard Hall, forever hiding behind those gold-rimmed glasses. Now that West was back on the case, Hall was like a bacon sandwich at a Jewish wedding and people kept away from him. Increasingly, all the Sussex man's time was spent at the school. The co-operative gulf was widening. 'What are the links between Pardoe and Robinson?'

'Both taught at the same school,' Berman kicked off with the brain storming.

'But Robinson only since January. They couldn't have known each other well,' DS Walters reminded everybody.

'Pardoe was a Housemaster,' West orchestrated their thinking. 'What about Robinson?'

Chapell shook his head. 'Not attached to any House. School policy apparently – PE staff aren't.'

'So what were they?' West wanted to know, drawing viciously on his ciggie. 'Ships that pass in the night?'

'With respect, guv,' DS McGovern was sipping her coffee in a corner. 'Are we definitely calling the Pardoe thing murder? And are the two necessarily linked?'

West's scowl could turn people to stone. 'Are you serious, Denise? Whether Bill Pardoe jumped or whether he was pushed is, I'll grant you, still up for grabs. But linked? Come on; I like, as they say, a laugh. Anything on the murder weapon for Robinson?'

'Still nothing, guv,' DS Walters volunteered. 'All the oars in the boat-house are clean.'

'What sort of oars are we talking here, Pete?'

'Sculls, guv, aptly enough.'

That earned him one or two guffaws and a few more grins. Nothing politically correct about Mark West's Incident Team.

'What are we talking? Six, seven feet long?'

'Thereabouts,' Walters nodded.

'Not something you'd carry about without being noticed.' West was thinking aloud.

'Unless you were a member of the rowing team,' Berman threw in.

'Go on, Sandy.' West lit a second ciggie from the first. He knew his DI was no slouch in the deductive department. More than that, he was lucky.

'Well, it's the old needle in the haystack bit. The best place to hide something is in the middle of a thousand similar things. No one would think it odd to see a rower carrying an oar; whereas if you or I...'

'Yeah, but it's the timing, isn't it?' Chapell reasoned. 'Forensic gives us a window of the early hours. Nobody's rowing at that time of night. Under the cover of darkness, it wouldn't matter who was carrying what; there'd be nobody to see.'

'We could drag the lake,' Berman suggested.

There were groans and chuckles at all points of the compass.

'I'm not sure the Chief Super's budget runs to that,' West grinned. 'But I'll think about it. Who's checked the boathouse itself?'

'I have, guv.' Denise McGovern held her biro in the air.

'And?'

'Bit of a knocking shop, by all accounts.'

'Oh?' Berman leaned across to her, winking.

169

'Semen-stained tissues.' The DS ignored him. 'Areas flattened by what appears to be human contact.'

'Analysis of semen?'

'Not Robinson's,' McGovern assured them.

'So what do we do?' Berman asked. 'Blood group every bloke in the school?'

'If it comes to that,' West nodded. There was a movement near the door and a rattle of wood and glass. Jacquie Carpenter dashed in, doing her drowned rat impression and apologizing silently with an awkward grin. 'Right, people.' West stubbed the ciggie out briskly. 'To work. Steve, keep on the background thing. I want photos circulated. Morgue ones if you have to, suitably cleaned up. Go house to house in Petersfield. I want somebody who knew who the bloody hell this Robinson was. Denise, the bike. Get the serial number. I want to know where and when it was bought. Sandy, get your team over to Robinson's house...'

All eyes had turned to Jacquie Carpenter now.

'I believe DCI Hall was working on that one, guv,' Berman said.

'Is that right, DS Carpenter?' West asked her.

Jacquie nodded.

'I think it's time we got to know each other, don't you?' And he nodded at the others to go into action, holding open the door into his inner office. She trudged in, dripping all over his lino.

'Smoke?' He held the packet out to her.

'I gave up,' she said, still wiping rain from her forehead, and arranging herself on the chair, dumping her bag on the floor.

'Good for you.' West sat on the corner of his desk. 'Coffee, then?'

'No, thank you, sir. I've just had one.'

'Yeah,' West was lighting up again. 'I've just had one of these, too. What difference does that make?' He inhaled. 'These bastards'll kill you in the end. It's Jacquie, isn't it?'

'Sir.'

'I'm Mark,' and he held out a stubby-fingered hand.

'Sir.' She took it dutifully.

'Let's get something straight.' West poured himself a coffee from the dead-looking brew on the side-counter. 'Your DCI Hall was seconded to my patch, stumbled on an incident and blew it. I was ordered off at first. "Let Henry Hall do it. He's a fucking whiz-kid" – this, in essence, was Chief Superintendent Mason's dictum. Except,' he sat himself down in the swivel, 'he was a little over-optimistic there. Your DCI bit off a little more than he could chew. So now, change of heart for the Chief Super, here I am.'

'We'll see you at Grimond's, then, sir?' Jacquie said.

'Er ... no,' West conceded. 'No, for reasons best known to the Chief Super, that's still Henry's province. My people can poke around in the shrubbery, check the bike sheds and so on, but Hall interviews the kids. I can, I'm sure, count on your full co-operation?'

'In the interests of closing the case, sir, yes, of course.'

'Good.' West leaned back. Jacquie still sat up-right, steaming slightly in the clammy atmosphere

171

of the office, as co-operative as a barracuda. 'Now, you went to Robinson's house?'

'Yes, sir.'

'And found?'

'Nothing.'

West blinked. 'Nothing?'

'I've never seen a place so clean, sir.'

'You talked to neighbours?'

'A mad old couple on one side.'

'And?'

'Didn't know anything. Like two thirds of the wise monkeys.'

'And the other side?'

'Nobody in. I'll call back.'

'No, no. I'll take over that one now. Can I see your report?'

'You'll have to ask DCI Hall, sir.'

'Now, Jacquie,' West's smile was like the silver plate on a coffin. 'Didn't we talk about full co-operation a minute ago?'

'I can assure you, sir, I'm not being unco-operative. It's just that DCI Hall has my only copy. I can get it for you if you like.'

'Tell me,' West watched his brown-ended fingers curling around the smooth white of the cigarette. 'Why did Hall send for you?'

'Support, I suppose,' Jacquie said. 'You know how it is, a long way from home.'

'He's got support here.' West waved to the hive of activity in his outer office, men and women on phones and photocopiers and computers.

'Has he, sir?' Jacquie said, wide-eyed. 'I know he'd like to think so.'

Meal times had become gloomy things at Grimond's. Everybody talked in low, subdued tones about little but Bill Pardoe and Tim Robinson. Maxwell, versed as he was in the Victorian obsession with death, expected to see the curtains drawn in the dining room and the grim black stallions pacing the gravel at the door; the white-faced mutes crying their glycerine tears and sable ostrich plumes gusting in the wind.

'Mr Tubbs not on the boarding staff?' Maxwell put the question to Tony Graham at his left elbow as both of them made fairly easy work of Mrs Oakes's apple crumble.

'Tubbsy? Lord no,' Graham told him. 'Hasn't the stomach for it, between you and me.'

'Needs stomach, does it, Housemastering?'

Graham slid the empty plate away from him, turning in his chair to face Maxwell on High Table. 'It may not be the right climate to say so at the moment, but consider your colleagues, Max. How many of 'em would you trust, say, with your own child?'

Maxwell's own child lay with her mother under the flowers in a cold cemetery to the north. No one would ever teach her, not now. 'My own child?' He could still see her dark, bright eyes and feel her trusting fingers tangling in his hair.

'That's the benchmark,' Graham nodded. 'Look around you here. Gallow, a miserable bastard with a smell under his nose; Helmseley, so dyed-in-the-wool it's pathetic. Maggie Shaunnessy, well, talk about a reincarnation of Jean Brodie ... oh, there are some decent types. Richard Ames is a good buddy, even Mervyn

173

Larson has his moments...'

'The good doctor?' Maxwell raised his eyebrows in the direction of Sheffield sitting a couple of chairs away behind Graham and lost in earnest conversation with his deputies.

The Head of Tennyson laughed. 'Sorry,' he said. 'That's probably enough character assassination for one day, isn't it? Unprofessional. I'm sorry. We're all a bit on edge.'

'Ah, we all do it,' Maxwell sipped his water, wishing it was something stronger. 'I've got this wax model of Legs Diamond at home I habitually riddle with pins every Sunday night. Doesn't do him any harm of course, but I feel a damn sight better for it. Who's your money on, Tony?' Maxwell had closed to his man.

'What?'

'Tim Robinson. Who bent an oar over his head?'

Graham looked appalled. 'For Christ's sake, Max. You're not serious.'

'Oh, but I am, Tony. You're rubbishing your colleagues for some slight, real or imagined over your years at Grimond's chalk face. But what if you *really* had cause? What if one of them is a murderer? Mervyn Larson? David Gallow? Michael Helmseley? George Sheffield? Richard...'

'No,' Graham was suddenly on his feet, throwing his napkin onto the table. 'Preposterous.' And all eyes on High Table turned at his exit.

Mad Max went home that afternoon. He hadn't planned to; it was a spur of the moment thing. Was it the lure of the bills that would be waiting for him in their buff anonymity in the hallway, kindly stacked by courtesy of Mrs B., who did for him every Wednesday? Hard to say.

Parker, Grimond's steward and Johannes Factotum, had called the taxi for him and he waited in the man's lodge office a little after lunch.

'Rum business, eh, Mr Parker?'

The steward, it had to be said, was a charmless nerk as a result of a lifetime of being looked down on by his betters and, latterly, his youngers. Nobody ever called him 'Mr', still less 'Eric'. So it came as rather a shock from this bloke from a school on the wrong side of the educational tracks.

'It is, sir.'

'How long have you been at Grimond's?'

'Since the old Headmaster's time, sir. Mrs Parker and I come here in '78. Different place it was, then.' It was indeed. Maxwell remembered it well: the Amoco Cadiz broke its back off Brittany, spilling thousands of tons of crude into the sea; Jomo Kenyatta, the Mau-Mau terrorist, shuffled off his mortal coil mourned as a great and wise leader; somebody pinched Charlie Chaplin's body out of his grave.

'No girls,' Maxwell watched a gaggle of them squealing their way out onto the netball pitch, incomprehensible letters bright on their backs.

'Right,' Parker snorted. 'And none of these kids still wet behind the ears.'

'Teachers, you mean?' Maxwell checked. 'Tell me about it. Mr Pardoe must have been a bit rough for you.'

'I've been serving Tennyson House for a quarter of a century now. I couldn't believe it when they told me.'

'Not the suicidal type?'

'Nah,' Parker shook his head, rummaging through a pile of papers.

'What drove him to it, d'you think?' Maxwell had piled his hat and scarf on Parker's counter and was leaning on it, arms folded like a genial gargoyle atop Notre Dame.

He watched the steward's eyes flicker left and right. 'I couldn't say,' he grunted.

'You handle all the school mail here, do you?' Maxwell asked.

'Mrs Parker and I do, yes sir.'

'What, it's delivered here and you distribute it?'

'That's right. Each House has its own pigeon holes as well as the Senior Common Room. Dr Sheffield's secretary takes care of his post.'

'Did Bill Pardoe get much mail?' Maxwell caught Parker's look. 'I mean, I know I do. Junk mostly. Addressed to the Head of Sociology, Psychology, Law – except that we don't teach those things where I come from. Nobody knows what they are.'

'He got a lot of blank stuff,' Parker was scowling. 'Anonymous, like.'

'Anonymous?'

'Well, when I say anonymous, it was addressed to him, like, but always in the same envelope, plain white.'

'I don't suppose one of them arrived after ... the accident?'

'Accident?' Parker snorted. 'You don't have to pussyfoot around with me, Mr Maxwell. The man killed himself. It's that simple.'

'Mr Parker,' Maxwell refolded his arms on the steward's counter, 'I don't think there's anything simple about it at all. And you just told me you thought he wasn't the suicidal type. The envelope?'

Parker hesitated, then he ducked out of sight, to a wooden locker near the floor, beyond a single-bar electric fire. When he stood up, he was holding a white envelope in his hand; it was bulging and it was addressed to Bill Pardoe.

'Why didn't you give this to the police?' Maxwell asked.

'They didn't ask for it,' Parker shrugged. 'Leaves a bad taste in the mouth, does this. Washing Grimond's dirty laundry in public. That ought not to be happening. I'm not making it any more public than it has to be.'

Maxwell nodded. He couldn't think of anybody that loyal to his native Leighford High School. Such things just weren't fashionable any more, not in the state sector. School was a place to be endured, not loved. 'Mr Parker,' he said gently, 'could I take this?'

'What for?' Parker asked.

Maxwell took a deep breath and launched himself. 'I didn't know Bill Pardoe,' he said, 'but I've been involved with sudden death now for more years than I care to remember.' He shrugged. 'Just follows me, I suppose. I don't know why.'

'So ... you're saying...?'

'I'm saying that I don't think Bill Pardoe killed himself, any more than you do. I think somebody

177

here did it. Somebody at Grimond's pushed him off the roof.'

'No,' Parker was growling, shaking his head. 'No, that can't be.'

'Let me prove it, then,' Maxwell said. 'I think the reason that Bill Pardoe died, or part of it, lies in this envelope. When did it arrive?'

'The day after they found him,' Parker said. 'Wednesday.'

'Time?'

'Bout nine, quarter-past, maybe.'

Maxwell checked the postmark. Petersfield. The date and time were all but illegible.

'Mr Maxwell,' Parker looked into the man's eyes as the taxi hooted outside the lodge. 'Can you sort this? Put Grimond's back on its feet again?'

Maxwell slid the envelope out of the man's hands. 'I'll give it my very best shot,' he smiled.

The sun had the nerve to come out as Maxwell's cab purred into Leighford. All day, it had been dull and dingy and cold and now, as dusk began to creep from the East, a red-gold glow bathed the flyover and the trees that ringed the common land called the Dam. On the way through Sunday Sussex, the driver had bored the Head of Sixth Form rigid with his views on the Euro, Hear'Say and the *Weakest Link*. It was a numb Peter Maxwell who stumbled out at 38 Columbine and remortgaged the place to pay the fare.

There were the bills, piled high by the hall phone as he knew they would be. Mrs B's less-than-elegant note lay beside them. He read it aloud. 'I done the kitchen and the bathroom. The bloke called about the guttering. That bloody cat brought something in. I couldn't make it out by the giblets. Have you had him done, by the way? See you later, Mrs B.'

He consigned the missive to the bin. 'Thanks, Mrs B. Did he? Well, it's in his nature. Yes, I had him done years ago. See you.' He checked his answerphone.

'Max, Deirdre Lessing. You do know there's an Options evening next Monday? I can't find the paperwork for the Sixth Form. Get back.'

Maxwell held up his fingers in the form of a cross. 'Get back yourself, winged harpy of the night. And behind me, to boot. And talk to Helen Maitland, there's a dear. She is after all, my Number Two and a bloody efficient one. Not that you'd acknowledge that. She's only a floor away from that cavern strewn with human bones you call your office – surely to God it can't be that difficult!'

'Uncle Max, it's Tiffany...'

'Tiff.' Maxwell chortled. 'My agony niece. How are you, darling?' He often talked to tape recorders.

'Just thought I'd tell you I've got an offer from Cambridge. Jesus. Sorry, I'm supposed to have phoned you in January. Oops. Don't tell Mum I didn't. Love you.'

'Jesus!' Maxwell shouted, ripping open envelopes with a well-practiced thumb. 'Well done! Nice to see a fine family tradition going on. Do *some* work while you're there, there's a good girl.'

'Max, pick up. It's Jacquie.'

He was halfway up the stairs by this time and caught himself a nasty one doubling back to get to it. 'Jacquie?'

'Max, you're home.'

'Correct, oh wise one.' It was good to hear her voice.

'I couldn't reach you on your mobile.' It was good to hear his too.

'And you thought I'd forgotten how to switch it on again. Come on, admit it.'

'Something like that.' Her voice sounded very far away.

'I'm sorry I couldn't let you know,' he said. 'I need time to think.'

'Are you going back to Leighford?'

'Lord, no. I'll be back at Grimond's tomorrow. We need to talk.'

'You're right. Look, Max,' her voice fluctuated, faded, broke up. 'Henry's up to something. I think he's falsifying evidence.'

'What? I can't hear you. Henry's what?'

But she'd gone in a crackle of static punctuated with bursts of silence. He dialled her number, stabbing out the numbers he'd learned by heart. Nothing. Dead air. 'Damn!' He threw the rest of the bills into the bin and took the stairs again.

On the settee as he flicked on the wall lights a great black and white beast yawned and stretched, fangs bright in the half-light. Maxwell drew the curtains on the embers of the sun dying in the fields towards Tottingleigh and he saw the street lights twinkle into life out on the Shingle. He'd only been away a few days but already he missed the sea. He who had been born in the Midlands about as far as it was possible to be from the sea. Now it was in his blood, salty and untameable.

He tore open the white envelope he'd carried in his briefcase all the way back from Grimond's and sat down heavily in his armchair. From time to time on the interminable journey, he'd glanced at the leather, fighting down the urge to open it and see just what had been sent to Bill Pardoe the day after his death.

'Evening, Count.' He wasn't looking at the animal, but he was sure he heard the briefest of purrs before the head cocked sideways and the nightly ritual of bum-licking began. 'You know, you'd make a wonderful member of the Senior Management Team – they can all do that; although to be fair it's usually Legs Diamond's they're working on, not their own. Good God.'

He'd never seen what lay in his lap before. It was a Swedish import, a full colour porn mag which left nothing to the imagination. Every model was male. Every model was naked and erect. None could have been more than seventeen. Too late he realised his fingerprints were all over the thing. Too late he wondered who else's were there.

'So,' the house lights on the Shingle had gone out now as one by one sleepy Leighford closed its eyes to brace itself for another week. Maxwell sat in his modelling chair in the dim lights of the attic, his gold-laced pill box cap on his head, his lamp lighting the accoutrements of Trumpeter

Perkins, 11th Prince Albert's Own Hussars. Maxwell was carefully painting the plastic man's cherry-coloured overalls, checking that the crimson mix was just right. 'What we have, Count, is two deaths. One school. Four days. Pretty cranky arithmetic, don't you think?'

The Count, of course, couldn't count. And there wasn't that much evidence that he could think. There was a rhythmic richness to His Master's Voice, though, and die rather than admit it, he had missed the old duffer over the past week. That foul old sow who removed his favourite smells each week was now coming in daily, scaring him witless with that thing she plugged into the wall and roared over the carpets with. Many was the tasty giblet she'd sucked up with that and just when he'd saved them for later.

'What do we have?' Maxwell rested his brush on the top of the paint pot and leaned back, hands behind his head and forage cap peak over his eyes. 'One William Pardoe, revered Housemaster of the old school, not a million miles, I suggest, from your beloved master in terms of the cut of his jib. But was he loved? Feared? Hated? You know what kids are, Count.'

Metternich lashed his tail, just the once.

'Private sector, public sector. Eton, Dotheboys Hall, Leighford, they're all the same. It's not considered cool to be keen or interested or smart if you're under nineteen. The junior schools have all that – smelly little buggers with their hands in the air, all shouting "Me, sir, me Miss. Me, me, me." Standing by you as you listen to them read and sticking their tummies out. At university, they're keen again. Oh, it's laced with smack and nights down the boozer, but they'll do their work on water when it comes to Finals and Seminartime. And in the middle? What've we got? In between are the teenage years,' he paraphrased the old Val Doonican song that only he could still remember, 'you'll remember all of your life. They're still sticking their tummies out, or at least the girls are, but that's just to show off their navel jewellery. And that, Count, is why they love you, or hate you, or fear you. Because they're teenagers. And you don't always know which.' He yawned and rubbed his eyes. 'I haven't talked to the kids yet. And that's what I've got to do.'

He sipped the Southern Comfort in the dim light. Across the room, the black tapering lances of the 17th prickled against the sky as the horsemen of the Light Brigade waited to ride into legend.

'If you wanted to end it all, Count, would you leap off a tall building? With your four feet and nine lives, of course, you'd be okay, wouldn't you? Bill Pardoe didn't have your advantages, unfortunately. But what was wrong with a bottle of pills? A one-way drive in the car? A razor to the wrists? Why didn't he walk, like Virginia Woolf, into the water with his pockets weighed with stones? Why was it all so bloody public?'

He took another swig, larger than the first.

'And then there's Mr Robinson, the poor marker, the indifferent fencer. Mr Nobody. Captain Nemo. No past,' he balanced the paintbrush on his index finger and watched it tip one way, then the other. 'No future. Now here,

Count, we have a different kettle of fish, can of worms, whatever culinary metaphor you care to conjure up. Mr Robinson didn't kill himself and there's no point pretending he did. Somebody stove in his head and dumped him in the boating lake. Let's assume for a moment that the same person was responsible for both deaths – that Bill Pardoe was pushed and by the same hand that caved in Tim Robinson's skull. Why so crafty the first time and so cack the second? Murderer losing his edge? Panicky? Frightened? Both bodies visible, no attempt to hide them. Two very public deaths.'

He emptied the glass of its amber liquid.

'Bill Pardoe received pretty strong porn through the mail. Mail that was posted in Petersfield. What've we got, Count, a thriving porn industry in downtown Petersfield? Beggars belief, doesn't it? Tim Robinson lived in down-town Petersfield. Is that the link? Something going on between the two?' He shook his head, going round in circles as he was. 'But why post this stuff when they saw each other every day? What would be the point? And where is it all now? I saw at least one similar mag on Bill Pardoe's desk. But the law went over his room like locusts and they didn't find any more. And then,' he found himself reaching for the Southern Comfort again, 'there's that tape. The blackmail tape or whatever that was. Who left that outside my door? And why me? Was it just a souvenir of Grimond's? Did somebody get the wrong room?'

He ran his finger round the rim of the glass, sticky now with the residue of the amber nectar and looked up at Metternich, the cat. 'You know, Count, and I don't say this lightly, sometimes I think you're no bloody use at all. No offence.'

Chapter Eleven

'A free afternoon?' Maxwell was incredulous. You didn't get those in the state system.

'Ah,' Jeremy Tubbs was already three sheets in the wind and it wasn't even half-past-one. 'There's no such thing,' he burbled, 'as a free afternoon. I'm on prep duty tonight.'

'Hmm,' Maxwell nodded, finishing off his Cheddar ploughman's. 'What a bummer.'

Jeremy Tubbs taught Geography, always, as a subject, the poor relation among the Humanities. There was something rather pathetic about him, an air of idiocy, as though he'd always been the butt of everybody's jokes and was only now becoming aware of the fact. He couldn't have been more than thirty-five but had the ample girth of a fifty-year-old and his hair was already deserting him. But he'd finished his ploughman's and the glass of water and the wine gum was already making him tipsy.

Peter Maxwell knew he was taking his life in his hands doing this. Tubbs had driven him out to the Swallow's Nest, the old coaching inn along the Portsmouth Road, refurbished courtesy of the Harvester chain and would have to drive him back. How would three G'n'T's register on the coloured straws of Mr Plod, waiting in the lay-bys of the back-doubles to pull over such as he?

'This chap Robinson,' Maxwell swirled the

186

Southern Comfort around the glass. 'What do you make of it all?'

Tubbs scowled at him. Perhaps Maxwell had been misinformed. Perhaps Gaynor Ames had got it wrong. Just how much of Maxwell's pitiful salary would it take to loosen this man's tongue?

'Well,' the Geographer leaned forward in their corner of the snug and Maxwell was about to find out. 'There was talk, of course...'

'Really?' Maxwell leaned back by the ingle-nook, for all the world as if he'd rather be talking about Byzantine foreign policy.

'Our Mr Robinson was rather a one for the ladies.'

'Really?'

'Does this sort of thing go on in your sort of school?' Tubbs wanted to know.

'This sort of thing?' Maxwell was all innocence in his fishing trip, an ingénue with a mind like a razor.

Tubbs nudged his elbow as if about to launch into an old Monty Python sketch. 'Wanderings in the dorm. Oh, but you don't have dorms, do you? Even so, there must be temptation. I mean, the sixth form sirens are only a few years younger than our new recruits.'

'Robinson was older, surely.'

'Well, yes, but it doesn't necessarily follow. Here we are, brains the size of the great outdoors, and shapers of young minds... They're bound to have crushes, aren't they? I remember one girl...'

'You were telling me about Tim Robinson,' Maxwell had no wish to wander down memory lane with this one.

187

'Was I? Oh, yes.' Tubbs grimaced as a jolt of gin hit his tonsils. 'Well, it all started with that tart Cassandra James, you know, of Austen House.'

'Yes, we've met,' Maxwell said.

'Trollope House, more like. Well, I must admit, she's a cracking bit of crackling, isn't she? I mean, all professionalism aside and ignoring the *loco parentis* business for a moment, I could imagine getting my leg over her.' He closed to the Head of Sixth Form. 'They say she goes like a train.'

'Who says?'

'They,' Tubbs shrugged. 'Everybody.'

'So, Robinson was getting his end away, was he?'

'Allegedly,' Tubbs smirked.

'What about Bill Pardoe?'

'Pardoe?' Tubbs blurted, causing heads in the snug to turn in his direction. 'Good God, no. If anything, Bill swung the other way.'

'Boys, you mean?'

'You know what they say, Max,' Tubbs sniggered. 'Choirmasters, Housemasters. Not so long ago, it went with the territory; virtually de rigeur. In the fifties, allegedly, it was on people's CVs.'

'Allegedly,' Maxwell smiled.

'No, I never heard of Bill showing the remotest interest in the fair sex.'

'There wasn't a *Mrs* Pardoe, was there?'

'Not that I knew,' Tubbs leaned back and shook his head. 'But I've only been at Grimond's for seven years. My God, what an apprenticeship.'

Maxwell was secretly impressed. A *Geographer* who knew the traditional length of an apprentice-ship was a rare phenomenon indeed. 'So, what's your evidence for Robinson and Cassandra then?'

he asked.

'The boat-house.' Tubbs rattled the ice in his glass. 'Grimond's equivalent of Lovers' Lane. Think about it, Maxwell. Robinson's a Games master, access to the boat-house keys. Probably took one of those PE mat things they use in the gym to lie down on. The Arbiters won't like...' and his voice trailed away.

'The what?'

'Look,' Tubbs was checking his watch, comparing it with the clock over the fireplace. 'I really ought to be getting back.'

'I thought you had a free afternoon,' Maxwell reminded him.

'No, I've just remembered; I've a meeting, with that appalling Shaunessy woman at three. Some wretched girl can't cope with A level Geography. I ask you...'

It did seem unlikely, Maxwell had to agree, but somewhere, somehow, he'd touched something of a raw nerve with Tubbsy and now wasn't the moment to pursue it.

They ambled out to the great outdoors, Maxwell hoping the fresh air would have something resembling a sobering effect on his driver. Briefly, their feet crunched on the gravel and they bundled into Tubbsy's battered MG and roared the country lanes, via various verges, to the Grimond's gates.

'Mr Tubbs!' a local journalist called out as the car jolted to a halt by them. 'Any comments for the *Echo*?'

'Yes,' Tubbs had wound his window down. 'Why don't you people get a proper job?' And his foot hit the floor as the crowd of paparazzi jeered and hooted.

'*Somebody* got out of bed the wrong side this morning,' somebody said.

'Who was that pissed man?' another asked, paraphrasing the question eternally put to the Lone Ranger all those years ago.

'Jeremy Tubbs; fat bastard teaches Geography.'

'Who was that with him?'

'Somebody Maxwell,' the *Echo* man confided. 'Larson told us he was seconded from somewhere else. Not actually on the team.'

'Worth a few lines, though.'

'Nah. Rumour has it he works in a comprehensive. It's the weirdos who teach at Grimond's we're after.'

DCI Hall looked over the rims of his specs. It was Monday afternoon and the end of the day seemed years away.

'I thought you'd be shorter,' he was saying to Peter Maxwell. 'In fact, let's not beat about the bush, I thought you'd be Jeremy Tubbs. We've been expecting him since the day before yesterday.'

'Mr Tubbs is a little indisposed.' Maxwell slid the chair out from under Hall's desk. 'He may or may not have a meeting with Miss Shaunessy about now, but I happen to know he's sleeping it off in the San. The Matron here is, apparently, a dab hand with black coffee. You've been avoiding me, Henry.'

'Jacquie,' Hall threw his pen down on the desk. 'Could you leave us?'

190

'Sir?' The girl hadn't expected this. Not Maxwell's gate-crashing nor Hall's reaction to it.

'Now, please.' Hall didn't care for the woman's hesitation.

She stood up, Maxwell smiling at her as she went. 'I won't be far away,' she said. And both of them thought she was talking to them. Maxwell slid a large white envelope across Hall's desk, littered as it was in Sheffield's anteroom, with depositions without number.

'What's this?' the DCI asked.

'Evidence,' Maxwell said, 'which may have a bearing on Bill Pardoe's death.'

Hall flicked through the book's pages with his biro tip, his face expressionless as always. He looked up at Peter Maxwell. 'Where did you get this?'

'Parker, the steward. It was unopened in Pardoe's post. Arrived the day after he died.'

'And you opened it?'

'Yes.'

'Mr Maxwell.' Hall leaned towards him, putting the pen away and clasping his fingers. 'I've lost count of the times you have taken it upon yourself to trample over police investigations. In the past, I've always thought twice about bringing charges against you. Now, I'm inclined to change my mind. This is not my patch and I don't have any hint of leeway.'

'You must do as you think fit, Chief Inspector,' Maxwell said. 'And if that means playing things by the book, then so be it. But you and Jacquie are woefully short-staffed here.'

Hall sat upright, frowning. 'Are you offering

your services?' he asked. 'Only, I'm not sure that the rights of citizens' arrest extends to carrying out interrogations of witnesses and suspects.'

'Do you have any?' Maxwell leaned back, fencing with the man as he had so often before. 'Suspects, I mean?'

'I'm looking at one right now,' Hall told him.

'Come on, Henry,' Maxwell laughed. 'Short-staffed you may be, but stupid you ain't.'

Hall looked at his man. 'You're carrying out an investigation of your own, aren't you?' he asked.

Maxwell shrugged. 'I'm asking questions, yes. Can't help myself, I suppose.'

'Getting any answers?'

'Some,' Maxwell nodded. 'You?'

Hall sighed.

'I'll tell you what,' Maxwell said. 'I'll do you a deal. Let's swap. Remember *Strangers on a Train?* Dear old Robert Walker trying to swap murders with innocent, stupid Farley Granger. Criss Cross. I'll give you one piece of information in exchange for one of yours. We can get round to swapping murders later.'

'Which one of us is the innocent stupid one and which of us is mad?' Hall asked. 'And anyway, I don't do deals.'

'Yes, you do,' Maxwell growled. 'That's why West's back in the saddle at Selborne and you're still here, on your own. What's all that about if it's not some sort of deal with the Chief Superintendent?'

'How the...' Hall had gone a deathly white, then his colour flooded back. 'Oh, I know.'

'No,' Maxwell shook his head, reading the

man's mind. 'This has nothing to do with Jacquie. I've got a little portable telly in my attic room, Chief Inspector. I watch the news. Your Incident Room is at Selborne. Last Tuesday you were interviewed by Meridian; yesterday it was West. That interview, by the way, I watched on my own telly, at home. When did you go home last?'

Henry Hall looked at Maxwell. The bastard had an infuriating way of being right. And perceptive. And prescient. He was an irritating shit. But in the past, he had caught killers.

'Bill Pardoe was married,' he said calmly. 'The photograph of the boy in his study is his son.'

'Who told you that?' Maxwell asked.

'Never mind,' Hall said.

'And what do you conclude from that?' Maxwell was fishing for England.

'Nothing, particularly. It doesn't preclude his homosexuality. All this,' he tapped the mag on his desk, 'could be a later manifestation. It could be reason why Mr Pardoe was no longer married.'

'Have you found the wife? The son?'

'Uh-uh.' Hall waved a finger. '*One* piece of information only. That was the deal. Your turn.'

Maxwell smiled. He didn't think for a moment that Hall would fall for that one, but it was worth a try. 'All right,' he said. 'Tim Robinson was having a fling with Cassandra James, Captain of Austen House.'

Hall frowned. 'Where did you hear that?'

Maxwell tapped the side of his nose, lapsing into his Magwich. 'I got me sources,' he rasped, 'and I ain't no grass, Mr 'All, sir.'

'No,' Hall sighed. 'And your information's not

worth much, either.'

'You don't buy the Robinson-James liaison?'

'Not for a moment,' Hall said. 'I'd hoped for more from you, Mr Maxwell. I expect if I acted on every bit of tittle-tattle I'd heard about Leighford, I could close the place down. You're chasing shadows.'

'Cassandra?' Maxwell popped his head around the study door, high in the eaves of Northanger. The dark-haired girl rose languidly from the seat next to the old fireplace and swayed across the room. 'Could I have a word?'

'It's prep period,' she told him, indicating the pile of history books she'd just left.

Maxwell cocked his head to one side to read the spine of one of them. 'Ah, Kershaw,' he smiled. 'Okay, let's talk Hitler, shall we?'

'Are you an historian?' she asked archly.

'History teacher,' he said. 'Is that close enough?'

She led him up a narrow flight of stairs that skirted Ms Shaunessy's domain, past the rowing trophies on the wall. The April sunset was still glowing beyond the cedars that ringed the lake where Tim Robinson died. The pair went into a corridor where Maxwell had never been before and through a door marked Prefects' Study. This was a slightly girlie version of Tennyson, where Maxwell had watched *The Witchfinder*, but it had less of the odour of liniment and one or two fewer jock straps. She sat down on a settee and waited for him to join her.

'So,' she said. 'What do you think of Ian Kershaw?'

194

'First rate,' Maxwell said. 'But I'm an Alan Bullock man myself. Besides, I'm here to talk about Tim Robinson.'

'Mr Robinson? Oh.'

What, Maxwell wondered, was buried in that single 'oh'? He looked into the girl's eyes and could certainly understand where Tubbsy was coming from. 'What did you think of him?'

'Why do you want to know?' she asked, curling up on the settee and slipping her feet under her bum.

'Intellectual curiosity,' Maxwell told her. 'Murders don't happen every day.'

'Nearly every day at Grimond's,' she said, wide-eyed. 'At least recently.'

'He taught you fencing,' Maxwell tried to steer her back to the point.

'After a fashion,' she yawned, stretching so that her breasts jutted out under her blouse and her navel jewellery came into view.

'You mean he wasn't very good?'

'No,' she said. 'No, he wasn't. Not a patch on Richard Ames, for instance.'

'So...' Maxwell was feeling his way carefully. 'It's *Mr* Robinson, but *Richard* Ames?'

'What are you inferring?' she frowned.

Maxwell had met girls like Cassandra James before. They were poison, enjoying playing games with teachers, male teachers in particular, flaunting their new-found sexuality, sure of the irresistibility of their charms.

'Nothing.' Maxwell had played the game before. 'Should I be?'

'I've known Richard since I was fourteen,' she

said, 'when we amalgamated with Grimond's. Robinson's only been here this term.'

'Did he, Robinson, that is, just in casual chat, perhaps, tell you anything about himself? Friends? Family?'

She shrugged. 'No. Strong silent type was Mr Robinson. I got the impression he didn't like us much.'

'Us?'

'Grimond's. Private schools. I don't know. He didn't seem the type.'

'Type?' Maxwell could play the ingenue to perfection.

'You know, a private schoolmaster. He seemed rather ... well, I know it's terribly un-PC to say it, but rather working class.'

'Like me, you mean?' Maxwell smiled.

'You're not working class, Mr Maxwell.' She smiled too, dimples flicking at the corners of her mouth. She ran a finger along the lapel of his jacket. 'I'd say you went to a school very much like this one.'

'Would you?'

Cassandra nodded. 'No girls, of course. Not done, then, was it?'

Maxwell laughed. 'In the Dark Ages? No, it wasn't. Tell me, Cassandra, Mr Robinson; did any of the girls have a crush on him?'

'A crush?' Cassandra snorted. 'Oh, God, what a 'thirties word. Do you mean was he fucking any of them?'

'Well,' Maxwell said, 'I wasn't going to be so direct, but thank you for saving time.' Nothing like cutting straight to the chase in a murder enquiry.

'I don't know,' she said, twisting her face in an effort to think. 'Pru Vallender's a possibility. Shy, quiet type. They're always the ones who've been doing it for years.'

'Not you, then?' Maxwell ventured.

The girl's eyes smouldered and her fingers splayed out on his chest. 'No,' she said archly. 'He wasn't my type.'

'John Selwyn more your man?' he asked innocently.

Cassandra looked deep into the man's eyes. 'John's very sweet,' she purred, 'but he's only a boy. I go for the older man.' She let her hand slide down to Maxwell's waistband, leaning across so that her mouth was inches from his and her sweet breath warmed his face. 'Would you like to fuck me, Mr Maxwell?'

He took her hand firmly but gently and placed it back on Ian Kershaw's book, where it could probably do less damage. 'I wouldn't like the lawsuit and the police investigation that would follow if I did, Cassandra,' he said. 'But thank you for the offer.'

She recoiled quickly, then her right hand snaked out and she slapped him stingingly across the face. No sooner had his vision cleared from that than the door burst open and Janet Boyce stood there, all jeans and outsize jumper. 'Cassie, I ... oh.'

'It's all right, Janet,' the taller girl snarled, jerking upright. 'Mr Maxwell was just leaving.'

Maxwell rose to his feet, smiled at them both and said, 'We'll talk again, Cassandra ... somewhere a bit more public next time.'

'You know, I had an offer I couldn't refuse today.' Maxwell stretched out on Jacquie's bed at Barcourt Lodge.

'Don't tell me Dr Sheffield's offered you a job?' She was pouring another glass of wine for them both.

'No. Cassandra James offered to sleep with me.'

Jacquie looked across at him. 'Did she now? And what did you say?'

'I said I'd think about it,' Maxwell beamed and winced as the cushion hit his head from the far side of the room. 'The point is, Woman Policeman, why the change of heart?'

'Max, you don't mean she was serious?'

He looked at her outraged. 'It isn't *so* far-fetched, surely? You do it.'

'I,' she curled up archly in the armchair opposite him, 'am the older woman. You could be her grandfather.'

'Thanks,' he leapt off the bed and strangled her with his glass-free hand, before squatting on the floor next to her, 'But you're missing the point, dear heart. Miss James has been all ice since the moment we met. Difficult. Stand-offish. Until this evening.'

'What does that mean?'

'I don't know. Tubbsy told me she and Robinson were having a fling. I was acting on information received.'

'And were they?'

Maxwell chuckled. 'I said Cassandra offered to sleep with me, not tell me the truth. I have absolutely no idea. Said she preferred older men.'

198

'I wonder if Ms Shaunessy knows about her,' Jacquie murmured.

'I wonder if Tim Robinson did.'

'You think there's something in Tubbs' idea, then?'

Maxwell nodded. 'Yes, I do. But I'm not sure it's quite as straight forward as all that. Have you talked to him?'

'No. He keeps ducking out, like the bloody Scarlet Pimpernel. He's on for tomorrow now. Ten-thirty. That makes him the last of the teaching staff. We begin the sixth form just before lunch.'

'Start with Cassandra. I'll be interested to know what you make of her.'

'Max, in all seriousness, you took a chance being alone with her. We have rules about interviews.'

'So do we, dear heart.' He raised his glass to her. 'But the day I follow them, Hell will freeze over. If a kid comes to me upset, I hug them. What could be more natural than that?'

'Nothing, unless she's a twisted little minx who wants to get inside your trousers and trot off to the *News of the World* with the glad tidings. I seem to remember when we met you were suspended for something similar – set up by a vindictive pupil.'

'Indeed,' Maxwell nodded. 'An occupational hazard, I'm afraid. And they've lightened up the rules since then. Little Cassandra is having a fling with John Selwyn, Captain of Tennyson.'

'Head Boy. Head Girl. How sweet. She told you this?'

He shook his head. 'I saw them. Or rather, heard them.'

'What?' Jacquie sat up. 'Where was this?'

'The boat-house.'

'The...'

He held up his hand. 'All right. I know, I should have told you.'

'When was this, Max?'

'The night before they found Tim Robinson.'

'Jesus, Max.' She was on her feet, pacing the room. 'You should have told me.'

'Yes, I just said that,' he reminded her. 'I didn't because I wasn't sure. In fact, I'm still not absolutely a hundred percent. It was after you'd dropped me at Grimond's, do you remember? I was passing the boat-house and I heard a couple at it. I recognized Cassandra's voice at once. The man's? Well, I thought it was Selwyn's, but now...'

'You think it could have been Robinson?'

He nodded. 'It's possible.'

'So what are you saying? Cassandra's two-timing Selwyn with the PE teacher. The lad finds out, loses it and caves in his head? Come on, Max.' Jacquie wasn't buying it.

'Most male-female murders are domestic, aren't they?' Maxwell pursued it. 'The eternal triangle, straight line, rhombus, whatever bloody trigonometrical figure you care to choose.'

'It's possible,' she admitted. 'But what about Pardoe?'

'Don't know.' Maxwell sipped the wine again. 'But then, until today, I didn't know he was married, either.'

She stopped pacing, turning from the window

to look at him. 'Who told you that?'

'Your Lord and Master.'

'The DCI? God.'

'One and the same. Look, what did you mean on the phone last night? It sounded like Henry was falsifying evidence.'

Jacquie was nodding, her eyes frightened, her face pale.

Maxwell sat up. 'That's not the Henry Hall I know.'

'Nor I.' She shook her head.

'What's the score, Jacquie?' He put down his glass and got up, walking across to her, taking her in his arms.

'Robinson,' she said, looking up at him. She broke away, pacing the room again. 'Look, I went out on a limb for Hall last night, Max. I went to the Incident Room at Selborne, talked to West.'

'And?'

'They're working on Robinson's bike, tracing its manufacturer. He's sending officers round to the Blundells...'

'Good luck to them,' Maxwell chuckled.

'No, Max, you're missing the point. Hall was disinterested. He could have done this already, *should* have done. The bike was standing here, in the sheds at Grimond's. He didn't go near it.'

'That's not exactly falsifying evidence, darling.' He crossed to her again, stroking her hair, looking into those worried grey eyes. 'Missing the odd angle, perhaps, but...'

'Why did we go to Robinson's, Max?' she asked him. 'Hall and I, I mean?'

'Looking for evidence,' he shrugged. 'Anything

that might explain his death.'

'Or removing evidence.' Jacquie held his hand. 'Oh, Max, I'm frightened.'

'Whoa, now.' He held her head as she hugged his chest, smoothing the tied-back hair. 'I don't understand.' It wasn't a confession many people heard from Mad Max.

She lifted her head, looking into his face. 'We were there far less than twenty minutes.'

'Yes, you told me.'

'Hall went straight upstairs when we arrived.'

'So?'

'So, I don't know what he did up there. What if he took something away?'

'What?' Maxwell asked.

'Christ, I don't know. A letter, photograph, diary, drugs, somebody's underwear, *something* which would tell us who killed Robinson and Hall's just sitting on it.'

He looked at her, in the half light of her hotel room, courtesy of the West Sussex Constabulary. Then he held her shoulders firmly. 'If Henry's sitting on something,' he said, 'we've got to get him off his arse.'

He wandered along the rubbish-strewn streets. Drunken couples lurched past him, making for an Indian or a KFC. He kept his collar turned up, his face in the shadows. The kid he was following stumbled into an alleyway. It was dark here, where the cats prowled by the dustbins. Monday was market day. There were pickings.

'Hello, son.'

The boy turned, slipping on potato peelings,

slimy under his trainers. 'Who are you?'

'Dave. You all right?'

'Yeah.'

He felt the man's hand steady his arm. 'You've had a few.'

'Just a few,' the boy chuckled.

'What do they call you?'

'Brian.'

'Okay, Brian.' Dave put an arm around the lad's shoulder. 'Let's get you home, shall we? Where do you live?'

'I'm all right,' Brian slurred.

'Course you are,' Dave grinned in the darkness, training his electronic remote on the dark car parked in the shadows. 'All the better for a little car ride, though, eh? Trust your uncle Dave, huh? Come on.'

'Cassie?' The voice was a hoarse whisper in the darkness.

'What?'

'You wouldn't let a man touch you, would you?'

Cassandra's face was lit by the moonlight through the half-open curtain as she sat up, chin on her knees. 'No way,' she said.

'Good.' The plumper girl turned to face her, nuzzling her nose into the soft warm heaven of her friend's side, kissing the petal skin tenderly.

'I don't like that Mr Maxwell, though.'

'Maxwell?' She broke off the kisses. 'He hasn't done anything to you?'

'No, no,' Cassandra said, glancing down at the plain, earnest face looking up at hers. 'No, it's just that, he might. I don't like the way he looks at me. You'll take care of me, though, won't you, Janet darling?'

Janet threw her arms around the girl, squeezing hard. 'Of course I will, my dearest, my dearest.'

Under the moon, she slipped off the dark bath robe with its Grimond's crest, feeling the sharp breeze of night prickle her skin. She raised her knife to the stars, clasping the hilt with both hands, then threw herself onto her knees, driving the tip again and again into the damp of the soil, moaning the words of hate.

'Die, Maxwell,' she rasped. 'Die.'

She didn't see the shiver in the shadows.

Chapter Twelve

'I'm sorry about the other day, Max.' Tony Graham was nibbling his toast. 'It was stupid of me, flouncing out like that.'

The sun of Tuesday was streaming in through the stained glass of Grimond's dining room, the dust particles whirling in the spring morning. A small bunch of freesias lay in yellow and purple at the place usually occupied by Bill Pardoe on High Table.

'No, no,' Maxwell was helping himself to a second cup of coffee. 'I was out of line. Nobody wants to think of their colleagues as homicidal maniacs, love to hate them though we do.' He winked at his man.

'You know the counselling starts today?' the Housemaster asked.

'Counselling?'

Graham chuckled. 'Yes, that apparently was the response of our revered Chair of Governors, although I understand it was suitably laced with expletives that would make a sailor blush – which is, of course, what rumour has it he used to be.'

'Doesn't approve of our caring, sharing twenty-first century then?'

Graham quaffed his orange juice. 'Fucking – and I quote – namby-pamby bollocks.'

'Is he still intending to close the school?'

Graham's eyes raked the room. There was no set

pattern to Grimond's breakfasts and it was not compulsory. John Selwyn was there with his House prefects from Tennyson and a scattering of younger boys. Only one or two girls from Austen had made an appearance and Maggie Shaunessy was selecting her Jacobs cream crackers from Mrs Oakes in the far corner. 'Rumour has it that Sir Arthur and George Sheffield had the mother of all rows last night. Damn near came to blows, apparently.'

'Really?' Maxwell couldn't quite see George Sheffield as something in the Red Corner, coming out fighting. 'Who won?'

'Suffice it to say Dr Sheffield still has his job and the shrinks are moving in at nine. My own house first. And the school's doors are still open. Wilkins will have made him pay however – you can be certain of that.'

'Who are the counsellors?' Maxwell asked.

Graham shrugged. 'Local social services, I suppose. I must admit, I'm not convinced. Oh, the boys are cut up, of course. That's inevitable. But Bill ... well, I'm afraid he was losing it a little.'

'He was?'

'May I join you?' Maggie Shaunessy had arrived.

Both men were public school; both men scraped back their chairs and stood up.

'Anyone seen Jeremy Tubbs?' she asked.

'Not since lunchtime yesterday.' Maxwell poured some coffee for her.

'Thank you, just black. What time was that?'

'He dropped me in the quad about two-fifteen, two-thirty. Told me he had a meeting with you.'

'Yes, he did.' She buttered her crackers with an elegance born of Benenden and Oxford. 'Or rather, he didn't.'

'No show?' Graham asked.

'Ah, I can probably explain that,' Maxwell said. 'When we parted, Mr Tubbs was a little ... shall we say, merry?'

'Ah,' Maggie said. 'No surprises there, then. One of his famous liquid lunches. Janet will have to wait.'

'Janet?' Maxwell repeated.

'Janet Boyce, one of my charges. A sweet child, but a martyr to a sense of inadequacy. Last year it was a crush on Jane Devereux, Head of Art and Design. This year she's falling flat in Geography. I wanted to run the situation past Jeremy. Legend has it he teaches her. Do you have this problem...?'

'At Dropout High?' he winked at her. 'Oh, yes, although we probably have fewer schoolgirl crushes than you do.'

'It's the hothouse environment.' Maggie took her coffee cup in both hands. 'It was worse when we all were at St Hilda's.'

'Now, presumably, you have the added complication of boys.'

Maggie glanced across at Graham. 'All men are beasts, Max,' she smiled. 'It's just a question of which are the worst, the men of Dickens, Kipling or Tennyson.'

'I can assure you, Madam,' Graham beamed, 'the men of Tennyson are above reproach.' He leaned across Maxwell. 'Strictly *entre nous*, Maggie dearest, my money's on Kipling.'

207

'Why Kipling?' Maxwell asked.

'Tubbsy's House,' Graham laughed.

'I didn't know he was a Housemaster.'

'Oh, he isn't, in the sense that he doesn't live in. But it's a Grimond's tradition that everybody except the Games staff are attached to a House. Tubbsy is Kipling.'

'Nuff said,' Maggie trilled.

'Miss Shaunessy.' All three of them looked up to see a solemn-looking Janet Boyce standing there, full English steaming on the plate in her hand. 'Have you spoken to Mr Tubbs yet?'

'No, Janet, but rest assured, I will later. Do you have him today?'

'This afternoon,' the girl said.

'I'll talk to him this morning,' Maggie nodded. 'I promise.'

'Thank you, Miss Shaunessy,' and the girl wandered away.

'Sad one, that,' Maxwell commented.

Maggie watched her go. 'Yes,' she sighed. 'Yes, I'm afraid she is.'

'This is ludicrous.' DCI Henry Hall whirled away from his desk. 'This is the third time he's stood us up.'

Jacquie was on her mobile. 'Hello, Miss Taylor?'

She heard the starchy tones of the school secretary at the other end. Jacquie could almost hear her pearl lariat clashing on her brillo pad cardigan. 'We've been waiting for Mr Tubbs for nearly half an hour now. Have you any idea where he is?'

'As I told you,' the harassed woman said.

'According to the timetable he was teaching until ten-fifteen. He usually takes break in the Senior Common Room. His free periods he spends in the Geography department. I have rung through there three times now. No one's seen him.'

'Since when?'

Miss Taylor had had a week and a half. They'd taken that silly slip of a thing off the switchboard after Bill Pardoe's death. What with the media pestering hourly, parents ringing up demanding George Sheffield's head and the Chair of Governors insisting on more or less the same, Millie Taylor had nearly given in her notice.

'Since I don't know when,' she hissed. 'He was not in his room Period One.'

'He wasn't?'

'Mr Larson had to cover for him.'

'So let me get this straight.' Jacquie was circling the ante-interview room. 'No one has seen Mr Tubbs today at all?' And she held the phone away from her ear rather than have it shattered by Miss Taylor's confirmation.

'Jacquie?' Hall could read the face of his favourite DS after all these years.

'No Tubbs,' she said, pocketing the phone.

'The last member of staff who stood us up...'

'...we fished him out of the lake.' Jacquie finished the DCI's sentence for him, remembering the moment all too well.

'Right. Get his home number from the front desk. I'm going to the Geography Department. Talking to us is not an optional extra.'

'Jenkins?' Maxwell was leaning against a lime

209

tree, the sun dappling through its buds onto the tarmac below. He looked for all the world like the sudden black appearance of Bill Sykes in the sunlit crescent when Mark Lester was buying a wonderful morning.

The blond lad stopped short, trudging between lessons as he was with his mates.

'Can I have a word?'

All three of them stopped.

'I've got lessons, sir.'

'Oh?' Maxwell took his hands out of his pockets. 'What lesson in particular?'

'History.'

'Really?' Maxwell beamed. 'You boys run along. Mr Gallow, is it?'

'Yes, sir,' the other two chorused.

'Tell him I'm keeping young Jenkins a minute – apologize for me.'

They hesitated, then trudged on.

'I won't keep you long,' Maxwell said. 'What are you doing in History?'

'The agrarian revolution, sir.'

'Ah, where would we be without dear old Jethro Tull, uh? Designer of the seed drill by day, wacky Luton-based rock band by night. What's your first name, Jenkins?'

'Joseph, sir.'

'Joe?'

Jenkins nodded.

'I've been wanting to chat for a while, Joe,' Maxwell sat himself down on the wooden seat named in honour of some long-forgotten Old Boy and patted the planks beside him. 'Ever since you left that tape outside my room.'

Jenkins' bum was already off the seat, almost before it had touched it.

'It's all right, Joe,' Maxwell held the boy's arm and sat him down again. 'It'll be our secret.'

Jenkins was staring at the ground, fumbling with his briefcase handle, unable to look Maxwell in the face. 'Two questions,' the Head of Sixth Form said. 'First, where did you get it? Second, why did you leave it for me?'

For what seemed an eternity, the boy sat there, frozen. Then he looked up at Maxwell, his face a pale mask of fear. 'I found it, sir,' he managed between gasps.

'Where?' Maxwell leaned back, talking softly, looking at Joe Jenkins with those smiley eyes as if the pair were talking about the weather.

'In the skip, sir, at the back of Tennyson.'

'Tell me, Joe, is that something you do often, rummage about in the rubbish?'

'No, sir,' Jenkins rumbled as low as he could for a lad whose voice has yet to break. 'I saw Mr Pardoe put it there, sir. He was upset.'

Still Maxwell didn't move. 'When was this, Joe?' he asked. 'It might be important.'

'I don't know.' The boy was staring at the ground again. 'A couple of days before ... you know.'

'You played it, obviously?'

Jenkins nodded, feeling the salt tears trickle into his mouth and wanting the ground to swallow him up.

'What did you think it meant?'

Jenkins was shaking his head. 'I don't know. Not really.' Then he was on his feet. 'Sir, I've got to go.'

'Why me?' Maxwell was on his feet too, his second question still unanswered. 'Joe, why did you leave it for me to find?'

The boy stopped, his back to Maxwell. The History Department, Mr Gallow's lesson, Jethro Tull and his bloody seed drill – it had never looked so appealing. The man behind him and the questions he was asking were the lad's waking nightmare.

'I thought you could help,' he said quietly. 'I thought you could end it.' He turned sharply, the tears streaming now down his cheeks. 'I thought wrong,' he shouted and dashed away.

They'd never had counsellors at Grimond's before. But then, they'd never had murder either. Peter Maxwell watched them arrive from the back of David Gallow's Lower Sixth History lesson on the second floor. Four lefty-looking types in anoraks and trainers. Neither of the men clearly knew what a tie was and the women looked like bag ladies, all no doubt designer-chic to put the children at their ease. The Head of History was talking about British Foreign Policy in the early nineteenth century to a less-than-gripped Lower Sixth set; Shelley's poem kept thumping through Maxwell's head – 'I met murder in the way; he wore a mask like Castlereagh.' Masks was what all this was about, whatever was happening at Grimond's. Everyone wore a mask, every day, but behind one of them lay evil, more sinister than even poor deluded Shelley imagined Castlereagh to be.

The counsellors were emptying from two

unmarked cars; even the vehicles had Social Services written all over them. George Sheffield greeted them at Jedediah Grimond's Greek portico with the briefest of handshakes and led the way inside. They would start with Tennyson House, the boys who knew Bill Pardoe best, then attempt to identify those who had not been shooed away in time from the lake's edge when they found Tim Robinson white and swollen in the water. In the meantime, another Range Rover was taking another child away in search of a school where the staff weren't dying.

Henry Hall had the tape. Henry Hall had the porn mag. But he had no access to forensics on his own. He'd dutifully passed both, via Jacquie, to DCI West at Selborne and the Hampshire boffins were working on it. Maxwell could have guessed the outcome on the tape. There would be four sets of prints – his, in that he was the last to play it before he gave it to the suitably-gloved police; Jenkins', in that the lad had retrieved it from the skip; Pardoe's, in that he had, presumably, played it, if only out of curiosity and A.N.other's. And it was A.N.other who was stringing them all along; Maxwell, Hall, Jacquie, West and everybody else touched by the death of Bill Pardoe. The forensic result of the porn mag was something else. Here the evidential chain of custody would be shadowier, more vague. Maxwell had handled it, Parker and some anonymous postmen. But again, it was A.N.other who had put it in the envelope. And again, he was will o' the wisp.

'It's a Swedish import, guv,' DS Walters

informed the Incident Room. 'The lads from the Dirty Squad say it's published in Oslo, usually distributed via Holland and is not available over the counter here.'

'Yet,' somebody grunted from the back, to murmurs of agreement round the room. Policemen, like teachers, were forever at the retreating edge of civilization, forced to pick up the pieces of its collapse.

'Pardoe on their mailing list, was he?' West asked, still leafing idly through the mag's contents.

'Tricky one, that, guv,' Walters went on. 'We'd have to work with Interpol and even then, I don't think we'd be sure of a result.'

'You're right,' West closed the book. 'Forget that angle. We've got other fish to fry and time isn't exactly on our side.'

'But isn't that what all this is all about, guv?' Denise McGovern wanted to know. 'Why Pardoe went off the roof?'

West sighed. The case was already only seven days old and he was ready to go *through* the roof. 'With respect, Denise,' he grunted, 'we still haven't the first fucking idea why Pardoe went off the roof.'

'What about the tape, Mark?' Sandy Berman chipped in.

'Ah,' West nodded, reaching for his packet of ciggies. 'Voice recognition. Steve, what've we got on that?'

DS Chapell riffled through his notes. 'Not a lot yet, guv,' he admitted. 'Forensic reckon it's a male voice, age unknown, worked through some sort of modifier.'

214

'How specialist would that have to be?' West asked.

Chapell shrugged. 'Any sound studio would have that sort of stuff.'

'Right. Let's see what they've got at Grimond's in their Music Department or maybe Physics lab.'

'I'm on it, guv.' Chapell was on his feet.

'No, Steve, I need you out here. Denise, you go. The Chief Super in his wisdom has left the school end of things to DCI Hall, so I'm definitely persona non grata. Maybe the surly bastard'll be more accommodating with a woman – Hall that is, not the Chief Super. If not,' he winked, 'you can always do the all-girls-together bit with DS Carpenter.'

The Luftwaffe had done their best to level Portsmouth several years ago. In place of the narrow cobbled lanes and the stout medieval walls, the City Council had built high-rise flats, car parks and the appalling Tricorn Centre, ashes rising from the phoenix. It was here, in the ring of flats that circled the old city that Jeremy Tubbs lived. He'd always promised himself and his colleagues that he'd move closer to Grimond's, but that meant the obscene property prices of Petersfield, Haslemere, Midhurst and the sleepy commuter villages in between. For the moment, he'd stay in Pompey. George Sheffield, or more accurately, Sir Arthur Wilkins, was not a generous man.

Jacquie Carpenter rang the bell on the third floor. Nothing. Just a dead-looking corridor with slightly peeling paint and a window lashed by muddy rain at its end. She'd already flashed her warrant card at the concierge who'd grumblingly given her the key and she was inside. True, she had no search warrant, but the concierge hadn't considered that and Jacquie wanted answers. Whatever else he was, Jeremy Tubbs wasn't there and he wasn't tidy. The mail lay scattered on the hall floor, unsorted, unopened. Breakfast dishes still lay unwashed on the kitchen-diner table, the relics of coffee and toast.

In the lounge she clicked on the answerphone.

'Jeremy, it's Mervyn. Are you in today? We've had no work set. Can you let me know?'

She recognized the stentorian tones of Grimond's Deputy Head. A second bleep. 'Jeremy, darling, it's Mummy. I hoped I'd catch you before you left. You won't forget Daddy's birthday, will you? A tie or something would be lovely.'

Jacquie took in the scattered clues. Jeremy Tubbs read the *Telegraph* and *What PC?* He didn't smoke and there didn't appear to be a Mrs Tubbs. The drinks cabinet was well stocked – Gordon's, London, a few mixers. She went into the bedroom; another tip. And somebody had left here in a hurry. Ties and jumpers were strewn over the bed and the bed was unmade. She felt the sheet. Cold. There was no razor in the bathroom, no toothpaste or brush. A pile of exercise books lay unmarked on a bedside table, next to a dog-eared copy of *Men Only*, the single man's companion.

She punched out the numbers on her mobile and waited, flicking aside the nets to watch the lunchtime traffic moving noisily three floors below. 'Sir?'

DCI Henry Hall was sitting at the other end, otherwise engaged. 'Jacquie. Anything?'

'My guess is he's done a runner. Do you want...'

'Not now,' Hall cut in. 'Follow your nose. I'm a little tied up at the moment.' And he hung up.

DS Denise McGovern was sitting opposite him in George Sheffield's ante-room. She wasn't the type to flirt, to hitch up her skirt or unbutton her blouse. She was a woman who worked in what was still a man's world and there was a job to be done. 'Tell me again,' Hall said.

'The Music Room,' she repeated. 'I've just come from there.'

'And?'

'I have reason to believe that the tape left outside Maxwell's room referring to Pardoe was recorded there.'

'Really?' Hall remained impassive behind his glasses. 'What makes you think that?'

'I tried it out. Allowing for the fact that my voice is rather higher than the original, the distortion is the same. I won't bore you with woofer and tweeter details.'

'Thank you for that,' Hall said. 'Whose permission did you obtain to carry out this little experiment?'

'Dr Sheffield,' the DS told him. 'Was that out of line?'

'No,' Hall told her. 'But it would have been ... politic to talk to me, as well.'

'I'm sorry, sir,' Denise said. 'I was told that you and DS Carpenter were busy interviewing sixth-formers. Looks like I was told wrong.'

'We're between interviews,' he told her. 'Social services have sent counsellors in. What with that and the school's timetable, it's slowed us down a bit.'

'And what with DS Carpenter not being here.'

Hall paused. He wasn't used to Detective Sergeants with opprobrium in their voices, but he took it in his stride for the moment. 'That's right,' he said. 'Jacquie's following up leads elsewhere.'

'Would you care to let me in on that one, sir? I understand we were supposed to be co-operating.'

'And who told you that?' Hall leaned back, pushing the latest statement away from him.

'My DCI,' she said.

'Ah,' Hall nodded. 'Yes. Of course. *Your* DCI.'

'Sir,' Denise twisted in her chair. 'Can I talk to you, off the record, as it were?'

Hall threw his hands out, shrugging. Where was the woman going with this?

'He's not *my* DCI in any but a figurative sense. In actual fact,' she looked steadily into the immobile face, 'he's a bit of a bastard. My interest is to solve this thing. I'm not concerned in inter-force politics, whose patch it's on or the colour of the scrambled egg on some bloke's peaked cap. I just want results.'

'You're ambitious, Sergeant.' Hall was paying Denise McGovern a huge compliment, had she but known it; he was smiling at her.

'Too right I am,' she acknowledged, pointing upwards. 'See that glass ceiling? Well, I'm going to push my way right through it – with your help, of course.' She smiled back.

'*My* help?' Hall frowned.

'What we've got here, sir,' she leaned towards him, 'is a lockout, a siege situation of our own invention. Or, at least, yours and DCI West's.'

'Is that right?' Only Jacquie Carpenter talked to Henry Hall like that.

She ferreted in the copious bag by her chair leg and slapped a form down on Hall's desk.

'And this would be...?'

'A complete breakdown of the Incident Room's status as of midnight last night.'

'Complete?' Hall leafed through it.

'Forensics. Post mortems. You name it, it's there.'

'Simplify it for me,' Hall said, closing the file. 'Cut out the middle man.'

'All right,' she said. 'We've traced Robinson's bike.'

'So have I,' Hall said. 'It's in the bike shed.'

'Yes, but I mean its provenance. Page eight,' Denise nodded, pointing to the file. 'It was bought in Southampton at the end of December, three weeks before Robinson started at Grimond's; but not by him.'

'Not?'

Denise shook her head. 'The retailer had never seen Robinson before. Didn't recognize the morgue photo, and as dead men go, it's not bad. He wasn't sure, but he thought two men came in to buy it.'

'*Two* men?'

Denise nodded. 'Weird, isn't it?'

'Is it?'

'Wouldn't you say?' Denise McGovern was used to a rather quicker uptake from her superiors.

'Two men go to buy a bike that is subsequently ridden by somebody else.'

'It happens,' Hall shrugged. 'My parents used to buy my Christmas presents like that, allowing for the gender difference of one of them.'

Denise thought this the moment to change the subject. 'Then, there's Robinson's clothes.'

'Bought by two strange men?' Hall was teasing the woman.

'We don't know who bought them, but they're new, all of them.'

'All of them?'

'Everything in his PE locker at Grimond's gym, everything at his home. Nothing's used, lived in. Even his underwear, all of it brand new. Of course, his CV doesn't pan out.'

'He wasn't at Haileybury?'

She shook her head. 'And he didn't go to Loughborough. And he wasn't in the army. Tim Robinson didn't exist before January 7th of this year, the day he started work at Grimond's.'

'I take it DCI West's gone house to house?' Hall asked.

Denise nodded. 'Except for his neighbours and a couple of shopkeepers in Petersfield who do remember him, nothing. We've even drawn a blank on his dental work. But somebody knew him.'

'His killer,' Hall nodded.

'Exactly, sir.'

'What about Pardoe?' It was Hall's turn to change the subject.

'We know he was married. We're trying to trace the family. Divorce apparently – back in ... eighty-one.'

'I'm impressed, Sergeant,' Hall was smiling again.

'I told you, sir,' she smiled back. 'The glass ceiling. You don't get through it by being a daffy cow. I've got to know my stuff.'

'So what do you want from me?'

'Whatever you find out here,' she told him.

'That won't take long,' Hall sniffed. 'There's no dossier like this one I can hand over, I'm afraid.'

'You've interviewed a lot of people. All the staff?'

Hall nodded. 'And some of the sixth form. I've got more views on Pardoe than the parson preached about.'

'Such as?' Denise leaned forward.

Hall hesitated.

'Sir,' she sensed it. 'I'm not going to be rushing out of here back to Mark West. Whatever you've got is yours, but I've got a game plan here. I need some support.'

'Very well,' Hall slid back his chair and wandered to the window where the early afternoon sun kissed Jedediah Grimond's pale portico with its Cotswold columns. 'Two-thirds of the staff thought the world of Bill Pardoe. He was Mr Chips, everybody's Favourite Teacher.'

'And the other third?'

'The other third are prepared to believe the scuttlebutt.'

'Scuttlebutt?' Denise frowned. 'What scuttlebutt?'

'Drugs.'

'Drugs?' Denise's frown deepened.

'Part of a big operation. That's why I'm here.'

'What?'

221

'Look ... er ... Denise, isn't it?'

She nodded.

'I shouldn't be telling you this, but right now, I'm getting nowhere and I could use a link to the outside. There's something claustrophobic about this school. It creeps into your pores, under your skin, like an infection. Jacquie and I, we're too close to it all. I need a fresh perspective.'

'You said "a big operation".'

Hall nodded. 'Officially, it's secondment, inter-force co-operation, good practice, all that sort of thing that gladdens the Home Secretary's heart. In reality, there's a major drugs problem here at Grimond's. Bill Pardoe was at the heart of it.'

'My God, I had no idea.'

'Quite. A clever man was our Mr Pardoe. But somebody outside was even cleverer.'

'Who?'

Hall looked at her, shaking his head. 'I can't tell you that.'

'What about Robinson?' she asked him.

'Sorry?'

'What have you learned about Robinson?'

'Less than you have,' Hall said. 'Baseless rumours. He wasn't much of a teacher, forged his CV, that's about it. He'd only been here a few weeks, no one knew him.'

'Who was Pardoe's outside link?' Denise was on her feet now, her eyes burning into Hall's.

'Denise... No one knows this. Not Mark West, not even Jacquie Carpenter...'

She joined him by the window. 'Go on,' she said, willing him to talk.

'Mason,' he whispered.

'The Chief Super?' Denise gasped. 'I don't believe it.'

'Of course you don't.' Hall turned to her. 'That's what he's relying on and that's precisely why I'm here. I told you it was a big operation. It comes right down from the top. Am I making myself clear here?'

'Right, sir.' Denise licked her lips. They were bricky dry.

'Denise,' the sound of his voice pulled her up sharply and she felt Hall's hands on her shoulders, saw his eyes bright behind those blank lenses. 'This must, repeat, *must,* remain our secret. Do I have your word?'

She nodded. 'Of course, Mr Hall,' she said. 'My word.'

She punched out the numbers on her mobile, waiting for the ring to connect.

'Guv? Denise.'

'Yes, Denise.' She heard DCI West's voice crackle at the Selborne end. 'What'd you get?'

'It's drugs.'

'Drugs?' he repeated. 'At Grimond's?'

'Yep. And there's more. Hall's working under-cover. We've got a bad 'un.'

'On the force, you mean?'

Denise could feel her heart thumping as she spoke. 'You'd better sit down, guv. It's the Chief Super.'

Chapter Thirteen

There was a knock on Peter Maxwell's door a little after lights out in Tennyson House. John Selwyn's call to sleep echoed dying through the old corridors, like some Western muezzin summoning the faithful to prayer. But Maxwell was facing south-west as he opened the door and he was facing an anxious-looking George Sheffield, sans gown and past caring.

'Headmaster,' Maxwell nodded.

'Mr Maxwell, may I have a word? I know it's late.'

'Please,' Maxwell invited him in.

'Are you ... comfortable here?' the Head asked him, looking around at the dingy room.

'Thank you, yes,' Maxwell smiled. 'Won't you have a seat?'

'Thank you.'

George Sheffield had aged a hundred years in the last week. And it was exactly a week ago that Maxwell had heard a scratching on the outer staircase; seven days since he'd seen a gowned figure flitting furtively in and out of the shadows with a lovely girl with long, dark hair.

'I'd offer you something, but...'

Sheffield shook his head. 'If I'd wanted a drink, I would have invited you to my rooms. No, Mr Maxwell, it's advice I want.'

Maxwell sat opposite the man, aware once

224

again why he'd never climbed those dizzy heights, the greasy pole to Headship. 'Advice?' he said. 'I doubt I have any that could help your situation, Dr Sheffield. Rest assured, though, you have my heartfelt sympathy.'

'Mr Maxwell, I've been Headmaster at Grimond's for fifteen years. The school has been my wife, my children, my everything. Now, I've lost it.'

'Lost it?' Maxwell repeated.

'Sir Arthur – Arthur Wilkins, my Chair of Governors – has asked for my resignation.'

'Ah,' Maxwell nodded. 'I'm sorry.' He glanced up at the man who in turn was watching him carefully. 'Are you bound to accept?'

Sheffield shrugged. 'I don't know. I don't think there's anything in the rule book to cover this. There isn't a sub-clause in my contract headed "Murders of Members of Staff". I'm at a loss.'

'Are you asking my advice as to whether you should fight this?'

'I've talked to Mervyn of course, my Housemasters, even Millie Taylor, my secretary.'

'What do they say?'

'Fight it,' Sheffield told him, shrugging. 'To a man and woman, they said "Fight it".'

'Sounds like good advice to me,' Maxwell said.

Sheffield looked at him. 'With respect, Mr Maxwell, you're an outsider. It's no skin off your nose if you say the wrong thing. Your career isn't dependent on any reference of mine. I'd value your honesty.'

'Dr Sheffield,' Maxwell leaned forward, his elbows resting on his knees. 'You must stay and

225

fight. Tear up whatever contract Wilkins has given you. And let me talk to your kids.'

'What?' Sheffield frowned.

'Just the sixth form,' he said, hand in the air and all too aware of the delicacy of the situation. 'I know sixth formers.'

'Mr Maxwell, Chief Inspector Hall...'

'...is an army of one,' Maxwell interrupted. 'And Bill Pardoe's death is already a week old.'

There was a silence. 'I have done this sort of thing before,' Maxwell said.

'But Hall must have ... what do the police call it? Back up? He must have back up outside.'

'Must he, Headmaster? Then where are the others? Since the SOCO teams left the lake last Thursday, there have been two police persons on site – Hall and Jacquie Carpenter. That's it. It would be like you and Mervyn Larson trying to cover the curriculum at Grimond's by yourselves. It can't be done.'

'But what you're suggesting...'

'Has no basis in law, will almost certainly upset your counsellors, several parents and not a few children; yes, I know. But it might just catch a murderer.'

Sheffield was shaking his head, open-mouthed. He was on his feet already. 'Mr Maxwell, in all my years in education, I don't think I've ever seen such arrogance.'

'Really?' Maxwell looked up at him and smiled. 'You don't get out much, do you, Headmaster?'

'I forbid it, Mr Maxwell,' Sheffield snapped. 'You may observe my staff's lessons until Saturday. Then you will leave Grimond's.'

'Dr Sheffield,' Maxwell was on his feet too, 'a few days ago you specifically asked me to stay. You've lost two members of staff already. How many more are you going to stand by and watch go under? You're the bloody Headmaster, for God's sake. Act like it.'

George Sheffield saw himself out.

'So, what gloss is Henry Hall putting on it?' Maxwell was alone under the eaves again. No scratching now, just the rain bouncing on the dark windows, driven by wind from the south-east. He hadn't got round to drawing the curtains.

Jacquie was alone too, in her comfortable-enough room at Barcourt Lodge, her spare hand curled around a cup of very average instant coffee. 'I think he thinks Tubbs might be our man.'

'And you?'

'I don't know,' she confessed.

'Talk me through it, heart.'

'All right.' She curled up on the settee. 'Tubbs' place looked like the Marie Celeste.'

'With a lifeboat missing?'

There was a pause. 'You've lost me there.'

'Never mind.' Maxwell was a middle-aged man in a hurry and he hadn't time to discuss Great Naval Disappearances of History. 'Were there signs that he'd left of his own accord?'

'I'd say so,' Jacquie told him. 'Toothpaste gone, razor, that sort of thing. The problem with something like this is that you're always looking for something that isn't there. There was one small suitcase in his wardrobe. Does that mean he took a larger one away with him? There were a couple of t-shirts and a jumper. Does that mean he's plenty of other clothes and couldn't get those into the larger suitcase? Or wherever he's gone he doesn't need them?'

'You mean, could he be under the floorboards somewhere?'

'It's possible.' Jacquie was thinking out loud. 'We'll know when DCI West's lot have finished.'

'He's in the picture?'

'Insofar as he knows Tubbs is missing. Henry Hall wanted it that way. Apparently the deal is that we handle everything at the school end; West does the external stuff.'

'Isn't that a little bizarre?'

'Tell me about it,' Jacquie kicked off her slippers and ambled across to the kettle for a refill. 'All right, in any murder enquiry, there has to be a division of labour. But we're so unequally divided it's laughable.'

'I tried to do something about that earlier.'

'Oh?'

'I tried to talk Sheffield into letting me interview the kids.'

'And?' Jacquie was all ears.

'He went a funny colour and told me, in the parlance of our American cousins, to butt out.'

'No surprises there, then. Pomposity is that man's middle name.'

'Stick with Tubbsy,' Maxwell urged her. 'What do you know?'

Jacquie settled back on the settee again. 'Single man. Still in regular touch with Mummy and Daddy. Teaches Geography. I get the impression he's not very well liked.'

'He's a pisshead and a gossip,' Maxwell told her. 'Does that make him a murderer?'

'He had the means,' Jacquie was thinking aloud. 'For both Pardoe and Robinson.'

'Did he?' Maxwell lay back on the pillow, staring at the discoloured artex of the ceiling, working it out as she spoke.

'He lives alone,' she said, 'so he could come and go as he pleases. He drives a clapped out MG...'

'Ah, so the private sector doesn't pay, after all,' Maxwell couldn't resist.

She ignored him. 'My estimation is that he could do home to school, especially at night, in about forty minutes.'

'But Grimond's gates are locked at ten-thirty.'

'Right. So he either arrived before that or ... no, he couldn't have. Unless he had a key to the padlock, he must have parked outside. That would be safer. Remember the paparazzi the other night? I parked around the corner and you got into the building without being seen. It can't be difficult.'

'Granted,' Maxwell said. 'Then what?'

'On the Monday night, he goes up to Bill Pardoe's room...'

'...on the floor below mine.'

'Takes him up to the roof...'

'...like you do.'

'All right,' she snapped just a little. It was late and she was tired. Tired of working on a case that was winding her up in its eternal circles. 'I'll be first to confess, I haven't a clue how all that was done. Assuming Pardoe didn't actually shin up there of his own volition intending to end it all, somebody must have lured him up there.'

'Cat stuck on the roof.'

'Maxwell!' Jacquie shrieked, reverberating through the man's eardrum, then, calmer. 'I'm doing my best.'

'Sorry, darling,' he laughed. 'Go on.'

'Tubbs gets Pardoe up there somehow, pushes him off. Then he sneaks back out of the building and drives home.'

'And the scratching I heard was him or Pardoe or both making his/their way up the stairs.'

'Right.'

'So who was the girl?'

'Sorry?'

'I have to confess, Woman Policeman Carpenter, that I have been withholding information from the constabulary.'

There was a pause. Then, 'Max, you shit.' Jacquie was sitting upright.

'I love you too,' he beamed. 'On the night in question, I saw two people – a girl and a man in a gown.'

'Where?'

'In the quad, not far from the chapel.'

'What time was this?' She was whirling round the room like a dervish, looking for her note pad.

'God, I don't know.'

'Max, you're an expert witness, for Christ's sake. You've done this before. *Think!*'

'Right.' Maxwell was sitting up now. 'Since you've asked me so nicely, it must have been about one, one-thirty.'

'Before Pardoe died, according to forensics.' Jacquie was thinking aloud. 'Could you make out faces?'

'No,' he was shaking his head, having asked himself the same question a thousand times in the past week. 'The girl could have been Cassandra James, Janet Boyce, any one of a couple of dozen others I've seen around the place. It could even have been Maggie Shaunessy or Gaynor Ames in a dark wig – and I haven't started on the secretariat yet. Sorry.'

'It doesn't matter.' She spoke softly, not angry any more, not scolding. 'What about the man?'

'Same problem,' Maxwell said. 'Remember I hadn't been here long. I didn't really know anybody. And it was dark. And it was in deep shadow. I remember thinking how odd that whoever it was should be wearing a gown at that time of night. Almost as if ... no.'

'What?' Jacquie was prepared to grab any straw at this stage in the game, mixing metaphors madly as she went.

'Well, it sounds ludicrous, but it was as though the whole thing was an act, a sort of *tableau vivant* for my benefit. Yet, how could it be? How could they have known I would be awake and looking out of my window?'

He was doing that now, having crossed the room in a couple of strides and was looking down at the same scene. No moon tonight, just the rain bouncing off the guttering and the wind shaking the heads of the cedars far beyond the chapel. 'But if that is the case, if it was a show put on for me, or anybody watching, then we can expect any kind of theatricality.'

'Sorry?'

'The gown was a con,' he said, working his way

231

through it. 'The long dark hair was a wig. Christ, I can't even be sure if it was a girl. We've just done Macbeth at Leighford High. The murderers who took out the Macduff family were pretty scary, rippling biceps, impressive cod-pieces and plenty of attitude. But they happened to be Sasha Austen and Penny Sutherland, two fourteen-year-old girls who usually play flute in the school orchestra. What you see ain't necessarily what you get. What about Tubbsy and Robinson?'

'Same thing,' Jacquie said. 'Except that somehow he had to get Robinson back on site at night as well. Pardoe was already here because he lived in; Robinson didn't.'

'So wouldn't it have been easier to kill him at home?' Maxwell reasoned. 'Stove in his head in his lounge or his kitchen; wait 'til he's gone for a pee and hope he hasn't locked the door?'

'But this whole thing has to do with Grimond's, doesn't it?' She was asking herself as much as him. 'Pardoe died because of the school; so did Robinson.'

'Tubbsy told me Robinson was playing fast and loose with girlie or girlies unspecified.'

Another silence. 'You really are a mine of information tonight, Max,' Jacquie said.

'I'm sorry.' He was reaching for his kettle now, trying to do that thing that the Mobile Generation do of tucking the phone in the crook of his neck. 'Like you, I assumed you'd be talking to Tubbs this morning.'

'Yeah,' Jacquie grunted. 'We've assumed that several times already.'

'Let's make a further assumption,' Maxwell

suggested. 'That he's our man.'

'Right,' Jacquie said, but it was obvious she wasn't convinced.

Maxwell went through the motions of making his coffee. 'Tubbs had the opportunity,' he said. 'Assuming he lured Pardoe and Robinson to their deaths. What about means?'

'Pardoe was easy,' Jacquie told him. 'All you need is a stout pair of hands with a bit of welly behind them. I can't remember clapping eyes on the man. Stocky, was he?'

'The same,' Maxwell said. 'Blubber rather than muscle, but gravity would have helped at that height. Robinson?'

'Heavy object, probably wooden, possibly oar, although we know there's not one missing from the boat house. Again, attack from behind.'

'And was it the water that killed him?'

'That's right. So chummy would only have had to hit him once.'

'Having got him to the water's edge in the first place,' Maxwell was running with her, 'by whatever subterfuge. Then he drops the oar into the lake, suitably weighted.'

'Weighted?'

'My dear, when you've wedged your bum into as many boats on the Cam as I have, you'll know every property of an oar. Believe me, they float, usually faster than you do and always in the wrong direction.'

'Okay.'

'So,' Maxwell was recapping. 'Shit!' He burned his top lip in his coffee.

'What?' she asked.

233

'Hot,' he told her. 'Let's recap.' He was talking through the pain. 'Tubbsy has the opportunity and he has the means. The sixty-four-thousand dollar question, darling mine, is motive. In that unholy trinity of murder, why should Tubbsy want these two men dead?'

'Jealousy?' Jacquie tried him out.

'Professional?' Maxwell parried. 'Sexual?'

'Sexual,' Jacquie opted. 'You said Tubbs was stirring it about Robinson's proclivities. Which may, of course, be why Robinson faked his references. Bit of a perv.'

Maxwell nodded. 'Yes, Tubbs was hinting, certainly.'

'What if that pissed him off? What if he, Tubbs, was after the same bit of skirt Robinson was?'

'That's possible.' Maxwell was sprawling on the bed again, resting his coffee cup on the bedside table. 'But what about Pardoe? All the evidence suggests he swung the other way.'

'Could Tubbs have swung both ways?' Jacquie was wondering.

'The Julius Streicher of Grimond's?' Maxwell knew his Nazis. 'Possible. But that would mean that Tubbs fancied the very people, of both sexes, that Robinson and Pardoe had targeted.'

'Unlikely?'

Maxwell laughed. 'This is the private sector, Jacquie. The world turned upside down. Never-never Land. Anything is possible. Let's go with Scenario Two.'

'Which is?'

'That Tubbsy is an innocent bystander. Why would he run?'

234

'Because he was scared.'

'Of what?'

'Maybe,' and it wasn't a word that Peter Maxwell ever used lightly, 'he thought he was next on the list. Pardoe, Robinson, Tubbs. An unlikely trio.'

'Is there a pattern?' Jacquie asked him, never quite sure where the Great Man's brain was taking either of them.

'Pardoe was the longest-serving teacher at Grimond's; Robinson the newest.' Maxwell was pondering it all. 'Where was Tubbs? In the middle?'

'You think there's some sort of ... what? Geometric pattern to this?'

'Murder by mathematics?' Maxwell reflected. 'No, it's preposterous. Several of my colleagues murder maths on a daily basis, but killing by numbers? A mere academic exercise? I can't see it.' He heard her yawning. 'What's happening tomorrow?'

'We'll finish the sixth form at Tennyson House,' she told him. 'Then we're moving over to Austen.'

'Start with Cassandra James,' Maxwell advised as he had once before. 'She's a deep one. Tubbsy fancied her.'

'So, I gather, does half the school,' Jacquie said. 'Not to mention the little offer she made you.'

'What an improper suggestion, Woman Policeman.' Maxwell was aghast.

'What've you got tomorrow?' Jacquie knew well enough when to change the subject.

'God, I don't know. Wednesday? There's an inter-house debate tomorrow night. But tomorrow morning, I think I'm going to find out a little more about our Mr Tubbs. You will let me know if he turns up, won't you, poppet?'

It was good drying weather the next morning. The rain of the night had given way to cotton-wool clouds scudding against a sky of spring blue. Gaynor Ames looked like an advert for Daz, straight out of the '50s, standing by her washing line, pegging out clothes in a loose, floppy jumper and pedal-pushers.

'Mr Maxwell,' she greeted him.

'That's still Max,' he said. 'I can see you're busy, Gaynor, but can I have a word?'

'Of course. I can walk and talk at the same time,' she smiled. 'I might even make you a cup of coffee. Inside or out?'

'The sun's kind,' Maxwell squinted up at it. 'Outside would be good. No kids today?'

Briefly, Gaynor Ames' smile vanished. 'They're at my mother's. She only lives in Haslemere. It's an awful wrench, Max, but ... well, I just didn't feel happy with them around, what with all that's going on.'

'What is going on, Gaynor?'

She'd popped through the patio doors into her kitchen and began digging out biscuits to accompany the coffee. 'I hoped you might tell me,' she said. 'I understand Jeremy Tubbs has gone missing. Richard says the children are full of it.'

'When we met last,' Maxwell sat down at her patio table, his back to the wall in every sense of the phrase, looking out of the garden gate and across the fields where the girls of Austen were bashing hell out of each other with their hockey sticks, 'you said Bill Pardoe had enemies. Was Jeremy Tubbs one of them?'

'Repellent little man,' Gaynor shuddered. 'I didn't like being in the same room as him.'

'Past tense?' Maxwell looked up at her.

'You're a naughty man, Max,' she scolded him. 'A terrible picker-up of innuendo.'

'I'm sorry,' he smiled. 'I have a naturally suspicious nature. What was/is so repellent about Tubbsy?'

'He's a voyeur for a start.'

'Is he?'

Gaynor Ames looked out beyond her garden gate and then down at Maxwell. 'If that was Jeremy Tubbs sitting there, he wouldn't be sitting there – if that doesn't sound too Irish – he'd be out on the touch-line making notes or watching from the cedars with a pair of binoculars.'

'Are you serious?'

'Oh, yes,' Gaynor said. 'Very. Richard tackled him about it once. Said he was just supporting the school and happened to be a keen ornithologist. All bollocks of course, and you'll excuse my French.'

Maxwell smiled. 'So where's he gone?'

'Tubbsy?' she sighed. 'Damned if I know. But I do know this much. Grimond's is better off without him.'

'Not a welcome guest here, then?'

She shrieked with laughter. 'The last time he was here, it was the Christmas party. I didn't want him at all, but Richard felt sorry for him. He got rat-arsed, of course, Jeremy that is and

237

when he hadn't got his nose in Cassandra James' cleavage, he was whinging how tired he was of – and I quote – being treated like a pissed up bastard.'

'Cassandra was at the party?'

'Yes, and John Selwyn. It's traditional. Head Boy and Head Girl. They make a lovely item, don't you think?'

'I hadn't really considered it,' Maxwell lied. 'Tell me, did Tubbs have any aspirations there?'

'With Cassandra? Oh, I expect so. Probably has a modest collection of the girl's underwear in his sock drawer.'

'Apparently not,' Maxwell corrected her, sure that if that had been the case, Jacquie would have mentioned it.

'Don't give the slime the benefit of too many doubts.' Gaynor vanished to pour the coffee. Maxwell heard her rattling cups and ripping open biscuit packets. She was soon back.

'I find all this difficult,' Maxwell was saying. 'If a male teacher looks at a girl funny in the state sector, that's grounds for suspension.'

'You mean nothing goes on? I find that hard to believe.'

'Oh, it does, of course,' Maxwell said. 'But we don't have the same opportunity – the whole boarding thing. By one minute past four my school's empty – of staff as well as kids.'

'Ah, yes,' Gaynor laughed. 'The boarding thing – sweaty fumblings in the dorm. Much of that is just adolescent wet-dreaming – every schoolboy's fantasy.'

'And that of a few members of staff, it seems.'

238

She sat down at the table opposite him. 'Allegedly,' she said.

'Curious,' Maxwell looked at her. 'That was the word Tubbsy used when I spoke to him.'

She looked at him under her eyelids, a smouldering woman who oozed sexuality. 'He hated Bill Pardoe, you know.'

'I didn't know,' Maxwell told her. 'Er ... you don't mind if I dunk?'

She didn't and he dipped the chocolate finger accordingly. 'Why did he hate Bill?'

'Bill was everything Tubbs wasn't – isn't: clever, successful, popular. People deferred to him. After George and Mervyn, Bill was Grimond's. Jeremy resented that. He'd been here for eight years or whatever and had made no mark whatsoever. No promotion, no impact. Still thirteenth in the geography department. And destined to remain so.'

Maxwell knew that that was the lowest of the low the wide world o'er. 'Seems a bit drastic to kill the man, though.'

'I didn't say he did,' Gaynor shook her head. 'But I have to say I think him capable of it.'

'Can I ask you a rather personal question?' Maxwell looked at her over his coffee-cup rim.

She nodded.

'Did Jeremy Tubbs ever try anything on with you?'

She shuddered again. 'No,' she said coldly. 'But only because, I suspect, I didn't give him the opportunity. You know what I think, Max?' She arched an eyebrow. 'I think you scared Jeremy off.'

'I did?' Maxwell frowned.

'You said you talked to him.'

'That's right.'

'When was that?' she asked.

'Er ... the lunchtime of the day he went missing, apparently.'

'Well,' Gaynor nodded in an 'I told you so' sort of way. 'Whatever you said to him did the trick. What's the secret of your success?'

'I'm not sure it was what I said to him,' Maxwell was suddenly remembering. 'More a case of what he said to me. Who are the Arbiters?'

'The what?'

'You don't recognize the term?'

Gaynor shook her head. 'No, I'm afraid not. Was that something Jeremy said?'

'Yes, it was. I didn't know what he meant and I haven't seen him since.'

'Has anybody?' she asked.

'That,' Maxwell felt his chocolate finger disintegrate and plop into the cup, 'remains to be seen.'

DCI Mark West was standing in his shirt sleeves, an inevitable ciggie dangling from his lips. Jacquie Carpenter was standing before him in his inner office at Selborne and the air was electric. The sun hadn't reached this part of the old village hall and it was oddly chill for a spring morning.

'I wasn't aware there was an embargo of any kind, sir,' Jacquie had been in these situations before. She knew a wide-eyed innocence, a ready smile and a hint of bust could work wonders. Except that the DCI seemed immune; perhaps he'd seen it all before.

'Yes, you were,' West boomed. 'You and Hall handle interviews at the school, I handle everything else. So why were you at Jeremy Tubbs' place?'

'He didn't show up for his interview, sir. I was just checking why not.'

West snorted, stubbing the cigarette on his ashtray. 'You have a phone, detective sergeant,' he snapped, 'as does your DCI. All you've got to do is pick the bugger up, which in fact you did to tell us Tubbs was missing. You didn't need to go there yourself. What did you find there?'

'Nothing,' Jacquie said.

West emerged from his side of the desk. 'Don't think for one fucking moment I'm going to let you and Henry Hall get away with soft soaping me. I know about the drugs bust and I know who's involved. Now let's cut the bullshit. What did you find?'

'Nothing of any value, sir,' Jacquie had not moved as his purple face closed to hers. 'It looks to me as if Tubbs left in a hurry.'

'Of his own accord?'

'Apparently,' Jacquie told him. 'Although I can't be sure about that.'

'You are sure, are you, of what the bloke looked like?'

'No, sir, I never saw him.'

'Christ Almighty!' West spun away, running an exasperated hand through his thatch of grey, spiky hair. 'All right. Car. What sort of car does he drive?'

'MG Midget. Bright yellow. Second hand.'

241

'Registration?'

'It's on the school computer.'

'Denise!' he roared over Jacquie's shoulder and his own DS appeared. 'Ring Grimond's. I want the licence plate of an MG belonging to Jeremy Tubbs, one of their geography teachers. And if they've got a photo of the bastard in their files, I want that too. Then I want an alert sent out, nation-wide. Tubbs is to be stopped and apprehended. Ports. Airports. That car'll be a sore thumb and I want it found. Got it?'

'Yes sir.'

West grabbed another packet of cigarettes and looked at Jacquie. 'You still here?' he grunted.

Chapter Fourteen

'This House believes that adoption of the Euro is the first step to the abolition of Britain.' David Gallow launched the debate that evening in the Great Hall at Grimond's. Maxwell remembered moments like this from his own school days. The Hall had been called Big School then, but it smelt the same, redolent of years of worsted trousers polishing hard wooden seats and the kind of furniture polish they only sell to old schools. Emblazoned on the walls in faded gilt were the names of Old Boys who had fallen, along with Edward Thomas, under the stuttering death of No Man's Land or those of the next generation, fluttering to ground zero around the bridges of Arnhem.

The theme of the debates had been different in Maxwell's day – whether public schools could survive the permissive barrage of the '60s; why Princess Margaret couldn't marry Group Captain Townsend; whither Brahms and Liszt after Bill Haley? Maxwell had spoken in most of them, either for or against or merely from the floor. He was impressed with John Selwyn, the smooth Captain of Tennyson, who spoke for the motion and equally delighted with the Europhile response of Cassandra James, using her tongue almost as effectively as she tended to down at the boat-house of a spring night.

243

The Tennyson prefects were there in their finery, Ape and Splinter and others Maxwell recognized from his sojourn in their House, braided badges on their blazers and striped ties, thundering with their black, polished boots on the floor every time Selwyn scored a point. It was the fencing practice bout all over again, but Maxwell noticed that Janet Boyce wasn't in tears this time, but whooping with the other girls when Cassandra hit home.

'They're good,' Maxwell whispered to Tony Graham. 'Bill Pardoe must have coached them well.'

'Oh, yes,' Graham nodded. 'I'm proud of my boys. Any news on Tubbsy?'

'You're asking me?'

'Come on, Max,' Graham smiled, still watching Selwyn's second punching home a few points to the thudding of his mates. 'I'm wise to you.'

'You are,' Maxwell gaped. 'That's bad news.'

'Jacquie Carpenter,' Graham tapped the side of his nose. 'Your woman on the inside.'

'Implying?' Maxwell raised an eyebrow.

'Implying,' to Graham this was like drawing teeth, 'that you have the ear of the constabulary.'

'Perhaps,' Maxwell conceded. 'But I haven't actually spoken to Jacquie since last night. The smart money is on Tubbsy doing a runner.'

Graham looked at him. 'Why?'

'Why indeed? I was going to ask you that. You must know the man pretty well.'

'Not really,' Graham shrugged. 'Oh, well done!' and he was clapping a particularly vicious aside from Selwyn's second. 'No, Tubbsy is ... well, you've got them at Leighford, I'm sure ... a sort of fly in the ointment, really. He thinks the world owes him a living. Well, he's lost that now.'

'His job, you mean?' Maxwell turned to the Housemaster. For all he had often told Metternich the cat that that was it, he'd had enough, over some trifling incident that had got right up his nose, actually *leaving* the profession was anathema to the Head of Sixth Form.

Graham nodded.

'Sheffield's given him the elbow?' Maxwell wanted confirmation.

'Not so much Sheffield, as that insufferable bastard Wilkins.'

'Ah, yes, the Chair of Governors,' Maxwell smiled. 'Not just part of the furniture, then?'

'I shouldn't say this,' Graham was earnest, leaning closer to Maxwell, 'but I've been very surprised at the way the Headmaster has handled all this. Or rather hasn't. He's gone to pieces apparently. Mervyn Larson was filling me in. Much more of it and we Housemasters will be running the place ourselves. Ever known anything like that?'

'I have, actually,' Maxwell told him. 'Not at Leighford but in another of my previous incarnations. The Head went doolally and the Year Heads took over. It's not ideal, but, like shit, it happens. And it might just save a school.'

'I can't see Sheffield surviving,' Graham was shaking his head.

'Deputy Headship for you, then?'

Graham chuckled. 'I'm only just getting used to running my House,' he said. 'How many dead men's shoes can any one person fill? By the way, after the debate, come along to the Fox and Grapes, will you? It's traditional. Losing House buys the drinks.'

There were whoops and cheers from the girls as Cassandra's second weighed in with a particularly unanswerable *bon mot*. Maxwell turned to Graham. 'Looks like you could cop a packet.'

The Fox and Grapes was within spitting distance of Grimond's. 'Only a yard of ale away' as Bill Pardoe used to say. It was a typical old coaching inn that had had the heart ripped out of it to become a fast-food outlet. The beams were a little on the plastic side and the beer somewhat characterless, but it was better than meths strained through a sock. The dead Housemaster was never very keen on his charges nipping to this or any other hostelry. Grimond's sixth form were immaculately behaved of course and the landlord had a tendency to blindness in one eye where the law of the land was concerned. He couldn't tell the time either, so it was well after eleven when the Fox and Grapes handbell was rung for last orders.

'Max, what'll it be?' Tony Graham was buying among the quietly inebriated hum of the night. 'One for the dorm, eh?'

'All right, Tony, thanks. I'll break the habit of a lifetime and have a small Southern Comfort.'

And the new Housemaster was gone into the hurly-burly of the bar.

'You know,' Maxwell turned on his monk's bench near the empty fireplace to John Selwyn, 'you were very good tonight. In the debate. You should have won.'

'Let's just say it was Cassandra's turn,' he raised the remains of his pint to her.

The Captain of Austen looked years older out of her school uniform, sitting with similar sirens around a far table. She winked and raised her Malibu and Coke to him.

'Oh, now don't tell me the whole thing was fixed,' Maxwell was appalled.

'Oh, no,' Cassandra was still all ice after her encounter with Maxwell the other night. 'John lost fair and square.' She beamed broadly at him. 'He usually does.'

'Bitch,' Selwyn grinned.

'How's the House coping without Mr Pardoe, John?' Maxwell asked.

'Oh, you know,' Selwyn said, a little grimly. 'The show must go on. He'd have wanted it that way.'

'Mr Graham settling in?'

'Oh, yes,' Selwyn finished his pint. 'He's a natural. In fact, I'm not sure we'd have quite got through all this without him.'

'Hear, hear!' boomed Ape from the next seat along.

'You're off to Cambridge, I understand?'

'Oxford. Merton,' Selwyn said.

'To read?'

'As little as possible,' Selwyn joked.

'And you, Cassandra?' Maxwell called across to her. 'Oxford?'

'Cambridge,' she told him. 'I shall be reading around the subject.'

247

She and Selwyn convulsed in laughter. It was the way she pronounced the word that caused it. Janet Boyce at her elbow stood up, her face a mask, and she flounced out into the night. A couple of other girls saw it and sidled out after her. After all, there was a maniac on the loose at Grimond's and Miss Shaunessy had given them all explicit instructions. No one was to go home alone.

'Tell me, John, do the prefects at Grimond's wear gowns?'

'Gowns?' Selwyn stopped laughing. 'No. Not in my time here, anyway. Why do you ask?'

'Oh, no reason. You know how it is when you're plunged into a strange institution; it's all new. It was just something I saw the other night, that's all. I don't suppose you know, either of you, what's become of Mr Tubbs?'

'Your very good health, Max,' and Tony Graham was back with the drinks.

It was David Gallow who ran Maxwell back to Grimond's that night. The others piled into Graham's Range Rover and the school mini-bus, the unmarked one without the school coat of arms specially kept for such outings. Miss Shaunessy had not joined them, a stress migraine overtaking her just at the moment of her girlies' triumph.

'You know, Mr Maxwell, it's not really on.'

'What? Under-age drinking? No, I suspect not, but if the sons of the Prime Minister and the Prince of Wales can do it, we teetotallers are swimming against the tide rather, aren't we?' and he winked in the dashboard glow of the car's interior.

'I'm not talking about that,' Gallow snarled his way through the gears. 'I'm referring to the way you pump my students.'

'*Your* students?' Maxwell looked at the man's face, illuminated by the glow of his fascia-panel lights. 'I had no idea you took it so personally.'

'I think these children have been through enough in the last ten days.'

'It's only going to get worse,' Maxwell told him. 'They've asked me to play rugger against them on Saturday.'

'Who has?' It was Gallow's turn to look at Maxwell.

'John Selwyn and the hearties of Tennyson.'

'Oh, the Arbiters. Well, there you go.'

Maxwell froze. 'The what?'

'It's the annual staff versus First Fifteen. Aren't you – forgive me for saying so – a little long in the tooth for that sort of thing? A man of your age – it might kill you.'

'Who are the Arbiters?' Maxwell wasn't listening.

'What? Well, Selwyn and co. of course. It's an old Tennyson House tradition, going back to the school's early years. The Arbiters were the first House prefects at a time when there was only the one House – Tennyson. They ran the place, acting as a sort of drum-head court martial for unruly fags. They decided guilt or innocence – hence Arbiters. And punishments. Why the interest?'

'Oh, nothing,' Maxwell said. 'It was just something Jeremy Tubbs said the day before he disappeared. We were talking about the boat-house in actual fact and he mentioned the Arbiters.'

'Right. Well, my point is that Grimond's is convulsed enough as it is, Mr Maxwell. We've got social services and policemen all over the place...'

'Two staff dead and one missing,' Maxwell interrupted. 'Don't you think it's time someone asked some questions?'

'Not you,' Gallow bellowed, in a viewpoint that oddly echoed his Headmaster's. 'Oh, shit!' and he snatched at the hand brake as he saw the host of paparazzi, decidedly smaller that it had been, but still loitering at the school gates, the lights of their cigarettes like tall glow-worms in the darkness. 'I can't believe these people are still here,' he said.

Maxwell unclicked the seat-belt. 'My place for a nightcap?' he smiled, wondering how hospitable a cup of hot water would seem. He really must see Parker about some top-up coffee.

'Thanks,' said Gallow flatly. 'I have places to be,' and he revved away along the lane.

'Who are you?' a cold and dispirited newspaper man hailed Maxwell as he plodded towards them, his shoes clattering on the tarmac.

'The Grim Reaper,' Maxwell said, raising a hooked finger and beckoning towards him. 'Y'all have a good night, y'hear?' and he was gone, over the wall as their trainers squeaked on the tarmac and cameras popped uselessly to the rhythm of barked expletives, capturing the brickwork on celluloid.

He sat in the car, his face lit by the fascia dials. He was talking into the cassette mike again. 'This one's aged about fifteen. But he's not alone. Seems to live along William Street. Can't make out the number. He was drinking at the pub earlier. Under-age of course. May be able to use that. Going on into Petersfield now.' And he switched off the machine and roared away into the night.

'What are we going to do about this Maxwell person?' Janet Boyce was dragging on the spliff, screwing her eyes up with the effort, fighting the smoke.

'Do?' Cassandra was still sipping her red wine.

'From last night. When he made that filthy suggestion.'

'Masturbatory fantasies,' Cassandra slurred. 'Middle-aged men have them. Gaynor Ames told me he doesn't have a wife. Probably gets his kicks with little girls.'

Janet frowned. She was easily confused anyway, but the contents of her roll-up were getting to her. 'But you're not a little girl, Cassie.'

'No, dear,' Cassandra sighed. 'But it's all one. And don't call me Cassie.'

'Sorry.' The large girl twisted in the armchair. 'Look, I was silly for storming out like that, from the pub, I mean. What with "reading" and all, I thought you and John were laughing at me.'

'I know, dear.' Cassandra looked at the lamp-light reflected in the carmine of her glass. 'You told me. We've been all through that. No, no, as far as Maxwell's concerned, John's got something in mind, apparently. They've asked the old pervert to play in the staff Fifteen match this Saturday. They'll give him a good hiding then.'

'Cassandra?'

251

'Hmm?' the Captain of Austen was sprawling on the bed in the upper storey of the girls' dorm. Lights out was hours ago and all was silent except for the gentle snoring from Maggie Shaunessy's rooms two floors below.

'What do *you* think happened to Mr Pardoe?'

'Pardoe? It's obvious, darling. He killed himself.'

'Why?'

'Oh, for fuck's sake, Janet,' Cassandra drained her glass. 'Don't you keep your ear to the ground at all? Bill Pardoe was a pederast. Makes this Maxwell bloke look like Mr Normal. He was caught with any number of boys in Tennyson.'

'Who?'

'Jesus!' Cassandra took a huge swig from her bottle. 'I don't know. Wait a minute.' She rolled over onto her stomach, still holding the wine and trying to focus on the fat girl slumped in the armchair opposite. 'Yes, I do. That little shit Jenkins in the Lower Fourths for instance. Pardoe used to get the little freak to strip off in front of him while he … well, I don't need to paint you a picture, do I?'

Janet shuddered. 'No, you don't,' and she inhaled deeply. 'How do you know all this?'

'Common knowledge,' Cassandra said. 'All the Arbiters know about it. John wanted to tell Tony Graham, but thought better of it. Can you imagine the stink it would have caused? In the end, I suppose, Pardoe did the right thing. It's all genetics, of course. People like that can't help it. If they'd caught him, they'd have cut his bollocks off and put him on a sex offenders' register for

252

life. Personally,' she reached across for Janet's happy-ciggie, 'I think he got off lightly.'

'Mr Maxwell?'

'Mr Parker?'

It was a little after seven-thirty and Peter Maxwell was on his way to breakfast. Dawn was still a purplish pink as it rolled the night away and the wind whipped chill around Grimond's cloisters. The school steward looked unusually perplexed this morning.

'Can I have a word, sir?'

Maxwell went with the man into his office. Had the steward read Maxwell's mind last night vis-à-vis the coffee? And was he now delivering the goods? Mrs Parker, looking more ferrety than Maxwell remembered her, hovered there for a moment and at a nod from her husband, scuttled away.

'You've had a phone call, sir. As you know, there's no way of putting you through in your room in Tennyson, so I took the message.'

'Who was it from?'

'He wouldn't say, sir.'

'Wouldn't say?' Maxwell frowned. 'Well, what *did* he say?'

'He said ... well, it's on the answerphone. I was already on duty, but the machine recorded anyway. I was tied up with me post and sorting out the boilers. We've got problems again.'

It was the universal mantra of school caretakers.

'Can I hear it?'

'Er ... yes, sure.' And Parker pressed the button.

'I've got a message for Maxwell,' the voice crackled, far away, frightened. 'Tell him it's got out of hand. I never meant for any of this to happen. And tell him ... tell him to get out. For his own good and for God's sake, get out.' Then the line went dead.

Maxwell looked at Parker. 'Mr Parker, do you know who that is?'

The steward stared at him with an odd look in his eyes. 'Well, I'd say it's from a mobile phone, sir,' he said. 'And the reception isn't too good, but I think it's Mr Tubbs.'

'Jeremy Tubbs?' Jacquie paused in mid-toast. Maxwell had met her as he crossed the quad from Parker's inner sanctum. She looked cold and drawn and she hadn't eaten. He marched into the Dining Hall, smiled at George Sheffield, who scowled at him, nodded at David Gallow, who did the same, winked at Tony Graham who winked back and smuggled out two breakfasts under his scarf flaps. He always knew those Jesus colours would come in handy one day.

They sat together side by side on Maxwell's bed under the eaves, munching Mrs Oakes' toast and slurping coffee. He handed the tape to her. 'Listen for yourself. You and Henry have a tape recorder for interviews, don't you? Play it and see.'

'Answerphones are a different size, Max. But there is one in Sheffield's outer office.' She handled it gingerly.

'Parker's prints will be all over it. Mine too. Mrs Parker's quite possibly. The call seemed quite kosher.'

'When was it made?'

'About six-thirty this morning. The irony was that Parker was in and out of the office, but he'd forgotten to switch the answerphone off and by the time he'd got to it, Tubbs had rung off.'

'What were his words again?'

'"It's got out of hand",' Maxwell remembered. '"I never meant for this, or any of this to happen." Then he said I should get out, for my own good and for God's sake. Quite a colourful turn of phrase for a geographer. Probably part-pinched from dear old Robert Falcon Scott, but there you are.'

'Parker thinks this was from a mobile?'

'Right.' Maxwell winced at the lukewarmness of his coffee and switched on the kettle for more. He was down to single grains. 'So there's no way of tracing it.'

'No.'

'There's something else, though, about the message, I mean.'

'What's that?'

'It sounded familiar.'

'Well, of course, it's Jeremy Tubbs.'

'No, no, I don't mean that. Run it alongside that tape young Jenkins left outside my room.'

'Young ... Max?' Jacquie shouted. 'I don't believe this.'

'Hush, hush, sweet Charlotte,' he smiled. 'I'm not sure female voices are allowed in Tennyson.'

'You didn't tell me about young Jenkins,' she growled, looking fiercely at him.

'Sorry, darling,' he grimaced. 'I really meant to.'

'Jesus! How did you find out?'

'Just a hunch,' and he leapt around the room like Professor Frankenstein's assistant, arms swinging and knuckles brushing the carpet. 'Your alter-igor.'

She threw a pillow at him.

'The lad admitted it, but it won't do any good now. He feels I've let him down. Haven't worked out who killed his Mr Pardoe.'

'*His* Mr Pardoe?'

'Hero worship,' Maxwell nodded, in his memory far, far, away, smiling. 'It doesn't happen any more, not in the state system, anyway. If a teacher appears to be a hero now, he's a pervert; there's a hidden agenda. The world's gone mad, Jacquie.'

She looked up. He hardly ever called her that. Only when the world really *had* gone mad.

'Anyway,' Maxwell sighed, 'I suspect young Jenkins has just turned thirteen. He's slipped over that fine line that demarks sanity and sagacity from testosterone-impulsed rebellion. Allowing for the tie and the blazer and the cut-glass accent, he'll turn into Harry Enfield's Kevin now; mark my words. I've lost him.'

'How did he get the tape?'

'He found it. Bill Pardoe threw it out. It was in the skip at the back of Tennyson.'

'Which explains his fingerprints.'

'And you'd have found young Jenkins' prints there too, I dare say, had Henry Hall had the balls and the manpower to fingerprint every-body.'

'You think Tubbs made that tape?'

Maxwell poured his second coffee. Jacquie

declined. 'I don't know. It's just ... oh, I know the Pardoe tape is distorted. But it was done apparently on the Music Department's machinery. Why shouldn't Tubbs be involved? According to Gaynor Ames, he couldn't stand the man.'

'Gaynor...?'

'Ames. The wife of the Head of PE. Haven't you talked to her?'

'Yes, we have,' Jacquie said, looking at her watch. 'Which reminds me, interviews in twenty minutes. Henry will want a briefing before we start.' She got up to go.

'Won't he have missed you at breakfast?'

'I pleaded the headaches last night. I was bushed. Gaynor Ames wasn't very forthcoming, incidentally.'

'Ah,' Maxwell tutted smugly. 'I've told you before about the matches under the fingernails technique. Softly, softly every time. With you and Henry it's Nice Policeman, Nasty Policeman. With me, it's just Nice Teacher, Nice Teacher. Gets results.'

'Bollocks!' she snorted. 'Where did you get to last night? I rang.'

'Sorry.' He wandered to the window to watch blazered youngsters in the quad below beginning to loiter on building-corners. 'I switched the thing off. I spent a happy hour in a state-of-the-nation debate, followed by a happy hour at the pub. What do you make of David Gallow, by the way?'

'Head of History? Bit up himself, I thought.'

'He's an assistant Housemaster, isn't he?'

Jacquie was rummaging in the pile on the chair for her coat. 'Yes, Kipling, I think. Why?'

257

'So, he lives on site?'

'Yes. As I understand it, all Housemasters and their assistants do. And the Head of PE.'

'That's what I thought.'

'Max,' she spun him away from the window. 'Is there anything else you'd like to share, anything else that's slipped your mind? So far we've had young Jenkins, Gaynor Ames and rather a lot of nookie in the boat-house.'

'No, no,' he laughed. 'It's just that Gallow dropped me at school after the pub and then drove off, heading somewhere else.'

'What time was this?'

'God, way after closing, but don't tell the law. Must have been nearly twelve.'

'Which way did he go?'

'Er ... let's see, past the gate ... East.'

'Towards Petersfield.'

'Could be.'

'Is he back?' It was Jacquie's turn to look down from the window. 'What does he drive?'

'Um, ah, now you've asked me.'

'Oh, Max, you're hopeless.'

'No, wait a minute. That's it. Green jobbie, next to the Range Rover.'

'Ah yes,' Jacquie smiled. 'What we in the real world would call a Proton.' She could have bitten her tongue. She, of all people, knew why Peter Maxwell didn't drive, couldn't tell one car from another. She knew about his wife and baby, the loved ones before he'd known her. She'd held him in the lonely watches of the night when he'd stirred, reliving it all in his mind, the roar of steel and the splinter of glass. She'd kissed the tears that trickled sometimes in the keenness of the wind.

'There's something else.' She broke away, making for his door, her public face on already. 'I talked to DCI West yesterday.'

'I suspect you deserve a medal for that,' he said.

'Hall's here working under cover.'

'Henry told you this?' Maxwell crossed the room to her.

'No, West. Max, stay with the plot.'

'What did he say?'

She sighed. 'Either he was fishing. Or he thought I know more than I do. Or ... Christ, Max, I don't know which way is up any more.'

'All right, all right,' he took her cheeks in his hands and kissed her forehead tenderly, leading her back to the bed and sitting her on it. 'Now, think, sweetheart. What exactly did West say?'

She blinked in concentration. 'He said "I know about the drugs bust and I know who's involved."'

'That's it?'

'Yes. But, Max, it has to be something like that. I never went along with all this inter-force co-operation, swappy-swappy cobblers. There may be forty-three police forces in this country, but we all operate on similar lines, for God's sake. What's to be gained?'

'What's to be gained from my being at Grimond's?' Maxwell was asking himself again.

'Don't change the subject,' she said. 'It only makes any sense if Henry's been drafted in to clean up a case.'

'And?'

'And that would only be necessary if there's

police involvement. Somebody on the Hampshire force is bent.'

'Drugs?' Maxwell was trying to piece it all together. 'Who?'

'Not West,' Jacquie said. 'He told me about it. Could be one of his team, I suppose. I've only met a couple of them.'

'Drugs, Jacquie,' Maxwell was crouching on his heels in front of her. 'You've interviewed all the staff now, a goodly proportion of the sixth form. Anything?'

'Every school has a drugs problem, Max. Christ, you know that, you teach at Leighford High, for God's sake.'

'Thank you for that, darling,' he sighed. 'It's difficult to soar with eagles when you're working with turkeys.'

'Yes, but it's usually worse in the private sector, Max,' Jacquie told him. 'They've got more money. They've already got the designer jeans and the platinum mobiles, so what other kicks are out there?'

'Tut, tut, Woman Policeman,' Maxwell scolded. 'Do I detect a teensy bit of the politics of envy there?'

'You get my drift, Max.'

'I do. But would you say it merits West's use of the word "bust"? Is it that major a problem?'

'I don't know,' Jacquie said. 'If that's Hall's aim, his questions have been pretty oblique. But one thing's for sure; I've got to tackle him about it. The DCI has some explaining to do. Thanks for the tape, Max. And thanks for the breakfast. Now, I've really got to go.'

Maxwell was still crouching in front of her. 'Of course you have, darling,' he said. 'And I'd love to let you, but unfortunately, my knees have seized up. And that's rather bad news bearing in mind I'm playing rugger on Saturday.'

Chapter Fifteen

Just another manic Thursday. Mark West was tetchier than usual, out of ciggies and out of leads. It was briefing time at Selborne and the team crowded around him, wreathed in smoke and hoping for something, *anything*, from their guv'nor. It was always the same ten days into a murder enquiry. Everybody'd tried the obvious. The house-to-house on Tim Robinson had elicited almost nothing. He'd shopped at the local Asda, had his bike fixed by the local bike-dealer. He probably went to the local cinema and the local library, but nobody remembered that. They tried the pubs, did Mark West's foot-sore coppers, in an attempt to resolve the dilemma over the drink question. A teetotaller with booze in the house. Kept for friends? If so, who? And did he go drinking with them, even if he was sitting at the bar sipping sarsaparilla with a dash of cherry? In the event, nothing. The morgue photo wasn't horrific, but it was clearly of a dead man who didn't look his best.

'Course, I wouldn't have seen him with his eyes shut,' was the banal, if predictable, response of many a landlord in Petersfield. 'Not unless he'd had a real skinful. Talking of which, we've got a special offer on Theakston's at the moment.'

The Blundells, Robinson's neighbours, had given useful descriptions of the men who paid the late PE teacher a visit one dark night. Or at least, Mr Blundell did, his wild-haired wife muttering the script at his elbow. But useful descriptions or not, they were just three blokes, needles in haystacks.

As for the missing Mr Tubbs, another resounding blank. His Mummy and Daddy lived in Harlow, on the probable grounds that somebody had to, and could not have been more helpful.

'Jeremy's a good boy,' the slightly dotty Mrs Tubbs had told DI Sandy Berman. She had a long chelonian neck and hair like a Gorgon's. 'We're enormously proud of him. I've got his graduation photo somewhere...' and by the time Sandy Berman left, he could have written the man's biography. Only one note had jarred. On his way out, the silent Mr Tubbs senior, still upright, still sprightly, had shown him to his car. 'Doesn't surprise me,' he muttered. 'Jeremy's a little deviant. Always has been. Had this cocker spaniel once ... well, you can fill in the details, I'm sure. Whatever's going on, he's up to his unpleasant neck in it, believe me. And to think, I wanted him to follow me into the Paras! I ask you!'

But Sandy Berman wasn't able to ask the old disappointee anything, because he slammed the door and Berman heard the bolts slide. Co-operation seemed to have come to an end.

'It's a bright yellow fucking MG!' West bawled, tired of brick walls and signs that read 'Road Closed'. 'How many of those can there be? Pete, what's the news from Dover?'

'Usual thing, guv,' DS Walters said. 'They're

snowed under with fighting the tide of illegal immigrants and asylum seekers.'

'I want a bastard who's trying to get out, not a load of foreign spongers trying to get in. Who's on airports?'

'Me, guv.' Chapell was waving a piece of paper at him. Clearly it was not peace in his time.

'Right, Steve. Anything?'

Chapell was shaking his head. 'No yellow MG,' he said. 'No one's answering his description.'

West looked at the sheet on his desk, the mug-shot faxed through from Grimond's and now distributed nationwide. Jeremy Tubbs smirked back at him, smug, defiant, as elusive as the scarlet fucking pimpernel. 'All right,' he said. 'Get me Grimond's. I want to talk to Hall. And, Lynda...'

'Yes, sir,' the dumpy little WPC looked up, pleased to be asked to do anything really.

'Get me some ciggies, will you? I'm out.'

'Well, well.' Henry Hall put the phone down and looked at Jacquie. It wasn't elevenses yet and they'd just started on Austen House. Cassandra James had arrived first, a fashionable few minutes late and had sat cross-legged in front of the Chief Inspector, swinging one foot and smouldering at him with those deep, dark eyes. It usually worked. Today was no exception. By the time she left, she had Henry Hall eating out of her hand. Or at least opening the door for her. Jacquie was less impressed. And less convinced.

'That was DCI West,' Hall told her.

Jacquie was adjusting the tape, ready for the

264

next interview. 'Oh?'

'He's got a proposition for us ... well, for you, really.'

'Oh.' Jacquie didn't like the sound of this already.

'He's proposing a swap,' Hall told her. 'In the interests of solving the case. Or cases or whatever we're actually dealing with here.'

'A swap?'

Hall nodded. 'I get DS Denise McGovern. He gets you.'

'I sound like a concubine,' she frowned. It was a word she'd learned from Peter Maxwell.

'I don't think it'll come to that,' Hall said with just a hint of a smile.

'Are you ordering me to go, sir?'

'No.' Hall rested his hands behind his head, lolling back in his chair. 'But I think it would be a good idea.'

'For whom?'

'For me,' he answered her. 'I'm too cut off here, Jacquie.' He flicked the clicker on his biro. 'I need a window on the outside.'

'And West needs one in here.'

Hall nodded. 'Phones and faxes aren't doing it, are they?'

Jacquie clicked in the new tape. 'All right,' she said. 'I'll do it. But I want some answers first.'

'Oh?' This wasn't like Jacquie Carpenter. She had a mind of her own, certainly. And there were times when, fleetingly, Hall had had cause to question the woman's loyalty. But that had usually been because somewhere in the back-ground, lurked the Svengali that was Peter Maxwell. Was that what this was all about? 'Answers to what?'

She took the bull by the horns. 'Something about a drugs bust. Something about a bent copper?'

There was a silence. 'Who's been putting those ideas into your head?' Hall wanted to know.

'DCI West,' Jacquie said. 'It was something he let slip when I was at Selborne last.'

'So the grapevine works,' Hall nodded.

'Sir?'

'DS McGovern was, as I suspected, a plant. Oh, I'm not surprised and it doesn't matter. It all works rather well, in fact.'

'What does?'

'You'd have done the same, I'm sure.'

'Sir, you'll have to excuse my French, but what the piss are you talking about?'

'It's not drugs, Jacquie,' he said quietly. 'It's a paedophile ring.'

Her eyes widened. 'Here at Grimond's?'

Hall nodded. 'Partly.'

Jacquie sat down. 'So that's why none of your questions were about possession ... or dealing, for that matter.'

'I'm sorry,' Hall said. 'I should have filled you in from Day One, Jacquie, but I wasn't sure who knew what. In fact,' he sat forward again, rubbing his eyes behind his glasses, 'in that respect, nothing's changed. I was called in by David Mason, the Chief Superintendent. One of his team is part of it.'

Jacquie didn't know whether to laugh or cry. Laugh because some, at least, of Hall's sloppy policework was falling into place. And cry because the cold-hearted bastard had left her out, sidelined her. 'Why did you send for me, then, if you weren't prepared to trust me?'

He threw the glasses down on the desk. 'Comfort,' he said softly. 'A face I knew. And I *do* trust you, Jacquie. You know that.'

She looked at the arsehole, in his three-piece suit, emotions wrestling inside her.

'You need a coffee,' he said.

'I need a Southern Comfort,' she corrected him.

'Ah,' he paused as he reached for the kettle. 'Mad Max.'

'What did you mean,' she asked him, 'a minute ago, when you said "so the grapevine works"?'

'Denise McGovern.' Hall rattled among the coffee cups. 'She came to see me the other day.'

It was a day of surprises for Jacquie Carpenter.

'She gave me a forensic file, on Pardoe and Robinson. In exchange, I gave her a lot of garbage.'

'The drugs connection?'

Hall nodded, clicking the sweeteners into his cup. 'I don't know, any more than the Chief Super does, who we're after. I just had instructions once Pardoe died, to keep all the local boys out of Grimond's. SOCO could come and go, West's people could root around in the bike sheds and the boat-house to their hearts' content. But only I – well, you and I – were to have access to the staff and kids. And I must say, it's not working. Too big a job. After Love died...'

'Love?' Jacquie repeated. It sounded as though

Hall were quoting a rather icky pop song from his youth, assuming he ever had a youth.

Hall looked at the girl, twisting in her chair to look up at him. This wouldn't be easy, either. 'Andy Love. His name wasn't Tim Robinson and he wasn't a PE teacher. He was working undercover too, seconded from the Met.'

'Jesus!' Jacquie whistled through her teeth. 'So Max was right.'

'What?'

'Peter Maxwell, sir...'

'Now, Jacquie...'

'I know.' Her hands were in the air and she was out of the chair, twirling round the office. She'd been here before on account of Maxwell, between the rock that was the man she loved and the hard place that was Henry Hall. 'But I didn't invite him here. That was just coincidence.'

'I'm beginning to wonder,' Hall said.

She blinked at him, 'You can't think Max is involved?' she blurted.

'No, I don't,' Hall sighed. 'Why was he right?'

'What? Oh, he said Robinson ... Love ... was a sloppy marker.'

'That accounts for about half Maxwell's profession, doesn't it?'

'And not a very good fencer.'

'Well, bearing in mind he'd only had a few weeks familiarisation, I think he did bloody well.'

Jacquie nodded. 'How was it done?' she asked.

Hall put their cups down on his desk. 'The Chief Super got a tip off last November, an anonymous phone call that said that a paedophile ring was operating in the area and that a teacher at Grimond's was at the heart of it. There's also a connection with his force, but he wouldn't go into details. There was a vacancy for second in PE at Grimond's – in fact, they were desperate, the last bloke having left in a hurry after a clash with Sheffield. Mason enlisted the aid of the Met, calling in a few favours and that's where Love came in. He applied and his rivals were leaned on. Don't ask me how Mason found out who they were, I don't know, but I suspect it was over a few double brandies at the Country Club with Grimond's Chair of Governors. That left Love as the new kid on the block. He was reporting directly to Mason.'

'And what did he report?'

'The bottom line is, not a lot. Clearly, Bill Pardoe was in the frame, but there was something about Tubbs. He'd only made two reports when Pardoe died.'

'And you were called in?'

Hall nodded. 'Mason didn't want the local team at Grimond's. Whoever the link is on the outside could have covered tracks, created new ones. I was originally just supposed to ferret about at operational level, but Pardoe's death rather scotched that.'

'So that's why you weren't very concerned about following up Robinson?' It was dawning on Jacquie.

'More than that, I wanted to play it down. I knew West's people would find that his references were faked. They were all written on Met PCs.'

'And when you went to his house...?'

'It was to collect his warrant card,' Hall confessed. 'I guessed he'd have it somewhere. It was in his wardrobe.'

'So, other than Mason,' Jacquie was still piecing it all together, 'nobody knows Robinson's real identity.'

'His wife,' Hall said soberly. 'And maybe, in a couple of years when she's old enough to understand, his little girl.'

'Oh, God. What about the blokes who came to see him?'

'Blokes?' This was new to Hall.

'Sir ... I went back to Rob ... Love's.'

'Really?' Hall sat back in his chair.

'Look, I didn't know,' she explained. 'You didn't talk to neighbours or any of the routine stuff. I didn't understand why. If you'd only told me...'

'Yes, all right, Jacquie. I'm not sure either of us has time for recriminations. What did you find out?'

'Three men visited Love on a couple of nights at least. They appeared to the next door neighbours to be friends.'

'Probably were,' Hall shrugged. 'Mates from the Met. It's a lonely job working undercover. You look at people in a different light.'

'Somebody looked at Love in a different light,' Jacquie said. 'But Pardoe was already dead by then. Do you think somebody sussed Love? Discovered his cover?'

'It's possible,' Hall said. 'Love was careful. Nobody at Grimond's, not even Sir Arthur Wilkins knew the real situation. He made no phone calls from school, cycled everywhere in case his car was seen and recognized. Apparently he was shadowing somebody.'

'Outside Grimond's?'

Hall nodded. 'That was the gist of his last communication with Mason. Whoever he was tailing drove around the towns, possibly as far south as Portsmouth...'

'Where Tubbs lives.'

'Right.'

'So,' Jacquie cradled the cup in both hands, 'Pardoe is the obvious link to the paedophile group.'

'He'd have access to boys, young, potentially vulnerable, away from home and trusting him.'

'He'd be their hero,' Jacquie said, remembering.

'Yes.' Hall hadn't quite looked at it like that. 'Yes, I suppose he would.'

'He recruited boys into the ring,' Jacquie was thinking aloud, 'introducing them to the others on the outside. But somebody had sussed him – the porn he had posted to Grimond's. Someone found out about that and was ... what? Blackmailing him?'

'We've got no vibes about that ... yet,' Hall told her. 'Unless I missed something in the rather long list of people we've spoken to in the last few days. You checked Pardoe's bank account?'

Jacquie had. 'He got his pay cheque here at the school, obviously. Banks with Lloyds in Petersfield. No large amounts going out. In fact, very little going out at all. He seems to have been the frugal type. West's people are still checking, but they can't find anything linking him to any sort of mail order company.'

'But someone knew about the porn,' Hall was reasoning. 'Hence that tape left outside Maxwell's door. Why would Pardoe need porn when he had access to the real thing?'

'There's another tape, sir.'

'Jacquie?'

She crossed to the corner and pressed the play button on the answerphone on the counter that ran the length of the room. A distorted voice scratched inside their ears, burning into their heads. "For your own safety and for God's sake, get out."

'What is that, Jacquie?' Hall was next to her now, staring blankly at the machine.

'It was a message left for Max this morning, sir,' she told him. 'About six-thirty.'

'Who is it?'

'Max thinks it's Tubbs. He also thinks it's the same voice as on the tape left outside his door, the one implicating Pardoe.'

'Sex, lies and sound tape,' Hall murmured. 'Right.' He flicked out the tape with his biro. 'Now, listen. You go now, before lunch, to Selborne. Report to West and take this tape with you. Tell him his forensic people need to dust it and check it for voice patterns against the other one. You know the drill.'

'Yes, sir.' Jacquie reached for her bag.

'And, Jacquie,' Hall looked into the girl's clear, grey eyes. 'You will *not*, I repeat *not* tell anybody outside this room about Robinson or the exact nature of the case we're working on here. Is that clear?'

'Perfectly, sir. Does that go for Peter Maxwell?'

'It goes double for Peter Maxwell, Jacquie. I mean it. This is not a grapevine job. This is for real. I don't want his great amateur feet trampling over this one. There's too much at stake.' She reached the door. 'And Jacquie?'

'Sir?'

'As I seem to remember they used to say on *Hill Street Blues*, "Let's be careful out there".'

And for the first time in her life, Jacquie Carpenter actually saw Henry Hall wink.

'I will, sir,' she smiled. 'Even though that programme was one my dear old mum told me about.'

'How goes it, Michael?'

'Max, won't you join me?' Michael Helmseley was mellow after a second helping of Mrs Oakes' plum duff. Maxwell couldn't believe anybody still made puddings that even Mrs Beeton found old hat. At Leighford, if it didn't come with chips and pizza, it wasn't on the menu. 'Many thanks,' and he took the proffered coffee cup.

Maggie Shaunessy was sitting in a huge armchair in the corner of the Senior Common Room, the midday sun filtering through the notices that covered the wall behind her.

Helmseley muttered under his breath, 'I can remember when that was my chair.' He looked at Maxwell, who tutted his sympathy and sat between them.

'I understand you're going to play in the match, Maxwell,' the Head of Classics said, making the best of an altogether smaller seat nearby. 'Is that strictly wise?'

'Tony Graham did point out that you're three men down, staff-wise,' Maxwell said.

'Oh, yes,' Helmseley reached for his pipe, then caught Maggie's disapproving look and thought better of it. 'Well, with no disrespect to poor old Bill, two. He was way past the ruck and maul stuff. As, I suspect, are you.'

'It has been quite a time,' Maxwell confessed. 'What position does Jeremy Tubbs play?'

'Tubbsy?' Helmseley frowned. 'Good God, Max, you wouldn't see Tubbsy anywhere near a rugger pitch. Seemed quite keen on hockey, though.' And he glanced up at the Head of Austen House who studiously ignored him. 'Oh, Dave,' and he waved to the Head of History who had just swept in.

'I'm late for a meeting, Michael. Walk with me, will you?'

'Scuse me, people,' Helmseley struggled to his feet. 'No rest for the wicked.'

'What position does he play?' Maxwell said, watching the man waddle off with Gallow.

'Both ends against the middle,' Maggie Shaunessy scowled. She caught Maxwell's look. 'Oh, I'm sorry, Max. That was unprofessional.'

'Ah, we all do it,' Maxwell waved his hand. 'I won't bore you with my views on some of my colleagues.'

'It's just that ... well, this merger was difficult enough as it was, without... To be frank, Michael Helmseley put the pig in chauvinist. I'm sitting, you may have gathered, in "his" chair. I probably ate my lunch off "his" plate and now I'm drinking from "his" cup. I feel like bloody Goldilocks.'

Maxwell laughed. 'Tell me about Tubbsy,' he said.

'Jeremy? What's to tell?'

'Well, where is he, for a start?'

Maggie shrugged. 'Yes, that is rather a facer, isn't it? I mean, colleagues don't just wander off, do they?'

'I've only known one,' Maxwell said, 'in three thousand years at the chalk face. Stress, of course. He was a geographer too, funnily enough. Just walked out one day, in the middle of a lesson. Halfway through plate tectonics, he was. Nobody saw him again – except, presumably, a team of nurses at the local psychiatric hospital, the keepers of the rubber rooms.'

'How awful! I suppose it must be something like that with Tubbsy.'

'Is he the type, do you think?'

'What, to go mad?' She sipped her coffee thoughtfully, frowning. 'I don't know.'

'Gaynor Ames has him down for an oddball.'

Maggie looked at Maxwell. 'Gaynor's usually pretty shrewd on these matters.'

'Says he hangs around the hockey pitches a little too often. I got the impression that Michael Helmseley was saying something similar a moment ago.'

'You know my views on him,' Maggie snorted. 'Max, do you think Tubbsy's involved in what's going on? I mean … well, I don't know how to put it.'

'You mean, do I think he killed Bill Pardoe and Tim Robinson?' Maxwell sensed a hush fall over the entire room, virtually empty though it was.

'That's possible,' he said. 'The police are certainly looking for him.'

'But what would be his motive?' Maggie asked him. 'What would he have to gain?'

'Perhaps he was covering something up,' Maxwell suggested.

'I'm sorry?'

'Maggie, you've been Head of Austen House since the merger, right?'

'That's right.'

'And at St Hilda's you were...?'

'Second Deputy. My two seniors, both rather elderly blue stockings, it has to be said, threw up their hands in horror when the merger was suggested. I mean, co-education? It smacked of co-respondence for people of their generation. They retired – and probably not before time. That sort of left me in the hot seat. De facto Head, I suppose, although that didn't last long.' She was still glancing in the wake of the Head of Classics.

'Ah,' Maxwell smiled. 'To some you were the tea girl.'

Maggie Shaunessy snorted with laughter. 'Oh, don't get me wrong. Dr Sheffield, Mervyn Larson, Bill Pardoe, they were fine. But Helmseley and David Gallow ... well, I might as well have been the Invisible Woman, except that those two would quickly point out there was no such person.'

'So, in all your time here,' Maxwell asked, 'did you ever get wind of Jeremy Tubbs acting, shall we say, improperly?'

Maggie looked at him, trying to fathom those dark, haunted eyes, that full mouth with the ready smile. 'Max,' she said, both hands in the air. 'You're not from Grimond's. I can't...'

'Precisely.' He leaned forward. 'And it's just because I'm not from here that you can trust me. You see, Maggie, Bill Pardoe and Tim Robinson might only be the first two in what is becoming a series.'

'God,' she growled, looking from side to side. 'And is Tubbsy the third?'

'No, Maggie,' Maxwell was shaking his head. 'I am.'

'God,' she growled again, looking directly at him this time. She took a deep breath. 'There was one occasion. And I never got to the bottom of it. Tubbsy had an accident and I let it go. Perhaps I shouldn't have.'

'What happened?'

'Let me see – this was early last term, late September, I think.' She closed to him lest Senior Common Room walls had ears. 'There'd been a few whisperings around the House. I suppose it's the same for you. You get the vibes.'

'I have a school nurse who keeps me posted,' Maxwell nodded, picturing Sylvia Matthews' face as he said it and feeling her toe crunching against his shin.

'Well, the rumour ran to the effect that boys were meeting up with some of my girls after lights out, nipping off to the boat-house for a bit of how's your father. I ignored it for a while, then thought I ought to investigate. Well,' Maggie sighed apologetically, 'I'm no Miss Marple, I'm afraid. It was a Wednesday, I remember and I waited until well and truly after dark, then went out to the boat-house myself. It was a beastly night, pouring with rain and the visibility was awful. There are no locks on the boat-house so anyone can get in. I looked through the window...'

There was a pause.

'Come on, Maggie,' Maxwell urged. 'I'm on the edge of my seat, here.'

'Oh, sorry,' she said. 'Well, there was a couple making love, on some mats in the corner.'

'Who?'

'Now there you have me. I just couldn't get a clear view.'

Maxwell sympathized. He'd had exactly the same problem the week before.

'But that wasn't all.'

'Oh?'

'There was someone watching them, apart from me, I mean.'

'Who?'

Maggie scratched her head. 'Well, as I said, it was dark. And it was raining.'

'Maggie...' Maxwell growled.

'It was the grunting I heard first.'

'From inside the boat-house?'

'No, from the bushes to one side. There's a better view from there, I imagine, on the lake side. I trod on a twig or something – I told you I was no Jane Marple – and the grunting stopped. Somebody dashed away from the bushes and was last seen legging it up the hill towards the wall.'

'Who was it, Maggie?'

'Well,' the Head of Austen was getting seriously flustered. 'Obviously a voyeur of some sort, and behaving in a perfectly revolting manner.'

'Who was it, Maggie?' Maxwell persisted.

'It looked like – and, mind you, I don't say it was – it looked like Jeremy Tubbs.'

'Bingo!' Maxwell nodded.

'And he wasn't alone.'

'What?'

'No, I couldn't swear to it in a court of law, but I got the distinct impression there was somebody else, watching.'

'With Tubbs?'

'No, no, there's a sort of annexe to the boat-house, a wing off to one side.'

Maxwell remembered it.

'While I was watching ... Tubbs ... running to the wall, I heard somebody else moving away in the opposite direction.'

'Around the lake?'

'Yes. It's about a mile all the way round.'

'Did you see this person?'

Maggie shook her head. 'No. No one. I just heard the rustle of grass and the pounding of feet.'

'And you didn't tackle Tubbs about it?'

She shrugged. 'Cowardice, I suppose. I had no actual proof. What if he said to me he was at home in bed at the time of the alleged incident? What was I supposed to do? Call the man a liar? A pervert? He'd be bound to deny the whole thing. Anyway, fate stepped in.'

'In what way?' Maxwell asked.

'The next day, Tubbs fell down stairs in Tennyson House, sprained his ankle, quite badly, apparently. He was off for a fortnight. I read the riot act in Austen, obliquely, of course, about curfews and sensible behaviour and so on. I had a word with the other Heads of House, omitting the boat-house incident of course and they had similar words with their lads.'

'This was September?' Maxwell checked.

'Yes, the last week, I think. Why?'

'So Tim Robinson wasn't on the staff then?'

'No.' Maggie shook her head. 'Why do you ask?'

'Tim Robinson wasn't Tim Robinson at all.' Jacquie's voice was a hoarse whisper on the other end of the mobile. 'He was Andy Love. And he wasn't a teacher. He was an undercover copper. And if you breathe one word about this, Peter Maxwell, my career is over and I will personally cut your bum off. What will I do?'

'Cut my bum off, Police Woman Carpenter,' and he waved to George Sheffield, flying across the quad in gown and mortar board.

The grapevine had swung both ways.

The sun was over the yard arm as Peter Maxwell climbed the open plan stairs to Maggie Shaunessy's Northanger. She'd invited him after their post-prandial chat and he was supposed to be talking about the alternative education available to the girls' sisters in the state sector.

Somehow nobody had the stomach for that, least of all Maxwell, and he talked instead about murder. For all Dr Sheffield had exploded with rage at the suggestion, here he was, with the serried ranks of girls in front of him, discussing the most delicate subject in the world. His defence would be, when news filtered through as it inevitably would, to the Headmaster's study, that he was not actually asking them questions, merely inviting open discussion.

He knew of course that it wouldn't work. Even among the confidence-oozing sirens of Austen, it was a brave soul who would confess anything at all in front of her peers and sure enough, there was silence. Maxwell talked about the tragedy of Bill Pardoe's death, what a loss as a man and a teacher. He talked about Tim Robinson, whom nobody had known at all. He asked them what kind of funerals should be held; should a company of the cadet force, for instance, carry a flag-draped coffin for a burial at night, perhaps somewhere out beyond the lake and the boat-house which, Maxwell couldn't help thinking, seemed to lie at the heart of what was going on at Grimond's.

When it was over, a slightly stunned Maggie Shaunessy led a desultory applause. The girls were used to missionaries and Oxfam represent-atives, chats on careers and makeovers. They were not asked to confront reality on their own doorstep.

'Why did you do that?' Maggie asked him as she saw him down the rowing-trophied stairwell out of Northanger.

'Do what?' he asked her in turn.

'Frighten them.' She was curt, frosty, like the first time they'd met when Maxwell was not showing what she considered due respect for Bill Pardoe.

'Did I?' he asked.

'I was watching a couple at the back,' she told

281

him. 'They were crying. We're losing enough students as it is, Max. You'll drive even more away now.'

'Not me,' Maxwell shook his head. 'The murderer.'

'And that's another thing,' she turned to face him at the bottom of the stairs. 'You're dishonest, aren't you?'

'Am I?' He looked into her blazing eyes.

'You know more about all this than you said tonight.'

He nodded. 'That's true. But then, so does somebody up there,' he pointed back to the auditorium, to the raked theatre seats where the girls still huddled in groups, whispering.

'Are you implying that one or more of my girls is involved in this appalling situation?' she snapped, jabbing him in the chest with a forefinger.

'They're Grimond's girls,' he shrugged. 'They're all involved. What's to be gained by pussyfooting around?'

'That's not what I mean and you know it,' she thundered. There was a movement overhead and a bevy of girls had collected on the landing, like those ominous crows on the playground climbing frame in Hitchcock's *The Birds*. They were all looking down at the teachers below.

Maxwell closed to the Housemistress. 'Watch their reactions tonight,' he said. 'I may know more than I'm saying, but someone in Austen knows a great deal more. That someone may call on you, in full confessional mode, or just tearful and confused. In that case...'

'In that case,' she growled at him, 'I will send

for the chaplain or I'll handle it myself. You, Mr Maxwell, will leave Northanger now. And you are never coming back.'

Chapter Sixteen

'Well, Denise,' Henry Hall was already making the coffee and already, in her eyes, a different species from Mark West. 'I'd normally get to know my detective sergeants, have a few preliminary chats. But then I usually appoint my own. Not quite the same here, is it?'

'Sorry, sir.' Denise McGovern was older than Jacquie Carpenter, with straw-like hair and a hard, angular face. She looked as though she could handle herself in a crisis; she looked as though she took no prisoners. But Henry Hall knew two things about her; she was efficient and she was utterly loyal to Mark West.

'No, no,' he said, handing her a steaming cup. 'It's just one of those things. You're the local officer; tell me about Grimond's.' He sat back behind the desk.

'You've been here for the best part of two weeks, sir,' she said. 'Nothing I can say's going to add to what you already know.'

'Don't be so sure. Where are you based?'

'Petersfield.'

'Grimond's kids get there much?'

'They're allowed passes at weekends – *exeats*, I think they call them.'

'And the sixth form on Wednesday afternoons, too,' Hall nodded. 'Well, don't be shy, Denise. Sit down.'

She arranged herself in front of his desk.

'What's their reputation?'

'Tea leaves,' she said, straight-faced.

'Are you serious?' Hall asked her.

'Ask any of the retailers. Churchers is the other private school, the one in the town. Bedales near-by. And they're straight as dies. No, there's something about Grimond's. There's been the odd run in with uniform.'

'Dealing?' Hall clung to the story he'd invented.

'I thought that was why you were here, sir.'

'It is. But to be honest, it's more the links with the outside I need a handle on. That's why you're here.'

'What can I tell you?'

'Who's your Dirty Squad Chief?'

'Locally, Sandy Berman, sir – DI Berman. Why do you ask?'

'Who's your drugs czar?'

'Joe Nelson. He's the one you should be dealing with, if you'll excuse the pun.'

'You know why I can't,' Hall became conspiratorial.

'Sir,' Denise put her coffee cup on the desk and let what little cleavage she had droop. 'I appreciate you can't say too much, but the Chief Super?' She was shaking her head. 'I just don't buy it.'

Hall leaned back. 'That's what he's relying on,' he said, sipping his coffee. 'David Mason is like Caesar's wife and he thinks we aren't going to snoop.'

'What've you got on him?'

'Ah,' Hall nodded solemnly. 'For the moment,

that's on a strictly need to know basis. And for the moment, that doesn't include you. Sorry, Denise.'

She shrugged, knowing how far down the pecking order detective sergeants came. 'That's okay.' She changed tack. 'What's the schedule today?'

'More of the same,' Hall told her. 'By lunchtime we should have finished the sixth form girls. Tomorrow it's Dickens House, then Kipling. By Sunday, we'll have interviewed all the staff and all the sixth form.'

'What about the younger kids?'

Hall threw his hands in the air. 'You know the drill there,' he said. 'Social services, parents present, video screen set-ups, the whole walking-on-eggs bit. I'm dreading it. It can slow an enquiry down by weeks.'

'Useful, though,' Denise said. 'In my experience, kids are good observers.'

'And better readers of moods than most adults,' Hall agreed, just for a fleeting moment wishing he had Peter Maxwell on board as consulting kid expert.

'This bloke Tubbs,' Denise changed the subject. 'The one who's gone walkabout.'

'What about him?'

'He's got form.'

'What?' Hall was sitting up.

'Just a caution, in fact. I came across it the other day, in records.'

'It wasn't in the file,' Hall waved it at her.

'The DCI didn't think it was important. No drug connection.' She could have bitten her lip.

'You told him, didn't you?' Hall looked levelly at her.

'Sir?'

'Why I'm here. You told him.'

For a moment, Denise McGovern toyed with trying to lie her way out. Then she thought better of it. 'Yes, sir. I'm sorry.'

'It had to come out one day,' Hall said, secretly loving it when a plan comes together. 'I'm too short-staffed to manage alone. Tell me about Tubbs.'

'It wasn't long after he'd started at Grimond's, maybe six years ago. He had a pad in Petersfield then, a rented place and he was in the habit of inviting local girls round, some from the local comp, others from St Hilda's.'

'That's the school that merged with Grimond's?'

Denise nodded. 'There was a complaint from a neighbour and uniform were called in. It all looked a bit sweaty, bottles of vodka and a few raunchy vids. All the girls were over sixteen though and no parents complained, so Tubbs just got a caution. He had backing from the school, apparently.'

'Sheffield?' Hall frowned.

'No. That wasn't the name. I can't remember, but somebody swore his life away for the sleazy bastard. Still, no hint of drugs, though.'

'Put yourself in his position, Denise.' Hall leaned back. 'Jeremy Tubbs. You're a third-rate teacher fast approaching middle-age in an obscure private school. You fancy young girls, but they probably don't fancy you. What do you do?'

'I don't think I'd kill a couple of colleagues,' Denise said. 'What would be the point? To increase my street cred? I saw the school mug-

287

shot; Ronnie Kray Tubbsy's not.'

'Agreed,' Hall nodded. 'But he ran anyway. For reasons we don't yet know. Where does he go?'

'Home to Mummy and Daddy?' Denise pondered the possibles. 'No, we've checked. Mummy thinks he's the best thing since sliced bread; Daddy thinks he's a weirdo with a history of pet abuse. No doubt the shrink counsellors you've got under your feet here would have a field day with all that.'

'No doubt,' Hall said. 'So where else does he go?'

'No brothers,' Denise told him. 'No sisters. We understand there's an aunt in Potter's Bar, but she hasn't seen him since he was ten and, I believe I'm quoting from her statement, "if I never see the little toe-rag again it'll be too soon". The Herts force seemed to think she was telling it like it is.'

'Nothing from airports? Ports? Eurotunnel?'

'Nothing, as yet, guv.' Denise was warming to her new DCI already. 'Course, he could have done a Lord Lucan.'

'Car at Newhaven?' Hall outlined the case with her. 'Lying doggo with the help of his friends? New identity in El Salvador? Shacking up on a farm in Kenya? Except that Tubbs hasn't got any friends. Do me a favour, Denise; find out who vouched for him at Grimond's, over that girls-in-the-flat business. That may have been good old-fashioned charity, but it may be he's the only guy who knows where he is.'

'Mr Graham?'

'Yes.' The new Head of Tennyson was hanging his gown on a hook at the end of another long morning.

She flashed her warrant card. 'DS McGovern. Hampshire CID.'

'Sergeant.' He shook her hand. 'What can I do for you?'

'Jeremy Tubbs,' she said.

'You've found him?' Graham asked.

'No, sir. I wondered if you knew where he was.'

'Me?' Graham frowned. 'You'd do better asking over in Geography or in Kipling House.'

'It was you who stood by him six years ago, sir, over an incident involving schoolgirls.'

'Oh, good Lord,' Graham laughed. 'Do you know, I'd forgotten all about that. Yes, that was a little embarrassing at the time.'

'According to our information, you were a character witness for him.'

'That's right. I'd only just joined Grimond's. Jeremy sort of latched on to me. I don't think he had many friends.'

'Were you involved with these girls?'

'Involved...? Oh, no,' Graham laughed. 'There was no "involvement" as you put it, Denise; it was all totally innocent. You'd have to be a teacher to understand.'

'Would I?' she arched an eyebrow at him. He'd picked up her Christian name. Here was a man who read warrant cards with great care.

'Look,' he took her gently by the arm. 'Won't you join me for a spot of lunch? Mrs Oakes' cottage pie is to die for.'

'Are you sure I'd be welcome?' she asked,

suddenly rather flattered by this man with the intense eyes and the cool charm.

'You're with me,' he linked arms with her, patting her hand. 'Besides, talking of welcome, we've already got Peter Maxwell!' and he winked.

'Who ordered the cheese and pickle?' Steve Chapell wanted to know.

'That'll be me.' Pete Walters was waving a hand in the air, left ear cradling a phone and his face glued to a computer screen. Friday lunchtime at the Selborne Incident Room was the most cursory of culinary delights.

'Who's your money on, Jacquie?' DI Sandy Berman was well into a turkey salad baguette.

'Sir?'

'Look,' he smiled with a face full of lettuce. 'I told you, if we're going to "Sir" and "sergeant" each other all over the shop, we're not going to get very far, are we? It's Sandy.'

'Sandy,' she smiled, chasing the last of her pasta salad around the plastic tub perched on her knees. 'What are you talking about?'

There were sniggers all round. 'I'm often confused about that,' somebody shouted.

'The murder at Grimond's.' The DI waved a couple of fingers in the shouter's general direction.

'Murder? Or murders?' she asked.

Berman looked around at the others. 'The smart money here,' he confided, 'is that Pardoe topped himself while the balance of his mind – and indeed his balance – was disturbed. We're only looking for one killer here – whoever finished

290

off Tim Robinson.'

'DCI Hall and I have interviewed all the staff,' she said. 'Strictly speaking, no one has a cast-iron alibi for the night of his death. Wives who live in have told us their husbands were with them, but then they probably would, wouldn't they? I think we can rule out outsiders, though. Whoever killed Robinson must have known the place pretty well and must have hidden the murder weapon pretty effectively.'

'That's the oar?'

'Probably.'

'I still say we should drag the lake,' Steve Chapell said.

'Where?' Peter Walters was shouting, clicking his fingers to attract everybody's attention. 'Right. Got it. I owe you one, Jim, and I want to marry you and have your children – oh, by the way, love to Rita and the kids.' And he threw down the phone. 'Tubbs' car. Portchester.'

'Yes!' the team roared as one. They were on their feet, giving each other high fives and slapping each other's backs. A breakthrough at last.

Jacquie was less impressed. She alone stayed in her seat, part of the team, yet detached from it. She knew what Henry Hall's response would be. Since when did officers applaud a mistake? There was a car, but there was no driver. So where was Jeremy Tubbs?

The sun kissed the mellow stone of Henry Plantaganet's keep at Portchester, and crows flapped their raucous way from the tall cedars to the corbelled crevices. The curtain wall was amazingly geometric for a medieval castle guarding England's south coast, but that, as Peter Maxwell could have told anyone who asked, was because it was once a Roman fort and the Romans knew a right angle or two.

In the visitors' car park where Henry V had once marshalled his bowmen on their way to Barfleur, Harfleur and the immortal glory of St Crispin's Day, a little yellow MG sat motionless, neglected near the rustic fence as other vehicles came and went; an ice-cream van, dog walkers, castle explorers and people busting for a pee. For five hours, DS Steve Chapell and WPC Lynda Reader, who didn't usually get out much, sat in their unmarked car and watched the MG. By then, they'd both lost the will to live.

'Nothing,' Jacquie told Maxwell over the phone from Barcourt Lodge. 'They waited there 'til six, then jemmied the MG and gutted it.'

'Anything useful?'

'The usual crap people collect in their cars – crisp packets, parking tickets, supermarket receipts. Nothing to tell who owned the thing, never mind any hint of guilt. But it's Tubbs' car all right. It's in the pound at Portsmouth now. Forensics will take it apart in the morning. Apparently, heads are rolling in Pompey.'

'Whose?' Maxwell was sprawled on his narrow bed under the Tennyson shingle. 'Why?'

'Some poor anonymous bastard of a PC should've noticed it. The fact is, of course, it wasn't there.'

'Sorry?'

'Come on, Max. A yellow MG must be one of

the most easily spotted cars in the world. Routine patrols would pick it up. The PC swears it wasn't there at nine o'clock this morning; by eleven, it was.'

'So which way did Tubbsy run from there?'

'Chapell and his WPC searched the grounds of the castle, the pubs nearby, the waterfront.'

'Nothing?'

'You guessed it, darling heart,' she said. 'There's an awful lot of coastline around Portchester. Maybe the tide will wash him up.'

'Maybe he's in France.'

'They'll be checking the harbour first thing tomorrow.'

'Of course.' Maxwell was thinking aloud. 'It could all be a feint.'

'What?'

'Tubbsy abandons his car on the coast. What are we supposed to think?'

'He's drowned or shipped out.'

'Whereas?'

Jacquie had caught Maxwell's drift. 'He could have gone inland.'

'And now he's lost the car, he won't be so easy to find. A fat, balding Geography teacher is by no means as conspicuous as a yellow MG.'

'Tell me about it. We had six sightings before lunch yesterday – anywhere from Wilmslow to Pitlochry. You don't disappear if you're bland; you turn up all over the place.'

'"I think there be six Richmonds in the field",' Maxwell quoted. 'How were West's people?'

'Not bad, actually,' Jacquie sounded brighter than she had for days. 'Devoted to Henry as I am, we were getting into a bit of a rut at Grimond's.'

'Wonder how he's making out with DS McGovern?'

'I hope you mean that figuratively, you suggestive old stirrer.'

'Madame,' he purred. 'I have the wooden spoon to prove it. Get any vibes?'

'As to who our paedophile link is? No. Sandy Berman's the vice officer. Seems a pretty straight sort of bloke, friendly enough. Bit too matey, in a way. Steve Chapell's a bit intense, workaholic type. He'll burn out by thirty-five. Pete Walters keeps himself to himself a little, although he got the break – if that's what it was – with Tubbs' car. He's got a sense of humour. The others ... well, if we're assuming our man *is* a man.'

'You tell me,' Maxwell said. 'Do women get involved in paedophile rings?'

'It's been known,' Jacquie told him, 'but usually because they're inveigled into it by the man in their life.'

'*Folie a deux,*' Maxwell nodded.

'Absolutely. They're useful, though.'

'Useful?'

'Myra Hindley, Rose West. Useful for their bloke to pick up innocents. Who'd suspect a man with a woman in the car? Even so, there aren't many women in the team – they're not exactly DCI West's bag, if I may use a sexist pun.'

'Pun away, *anima divida mea.*'

'WPC Reader hasn't got the imagination for it – no offence. Mind you, Denise McGovern's a different kettle of fish.'

'You've met?'

'Ships in the night,' she said, 'but her reputation goes before her – and in every other direction.'

'Ah, a medal-hunter,' Maxwell mused, familiar with the obsessions of the late Sir Winston Churchill.

'And pushy with it, apparently. Sharp, though. And damned good at her job, by all accounts.'

'Not our link, then?'

There was a sudden knock on Maxwell's door, sharp, staccato.

'Darling, I have to go. My time's up. Sweet dreams, heart. Talk to you tomorrow,' and he heard her blow him a kiss.

'Mr Maxwell?' A straw-haired woman was standing on the landing in front of Maxwell's open door.

'Ms McGovern?'

'Denise,' she held out a bony hand. 'Do you know me?'

'I saw you at lunch,' he reminded her. 'You were with Tony Graham at the other end of High Table from me. What can I do for you?'

She looked along the lonely semi-dark of the corridor. 'Perhaps I could come in? I know it's a little late.'

'They'll have locked the gates,' Maxwell invited her inside. 'How many hours do you people put in?'

'I thought you knew all about that,' she smiled. 'Word is your partner is a copper.'

'My partner?' Maxwell beamed. 'No, I have a whist partner once in a blue moon and even more rarely a dancing partner when I can't find the escape route in a night club. But a partner?' he shook his head. 'No, I haven't got one of those.'

'I've been misinformed,' she smiled.

'Comes with the territory, doesn't it?' he asked her. 'Look,' he closed the door, 'would you like a truly awful cup of instant coffee?' Parker had come up trumps and the supplies had got through.

'I've actually been on the go since eight this morning. Right now, coffee would be fantastic.'

'You're working with Henry.' Maxwell rummaged in his cups. He knew he had a spoon somewhere.

'I understand you've done some of that. Smoke?' She thrust a ciggie at him.

'No, thanks,' he said. 'Along with work, I gave it up a long time ago.'

'You don't mind if I do? As I said, long day.'

'No, please.' He ferreted around for an ash-tray.

'So what's a comprehensive teacher from Leighford doing at a place like this?' Her face glowed briefly in the lighter flame.

'I bet you say that to all the suspects,' Maxwell drawled, swaying from side to side like an embarrassed hillbilly.

'Do you think that's what you are?' Denise drew forcefully on the cigarette. 'A suspect?'

'You tell me.' He waved a packet of sugar at her and she shook her head.

'Well,' she said, narrowing her eyes beyond the curling smoke, 'things started jumping, if that isn't too sick an observation, when you arrived. Has DCI Hall interviewed you?'

'I'm sure you know he hasn't.'

'No milk either, thanks.' Denise leaned back on both elbows on Maxwell's bed. 'Why is that, do you think?'

Maxwell paused in mid-pour. 'Why hasn't Henry interviewed me? I really don't know. You'd have to ask him.'

'I have,' Denise said. 'They call you Mad Max, don't they?'

'Only behind my back.' It was a perfect Mel Gibson.

'And you've been interviewed by DCI Hall before.'

He passed her the cup. 'Denise,' he sat down slowly in the chair opposite her. 'I hope you aren't implying any impropriety on Henry Hall's part. It's true that he and I have met professionally before, several times. He's a damned good copper. And he's straight as the Dardanelles.'

The historical allusion was lost on Denise McGovern; at school she'd opted for Business Studies instead. 'I'm not implying anything,' she shook her head, 'but DCI Hall did say you have something of a reputation, Mr Maxwell.'

'Did he now?'

'Let's see.' Denise sat upright, flicking her ciggie ash into her saucer and fixing the Head of Sixth Form with a stare that could have turned a lesser man to stone. 'You're a Cambridge graduate – Jesus College. You're an Historian. Been teaching since...'

'...before the flood,' Maxwell smiled.

'And one of your own sixth form was murdered a few years back. You've seemed to have a penchant for it ever since.'

'The only game in town?' Maxwell raised an eyebrow. 'Unlike you, I'm not paid to solve crimes,' he said. 'But if they happen on my doorstep – and that has, literally, happened before now by the way – I can't just walk away.'

'You're an amateur, Mr Maxwell,' Denise told him. 'You do incalculable harm. Here's an analogy you might understand. An archaeologist, right? A bloke trained to know about the buried past, post-holes, soil composition, pollen grains, Christ knows what. That's us. The law. The professionals. The experts. You, you're the metal detector anorak crashing about over our valuable evidence, destroying everything the rest of us are trying to get right. Murder isn't a game, Mr Maxwell. It's not a toy you can play with and throw away when you're bored.'

'So this isn't a social call, then?' Maxwell asked.

'Fucking right it's not,' she snarled. 'Where were you on the night William Pardoe died?'

'Here,' Maxwell told her. 'Or rather, there,' he pointed at the bed.

'Alone?'

'Home alone,' Maxwell confirmed, but it wasn't his best Macaulay Culkin.

'No alibi then?'

'None.'

'What about the night Timothy Robinson was killed?'

'Ditto,' Maxwell said. 'But then, that applies to a lot of other people at Grimond's, doesn't it? People sleeping alone in their beds. It's a sad, sad world, my masters.'

'Sure,' she conceded. 'Except that most of the

kids sleep together in dormitories, a lot of the staff are offsite and you have a reputation for getting involved in other people's sudden deaths.'

'Should I cancel my foreign holiday, then?' he asked her.

'What you should do, Mr Maxwell, is stop being so fucking flippant and consider your options. DCI Hall might think you're as white as the driven, but you and I don't go back aways. Tomorrow morning, I would like you to present yourself for an official interview in the Head's outer office. Would nine-thirty suit?'

'Wonderful,' Maxwell beamed. 'Should I have my solicitor present?'

She stubbed her cigarette out in the empty cup. 'Do you have one?'

'No,' he told her.

'Then the question, like you, is academic.' She passed him the cup. 'Thanks for the coffee. You have a good night's sleep now, y'hear?' And she slammed her way out as John Selwyn was beginning his nightly rounds, Ape and Splinter at his elbows.

'Everything all right, Mr Maxwell?' he popped his head round the man's still partially open door.

'Just a little run-in with the law, John,' Maxwell joined the Captain of Tennyson and his henchmen as Denise McGovern disappeared down the spiral stairs. 'Thank you for asking. What time tomorrow?'

'Kick-off's at two. It's good of you to stand in like this.'

'No problem. Now, you are going to be gentle

with me, aren't you?'

Ape and Splinter sniggered.

'Don't you worry, Mr Maxwell. Playing rugger's a bit like falling off a bike, isn't it?'

'What? You mean it hurts like hell? Yes, I suppose you're right.'

'Goodnight, Mr Maxwell,' the three chorused.

'Goodnight, gentlemen.'

Peter Maxwell locked his door. He'd taken to doing that since the death of Tim Robinson who was Andy Love. He shivered the curtains aside to watch Denise McGovern striding for the car park. She'd have to knock up Parker at the lodge and fight her way through the diehard rear-guard of the paparazzi still camped at the gates, still hungry for a story. She'd probably run over three or four of them on the way.

He punched out the number on his mobile. 'Hello, Count.' He was talking to the cat. 'Pick up if you're there, will you? Blast. Out on the tiles, eh? I've just had a visit from a horrid policewoman who really wasn't nice at all. In the meantime, they've found Tubbsy's car, but not him. And Jacquie's met some very nice people at the Incident Room. Your Master's playing rugby tomorrow, so this might be the last time you hear my voice. Give a message to Mrs B for me, will you, you old bastard? Tell her, haemorrhage and traction permitting, I shall be back at Columbine tomorrow night. Missing you already.' And he hung up.

It must have been nearly one-thirty when he heard it. It was a bell. Slow and solemn. And it only tolled three times. Even so, it woke him up and groggily, he made his way to the window. Below, in the silver moonlight of the quad, a uniformed detachment was making its way again, berets dark and backs ramrod straight as they carried the flag-draped coffin. There was no sound of their boots on the tarmac, no muffling of drums, just the ghastly, sad ritual of the slow march.

'Ask not to know,' he whispered in the shadows, 'for whom the bell tolls, Maxwell. It tolls for thee.'

Chapter Seventeen

'Here,' he thrust a small folded wad of notes into the boy's hand. 'That's for you, son.'

'Thanks, Dave.' The lad tilted his baseball cap back into position and clambered out into the night.

Dave watched him go, fastening his jeans belt as he dashed away across the car park. He rummaged in his glove compartment and hauled out the cassette recorder. 'Not bad,' he croaked into it. 'Uses the handle "Janet". Sixteen or so he claims. Seemed to like the porn. I'll probably use him again. Not sure he's your type, though.'

He flicked out the tape and slipped it into an envelope. Then he stuck a row of stamps on it in the dim light and hit the ignition. This wasn't his own patch and he moved warily. Didn't want to come to the notice of the law parked in their out-of-the-way places. He drove slowly, but not too slowly; with care, but not with paranoia. He knew the game. Too fast and they'll pull you over. Too slow, the same. And the stash of mags in the well of the back seat would take too much explaining.

The black excrescence of the Tricorn Centre loomed to his right as he waited patiently for the lights. A white patrol car was prowling the roundabout and tucked in neatly and noiselessly behind him. There shouldn't be any trouble. He knew his rear brake lights were in order and his

302

tax disc in date. He waited for the emerald flash before cruising forward, keeping at a steady twenty nine miles an hour.

He was already out on the M275 and purring north when the patrol car swung off to the left on the brave bend that led to Portchester, Henry Plantagenet's castle black against the purple of the night sky. He pushed his foot to the floor and drove for home.

'I'm up before the beak this morning,' Peter Maxwell was tucking into his scrambled egg.

'DCI Hall?' Tony Graham asked.

'Worse. His new henchwoman, Gauleiter Mc-Govern.'

'Tut, tut,' Michael Helmseley scolded him over his full English. 'What a chauvinist remark.'

'I had the delightful DS Carpenter,' Graham smiled. 'Oh, not in the pejorative sense, of course.'

It was Saturday and Grimond's seemed more relaxed than it had for days. Spring was springing in the grounds outside, the daffodils nearly over and the buds bursting on the limes. Before too long, it would be the cricket season and David Gallow would come into his own again, leather on willow on a lazy Sunday afternoon.

'Oh, by the way,' Graham was helping himself to more coffee, 'I passed Richard Ames on the way up to hall this morning. How do you feel about playing Second Row, he asked me to ask you?'

'Did he now?' Maxwell swallowed hard. 'Where will you be, Tony?'

'Fly half, as usual.'

303

Maxwell nodded. 'Who's hooker?'

And both men glanced up at Cassandra James who was sidling past, as if on cue. They both shook their heads and looked away, slightly ashamed of themselves.

'Anybody hear the bell last night?' Maxwell asked, happy to change the subject.

'Bell?' Helmseley repeated.

'Hmm,' Maxwell munched. 'The school bell. About one, half-past.'

'What, in the early hours, you mean?'

'Yes. Or perhaps you saw the burial detail?'

'Max,' Graham frowned. 'I've heard of the odd hallucination after a game of rugger – concussion, that sort of thing. But never before. Perhaps you'd better have a little lie down.'

'Yes,' Maxwell smiled. 'Perhaps I should.'

'Please state your name for the record.' The tape was whirring.

'Peter Maxwell.'

'Address?' Denise McGovern was asking.

'Thirty-eight, Columbine Avenue, Leighford, West Sussex.'

'Interview in the presence of DCI Henry Hall and DS Denise McGovern, Saturday, 4 April.'

The tape was still whirring. 'Why are you here at Grimond's, Mr Maxwell?' It was Hall posing the question now.

'An exchange of sorts,' the Head of Sixth Form told him. 'This school and mine.'

'And you've been here since...?'

'Two weeks tomorrow.'

'Did you know the deceased, William Pardoe?'

'I spoke to him, yes. I'd only been here for a day and a half when they found his body.'

'Did you form any opinion of him?' It would not have been allowed in a court of law, but police interviews, Maxwell knew, had different parameters.

'He seemed a decent sort,' Maxwell shrugged.

'Apart from the porn addiction, you mean?' Denise McGovern chipped in for the first time.

'I didn't know about that,' Maxwell reminded her. 'Still don't.'

'Still don't?' Denise frowned. 'You were not aware that Pardoe regularly received pornographic material in the post?'

'I regularly receive offers from Saga Holidays,' Maxwell said, leaning back in his chair. 'That doesn't mean I actually go on them.'

'Did you know Tim Robinson?' Hall moved the matter on. He knew that Mad Max could fence with this woman all day.

'No,' Maxwell looked levelly at him, each knowing what the other knew. 'No, I didn't know Tim Robinson at all.'

'You didn't talk to him?' Denise followed up.

'Briefly,' Maxwell nodded. 'During a practice fencing bout in the gym.'

'How did *he* strike you?' Denise took a leaf from her new boss's book.

'Not much of a fencer,' Maxwell confessed.

'Sorry?'

'He mixed up his foil strokes and his sabre cuts.'

'Hush my puppies.' Denise was shaking her head.

'You asked,' Maxwell shrugged.

'Thank you, Mr Maxwell,' Hall said. 'Interview terminated at nine-thirty-eight.' And he switched off the tape.

There was a pause. 'Is that it?' Denise was only just reaching for her ciggies, preparing for quite a session.

'For now,' Hall turned to her for the first time.

'Mr Maxwell,' Denise shot forward in her chair, her cigarette hand poised over the ash-tray, ignoring the DCI's decision, ignoring the switched off machine. 'When do you plan to leave Grimond's?'

'Tonight,' he told her. 'Pretty soon after the match.'

'Do you not find it odd,' she leaned back, 'that *two* deaths should have occurred in the very twelve days you've been here?'

'Extraordinary,' Maxwell agreed. 'I've always thought somebody should do some serious research into synchronicity, serendipity, call it what you will. Although there's probably a Chair of it in some South-Western American University.'

'Thank you, Mr Maxwell.' Hall slid back his chair and stood up. 'That's all. Enjoy your game this afternoon.'

'Thank you, Mr Hall.' Maxwell bowed low while he still could and winked at Denise, before exiting left, out into the echoing main corridor of old Jedediah Grimond's house.

'That bastard's insufferable,' the DS growled, flicking ash all over George Sheffield's carpet, too furious to watch him go.

'Isn't he, though?' Hall was changing tapes.

'But take a tip from me, Denise. Don't go head to head with men like Peter Maxwell. He'll have you every time.'

No one at Grimond's had seen Peter Maxwell's knees before. Nor anyone at Leighford. It had been quite a time since Peter Maxwell had. When other foolhardy colleagues had had their legs waxed for charity some years ago, Maxwell had stumped up a small fortune *not* to roll his trousers up. They were nevertheless on display at a little before two o'clock by the sun on the First Fifteen pitch. Quite a crowd had gathered, stomping and whistling along the touch lines and on the make-shift terraces on the slopes that led up to the hallowed turf of the First Eleven Square and Jedediah Grimond's great house beyond.

Maxwell saw George Sheffield at his French windows, looking at the field of battle below him. The Headmaster would normally have been present at this annual event, presenting a cup at the end. But George Sheffield, it had to be said, was not the man he used to be. He felt alone, vulnerable, the precursors of full-blown paranoia. Scarves flashed everywhere on the field and the impromptu cheerleaders of Junior Austen were urging on the objects of their pubescent desires in the First Fifteen back line. Why was it, Maxwell wondered again, as he had as a boy, that girls never fancied the pack? Was it their knuckles dragging on the ground, the shaking of the earth when they moved, or the rather unflattering scrum caps half of them wore these days?

A rather surreal episode had transpired in the

changing rooms when referee Richard Ames had tried to force Maxwell to wear a gum shield. They didn't have them in Maxwell's day, when men's shorts reached their knees and Billy Webb-Ellis didn't know the rules. 'Thank you, no, Richard. I'll stick to my jock-strap.' And before he felt the turf springing beneath his studs, that's exactly what Maxwell was doing.

John Selwyn, scrum half and First Fifteen Captain, won the toss and David Gallow marshalled his team. It was the closest the staff at Grimond's would ever come to a group hug. They huddled in a tight circle.

'Counting on you, Jeff,' Gallow nodded solemnly to one of the Science staff. 'Remember, it's only thirty minutes each way. And watch for the offside rule. Ready, Tony?'

'As I'll ever be,' Graham said.

'How's your boot, Eric?'

Eric glanced down. 'I'll let you know,' he grinned.

Across the turf, the First Fifteen were doing the same. Selwyn, Ape, Splinter, other hearties Maxwell had met in the days that had gone, were psyching themselves up for the fray.

'Are you ready, staff?' Richard Ames had his whistle in his left hand, his right hand in the air.

The Fifteen's full back had his ball in his hand and the crowd set up a roar as his boot collided with it and it sailed high over upward-looking staff heads. There was a thud as it was taken cleanly by Number Twelve and the whole line moved forward. John Selwyn was quicker however and his pack charged the staff. Maxwell had forgotten the pace of all this. He was the wrong side of fifty, hell, the wrong side of fifteen large, fit young men, all of them hurtling for him. His lungs felt like lead and already he couldn't feel his feet.

He saw David Gallow flash across him, sliding the ball into his hands. Maxwell grabbed it instinctively, dummying to one side and swerving round their Number Eight. Number Two caught him full in the ribs and he twisted free before thudding into Grimond's mud.

'Get off it, staff!' he heard Ames roar and tried to roll clear, but the weight of bodies held him down. The whistle blasted. 'Scrum down,' Ames shouted. 'Fifteen ball.' And as the ref passed the dazed Head of Sixth, Maxwell heard him mutter, 'You've got to get off it, Max.'

'That's another new rule since 1823,' the Second Row wheezed, his vision reeling.

An arm hooked around his waist and Ronald from Geography had him fast. Bugger, Maxwell groaned internally as his head clamped between the buttocks of the Hooker and the Tight Head Prop. He could see the chewed Grimond's turf looking up at him, soon to be strewn, no doubt, with blood and teeth. He heard the wheezing of the less-than-fit pack all around him and felt his ears crush against somebody's loins. Much more of this and he'd be sporting cauliflowers.

'Engage,' Ames roared and the packs collided, with a shock of muscle and sinew, shoulder thudding into ham and teeth grinding. 'Shit a brick!' somebody hissed and Maxwell felt his back jack-knife. The ball was loose, rolling like

309

Richard Crookback's crown under the scudding boots on the field. Their Hooker had it, the pack swaying forward to carry the staff back and long before the front row collapsed, the ball was in Selwyn's capable hands and the back line were flying.

Maxwell rolled away from the wreck of the scrum as the attack hurtled downfield. There were shouts from the Fifteen.

'Here, Ape. On your left.'

'Miss him out, John.'

'Splinter. Go. Go. Splinter. Go.'

But Splinter had hit the brick wall that was the Head of Physics and he went down as the Fifteen mauled over him and the ball was free again.

Boots and hands were everywhere, bodies sprawling in the melee.

'Keep away, Fifteen,' Ames roared. 'Don't go in over the top.'

To Maxwell, the whole thing was over the top. The Fifteen did this sort of thing before breakfast and at least twice a week and they did it with legs and lungs that were new and egos that, while bruised, could bounce back.

'Close in there, Max,' Gallow was bellowing. 'Shut them down.'

It was the last thing Peter Maxwell heard for a while as he tackled John Selwyn. An articulated vehicle had careered across the pitch and slammed into his head, which exploded with a cacophony of echoing thuds, slowly dying away. Then the world was black and slimy and silent.

Something was twirling above his head, like those

fans in the films noirs of the '50s where Akim Tamiroff or Peter Lorre sat sweating in downtown Tunisia, or was it Mexico? Maxwell tried to focus, feeling the cold iron frame under his left hand. He was in an off-white room and a geisha was bending over him, green tea in one hand and his decapitated head in the other.

'Mr Maxwell, how are you feeling?'

'That depends,' Maxwell hoped he said – he couldn't be sure.

'You've had a nasty knock.'

'Christ, Max, you gave us a turn.' That was a voice Maxwell recognized. A second face swum into his vision. It was Richard Ames, still in his black reffing kit, whistle dangling around his neck.

'Don't tell me I didn't roll away quickly enough again,' Maxwell moaned.

'You didn't roll at all,' Ames told him. 'That's what was so bloody worrying. Poleaxed. It was an illegal move, of course. I should have stopped the match there and then. Rest assured the Fifteen had the wigging of their young lives.'

'I thought so,' Maxwell tried to nod. 'All of them hit me, right?'

Ames laughed. 'I'm sure it felt that way. No, actually, it was only three of them, but that was enough. Selwyn, Splinter and Ape. They're grounded.'

'That is just too apposite. Hit by an ape and something,' he winced, 'feels distinctly splintered.'

'There's no excuse for that kind of tackle. They could have killed you. We've had enough sudden deaths at Grimond's to last us all a lifetime.'

'Would you like some tea, Mr Maxwell?'

'Have we met?' Maxwell was still trying to focus on the two geishas in white.

'I am Suki Lee, the school matron.'

'Delighted,' Maxwell risked a smile. 'Is that Oolong Lapsang?'

'Brooke Bond,' the Matron said. 'Sorry.'

She and Ames helped the man sit up and waited until his head stopped spinning. Even so, the Ames and Lee twins were still blurring at the end of a long, dark tunnel. 'I'm afraid I wasn't much use out there. What was the final score?'

'Thirty-four, eighteen to the First Fifteen. And don't feel badly about it. Tony Graham's game was off and Eric Bolsover fluffed virtually every line out.'

'Did you have any subs to replace me?'

'Max, you're irreplaceable.' The Graham Twins had arrived, leaning over him, fussing. 'Jesus, that's a bruise and a half.'

'You've arranged for the official apology from your House, Tony?' Ames said.

'I'm sure there was no malice in it, Richard,' Graham said. 'I'm just glad to see Max is okay. And I'll see you afterwards about your less-than-flattering comments on my game, by the way.'

'No malice, my arse. I wouldn't blame Max if he sued.' Ames scowled at the Housemaster, 'I don't think you can laugh this one off, Tony.'

'No, no,' Maxwell chuckled. 'It's nothing to Chillianwallah.' But the historical allusion was lost on the Sports Master and the linguist. 'No worse than fighting my way through the lunch queue at dear old Leighford High. Talking of which, that's where I must be the day after tomorrow ... er ... it is still Saturday?' he tried to focus out of the San's windows. It was getting dark.

'Max, I'm not sure you should travel,' Ames was saying, looking into his eyes. 'Suki, what do you think?'

Matron held up one finger. 'Follow this,' she said to the English patient. It hurt like hell, but Maxwell rolled his eyes left and right, in what he hoped was vaguely the right direction.

'You've had a nasty blow to your head, Mr Maxwell,' she said. 'And I suspect you've got concussion. You were out for nearly ten minutes.'

'It seemed longer.'

'That was the first time,' she plumped up his pillows. 'You ought to go to X-ray.'

'I will.' Maxwell kicked one leg free of the covers in an attempt to find the floor. 'Just as soon as I go home. Tony, I couldn't ask you to help me to my room, could I? I've got some packing to do.'

Nobody was happy for Peter Maxwell to go, least of all Peter Maxwell; although George Sheffield took his leave only peremptorily and of Maggie Shaunessy there was no sign. As the taxi took off along the driveway towards the gates of Grimond's, he knew he was leaving two men dead behind him and his own blood on the turf of the First Fifteen pitch. In the end, he was leaving the place with a whimper rather than the bang he'd promised himself.

The knot of paparazzi had dwindled to a mere three, the rump of the Fourth Estate huddled around a makeshift brazier in the still chill of the spring night, like diehard strikers whose comrades have all gone back to work. One of them peered in through the taxi window, but didn't recognize him for the grim reaper who had nipped so adroitly over the wall the day before yesterday. Clearly, he hadn't seen Matron's bandage under Maxwell's hat or he'd have leapt for his laptop with the headline 'Third Teacher Murdered at Grimond's.'

Mercifully, the driver wasn't a talker and Maxwell was fast asleep long before the car was swinging around the one-way system that skirted Petersfield. And he certainly didn't see the dark car cruising the back doubles around the bus station where the lads sat laughing with their lagers.

Not until Columbine did he jolt awake and the cab driver helped him in with his suitcase. He locked the door, stumbling over the mail that had hit the mat that morning, ignoring Mrs B's neat stack of the rest. His answerphone was flashing green to his right, but it flashed in vain and he somehow climbed the stairs. One floor level was his limit however and he dumped his hat and coat on his way to the settee, easing himself down and wrapping himself in his armchair throw.

Metternich padded silently down the open-plan stairs from Maxwell's inner sanctum, the War Office where his beloved Light Brigade pawed the plastic ground, eager for the Balaclava fray. He raised his exquisite feline head, whiskers and eyebrows twitching, scenting the wind. Just as he thought, nodding at the heap on the settee; pissed again.

An odd thing happened to Peter Maxwell on Sunday. He didn't wake up at all.

Monday. The great adventure was over. Maxwell knew that once he was back at Leighford High, his time at Grimond's would seem a dream, like the shooting of JR in *Dallas* all those years ago. Or was it Bobby? Either the knock he'd taken had wiped his memory cells completely or *Dallas* was longer ago than Maxwell cared to admit.

His mouth felt like the bottom of a budgie's cage and his head as though a vice was squeezing it. He couldn't face breakfast and thought he might drown in a bath, so he risked a shower and wished he hadn't. He unwrapped the bandage that Suki Lee had lovingly wound round his temples and winced as the water stung the jagged gash that followed his hairline. This was odd. He'd lost count of the games he'd played at school and university, but he'd never known a wound like this. He even neglected to rinse his important little places in his eagerness to see for himself the result of sending a man to play a boy's game.

His face looked green in the bathroom mirror and there was a still-bloody slice running dramatically from his hair to his eyebrow, swollen and bruised. 'Here's looking at you, kid.' At least his Bogart hadn't lost its edge.

As if still in a dream, he heard the door bell. Shit. He checked his watch on the bathroom shelf. That would be the postman needing his signature. He wasn't sure whether he was up to that – the man may have to settle for his mark this morning. He lifted down the towelling robe that was made of lead and staggered down the stairs. The post lay scattered on the mat, but there was a figure beyond the frosted glass of his front door that he recognized. And it wasn't the postman.

'Max, for fuck's sake!' and Jacquie's arms, strong and frightened were around his neck.

'Well,' he said softly, trying to close the door and hold on to her at the same time. 'Now all Columbine knows I'm back. Thanks, heart of darkness.'

She stood back, wincing along with him as she ran her fingertips so gently over his forehead. 'Jesus, you silly, silly man,' she was saying, the tears brimming from those clear, grey eyes. 'What possessed you to play in that stupid, stupid match?'

'It's a man thing, Woman Policeman,' he said and let her help him back upstairs. 'Liniment and jock straps. It's what made the public school system great.'

'You didn't check your messages.' She was pointing back at the flashing lights. 'They're probably all from me.'

'Sorry,' he managed. 'The weekend's been something of a blur, I'm afraid.'

She got him into the lounge and sat him down, turning off the table lamp and tucking his feet up on the pouffé. 'When I couldn't get a reply on your mobile, I rang Henry Hall. He said you'd been hurt, knocked out. By the time I got to Grimond's, you'd gone. I'd have come yesterday, but...'

And he held his finger to her lips. 'But you're up to your eyes in a murder enquiry,' he said softly. 'This is only a tap on the head, to paraphrase the old joke. You shouldn't be here, darling, you should be in Selborne. Anything broken yet?'

'I should be asking you the same question,' she fussed. 'Let me get you to bed.'

'I'm not sure I'm up to that,' he whispered, glancing down to his lap. 'Could be a soft tissue fracture. Besides,' he sat up, 'what day is it?'

'Monday.'

'Precisely. Let me see ... ah, how soon they forget. Twelve Bee on the Ulster Question, followed by Seven Eff Twenty Eight on Walking and Chewing Gum.'

'Max, you can't seriously be intending to go to work?'

'Got it in one, WP. I can see why you made sergeant.'

'I forbid it,' she shouted, immediately wishing she hadn't.

His eyes widened as he struggled to his feet. 'Saddle White Surrey for the field today,' he swung himself round as best he could, giving her his second-best Olivier.

'No, no,' she was shaking her head. 'No bike. You leave Surrey in the shed. If you insist on being daft, I'm taking you in.'

'Ah, ever the policeman,' he smiled. 'And all right, I accept. I think I've got a loose chain on old Surrey anyway, otherwise I wouldn't be giving in so easily. Help me upstairs, heart and while I struggle into my underpants, tell me the news.'

She tucked her arm under his and they made for the bedroom. She knew her Mad Max; how pointless argument was at moments like this. If she pushed it, he'd be telling her how Leighford High had never had to do without him for so long and that it must be on the point of collapse by now.

'Let it go, Max,' she said, propping him by the bed and hunting for a shirt. 'It's over now.'

'Over – and you'll excuse my French – my arse,' he growled. 'I had to walk away, Woman Policeman. There were two men dead at Grimond's and I walked away.'

'I suspect,' she put him right, 'you had to be carried. How on earth did you get that wound on your head?'

'Selwyn, Ape and Splinter,' he told her. 'The rough equivalent of an artic.'

'Do you remember it?' She was sitting by him on the bed now, looking closely at his head.

'Not exactly. It was all a bit of a blur, as I said.'

'And this,' she tweaked the jagged wound and Maxwell saw stars.

'Jesus Christ!' He doubled up.

'I'm sorry, darling.' She looked as pained as he did. 'It may have been an artic that hit you, but it was an artic carrying a pencil.'

He looked down at the piece of broken graphite in the palm of her hand.

'An inch or two to the right and you'd have lost an eye. Is that how Grimond's win all their matches?'

'Maybe,' he said, recovering from the pain through a mist of tears. 'I wish we could ask Tim

Robinson. How did West's team react to that by the way? The undercover man?'

'I haven't told them,' Jacquie said. 'Hall insisted that I didn't. I may be on loan to West, but I'm not an open book. If West wants to know that, he'll have to ask Hall himself. I'm not doing it. Oh, Max,' she put an arm around his neck. 'Won't you please reconsider this? Going to Leighford is madness.'

'Ah,' he smiled. 'If only somebody had said that to me twenty-three years ago. It is, I fear, too late now. Come on,' and he staggered to his feet. 'Last one in Legs Diamond's office gets 'em in.'

Chapter Eighteen

'Good God!' Dierdre Lessing, Senior Mistress at Leighford High, was staring out of the staff room window at the apparition inching its way across the car park. 'Is that Peter Maxwell?' It was a Monday morning in late spring and the endless round of life in a comprehensive school some-where on the south coast was about to be disturbed.

Ben Holton, the Head of Science, was just col-lecting a much-appreciated lesson-cover slip from his pigeon hole. 'Good God, yes. Stroke, d'you think? He's a funny age.' Ben Holton had known Peter Maxwell, as had they all, for years. The Head of Science had had hair when they'd first met. Now it was merely a monkish fringe above a perpetually furrowed forehead.

'Funny colour, too.' Paul Nicolson, the Head of Drama had joined the others. Still reeling from the partial success of his Macbeth he now faced the grim reality of the Practical Drama Season. 'Where's he been?'

Dierdre turned away. 'Poncing about at some private school or other. One of Mr Diamond's less than sensible suggestions.' It was an un-usually disloyal remark from Dierdre Lessing.

'That's right,' Nicolson clicked his fingers. 'It was in the papers. Grimond's in Hampshire. They've had a couple of suspicious deaths, among the staff, I mean. Makes Leighford look quite normal. Didn't you read about it?'

'I saw it on the News,' Holton said, his only reading matter being *The New Scientist*. 'Why am I filling in a French lesson *again*, pray?'

Dierdre patted him on the shoulder. 'No problem for a multi-tasker like you, Ben,' she said. 'Maxwell did it.'

'Did what?' Nicolson asked, checking the mail that had arrived that morning.

'The suspicious deaths. They'll turn out to be murder and Maxwell's the culprit.'

'Right.' Nicolson nodded, well aware of the Senior Mistress' view of the Head of Sixth Form.

She gave him her iciest stare. 'Just wishful thinking,' she purred.

On the tarmac below them, Maxwell made it to the front door and stood there for a moment, stock still. He'd just climbed six steps and it felt like the Matterhorn.

'You all right, Mr Maxwell?'

The Head of Sixth Form turned to his inquisitor, a pretty, blonde GNVQ student in Year 12. 'I am, Ellen,' he smiled, 'and thank you for asking. Just getting used to the smell of the old place again. How was it for you?'

Ellen had never really known what Peter Maxwell was talking about, even before he became her Year Head and was just her History teacher. But that was because he was Mad Max. He did look a funny colour, though. Maxwell waved to her as he passed on and made it to the mezzanine floor, too and to his office. Nothing seemed out of place. Still the same chaos of paperwork, the waiting piles of marking, the unread memos from the Senior Management Team, that spider's web from the Cretaceous period that Mrs B. his cleaner, seemed to find invisible.

Helen Maitland, known to generations of sixth formers as 'The Fridge' on account of her white bulk, looked horrified when she clapped eyes on him. But then, that was her usual reaction, whether it be to the electricity bill or Year Ten's summer exam results.

'I was going to ask you how it all went, Max,' she said, patting his tweedy shoulder. 'Now, I don't think I will.'

'This little thing?' he pointed vaguely in the direction of his head, 'Why it ain't nuthin' at all, honey-chile. Just the result of banging my head against the bastions of privilege.'

'Huh, huh,' she smiled, nodding patronizingly. 'I'll buy that. Sit you down. What've you got first?'

'Year Twelve.'

'Wait here. I'll get you some coffee.'

He sank gratefully into the low, soft chair in the corner of her office, the one next to his. He heard the bell, the damned one without mercy, clapping electronically in his ears and away down the corridors of power. He was vaguely aware of kids clattering past in ones and twos, back packs and carrier bags in their hands, but mostly the latter, on the grounds that Tesco was cheaper than Nike. He picked up their usual Monday morning conversation.

'What about *EastEnders*, then, eh?'

'That Nicholson's a real wanker. I hate him.'

And comments like that even a concussed Maxwell couldn't let go. He swung upright, leaning out of Helen's doorframe with difficulty. 'Not as much as he hates you, Morgan, you freak.'

Morgan stopped in his tracks. 'Oh, hi, Mr Maxwell. Didn't see you there, sir.'

'Clearly,' Maxwell agreed and was grateful to sit down again, young Morgan an altogether more careful lad from now on.

Maxwell didn't know how long he waited there. He only knew he should be up to his elbows in Sir Edward Carson and Ulster by now and he was still sitting. Year Twelve would be gibbering. They'd had supply teachers for a fortnight, that strange band of unaccountables, the hand-holders and the breach-holders who daily patched up the crumbling edifice that was British education. Time they had some real teaching.

'No, you don't.' It was Sylvia Matthews, the school nurse, holding him down in his chair, very gently with a single finger. 'Good God, man.'

Maxwell saw Helen Maitland at Matron's elbow. 'Traitor!' he hissed, 'I thought you were an unconscionably long time making coffee.'

'That needs stitches, Max,' Sylvia was fussing. 'I'm taking you to Casualty.'

'I can't bear the soaps,' he muttered, 'you know that. But perhaps – just perhaps, mark you ... a day at the chalk-face is a bit much at this moment. Call me a cab, Nursie and I'll find somewhere to sleep it off.'

'Cab be buggered,' Sylvia said. 'Helen, tell Reception, will you? I'm taking Max home. Christ, you didn't cycle here, did you? Tell me you didn't.'

'No, I didn't,' he said. 'Jacquie dropped me.'

'And if I know her,' Sylvia was bundling the Great Man up and out of Helen's office, 'that wasn't her idea either. Come on.'

'Can I at least check my mail first? Pension plans, begging letters from Lord Puttnam and Estelle Morris – none of these will be there, but there's bound to be a load of crap from the NUT and exams boards various.'

'Here it is.' Helen Maitland had read her boss's mind and stuffed it all into a folder under his left arm.

'Ah, what would I do without you ladies?' He tried to put an arm around them both, but only succeeded in dropping his folder.

'Get him out of here, Sylvia,' Helen sighed. 'Max, for God's sake take care of yourself. How *did* you do it, by the way?'

'I stuck my nose in,' Maxwell told her, patting the side of it gently. 'Somewhere it wasn't wanted.'

Helen watched him go, sighing. 'Nothing new there, then.'

Dierdre Lessing was still at the staff room window when she saw Maxwell and Sylvia hobbling out to her car. 'Ten minutes,' she checked her watch. 'That's a record, even for Maxwell. Perhaps he left the iron on. Why that woman wastes her time on him, I have no idea.'

'That's not very fair,' Ben Holton said, still rummaging through his Science correspondence. 'Max is a cornerstone of this place.'

She looked at him witheringly. 'Should you still be here? I thought you had a French cover.'

It wasn't until Maxwell was sprawled on his settee that he bothered to check the folder Helen Maitland had given him. He'd only left his lounge an hour ago and it seemed like years. He'd toyed with getting back to his creation of Trumpeter Perkins of the 11th Hussars, still waiting, half-assembled, in his attic, but the thought of focussing on minutiae with a head like his wasn't really likely to happen. So, feeling guilty as he always did when he wasn't chipping away at his own chalk face, he began rummaging in the post.

'Jesus!' he whistled through his teeth and reached for his cordless, punching out the only number sequence he'd ever managed to commit to memory, except of course every date known to man.

'Jacquie?' he heard her voice. 'Can we talk?'

'Not now, Max,' she whispered. 'Are you all right?'

'Yes, yes, I'm fine. Helen and Sylvia insisted I took the rest of the day off.'

'Good. Talk later.' And she'd gone.

Shit. That wasn't what he'd hoped for at all. He'd hoped to discuss the plain white envelope that was lying on his lap, the one he'd just torn open, the one with the Petersfield postmark. He'd hoped to discuss the Swedish porn import that had fallen out of it and the note appended to it that read 'We know all about you, Maxwell.' In the event, he'd have to go it alone.

He staggered back into his shoes and got himself gingerly down the stairs again. There was no doubt about it, a town house was not the most sensible proposition for a man who saw double. He knew he'd just negotiated only fourteen stairs, but he could have sworn there were twenty-eight. He was still fumbling for his Barbour in the hall when he realized his answerphone was flashing again. He remembered Jacquie deleting all her messages before they set off for school, so this was something else, probably that officious bastard Bernard Ryan, First Deputy, demanding Maxwell send in some work.

'Mr Maxwell? This is John Selwyn of Grimond's. Mr Graham gave me your number. I hope you don't mind me ringing you at home like this and I hope you're not feeling too rough after the match. We'd like to invite you to a debate, tonight if you can. Start at eight o'clock, after prep, in Tennyson. We hope you can be there. You're our guest of honour. Ciao!'

'Well, what a coincidence, John,' Maxwell murmured. 'I was just on my way to see you too.'

The cab took him north-west again, along wet lunchtime roads, the tyres hissing on the tarmac. He was awake this time, his head still throbbing, but his brain fully operational. And he had some questions to ask. He had some ghosts to lay.

'That's it, sir,' Denise McGovern said. 'The last one. Now it's the main school.'

Henry Hall was sitting in George Sheffield's chair in George Sheffield's outer office. He had hours of taped interviews, thousands of words. But nothing concrete. Nothing to tell him who pushed Bill Pardoe off a roof or caved in Tim

Robinson's skull. Nothing about a paedophile ring. Just nothing.

'Now that you've seen the staff, where are we on all this?'

'I wish I knew,' Hall said, tapping his teeth with his pencil. 'I...' But he never finished his sentence. There was a knock at the door. 'Come in.'

'I'm sorry, sir,' Parker, the school steward, stood there. 'But, might I have a word?'

'Of course,' Hall ushered the man to a chair. 'It's Mr Parker, isn't it?'

'That's right, sir.' Hall and Jacquie had interviewed the man days ago, along with his wife, Mrs Oakes and her kitchen staff and the groundsmen. Hall had the impression that all the domestics were as tight-lipped as buggery. They were Grimond's through and through and they weren't talking to the law. Parker sat down, awkwardly, uncomfortable with senior police officers he considered his betters. 'We spoke last Tuesday, if I remember right.'

'What can I do for you, Mr Parker?'

'Well, sir, one of my jobs is to sort out the stationery and get it out to the Departments, you know.'

Hall nodded. Denise McGovern was watching the steward intently.

'Well, we had a new consignment of envelopes in on Saturday. We've got our own crested paper, of course, but the envelopes are plain.'

'And?' Hall wasn't following.

'Well, I took a load out to replace the old ones that had nearly run out.'

'Could you get to the point, Mr Parker?' Hall

asked. His case would be two weeks old tomorrow and he was treading water.

'Well, when I checked the old stock, sir, in that department where I went, I noticed, well ... couldn't help noticing, really, the old stock, sir, it was the same as ... just the same as the envelopes that used to come for Mr Pardoe, sir.'

Denise McGovern sat up, but Henry Hall's hand was in the air, waving gently, keeping her in her seat.

'These would be the packages that arrived for him, the ones that came ... what, once a week?'

'About that, sir,' Parker nodded. 'But it wasn't that regular.'

'And which department was this?' Hall asked. 'Where you found the old envelopes?'

'Well, it wasn't exactly a department, sir. It was a House. Austen House.'

The rump of the paparazzi left the wrought iron gates of Grimond's that Monday morning. They'd been moved on by the police, not because they were beginning to resemble a miniature gypsy encampment and give off noisome odours but because DCI West wanted a word. One by one he put them through their paces in his inner office at Selborne, watching them as they strained their story-hungry necks to catch a glimpse of something, *anything* flapping on the display boards.

'Ghouls,' he said to Martin Skinner, lighting up his umpteenth ciggie that morning. 'That's what you people are.'

'Doesn't sound like you want my co-operation after all,' the hack said, getting up to go. He was the last of the four to be seen and the most forthcoming.

'All right,' West cracked his mirthless smile and shook loose another ciggie from the pack, pointing it in the man's direction. 'Let's stop pussyfooting around. You're a freelance, Mark...'

'Martin.'

'Martin. And you've got to make a buck, just like the rest of us. You don't mind if my detective sergeant takes the odd note?'

Skinner glanced across to where Jacquie Carpenter sat, one knee hooked over the other. The view was fine from where he sat and he shook his head. 'As odd as you like,' he said.

'You were in the school grounds?' West watched the man's face light up as he flicked his lighter for the cigarette.

'Now then,' Skinner inhaled deeply and sat back, his smile wreathed in smoke, 'that would be telling, wouldn't it?'

Mark West had worked with slime like Skinner before. They wanted it all, all the dirt, all the gut-wrenching horror of a murder enquiry details, but they didn't want to give much back.

West drew on his own fag and carefully placed the lighter on its end among his copious paperwork. 'We have ways of fudging these things,' he said. 'Depending on the nature of your evidence.'

Skinner looked at Jacquie who had yet to put pen to paper. Sneaking into Grimond's grounds to get a story was one thing. Obtaining potential trial evidence illegally was something else. 'I will get an exclusive, won't I?'

'Do bears shit in the woods?' West asked him, but the man was freelance so the answer might take a little longer.

'There's something ... uncanny going on at that school,' Skinner told him.

'Uncanny?' West frowned, spitting a sliver of tobacco out from between his teeth. 'That's an old-fashioned word you don't hear much these days. Do you, Jacquie?'

His hired DS raised both eyebrows at Skinner, waiting.

'Perhaps you could be a little more explicit?' West hoped.

'All right. Incantations. Spells. Surreal, really. Like a bad B feature. Sub-Hammer, you know?'

Jacquie knew that Peter Maxwell would.

West sighed. 'I'm going to have to ask you for some sort of chapter and verse, I'm afraid, Mr Skinner.'

'All right.' The hack leaned back, enjoying centre stage. 'Thirteen nights ago. Tuesday night to be exact, I'd drawn the short straw and was on duty. You know, we've got a little hut thing down the road from the gates? Well, I was on the midnight to eight haul; wee small hours, you know.'

'That was the night after Pardoe's body was found,' Jacquie said.

'And?' West ignored her. He was still resting his elbows on his desk, holding his ciggie inches from his face, watching his man through narrowed eyes and a haze of smoke.

'I went over the wall, you might say. Oh, yeah, we had a gentleman's agreement with Dr Sheffield, what with him being a gentleman and us being gentlemen of the press and all, but hey, this is the twenty-first century for fuck's sake. I've got a mortgage, kids.'

'Yes, I'm sure your motives are understandable.' West was nodding. Jacquie could believe the mortgage, but she was less convinced about the kids. 'But it would help my enquiries enormously if you'd get to the bloody point.'

'I wanted to see the scene of crime,' Skinner told him. 'Or at least one of them. I drew the line at sneaking around the buildings, which you blokes might look on as breaking and entering, but the details of the Press Conference on Robinson said he was found in the boating lake. That's where I went.'

West and Jacquie were still looking at him, still waiting.

'There was nothing at the lake. But from there there's a path that winds up to the cedars. It used to be an orchard, apparently. I could see somebody in the trees. Stark fucking naked.'

West looked at Jacquie.

'What sex?' she asked.

'Female,' Skinner leered at her. 'Big with it.'

'What was she doing?' West wanted to know.

'Some sort of weird dance thing. She was swaying round in a circle, a sort of spiral, getting tighter, singing to herself.'

'What time was this?' the DCI checked.

'Two, half-past. Well after lights out, I reckon.'

'Did she see you?'

'Christ, no. I hid behind the bushes out by the boat-house. She seemed to be waving some sort of knife in the air. I couldn't make it out. Then she

331

knelt down, looked like she was burying something.'

'What?' Jacquie asked.

'Couldn't make it out.' Skinner was shaking his head.

'What happened then?' West asked him.

'The girl had a coat, a wrap of some kind, on the ground. She put it over her shoulders and was clearly heading back to the school. I did a runner.'

'This girl,' Jacquie asked. 'How old would you say she was?'

'Hard to tell in the dark. She was pretty well formed, though, big tits. I'd say, seventeen, eighteen.'

'Would you know her again?'

'What are you suggesting?' Skinner grinned. 'A naked line-up?' He winked at Jacquie. 'Well, it's a shitty job, but somebody has to do it – in the interests of solving a crime, of course.'

'DS Carpenter,' West stubbed his cigarette out. 'You're persona grata at Grimond's. Take Mr Skinner onto school premises, will you? I want to know *exactly* where you saw this girl. And if there's anything buried there, I want it excavated.'

'What about my exclusive?' Skinner knew the bum's rush when he was being given it.

'In the fullness of time,' West snarled on his way out. 'Right now, I'd like you to accompany my sergeant. There's a constable outside the door who'll see you off the premises, should that become necessary.'

'It won't sir,' Jacquie assured him, picking up her coat. 'Where'll you be, sir?' she asked.

'It's time I stopped this nonsense with your DCI,' he said, checking his watch. 'I'm going to the Country Club; I'm going to see the Chief Super.'

The drone of a vacuum cleaner welcomed Maxwell back to Tennyson House. Grimond's own Mrs B was skimming over the floors below the spiral stairs that led to what had been his room and beyond that, to the roof. The cab had left him at the gates and he was surprised to find them unlocked, if not exactly open and the paparazzi gone. He nodded to the cleaner and edged past her into the Prefect's Study, the abode of Selwyn, Ape and Splinter, the dauntless three. It was deserted. Like the *Marie Celeste*. Like Jeremy Tubbs' flat and Tim Robinson's house. An emptiness where there should have been bustle. Deadness where there should have been life.

Maxwell checked his watch. Four-thirty. He'd broken his journey in Petersfield, prowling the bookshops, lingering over a late lunch and a long coffee, planning his next move, thinking things through. His head ached like buggery and his vision still blurred if he moved too quickly, but he had no intention of doing that too often.

It was happy hour at Grimond's. Through the window, from the second floor where he was now, he saw the stragglers of the day students making their way home, carefully watched from the side gate by Mervyn Larson and David Gallow, guardians of the good, protectors of the privileged, lest the paparazzi merely be lurking around the corner. They had been there, at these wrought iron gates, man and boy, for nearly a fortnight. Grimond's was old news now. There were other shock horror stories out there for the cheque-booking.

'Max?' The Great Man turned slowly at the sound of his name.

'Hello, Tony.'

The Housemaster shook him by the hand. 'How the hell are you? And if it isn't too rude a question, what are you doing here?'

'I've come for the debate,' Maxwell told him.

'Debate?' Graham looked confused. 'What debate?'

'I don't know the motion, I'm afraid. John Selwyn invited me.'

'John?' Graham's confusion was deepening. 'When was this?'

'This morning,' Maxwell said. 'There was a message on my answerphone.'

'Well, that's odd.'

'What is?'

Graham looked at Maxwell. The man didn't look at all well. 'There's no debate, Max. At least, not today. In fact...' he brushed past him to check notices on the study wall. 'Not 'til next week – "This house believes that the House of Lords reform has gone far enough".'

'Selwyn was definite about the date,' Maxwell remembered. 'Said it was due to begin after prep at eight. He said "tonight if you can".'

'The time's right,' Graham said, 'but the date isn't. I don't know what's got into Selwyn at the moment. He's not himself. Skipped my French lesson this morning. Come to think of it, I didn't

334

see him at lunch, either.'

'Do you recognize this writing, Tony?' Maxwell ferreted in his briefcase and produced the note that had arrived that morning with the mail.

Graham was shaking his head. '"We know all about you, Maxwell",' he read aloud. 'That sounds cryptic. What does it mean?'

'Don't know,' Maxwell shrugged. 'It was in my pigeonhole this morning. Along with this,' and he thrust the porn mag into Graham's hand.

'Good God!' The Housemaster had turned pale and was glancing frantically around him. 'What the hell is this?'

'A glimpse of a way of life I don't want to go into,' Maxwell said.

Graham checked that the two of them were alone, leading Maxwell down the corridor into what had been Bill Pardoe's study. The place had changed with new trophies everywhere, different photographs and memorabilia from another life, another time. '*This* was in your pigeonhole?'

'In the post,' Maxwell nodded as best he could. 'In a plain white envelope with a Petersfield post-mark. Silly, really, on my way here, I stopped off in the town, hung around the Post Office like some sort of ghoul. What I hoped to see, I don't know. That was the stuff Bill Pardoe used to get regularly.'

'Bill? No, I don't believe it. How do you know?'

'Jacquie, remember? My woman on the inside? But *that* piece of information will cost you.'

'It will? What?'

'A strong coffee.'

'Here,' he stuffed the mag back into Maxwell's

hand. 'I don't really want this.'

'No,' Maxwell said. 'And it's my guess neither did Bill Pardoe.'

'You've lost me.' Graham rattled among his coffee cups.

'I think the senior law have labelled Pardoe as a paedophile, molester of boys, collector of porn.'

'It pains me to say it, Max,' Graham sighed, 'but there were rumours.' He flicked on the kettle.

'Really? From whom?'

'Well, I don't know … er … Tubbsy, for one.'

'From what I know we can't take much of what Mr Tubbs says as gospel.'

'Maybe not.' Graham conceded. 'But the thing about Tubbsy is that he's an inveterate gossip. Such people notice things – it's their stock-in-trade.'

'The fact is, Tony,' Maxwell said, easing himself into a leather chair, 'the police found nothing here in Pardoe's study or anywhere else where he operated. Nothing in his classroom, his filing cabinets, under his carpets, in the lining of his mattress.'

'I don't see…'

'When I first came to Grimond's, I saw another mag like this over there, on his … your … desk.'

Graham was looking blank.

'If you collect porn, you don't have it sent to your place of work, even if your place of work is also your home. What if somebody else opened it in error? Parker when he sorted the mail? Sheffield if he had a penchant to check on his staff?'

'I'd be fairly appalled if George went through my mail,' Graham said.

'You don't get out much, do you?' Maxwell

grunted. 'Believe me, it happens. Then, there's the erratic pattern.'

'Sorry?'

'Mags, even porn mags, are published regularly. If Pardoe had an account with a friendly neighbourhood Pederast Peddler in downtown Upsala, wouldn't that have come at regular intervals, say every week, every month?'

'Perhaps.'

'According to Parker, they came at all sorts of times, two days apart, three, five. No rational pattern at all. What I got this morning confirms it.'

'It does?'

'Contrary to what some will tell you, I am a white, Anglo-Saxon denizen of Middle England. Cranky, tetchy, eccentric even, but heterosexual as Casanova – if not quite so lucky. So why is someone sending me this stuff? An introductory offer, perhaps?'

'You can be arrested for receiving that, can't you?'

'Probably,' Maxwell nodded. 'But I've got an almost live-in lover and a string of broken female hearts from here to ... ooh, your study door. Ah, thanks,' and he gratefully accepted Graham's steaming mug. 'Not that either of those criteria make me snowy white, of course. Bill Pardoe had ... what? Years teaching in a boys' school, irrespective of his previous experience in a comprehensive. You know what the world at large thinks about Housemasters, don't you? Especially Housemasters in private schools?'

Graham was nodding. 'I'm afraid I do,' he said. 'But what's the point of it all, Max? Everybody loved Bill. Who'd stitch the poor sod up like that?'

'The same person who killed him,' Maxwell said.

'All right,' Graham winced as the hot coffee hit his tonsils. 'Why send it to you?'

'Because I'm close, Tony. So close I can almost taste it. And chummy's scared, if I don't sound *too* much like Jack Hawkins' Superintendent Gideon. He's sending a shot over my bows, in naval parlance, hoping I'll back off, sail to leeward. Well, damn the torpedoes, as dear old Admiral Farragut was wont to say steaming into Mobile Bay. It's a case of full speed ahead, I'm afraid.'

'Here,' Martin Skinner was getting his bearings, lining up the cedars from the boat-house down below them. One or two curious kids, still in their uniforms, watched them intently from the water's edge, dawdling before wandering in for supper.

'You're sure?' Jacquie wasn't about to embarrass herself in the damp grass for nothing.

'As sure as I'll ever be,' he told her.

She knelt down, driving in the trowel she'd brought for the purpose into the moist earth, flicking out clods left and right. For a while there was nothing but soil springing out over her sleeve and Skinner's shoes, then she felt the cold metal strike something hard. She looked at the hack, hovering triumphantly over her below the cedar's spreading arms. Jacquie dug with both hands now, abandoning the trowel and felt something soft that was not earth. It was cloth. She pulled it free of its shallow grave and held it upright.

It was a heart, dirty and torn, but lovingly handstitched with sequins forming the intertwined initials J and C.

From the school they heard the bell calling the boarders for supper as the light faded and the wind rustled in the cedars. Night was coming to Grimond's.

'Course,' Skinner crouched down beside Jacquie, 'there's a lot more I could tell you 'bout this place.'

'Really?' Jacquie looked at him with contempt. 'And what would that cost me, exactly?'

Skinner looked at the woman's spread thighs and the cleavage above her blouse. 'Oh,' he grinned. 'I'll think of something.'

Chapter Nineteen

'My darling,' Chief Superintendent David Mason raised his glass to the elegant, coiffured woman sitting opposite him. 'Here's to the next twenty years,' and their glasses clinked in the candlelight.

'Mr Mason,' the Maitre d' was at his elbow, penguin-suited, embarrassed. 'I'm sorry to bother you...' and he bent low to whisper in the man's ear.

The elegant woman put down her glass. She'd lost count over the last twenty years of the times that this had happened. Interruption after interruption. Weddings, christenings, parties, there'd always been that bloody phone call, that dark, usually helmeted bulk in the doorway. This time it was DCI Mark West. No helmet, but bulk nonetheless.

'That obnoxious man,' she hissed. 'What's he doing here, Dave?'

'What he's always doing, dear,' her husband sighed. 'He's working. I won't be a minute. Have the sorbet, will you? I'll try and get rid of him.'

He dropped his napkin on the table and reached across to kiss her forehead. The Maitre d' held his chair aside for him and he crossed the dining room in three strides, taking West into the vestibule where ball-gowned ladies strolled with ancient, florid-faced county types.

'This had better be important, Mark,' Mason

muttered. 'It's my wedding anniversary, for God's sake.'

'I'm sorry,' West said. 'I didn't know.'

'No, of course not,' Mason sighed. 'Why would you? Developments?'

'We need to talk,' the DCI nodded sulkily to a couple he vaguely knew. 'It's about Hall.'

Mason glanced through to where his wife was being accosted by an elderly woman with lariats of pearls around her neck.

'You're in luck,' he said. 'Fiona's just been got by Lady Whatserarse. That should give you a clear window of two hours or so.'

'Can we do this in private somewhere, Dave?' West asked. 'It's like Piccadilly fucking Circus out here.'

'That's because it's the Hampshire County Club, Mark. They do an impressive house red and a mean crown roast, which I'd quite like to get my teeth into round about now, by the way, now that I can.' He patted his jaw, from which Dr Josef Mengele had ripped his throbbing tooth only the week before. 'What's in here?'

What was through the door the Chief Super had just opened was an empty room with stacked chairs and music stands. Mason closed it behind them. 'What about Hall?'

'What's he really doing here?' West asked.

Mason looked at the man in the half light. Beyond the double doors the world and his wife were still passing by, between bar and ballroom.

'I don't believe this,' the Chief Super said. 'You drag me out on my bloody anniversary...'

'Don't bullshit me, Dave,' West snarled. 'We go

341

back too far, you and I.'

Mason hesitated. 'What are you saying?'

'Interforce co-operation, my arse,' hissed the DCI. 'That's for outside consumption, media, maybe even the Home Office. But we're in here now, Dave. You and me. This is Marky, remember?' He hauled up his shirt sleeve above the wrist strap. 'I took a fucking bullet for you,' he shouted. The purple scar shone in the dim light from the distant twirling glitter balls.

'I know, Mark,' Mason nodded, patting the man's shoulder. 'I know.'

He still saw it in all his waking nightmares. A kid on the run, scared, alone, out of his mind on acid. He'd gone in alone on a tip-off from West. The DCI had been a sergeant then, Mason a DI. He hadn't realized the kid was armed, didn't think he'd use the gun even when he had. It was only West's presence of mind, working as back-up, that saved his life, brought the kid down. He was fifteen with a neat black hole just below his hairline, lying on a spreading pillow of black-red blood. All David Mason's nightmares were about that.

'I never thought I'd say this, Dave,' West growled, looking the man straight in the face, 'but you owe me.'

'My life,' Mason acknowledged. He looked back through the round window in the door to where Fiona sat chatting to her old friend. 'All right,' he said. 'What do you want?'

'The truth,' West told him.

'Ah,' Mason smiled. 'That old thing.' He wandered across to a stack of dining chairs and

342

pulled a couple out, before sitting himself down. 'How long have you got, Mark?' he asked.

'Are you going to tell me what we're doing here?' Jacquie Carpenter was getting edgy. She looked at the ferret-faced man with the roll-up and the terminal acne in the green glow from his dashboard lights.

'Like I told you,' Martin Skinner said. 'Waiting.'

'Mr Skinner,' Jacquie turned to him. 'I could, of course, do you for wasting police time.'

'Now then, darling...'

'That's sergeant to you, slime,' she growled.

'Well,' he bridled. 'So much for police co-operation.'

'You said you had something important. We've been sitting here now for the best part of an hour.' Skinner's car was not exactly state of the art. Jacquie was cold and couldn't feel her left buttock at all.

'Yeah, well,' Skinner chortled. 'That's the name of the game, isn't it? We both play it, Jacquie...' He caught the look on her face. 'Oops, sorry, DS Carpenter. We both sit and stand around, don't we? Stake-outs, tip-offs, surveillance. Lots of shoeleather, lots of bum-ache. Doesn't always pay off, does it?'

'Get me back to Selborne,' she said, reaching for her seat-belt. 'Do it now and I'll go easy on you.'

'Oh, yeah?' Skinner's ciggie bobbed up and down in his tight lips. 'How easy's that, then? Aye up,' and he shuffled down in his seat. 'There he is.'

'Who?' Jacquie was looking through the windscreen into the darkened square ahead.

'There, in the corner by the church. That's Brian.'

'Who's Brian?' Jacquie couldn't see anybody.

'That lad. Jeans, bomber jacket, baseball cap.'

'What's he doing?' Jacquie asked.

Skinner sat up again. 'Christ, love, I thought you were the filth. Where's your career been up to now, then? Tracking people down for non-return of library books? Brian's obviously waiting for a bus.'

Jacquie ignored the sarcasm. 'What's he got to do with what's been going on at Grimond's?'

'Maybe nothing. Maybe everything. He used to go there. Before they gave him the elbow. Goes to the local comp now.'

'I don't see...'

'Look,' Skinner was stubbing out the butt on his dashboard, 'Do you want to talk to him or not?'

Jacquie hesitated.

'He's a rent boy, as my colleagues in the Sundays put it,' Skinner explained. 'Bum bandit, fudge-packet. Do I have to spell it out?'

'Thanks,' Jacquie frowned. 'I think you already have.' And she got out of the car.

'Oh, no,' Skinner was with her. 'This is *my* story, sergeant dear. You don't talk to Brian unless I'm with you.'

But it was too late. The lad was looking in their direction, turning, running into the night.

'Shit!' Jacquie gave chase, then stopped. 'Can we use the car?'

'No chance,' Skinner shouted. 'We'll lose him in the back doubles. Come on then, let's see what you lady coppers are made of.'

Their boots rattled on the cobbles, then the tarmac. Skinner was slim enough for a night exercise like this, but the years of roll-ups and Scotch had done him no favours and Jacquie was soon outrunning him. Her head felt like bursting and her lungs were torture as she clattered around corners into the darkness, skidding in those little bits of nastiness with which urban dwellers decorate their towns. The bright lights of the square had gone now and there was no passing traffic. Ahead of her was a park, its gates locked, its trees black against the night purple of the sky. She stopped, listened. Somewhere, a dog barked, a distant train rumbled. She was walking softly now, head tilted to one side, trying to catch breathing, rustling, anything that gave her a scent of her quarry.

The infuriating thing was she seemed to have lost Skinner too. Perhaps that was for the best, but even so, if she found this boy, what was she going to ask him?

Then, none of it mattered, because he broke cover, hurling dustbins over as he leapt at the park railings, hauling himself up and over, ripping his jacket and shirt on the spikes before crashing into the bushes on the other side. Jacquie was slower, less desperate perhaps and she couldn't manage the climb. Twice, three times, she threw herself at the cold, rusting metal, only to fall back again.

'You lost him!' Skinner was at her side now, panting, holding his ribs. 'Christ Almighty!'

'I didn't notice you breaking any speed records!'

Jacquie snapped, resisting the urge to smack the hack around the head, chain him to the railings with her cuffs and leave him there overnight. Above all, she wasn't going to give him the satisfaction of letting him know she'd broken a nail. 'All right, so he's gone. What happens now?'

Skinner shrugged. 'I could tell you what I know,' he said. Jacquie straightened her jacket, peering one last time into the darkness of the park. 'All right,' she said. 'Where?'

'Well,' Skinner was still getting his breath back. 'There's a lot of pubs in Petersfield.' He closed to her, taking in her warmth, her scent. 'Or we could go back to my place.'

Jacquie was momentarily between a rock and a hard place. She wouldn't usually be seen dead in public with a reptile like Skinner. But the prospect of 'his place' and all that that entailed didn't bear thinking about. She stood up to her full height, looking down on him. 'We might wake the wife and kids. First round's on you,' she said.

'It's only me.' Denise McGovern was peering round Henry Hall's door, and it wasn't a very good Harry Enfield.

He was in his shirt-sleeves, looking at his watch. 'I was just going to bed,' he said.

'Yeah, I know,' she said. 'I wouldn't have come unless it was important.'

Hall held the door open for her. All in all, he'd had a bitch of a day. Steadily, the two of them had begun working through the younger lads of Tennyson House, asking about Bill Pardoe, Tim Robinson, the whole sorry episode of the last two

346

weeks and before. Alongside each kid was a bewildering, ever-changing rota of minders – parents, solicitors, social workers; all the cloying cotton-wool of the nanny state that conspired to wrap up the innocent and let the guilty go free.

Barcourt Lodge was typical of hotels of its type. After dark, they became empty, soulless. Who stays in these rooms? What dramas and tragedies go on behind these doors? No soap can ever do it justice, no painting and no photograph can capture the essential loneliness of a place like that. And Henry Hall had been there for two weeks, to the day. The police house he'd been in before they found Bill Pardoe was too far out. Barcourt was handy for Grimond's, but Barcourt had no soul. He'd die rather than admit it, but Henry Hall missed his wife and he missed his kids. In his own three-piece, anal way, he even missed Leighford.

'This isn't about drugs, is it?' Denise took his offer of an armchair.

'Sorry?'

'Look, guv,' she sighed. 'I've been in on a lot of interviews in my time. Some of it's boring, some of it's slow, some of it turns your stomach. But I've never been on interviews when the questioner doesn't get to the point.'

'It's a murder enquiry, Denise,' Hall told her. 'I don't think I've been too obscure. You've got to keep all the options open.'

'But the drugs, guv,' she persisted. 'The source of it all. You've got nothing.'

'Nothing, Denise,' Hall shrugged. 'That's how enquiries go, sometimes.'

'Yeah, well,' the DS said, reaching in her bag for the inevitable ciggie. 'Like I told you, I'm in a hurry. Got a glass ceiling to crash through, remember. And I've got an idea...'

Earlier in the evening, a solemn bell had sounded through the corridors of Grimond's, tolling the faithful to supper.

'Vespers,' Tony Graham stood up. 'Max, I'd invite you to dinner, but...'

'Thank you, no,' Maxwell reached for his coat and hat. 'I'm not sure George Sheffield's speaking and Maggie Shaunessy would probably have my throat out.'

'What'll you do?' Graham asked. 'Head home tonight?'

'No, I tried getting through a day's work this morning,' Maxwell told him. 'Couldn't take it. I'm afraid the old get up and go etcetera etcetera...' The immaculate Yul Brynner was lost on the Housemaster, film buff though he claimed to be. 'No, I think I'll catch me a cab to Barcourt Lodge. They do a mean cocoa there, I understand. Could I just use your phone, Tony?'

'Be my...' but Tony Graham never finished his sentence. There was a thud at his study door and it burst open. Roger Harcross stood there, still in his blazer and tie and crimson in the face.

'Ape?' Graham looked at the lad. He was sweating and clearly in a hurry. 'Something amiss?'

'John Selwyn, sir,' the lad blurted. 'We can't find him. He's gone.'

'Gone, Ape?' Graham echoed. 'What do you mean?'

348

'He's not in his room, sir. He's not in the Pre-fects' Study or anywhere in Tennyson. Splinter's tried the gym, the CCF hut.'

'Has he tried the boat-house?' Maxwell thought it politic to ask.

'The boat-house has been locked recently,' Graham said, stony faced. 'Too many goings-on going on.'

Maxwell took in the anxious faces on both men, the Housemaster and his prefect. 'Has John done this before?' he was asking them both.

'No, sir,' Ape was adamant.

'Never.' Graham was shaking his head. 'And ordinarily I wouldn't concern myself. But with all this going on ... Ape. Catch supper later, will you? You and Splinter take the Houses. All of them. If Miss Shaunessy tackles you in North-anger, don't mix it with her. I'll sort that later. You were ringing for a cab, Max...'

'I think you need help on this one, Tony.'

'No, really...' Graham began.

'Tony...' Maxwell looked at Ape.

'Double-up, Ape,' Graham said. 'You and Splinter meet me back here in ... what, half an hour? And softly on this one, eh? We don't want the world and his wife to know.'

'Yes, sir,' and Ape was gone, flying down the dimly lit corridor.

'Like a bull in a china shop,' Graham tutted. 'Max, there's no...'

'Look, Tony,' the Head of Sixth Form closed the door. 'I'll eat my hat afterwards if I have to, but I think John Selwyn's involved in all this.'

'You mean...?'

'Pardoe. Robinson.'

'Come off it, Max,' Graham guffawed. 'You're talking about my Captain of House here.'

'More especially,' Maxwell said, 'I'm talking about Bill Pardoe's Captain of House. Who, coincidentally, had a pretty public stand-up row with Tim Robinson in the gym the day before the man died.'

'No,' Graham was shaking his head. 'No, I can't accept that, Max. It's nonsense.'

'It may be,' Maxwell nodded. 'And I very much hope it is. But the fact, according to Ape, is that he's vanished. What are we talking about here? A fairy ring? The Bermuda Triangle? I'd like to help you look.'

Graham hesitated. 'All right,' he muttered. 'But you don't know Grimond's like I do. Two pairs of eyes are better than one, I suppose. Stick with me. Head okay for walking?'

'I don't walk on my head, Tony,' Maxwell reminded him. 'But thanks for asking.'

They combed the corridors on their way down, beyond Maxwell's old landing, past the staircase that led to his room. 'He wouldn't be up there, I suppose?' the Head of Sixth Form asked.

'We only use that for the odd guest, Max,' Graham said, perhaps privately conceding they didn't come much odder than Maxwell. 'No, that's locked now. Come on; we'll do the grounds.'

There was a mist in the hollows, wreathing the dip below Sheffield's French-windowed study and snaking around the bases of the rugger posts, white and ghostly in the evening dark. The timing for the search was perfect. Everyone except Ape and Splinter would be indoors, having supper in the Dining Hall, Dr Sheffield sitting with his staff at High Table, wondering how long he'd got until his Chair of Governors threw him out and he saw his own job advertised in the *Times Educational Supplement*. From there, everyone would troop back to their prep bases, their studies and dorms. There should be no one out on the field at all.

'So what's going on?' Maxwell was finding it quite difficult to keep up with the younger man's stride.

'I wish I knew,' Graham muttered, peering into the line of the hedges as they approached them.

'You said Selwyn missed your lesson today.'

'That's right, he did. And lunch, too.'

'And he rang me to invite me to a non-existent debate, at, I might add, incredibly short notice.'

'You came,' Graham observed. 'Did he know you would?'

'Meaning?' Maxwell had stopped, his head thudding with the exertion. The pair had left the level of the pitches now and were striding over the tufted grass that led to the lake. It was dark here with only the mist for horizon and the odd squawk of disturbed ducks breaking the stillness.

Graham threw his hands in the air. 'I don't know,' he said. 'This is all crazy. Selwyn, Ape and Splinter are usually joined at the hip. If they don't know where he is, then something's really up.'

'When do we call in the police?' Maxwell asked.

'No,' Graham said emphatically. 'No police, Max. Not yet. Those kids have been through enough in the last fortnight, God knows.'

'And what if,' Maxwell looked hard into the

351

Housemaster's face, 'what if John Selwyn is a victim? What if he's Number Three?'

Graham twirled away, waving his arms in the darkness, listening to the little splashes of the ducks at the water's edge. It was getting cold down here and both men felt it.

Maxwell didn't give the man an inch. 'What is it, Tony? You're Head of Tennyson, for Christ's sake. If you don't know what's going on, then nobody does.'

Graham stopped pacing and turned to face his man. 'All right,' he said. 'For what it's worth, I think Bill Pardoe was a pederast. And I don't think he was working alone.'

'He wasn't,' Maxwell said quietly.

'He had a collection of porn,' Graham went on, piecing together what he knew, collecting scraps. 'Hanging around the showers, that sort of thing.'

'Did you see this?' Maxwell asked.

'No,' Graham shook his head. 'He was too fly for that. But the boys don't miss much. Two or three of them came to see me.'

'They did?' Maxwell frowned.

'What could I do?' Graham asked. 'Take ... take your Dierdre Lessing at Leighford.'

'Must I?' Maxwell shuddered.

'What if one of your sixth form girls came to you and told you Dierdre was a lesbian? Had made advances to her? What would you do?'

'Say I told you so and run to the editorial offices of the *News of the World*, I suppose.'

Graham was shaking his head again. 'No, you wouldn't,' he said. 'Like me, you'd agonize over it, weigh up the pros and cons. I was on the point of deciding when all this ghastliness happened.'

'You were?'

'I chickened out, I suppose,' Graham confessed. 'I should have seen Sheffield earlier, but when the Leighford exchange came up, I thought I'd just do that first, give myself a little breathing space. Then Pardoe jumped.'

'So that's it?' Maxwell asked. 'Neat and tidy?'

'Hardly that,' Graham muttered. 'And before you ask, I haven't the first idea how Tim Robinson fits into all this. My guess would be that's a horse of a different colour.'

'Now there, Tony,' Maxwell nodded, 'you have my full agreement. Come on, we've got a Captain of House to find.'

She watched him crossing the park in the early morning, a grey light failing to break the clouds to the west. His Tesco bag was slung nonchalantly over his shoulder. He was wearing trainers and it was her guess that the bag contained his school shoes. That would figure; he was rebel enough not to fit in with Grimond's rigidity, but old habits die hard. He'd taken his shoes just in case, in case the rebel lost his nerve. He looked younger in his black school sweat shirt and he wasn't wearing the baseball cap. She waited until he'd reached the gates and then she dashed from the bushes and stuck her warrant card under his nose.

He gasped in surprise. 'I'm Detective Sergeant Carpenter,' she told him, 'and I have absolutely no intention of chasing you all over Petersfield again. We need to have a little chat, Brian, you and I.'

353

'I'll be late for school,' he whined.

'I don't somehow think that's going to break the habit of a lifetime,' she said. She took him by the arm and yanked him down alongside her on a park bench. It was out of sight of the main drag and anyway, most of Brian's classmates had gone now, hurtling with the pure exhilaration of learning, the joy of the comprehensive chalk face. Sometimes, in fact, she wondered how Peter Maxwell stood it.

Until well after closing time, Jacquie Carpenter had sat with Martin Skinner in the Dawlish Arms, one of the many places the hack called his local. She promised him exclusives left, right and centre and was feeling pretty guilty about that until he started slobbering over her and making a grab for her breasts. Instead, she'd grabbed his car keys and driven his car back to Barcourt Lodge to get a well-earned zizz, leaving the reporter swaying confusedly in the Dawlish doorway. For all of four minutes, she felt guilty about that too, but she had told him where he could pick up his vehicle and since she'd protected him from losing his licence by being in charge of a vehicle while under the influence, reckoned they were more than quits.

'How long have you been on the game, Brian?' Jacquie asked, sliding the warrant card away.

'What?' The lad looked confused. 'How do you mean?'

'How old are you, Brian?' The question was softer, more mumsy.

'Sixteen,' he told her.

'Year Eleven, right?'

'That's right.'

'Okay, so there's no law against homosexual acts involving sixteen year olds.'

'I'm not a poof!' he shouted, then quieter, glancing around him, 'I ain't.'

'You can drop the street talk, Brian,' she told him. 'I know you used to go to Grimond's. I can't imagine Dr Sheffield tolerating "I ain't".'

'All right then,' Brian was prepared to concede. 'I'm not.'

'That's a bit like saying you're not a murderer while you're tightening your hands around someone's neck, isn't it, Brian?'

'You said there was no law against it,' he reminded her.

'Not exactly, Brian,' she patronized. 'The law covers consensual sex, in private and must not be for gain.'

'You what?'

'It's my guess you charge for your services. What? Ten quid for a wank? Twenty for a blow job? And the stalls of a gents' loo aren't exactly private, are they, Brian? Hence the correct term for them, *public* conveniences.'

'Are you going to arrest me?' The lad was shaking from the lips down.

Jacquie looked at him. Brian was an unlovely child, pasty with hair the same colour as his skin. 'You see, son,' she leaned towards him. 'You're on the slippery slope. First it was Grimond's. Now Dotheboys Hall. Next it'll be the dole queue and you're already hanging around loos and bus shelters for dirty old men. I'm the only brake in all this you've got.'

'So are you going to arrest me?'

'Been arrested before?' She saw his eyes fill with tears as he shook his head. 'Tell me about Grimond's,' she said.

'What?'

'And tell me the truth, Brian or you and I will take a little stroll to the police station. The judge might go easy with you, first time and all, but your mum and dad will have a pretty whacking fine to pay and your name, depending on when you're seventeen, will be in the papers. And even if it's not, you know how these things have a habit of getting out, don't they? There again, if you're unlucky, we're talking about a custodial sentence and you don't want to know what'll happen to a young thing like you inside.'

'What do you want to know?' Brian asked quickly.

'Why did you leave Grimond's?'

'Thieving,' he said. 'I stole a wallet.'

'Whose?'

'Graham's. Mr Graham. He was a bastard.'

'No doubt,' Jacquie nodded. 'Which House were you in?'

'Tennyson,' Brian said.

'Mr Pardoe's House?'

Brian nodded. 'That's right.'

'Tell me about Mr Pardoe. Did you like him?'

'Yeah, I did. He was a good bloke. Not like Graham and that bastard Sheffield.'

'How long have you been on the game, Brian?'

The boy's gaze faltered. 'About two years,' he said.

'You were still at Grimond's at the time?'

Brian nodded again.

'How many "clients" would you say you've had in that time?' she asked.

The lad shrugged. 'I don't know.'

'But enough,' Jacquie suggested, 'to know the type.'

'There's no special type,' Brian corrected her.

'Maybe not, but you know, don't you? The bloke driving slowly in his car, you know whether he's a punter or just somebody looking for directions?'

'Oh, sure,' Brian said.

'Mr Pardoe, then,' Jacquie pursued it. 'Was he that type?'

Brian looked at her. 'Pardoe?' he frowned. 'No, never in a million years. He was about the only decent teacher they had at Grimond's. I couldn't believe it when they said on the news he'd killed himself.'

'You shouldn't believe everything you hear on the news, Brian,' she said.

'So?' He looked at her, still shaking, still unsure. 'You going to arrest me, then? 'Cos if you do, I'm taking a few of them with me.'

Jacquie knew this game. How easy it would be for Brian to name names. Anybody he didn't like, anybody who'd ever looked at him funny. It sounded as if Tony Graham might be top of the list.

'I thought you might,' she said. 'Anybody in particular?'

Brian thought for a moment. 'There is one bloke,' he said. 'Not a regular exactly, but I've met him two or three times now.'

Jacquie wasn't really interested in this, but she'd need to talk to the boy again and needed to keep whatever trust he had in her. 'Go on.'

'Well, he keeps a record, like, about me, about other lads, I expect.'

Jacquie frowned. Suddenly she was interested. 'How do you mean, Brian, "keeps a record"?'

'Uses a cassette. You know, a tape recorder. I've seen it in his car, seen him use it when we've finished.'

'This man,' Jacquie said. 'Does he have a name?'

'Dave,' Brian said. 'He calls himself Dave.'

'Can you describe him?'

Brian shrugged. 'It's been pretty dark when we've … you know. He's a big bloke, solid like, spiky grey hair. Drives a big, dark car. Sorry, don't know the make.'

Jacquie was already on her feet. 'Brian,' she said. 'I want you to do something for me. Will you do it?'

'What's that?' he stood up with her.

'Have you arranged to meet this man again?'

'No,' Brian said. 'He don't work like that. I may see him, I may not.'

She fished in her handbag. 'Here's my mobile number,' she said, aware of the risk she was taking. 'If you see this man again, anywhere, anytime – I don't care if it's three in the morning, you ring me. Got it?'

'I don't know…' Brian said.

Jacquie closed to him. 'I know the school you go to, Brian,' she said, levelly. 'And I know where you live. Remember that slippery slope we talked about? And that brake? You think about that, Brian. Now,' she glanced up at the Petersfield day going on around them. 'Hurry up or you'll be late for school. And Brian ... this man...' She looked deep into his eyes. 'Do yourself a favour. Don't get into the car with him. All right?'

Chapter Twenty

They didn't find John Selwyn. Ape and Splinter met Graham back in his study at the appointed hour and had drawn a blank. They'd got into Northanger unobserved by everybody except Janet Boyce who had attempted to wither them with her glance. Selwyn wasn't there.

'What about Cassandra?' Graham asked the obvious.

'She was there,' Ape remembered.

'We met her coming back from supper,' Splinter added. 'No John.'

Graham and Maxwell had produced nothing either. There was no one by the lake or the boat-house, no one at the CCF hut that Ape and Splinter had already checked. The chapel was locked and dark in its nightly neglect with a solitary red flame burning somewhere in its nave. On the way back through Tennyson the pair had checked all the obvious places – the little theatre that doubled as the film studio where rows of videos lined the walls; Prefects' Study where the lockers were lined with photos of Britney Spears, Kylie Minogue and, in one case, Will Young. Of Selwyn there was no sign.

Neither of them wanted to risk a journalistic incident by enquiring of the two furtive geezers, the rump of the moved-on paparazzi who were slowly crawling back, on the off chance that something broke. A missing prefect would be grist to their mill and it was not something either Graham or Maxwell wanted to hand them on a plate.

At shortly after two o'clock, they'd called it a night and Tony Graham had run Peter Maxwell out of Grimond's, courtesy of the Housemaster's key, through the silent country lanes to Barcourt Lodge.

'Thanks Tony,' Maxwell waved to the man. 'And don't worry. When you get back, it's my guess John will be there, large as life and twice as sassy.'

'I've never lost a lad yet, Max,' the Housemaster said, crunching into gear. 'I don't intend to start now.'

'Good for you.'

The man on the desk was the very antithesis of Anthony Perkins' Norman Bates; in fact, he was rather more Oliver Hardy's Oliver Hardy. With that old skill he'd picked up in the classroom years ago of reading inappropriate notes upside down, Maxwell found Jacquie Carpenter's name and room number. Had he been of a different disposition, or a funnier time of life, he might have sought DCI Henry Hall's company. As it was, he made for Room 26, knocked and waited. Even with a head that still thudded for England, he had noticed her yellow Ka was not in the car park. After Tubbsy's MG it was probably the second-most-noticeable vehicle in the world. And it wasn't there. No one answered his knock. He checked his watch. It *was* very late. And Peter Maxwell turned in.

'A search, Chief Inspector?' George Sheffield was due to teach his one lesson of the week that Tuesday morning. It had been two weeks since he'd stood in that ghastly white tent they'd erected over the dead body of Bill Pardoe, but the grey face of the man and the colour of his congealed blood had never left him. He couldn't forget Tim Robinson either, purple-blue and waterlogged, lying inert under the frantically working body of that policewoman.

But it was another policewoman who stood in front of him now, across the desk that had become his last refuge in the past fortnight. This was Denise McGovern, all bark and no less bite, a frosty-faced bitch who meant business. Hall was more benign, Sheffield knew and he *was* in charge, so perhaps sanity would prevail. 'What are you looking for?'

Denise opened her mouth to tell him, but Hall was faster. 'Anything,' he said. 'It's standard procedure.'

'Standard procedure?' Sheffield pulled off his glasses and began to fuss around, cleaning them with a cloth. 'You'll forgive me,' he said. 'I don't know what that is.'

'It's routine,' Denise explained with as much patience as she could muster, 'to search a murder scene. You'll agree that your school is that twice over.'

'But,' Sheffield persisted, 'isn't that an infringement of human rights? Privacy and so on?'

'Denise,' Hall said and the woman pulled a piece of printed paper out of her handbag.

Sheffield took it, putting his glasses back on.

'That's a search warrant, sir,' she said. 'Mr Hall and I thought we'd get one in case you adopted the difficult approach you, in fact, have.'

'Difficult?' Sheffield frowned, still checking the fine print. 'Oh, no, I assure you, I want all this cleared up as much as you do. More. Er ... where would you like to start?'

'Here would do nicely,' Hall said.

'Um ... of course. The planning room next door you know all too well by now I should think. There's this room, and through that door a staircase leads to my private apartments – three bedrooms, a sitting room, dining room, usual offices.'

'Must be quite pushed for space,' Denise scowled.

'Look, Chief Inspector,' Sheffield closed to the larger man. 'Would you mind if my secretary stayed with you? There are private records, student files and staff information here. You've read those on Bill, Tim and Jeremy Tubbs already, I know. I'd just like her to put things back, otherwise it's hours of paperwork.'

'Where will you be, sir?' Hall asked.

'Well,' Sheffield said. 'I wonder if I might crave your indulgence here? I understand the compulsion of your search warrant, but this won't go well with some of my staff. May I tell them in person, the House staff at the very least?'

'Be my guest,' Hall nodded.

'Thank you.' Sheffield flicked the intercom on his desk. 'Millie, come in here a moment, will you?'

In the adjoining office, the Head explained the situation to an appalled-looking Millie Taylor.

'What did I tell you?' Denise hissed to Hall out of the corner of her mouth. 'It's ruffling feathers already.'

'Not half as many as were ruffled on the magistrate whose door bell I leaned on at half past one this morning,' Hall hissed back. 'Next time that's *your* job.'

While the DCI and his loaned DS began the mind-numbing process of ransacking Sheffield's study and private rooms, the great man himself hauled on his gown and strode across the quad. It had all the makings of a marvellous spring day, the cloud clearing and the sun sparkling on the day boys' bikes in their shed. The light was flooding in through the golden stained-glass of the chapel, and Sheffield found himself wondering whether God was really in His Heaven when all was clearly not all right with the world.

'Michael, could I have a word?'

'Headmaster?' Michael Helmesley was about to leave his study for the next lesson. They nearly collided in the doorway.

'DCI Hall,' Sheffield said, grim-faced, 'and that unspeakable siren he's got in tow are searching the premises.'

'Good Lord!' the Head of Classics was suitably horrified. He hadn't known anyone behave like this since Nero and even that man's excesses had been greatly exaggerated by legend.

'I know,' Sheffield nodded, his fingers drumming on the jamb of Helmesley's open door, 'but unfortunately they have a search warrant. They're ... what's the colloquialism ... turning over my place as we speak.'

'Outrageous!' Helmesley snorted. 'Well, thank you for the warning, Headmaster. Better lock up my Scotch, d'you think?'

'Not a bad idea,' Sheffield said. 'Oh, Michael, need your coat?' He handed it down from the peg behind the door.

'No thanks, Headmaster. Quite mild, I fancy, for a stroll over to Tennyson.' And George Sheffield hung it back up.

As Henry Hall expected, there was nothing in Sheffield's suite at all. And at that point, as agreed, the detectives went their separate ways. Hall took Tennyson; Denise, Kipling.

'Is this strictly in order?' Tony Graham felt obliged to ask. 'I've got a sick Captain of House this morning. Don't really want great plates of meat – no offence, Chief Inspector – traipsing all over the place.'

'None taken, Mr Graham,' Hall said. 'If you tell me which room the lad is in, I'll traipse in the opposite direction. It's not a problem.'

'Up the stairs,' Graham told him. 'Along the corridor and then up again.'

'Your Captain of House – that would be ... John Selwyn?'

'That's right.' Graham was impressed. 'How clever of you to remember the name.'

'Goes with the territory,' Hall nodded. 'And,' he was standing in the corridor on the first floor trying to get his bearings, 'that would be above Bill Pardoe's rooms, wouldn't it? Your study as is?'

'That's right too.' Graham grinned. 'Do you want to start there, by the way? My study?'

'No, I think I'll take the dormitories first. Do you have a master key to the lockers?'

'Sure,' and the Housemaster handed it over. 'Look, would you like someone to show you around? One of my Prefects...'

'No, thanks,' Hall said. 'I'm fine,' and he made for the stairs.

One thing that Peter Maxwell always said about Henry Hall. Tell him what not to do and he'd do it; tell him where not to go and he's there. And so it was that the DCI ignored the Tennyson dorms and made for the tight spiral of the stairs above Bill Pardoe's rooms, to the little room under the eaves that had housed Peter Maxwell briefly and now housed an ailing John Selwyn. He rapped on the door. No response. He tried again. Nothing. He briefly toyed with using his credit card on the lock, but this was a Victorian door and that would be a waste of time. So he put his shoulder to it and the thing burst open with a crash.

A figure crouched half in, half out of the window opposite him, caught like a mongoose facing a cobra. And if it was John Selwyn, whatever he'd got had aged him fifteen years and changed his hair colour.

'Hello, Mr Tubbs,' the DCI said, holding up his warrant card. 'I've been trying to interview you for quite a while. Do you have a moment now?'

'I ... er ... I've never been interviewed by the police before.' Jeremy Tubbs was sitting opposite

366

Henry Hall in George Sheffield's outer office. The tape was running, although Hall was aware that he had no second officer, neither had he cautioned his man. This was, for now, in the nature of a friendly chat.

'That's not quite true, is it, Mr Tubbs?' Hall was at his blandest, hiding behind those blank lenses that were his stock-in-trade in interviews. 'A little matter of under-age parties involving schoolgirls... I don't have to cross too many t's do I?'

'They were not under-age,' Tubbs protested. 'And that was a long time ago.'

'Indeed it was.' Hall took in his man. Jeremy Tubbs was heavier in the flesh than he appeared from his school mugshots and he was sweating profusely. Hall didn't need the spotlights and rubber hoses on this one. 'All right,' the DCI leaned back in his chair. 'Let's bring all this up to date, shall we? Where have you been for the last eight days, Mr Tubbs?'

'Been?'

Hall looked bored. 'It's a perfectly standard past tense, Mr Tubbs,' he said, aware that Peter Maxwell would probably be able to codify it further.

'Well, all this,' Tubbs whirled his arms in all directions. 'Call me a coward if you like, but I suddenly couldn't stand it. I felt ... well, threatened...'

'By whom, Mr Tubbs?'

'Well, no one in particular. I mean, unless you people have caught the bastard.'

'No, no,' Hall shook his head. 'No, we haven't caught anyone yet. But I've been in this game a long time. You get a nose for when things are about to happen. I somehow think we're pretty close, now.'

'Um ... good,' Tubbs grinned inanely. 'That's good.'

Hall flicked open a file on his desk. 'Your vehicle was found at Portchester Castle last Friday. And when I go looking for a sick sixth former, I found you, hiding in a room which is not yours and, if my memory serves, attempting with some futility to escape through a window which is three storeys up.' He leaned across the desk. 'Bill Pardoe fell from only a few feet above that,' he said. 'Did you happen to see his body at all?'

'Look, Inspector...' Tubbs had resorted to mopping his forehead with his handkerchief.

'That's *Chief* Inspector, sir,' Hall knew when it was time to tighten the screws. 'Can you, above all, tell me why it is that, having felt threatened at Grimond's, you should return here, I assume voluntarily? Or were you being kept in that room against your will, like something in Glamis castle?'

'No, no, it was nothing like that...'

'But of course,' Hall interrupted, 'what I really want to know is your relationship with the dead men, Pardoe and Robinson.'

Jeremy Tubbs had gone a very strange colour. 'I want my solicitor present,' he said, wiping the spittle from his lips.

'That is your right, sir,' Hall leaned back. 'And don't let it bother you that statistically, eight out of ten people who make that request have something to hide.'

It was then that the planning office door burst

open and Denise McGovern stood there. She had a tape in her hand. 'Jesus!' she said.

'Not exactly,' Hall corrected her. 'For the benefit of the tape, DS McGovern entering the room at ten-thirty-four. Meet Jeremy Tubbs,' and he switched the tape off.

'And where do you think you've been?' Denise snarled at the man, suddenly smaller than he had been and almost cowering in his chair.

'You can do the rolling pin bit later, Denise,' Hall said. 'Right now, Mr Tubbs would like to see his solicitor. Could you arrange that on your way to Selborne, please? See if DCI West wants a word with Mr Tubbs. And Denise,' he stood up and looked the woman squarely in the face. 'Make sure that DS Carpenter attends the interview too, would you?'

'Of course, sir.' She stared defiantly back.

'What's that?' Hall was pointing to what was carried triumphantly in the Sergeant's hand.

She motioned him outside. 'Could you give us a moment, Mr Tubbs?' he said as he closed the door.

'Where the fuck's he been?' Denise hissed as Millie Taylor looked up from her typing.

'Here, most of the time would be my guess.'

'But why...'

'It was inspired, really. We've got blokes out combing the county for him and he was right here under our noses all the time. Pretty clever. What's that?' he asked again.

Denise positioned herself so that she had her back to the secretary. 'I found it in the coat pocket of Michael Helmseley, Head of Classics. I don't know what it is yet. Some harmless languages tape. Maybe. But if that's the case, what was it doing in his coat pocket?'

'*You* found it in his study?'

'Behind the door,' Denise nodded.

Hall took it. 'Okay, I'll play it. Get Tubbs across to Selborne, Denise. Tell West ... ask your DCI to play him along. Mr Tubbs has got some talking to do.'

Jeremy Tubbs' solicitor was actually one his mummy had retained aeons before and he'd known the lad for years. He was no longer a lad of course, but a rather repellent geography teacher and he was in trouble. Over the years, the solicitor had rather come to Tubbs' père's view of his son, that he was a degenerate who deserved, in police parlance, a good smacking. He was not inclined to be too officious on his client's behalf as he sat in the makeshift interview room at Selborne, facing DCI West and DS McGovern.

'So ... Jeremy...' West was rolling a piece of Nicorette gum around his molars in a sporadic and vain attempt to give up smoking. 'Where've you been, old lad?' The 'nice' policeman bit didn't come easy to Mark West, but looking at Denise McGovern across the table from him, Tubbs was ready to clutch at any straw.

'Around,' he said, glancing across at his solicitor and seeing no help there. 'Just driving around, you know.'

'No,' Denise said flatly. 'We don't know. Suppose you tell us.'

'Tell you what?'

370

'Precisely where you've been,' West said.

'Well, now you've asked me....'

'Yes,' West nodded. 'We have. And we've asked you now four times one way and another.'

'Well, I went to Portchester, obviously...'

He'd dried up already and it wasn't even mid-afternoon.

'All right,' West raised both hands and placed them behind his head. 'We'll get back to that. Why Grimond's, Jeremy? Why did you come back?'

'I was going to resign,' Tubbs told him. 'I'd come to pick some things up.'

'From an empty room?' Denise chased him. 'A room used only by guests? That's where DCI Hall found you, wasn't it?'

'Well, I...'

'Come on, Tubbs!' West had stopped playing nice policeman. Nicorette wasn't doing it for him this afternoon and his was a short fuse indeed. 'You're giving us zip here, mate, whammo. What I want is answers.'

'He can't talk to me like that ... can he, Gerald? Tell him.'

The solicitor rolled an eye in his client's direction. 'You tell him, Jeremy.'

'All right ... all right, I will. They call me *Mr* Tubbs,' he said, his face scarlet, his cheeks wobbling, 'for a start.'

Peter Maxwell would have appreciated the filmic irony; Mark West didn't. 'Jeremy Tubbs, I am arresting you on a charge of wilful murder...'

Gerald looked vaguely interested for the first time.

'All right!' Tubbs almost shrieked. 'All right, I'll tell you. It was never supposed to happen the way it did. Never.'

'Would you like to caution your client, sir?' West asked the solicitor.

Gerald leaned towards him, beaming. 'Would you?'

'I *do* have another class in a few minutes, Chief Inspector.' Michael Helmesley was checking the cut of his bow tie in the mirror. 'Can it wait?'

'No, sir.' Henry Hall was stone faced. 'I'm afraid it can't. Do you know what this is?'

'Looks like an audio tape,' the Head of Classics said, rummaging through a pile of books on his study desk.

'Is it one of yours?' Hall asked.

'Mine?' Helmseley reached for it, but Hall pulled back. 'Well, I can't tell you if I can't examine it, can I? Is it labelled?'

'No, sir. It's plain.'

Helmseley shrugged.

'Do you know anyone called Brian?'

'Brian? Brian?' Helmseley was thinking. 'There was a Brian Hedgepath who taught here a few years ago. I expect there are one or two Brians in the school now, among the student body, I mean. I'm afraid I'm the old-fashioned sort, Chief Inspector, I use their surnames. Now, I really must...'

'Do you use their surnames when you pick them up, sir?'

Helmseley stopped in his open doorway, turning to the man, blinking. 'I beg your pardon?'

'Where do you find them? Oh, I know it's Petersfield, Petworth, Portsmouth – the three Ps. But I'm talking details here – gay pubs, public loos, parks?'

Helmseley slammed the door, horrified. 'What the Hell are you talking about, man?' he croaked.

'I seem to remember from our last little chat, Mr Helmseley, you aren't married.'

'Neither is the Pope,' Helmseley snapped. 'What's the relevance of that?'

'May I use your cassette player, sir?' Hall asked him.

'All right,' Helmseley nodded. 'Be my guest.'

There was a machine on Helmseley's desk and Hall flicked it into position and pressed the play button with a latex-gloved finger. There was silence for a moment, just the soft whirr of the tape coming into play, then a gravel voice, intense, calculating. 'Ten-thirty-four,' it said. 'He's reaching his front door now. Age about fifteen, possibly younger, blond. Nice looking lad. He seems pissed. This is quite promising. I'll keep you posted on this one ... I think he's a natural.'

Hall clicked the pause button. Helmseley sat down.

'Good God,' the Head of Classics looked at the Chief Inspector. 'Where did you get that?'

'A few feet behind you,' Hall said, pointing at the study door. 'In the pocket of your coat.'

'My...'

'Perhaps you'd like to hear some more,' Hall was pushing switches again. 'This one's aged fifteen. But he's not alone. Seems to live along William Street. Can't make out the number. He was drinking in the pub earlier. Under-age of course. May be able to use that.'

Helmseley stood up, shaking, but staring Hall in the face. 'I have never heard this filth before in my life,' he said solemnly. 'That is not my voice.'

'Oh, no, Mr Helmseley. I know that.'

'You do?'

'Yes,' Hall nodded. 'I know whose voice it is. What I want to know is what this tape was doing in your coat pocket.'

He pressed the button again. 'Not bad,' the voice grated. 'Uses the handle "Janet". Sixteen or so he claims. Seemed to like the porn. I'll probably use him again. Not sure he's your type, though.'

Hall released the tape. 'There are other references,' he said. 'More mentions of "Janet", some to someone called Brian. What was wrong with "Janet" then, Mr Helmseley? Why wasn't he your type?'

'This is appalling,' Helmseley was sitting down again, staring at the floor. 'Absolutely appalling.'

'The porn that the tape refers to.' Hall pocketed the evidence. 'Would that be the magazines that Bill Pardoe was getting in the post? Compare notes, did you?'

Helmseley looked up at him. 'You utter shit!' he growled. Hall's phone shattered the moment, vibrating in his pocket. He turned his back on the Head of Classics.

'Sir?'

'Jacquie. I've been trying to reach you. Are you at Selborne?'

'Yes. I'm sure Denise McGovern just brought

in Jeremy Tubbs.'

'You mean you're not in on the interview?' Hall frowned, suddenly aware that he'd been double-crossed.

'No. Should I be?'

'Get in there,' he ordered.

'Sir, there's something else. I tried a long shot last night. I've been trying to reach you too. I spoke to a lad in Petersfield, a kid on the game.'

'Really?' Hall straightened. 'What's the lad's name?'

'Brian,' Jacquie told him.

'Brian.' Hall turned to where Helmseley was still sitting. 'Tell me, Jacquie, did Brian mention Michael Helmseley at all?'

'No, guv,' Jacquie said. 'Though he is an Old Boy of Grimond's. What interested me more, sir, was one of his punters. Drives a big, dark car and has spiky grey hair.'

'Oh, yes?' Hall said. 'And who does that sound like to you, Jacquie?'

'Well, I know this is going to sound pretty pre-posterous, sir, but it sounds like ... it sounds like...'

'DCI West?'

Peter Maxwell had had a fruitless day. There was no Jacquie over breakfast. And she wasn't answering her phone. For a while he toyed with getting a cab to Grimond's and loitering with the paparazzi pair outside the gate. He wasn't up to hauling himself over the wall again and anyway, was rather concerned that if George Sheffield or Maggie Shaunessy saw him, he'd be shot on sight.

So he'd loafed around in Petersfield again, chatting up barmen over Southern Comforts and picking up what tittle-tattle he could about Grimond's. Then, having failed to raise Jacquie for the umpteenth time, hailed a cab to Selborne, partly to commune with the shade of the naturalist Gilbert White and partly to meet the ogre with whom his light o' love now worked.

'I told Mr Maxwell you were busy, sir,' Denise McGovern's hard face appeared round the door, hot on the heels of the Head of Sixth Form. 'Come on, you,' she barked at him. 'Out!'

'Maxwell,' West had abandoned the Nicorettes as a lost cause and was back on the hard stuff, smoke wreathing around his flaring nostrils. 'No, no, Denise. I've heard a great deal about Mr Maxwell one way or another over the last few days.' He pointed to a chair. 'I've got a little windowette in my schedule at the moment. Have a seat, Mr Maxwell. Tell me where you fit into all this.'

'Oh,' Maxwell pulled up a chair that was still faintly warm. 'You know, just passing,' he smiled.

'Just bollocks,' West was smiling too.

'Ah, I just knew I'd enjoy meeting you,' Maxwell winked at the DCI.

'You arrive at Grimond's, and people start dying, Mr Maxwell. Bill Pardoe goes off a roof. Tim Robinson falls into a lake. And old Tubbsy sends you a warning phone call to get out just after his own disappearance. Now, I understand a sixth former's gone walkikins. Tell me, Mr Maxwell, is any of this down to you?'

'Sir,' the door crashed back and Jacquie Car-

376

penter stood there.

'Not now, sergeant!' West bellowed, 'Your boyfriend here is about to fill in a few blanks for me.'

'Jacquie.' Maxwell crossed to her.

'Look at me!' West snarled. 'I've been talking to an old friend of yours this afternoon.' He was on his feet, confronting them both. 'A sad bastard of a geography teacher called Jeremy Tubbs.'

'Tubbs?' Maxwell repeated.

'He was most helpful,' West smiled, before blowing smoke rings to the ceiling. 'He's been staying in your old room, apparently, at Grimond's. But I've got a feeling he doesn't know the half of it.'

'Sir,' Jacquie interrupted. 'Mr Maxwell...'

'Is your sugar daddy,' West finished the sentence for her. 'Your bit on the side. Yeah, I know. But he's also up to his fucking neck in what's going on at Grimond's and I intend...'

But another voice was filling the Incident Room at Selborne. Another voice, but not another voice. And it was getting louder.

'Not bad,' it was saying. 'Uses the handle "Janet". Sixteen or so he claims. Seemed to like the porn. I'll probably use him again. Not sure he's your type, though.'

DCI West walked numbly past Maxwell and Jacquie, out of his Inner Sanctum, the cigarette trailing in his right hand. His team were out there, all of them – Sandy Berman, Steve Chapell, Pete Walters, Denise McGovern. Most of them were on their feet and he seemed to be walking in slow motion. His mouth wasn't moving, but his own voice was filling the room, with an electronic hiss behind it. His team were all there and they were

377

all looking at him, recognizing the voice and what it meant. Then, quite suddenly, the voice stopped in mid sentence with a click and DCI West was staring into the blank, expressionless face of DCI Hall.

'Mark,' he said softly. 'Can I have a word?'

Chapter Twenty-one

They met briefly in the car park as the rain began, kissing under the narrow, unforgiving eaves of the Incident Room.

'DCI West,' Maxwell shook his head. 'So Henry's got his man, then?'

'One of them,' Jacquie said, looking back through the Inner Sanctum windows where Hall was lowering the blinds and a shattered Mark West sat with his head in his hands.

'You're staying here, aren't you?' he squeezed her hand.

'There are a lot of hurt people in there, Max,' she said. 'Some of them will have kids of their own. You work with a man for years, trust him, believe in him. Maybe, in our line of work, you put your life on the line for him, or he does the same for you. And then...' she sighed, 'At the very least, Henry will need help with the paperwork.' She turned back to him. 'What about you?'

'Me?' he shrugged. 'Home, I suppose. Time I got Grimond's out of my system. I've got a Sixth Form to run.'

'Call me,' she said, pecking him on the cheek, and she was gone.

Maxwell called a cab and waited in the lee of the Incident Room. He hated loose ends. They were like unfinished jigsaws and they irked him. And answer came there none. Patrol cars came and went, but it couldn't be called business as usual. At Selborne a murder inquiry hung in the balance, like a film frozen in mid-frame, while the team leader's career was being shredded. Dumpy Lynda was trying to make tea for the two DCIs locked in the Inner Sanctum, but she kept crying and her tears were wetting the sugar. Sandy Berman watched the others, numbly going about their business, avoiding eye contact, staring at the paperwork, or the VDU screen or the ground. He knew he'd have to snap them all out of it, pull the team together. But that would have to come later. He was having trouble pulling himself together first.

Outside in the rain, Maxwell's phone warbled in the gathering dusk.

'Max?'

'Yes.' Triumph! He'd pressed the right button again.

'It's Tony Graham. Look, we've found John Selwyn. I can't talk over the phone. Are you back home?'

'No, I'm in Selborne as a matter of fact.'

'Really? Well, look, I hate to ask you this, but you couldn't come over, could you? There's a problem. With John, I mean.'

'Yes,' Maxwell nodded. 'Yes, Tony, I expect there is.'

Old Jedediah Grimond's opulent pile looked black and oddly lonely in the purple of the night sky. There was a frost of stars shimmering in God's Heaven now that the evening cloud had cleared. Peter Maxwell paid his taxi fare and sauntered through the open gates. This was odd. Even the two remaining paparazzi had drifted away to chase other stories, make other people's lives a misery. The wrought iron was thrown back, chained against the stone pillars and the rampant lions snarled soundlessly in the still of the night. His feet crunched on the gravel until he reached the limes that formed an avenue into the main quad. He saw a light burning in Parker's window and the moon cold on the parked cars. He checked his watch as he passed the chapel. Gone nine. Supper would be over. Prep should be done too, except for the late bird, the anorak to whom good grades were everything and who would be burning the midnight oil.

He heard the chatter of the younger boys in the lower Tennyson corridors as he rounded the corner. A clutch of lads were laughing and rough-housing on their way to the television room. One of them, less happy than the rest, a quiet-looking blond boy the wrong side of thirteen, stopped for a brief moment, looking solemnly into Maxwell's eyes. Then he was gone.

'Courage, Jenkins,' the Head of Sixth Form muttered to himself. 'It won't be long now.'

He heard his feet echo on the wooden stairs and turn to a clatter as he reached the stone. In front of him was the solid oak door of Tony Graham's study; Bill Pardoe's study. He knocked.

'Up here, Mr Maxwell.'

He turned at the sound of his name. Roger Harcross stood there, dressed to the nines in his CCF uniform, boots polished, buttons gleaming, a corporal's stripes on his sleeve and a black beret

381

across his forehead.

'Evening, Ape,' Maxwell said.

'Up here, sir,' he said. 'We're waiting for you in the theatre.'

'Ah,' Maxwell said. 'Special showing of the Film Club tonight?'

'Not exactly, sir,' Ape said, as the Head of Sixth Form reached him on the upper landing. 'More of a debate, of sorts. You'll see.'

Maxwell walked with the boy along the gloomy corridor that led past the stairs to his old room, past the door that led to the roof, to that cold lonely place where Bill Pardoe had said his farewells to the world. 'I gather John Selwyn's returned to the fold,' Maxwell said.

'He has, sir,' Ape smiled. 'He strayed a little yesterday, but he's back now. One of us again.'

Ape led the way up the small flight of steps that led into the theatre. The auditorium was in darkness, the rows of plush seats silent and black in the gloom. On the little stage below them, in front of the huge white screen, a knot of cadets sat facing the newcomers. John Selwyn was there, in his sergeant's uniform and crimson colour-sash, his face pale and grim under the beret. Antonio Splinterino was on his left, grim-jawed and jackal-eyed in khaki, watching Maxwell make his entrance. And in the centre, in his mortar-board and gown, smiling benignly, sat Tony Graham, the Head of Tennyson House.

Maxwell heard the door click and lock behind him. In the state sector, nanny state regulations would insist on at least three exits from this room. But this was the private sector. This was

Grimond's and the only way out was locked. He felt Ape at his shoulder. 'Could I have your mobile please, Mr Maxwell?' he asked.

'Never carry one, dear boy,' Maxwell held out his arms to allow a body search. Ape hesitated, glancing down to the stage, but Graham nodded and the lad rummaged through the man's pockets, patting his chest, ribs and back.

'He's clean, sir,' Ape called, his voice sounding hollow in the echo-chamber of the Tennyson theatre.

'Which is more, I suspect, than any of you are,' Maxwell said.

'Now, Max,' Graham chuckled. 'You're not going to start moralizing, are you? So early in the proceedings.'

'Proceedings?' Maxwell repeated.

'The debate,' Graham explained. 'Well, not really a debate. More a trial, really. Well, actually, a Court Martial. I'm sorry about all this theatricality – dressing up, I suppose you'd call it. But you see, it's what we do at Grimond's, isn't it, Arbiters?'

Ape had joined the three on the stage now and as one their boots thundered on the woodwork, reverberating around the auditorium.

'But if you want a debate,' Graham turned to his left, 'Cassandra.'

There was a shiver in the half-drawn tabs and the lithe Captain of Austen sauntered across the stage, wearing her braided Prefect's blazer and tie and smouldering with contempt at the Head of Sixth Form.

'This House believes,' she said in a clear, cold

voice, 'that Peter Maxwell has outlived his usefulness in this life and deserves to die.'

The thudding boots took up the mantra again. Maxwell waited until they died down. This was all so surreal. 'Are you seriously going to kill me?' he asked, 'with Tennyson lads running all over the place and various House staff on the prowl?'

'Tennyson lads,' Graham said, 'will do as I tell them, Maxwell. Without question. Without thought. And House Staff? Who had you in mind? Dear old Dr Sheffield left us quite precipitately this afternoon. Gave no explanation. Just drove away with a suitcase. Jumping before he was pushed, I suspect.'

'A bit like Bill Pardoe?'

'Can you defend yourself, Maxwell?' Cassandra asked. 'Can you give us a reason why we should let you live?'

'None at all,' Maxwell laid his hat and coat down carefully on a chair in the front row and sat next to it. 'In fact, if you'll indulge me, I'll give you plenty of reasons why you have to kill me.'

'Really?' Cassandra's disdainful eyebrow said it all. 'God, you're so boring.'

'No, no,' Graham smiled. 'Go on then, Max. Consider yourself indulged. Tell us what you think this is all about. I know you're dying to.'

And Ape and Splinter sniggered at their Housemaster's side. Cassandra took the vacant chair on stage and sat facing the man who was signing his own death warrant.

'Are you sitting comfortably?' Maxwell asked. 'Then I'll begin. Once upon a time there was a complete shit called Anthony Graham. He impressed people. He listened carefully, made them believe he cared. There was no one quite like him, in fact. He was a one-off. The sort of character, larger than life, you might say, we've long ago lost in the state sector. They broke the mould, etcetera, etcetera.' It was still a brilliant Yul Brynner and still Tony Graham didn't appreciate it.

'Get to the point, Max,' he snapped. 'We've all got a busy evening in front of us.'

'Oh, but that *is* the point,' Maxwell said, spreading his arms along the seat back. 'This whole thing is about you, Tony. Your ability to manipulate people. Your megalomania. How does it go? Today, Tennyson; tomorrow, the world? And now George Sheffield's gone, well ... the world's your lobster, isn't it?' Maxwell clambered to his feet. He did it a little too sharply and his vision wobbled, but he didn't let it show. 'Vaulting ambition, boys and girls,' he strode backwards and forwards in front of the stage, just out of the limelight. 'My own humble little educational establishment...'

Graham snorted.

'...Leighford High, put it on not five weeks ago – the Scottish Play by William Somebodyorother. Macbeth, obsessed with a need for power, kills those who stand in his way – "I have no spur to prick the sides of my intent, but only vaulting ambition, which o'erleaps itself and falls on the other". Well, people, there's going to be a lot of o'erleaping and falling tonight, I fancy.'

'Is that right?' Splinter mocked him.

'Oh, yes. Now, let me see if I've got this right.

John, you're an intelligent young man, Captain of House, fencing champion, rugger hearty and,' he glanced at Cassandra, 'super-stud. Tell me, what are the two things a teacher can lose his job over?'

Selwyn frowned under the beret, glancing at Graham to his right.

'No?' Maxwell was in full flight. 'Well, let me tell you. Fingers in the till and fingers in the knickers. Not much else. You can be a crap teacher like dear old Tubbsy or an indifferent one like poor old Tim Robinson and you won't lose your job over it. But naughty happenings in the dorm, now, that's different. So that's what Mr Graham went for in the case of his House boss, Mr Pardoe. He framed him. Poor old Bill was an ingénue, a Roger Rabbit caught in the brilliant headlights of a clever, ruthless bastard out to get him. Mr Graham opened a subscription to a Swedish porn company and had their samples sent to Mr Pardoe here at the school. To be exact, of course, they were sent to Mr Graham under an altogether more innocent-looking cover. He stole some plain stationery from Austen House to package them and re-posted them in Petersfield. That created a certain muddying of the waters, a widening of the net. When Pardoe took to burning the envelopes without opening them, he placed them open on the man's desk – I know; I saw one. Not content with that, he rang the coppers; Chief Superintendent Mason, no less, and told them there was a paedophile ring operating out of Grimond's. And to put the icing on the cake, he cut his nasty tapes, accusing Pardoe of God knows what and suggesting suicide. All very professional, all very supportive, in a colleaguey sort of way.'

'You're reaching, Maxwell,' Graham sneered.

'You were, of course, aided and abetted in this by your less-than-able henchman, Jeremy Tubbs. You bailed him out, literally, years ago, from a potentially sordid sex scandal and he owed you one. So I suspect the voice on the tape, suitably distorted electronically, is his.'

'Mr Graham...' Selwyn was frowning, looking at his Housemaster.

'Shut up, John,' Graham said. 'Mr Maxwell is, I fear, clutching at straws.'

'*Endoslung*, John,' Maxwell shouted. 'You're an historian, dammit; what does it mean?'

'Er ... it's the German for the final solution,' Selwyn remembered. 'The Nazi extermination of the Jews.'

'Excellent!' Maxwell clapped. 'You might have gone somewhere if you hadn't had the misfortune to be in Tennyson House. Mr Graham hit upon the final solution for Mr Pardoe. You see, it wasn't really working.' Maxwell was wandering to the steps that led to the stage. 'The porn, the tape, the rumours, the call to the police. Against all the odds, Bill Pardoe was coping as best he could. He might survive a campaign like that and he had, what, another fifteen years to go in the job? Mr Graham couldn't wait that long. So he hatched a plan. And his timing was immaculate. On the afternoon after Bill Pardoe's body was found I overheard a sweet little conversation in the library from some Year 9 ... er ... sorry ... Lower Fifth kids, I believe. They were speculating on who might have pushed the poor bastard off the roof and one of them said, "There's only one of them in the clear. Mr Graham. He's the only one not here." How true. Mr Graham was miles to the south-east, kipping peacefully under the eaves of my very dear friend Mrs Sylvia Matthews, Matron of Leighford High. What an alibi. But he didn't need to be here himself, did he Cassandra?'

'Look,' Selwyn said. 'What's going on?'

'Shafting, John.' Maxwell had reached the stage. 'You, Ape, Splinter, even dear old Cassandra, the ice-maiden of Austen House. You've all been shafted by Mr Graham here.'

'All right,' the Housemaster was on his feet. 'That's probably enough, I think. Arbiters, do we have a decision?'

'Oh, but you haven't indulged me yet, Tony. Not fully. Cassandra here is such a consummate actress. A woman for all seasons. One minute she's a poor little heroine, a fragile Joan of Arc battling against the evil bully John Selwyn. Her girlies whoop and shout for her and sad little misfits like Janet Boyce cry. The next minute she's shagging John Selwyn in the boat-house – and offering me the same services, by the way.'

'Shut your fucking mouth,' the girl hissed, standing up now, her face a mask of fury.

'You almost certainly made the same offer at least to Jeremy Tubbs, didn't you? That's how you got Pardoe up on the roof that night. You and Tubbsy acted out a little charade in the quad. You'd sowed the seeds earlier, at Mr Graham's suggestion. What did you do? Go and see Pardoe? Turn on the water-works? "Oh, Mr Pardoe" – it was a damn good Cassandra James – "Mr Tubbs keeps pestering me. He's threatened to come to Austen tonight, to take me to the boathouse" and...'

'Bastard!' Cassandra flew at Maxwell, all teeth and claws. Graham clicked his fingers and Ape and Splinter leapt up to hold her back. 'Enough!' he barked and she stood still, spitting blood, but not moving.

'Very impressive,' Maxwell nodded, eyebrows raised. 'I could use you with Nine Eff Twenty-Four last thing of a Friday afternoon. So Mr Pardoe was primed, ready, on the look out. It was stupid of me, really. I thought you and Tubbsy were putting on a show for me. Then I realized – it was for Pardoe. Pardoe's room was directly below mine. He had the same view out of his window that I did. Wicked, evil Tubbsy dragging poor Cassandra to a fate worse than death.'

'Tell him he's talking bollocks, Cassandra!' Selwyn shouted, pale under the lights and shaking.

Nothing.

'Oh, but I'm not, John. Look at her. Look at her face. She knows I'm right. She left poor deluded Tubbsy back in the quad with ... what? The promise of a grope later? Then she doubled up to Pardoe's corridor, hovering just long enough to let him see her. He followed her up to the roof. It's odd how sound distorts up there. It sounded like scrabbling in the wainscoting, rats in the attic. It was Cassandra on her way to the place of execution. It was Pardoe, following like a lamb to the slaughter. Once up there, what could be easier? There's a chimney on that side of the roof – I know; I've looked. Plenty of space for a slim young filly like you to hide, Cassandra. Bill's up there, still in his jammies, poor bugger. Rather crankily, when he saw the scene in the quad, he just grabbed the nearest overcoat he'd got, his gown. But he didn't put any shoes on. All you had to do was wait until he was near the parapet and ... push.'

There was a silence in the auditorium.

'No.' It was John Selwyn's voice. 'No, it's not true.'

Maxwell was alongside the lad now. He laid a gentle hand on his shoulder. 'Yes, it is, John,' he said softly. 'You know it is. You'd put all this together, hadn't you? You'd seen through Svengali here for the devious, murderous bastard he is.'

Graham rose to his feet, looking Maxwell in the face.

'That's why you rang me, wasn't it? Asking me to come for the debate? You wanted to talk. Only Mr Graham found out, didn't he? You were wavering. You,' Maxwell patted the shoulder, 'the brightest and best.'

John Selwyn was crying softly.

'You're pathetic,' Cassandra sneered and turned away, folding her arms tightly across her breasts.

'You ran,' Maxwell went on. 'Where, God knows. But you had to get away. That rattled you, Tony, didn't it? For the first time last night I saw you confused, worried. You, Ape, Splinter, you really didn't know where he'd gone. Then you found him. And you could probably shut him up. Honour of the House and all that. And anyway, he didn't know the exact details, any more than Ape and Splinter did.'

Maxwell was wandering the stage, watched intently by them all except Cassandra, who had resolutely turned her back. He was pointing at the rows of videos that lined the far wall. 'What really gave it away was all this,' he said. 'When you invited me for the screening of *The Witchfinder General* I took a little peek at your collection. And three of them just leapt out at me. There was *Dead Poets Society* of course, an over-rated little number with Robin Williams as the schoolmaster exhorting his pupils to "seize the day". Well, that was Mr Graham here, wasn't it? One of those mercurial one-offs, a charismatic teacher who is, God knows, so rare in the profession today.' Maxwell turned to face him. 'Tony, you could have been so good. But these days people kill each other for a mobile phone, for a pair of trainers. Why not kill for something worthwhile, like a House? Then there was a real little oddity in your Film Soc collection called *Unmann, Wittering and Zigo* – Paramount, I think you'll find, 1971. Naïve young teacher David Hemmings discovers that his predecessor was murdered – killed by the boys – in a British private school. The spooky thing is that the eponymous heroes never appear – Hemmings just reads their names out at registration, but they're never there.' He turned to face the little company on stage. 'But here you are; John, Ape, Splinter – Unmann, Wittering and Zigo. And finally, a creepy little number called *Child's Play* – oh, not that many-sequelled tosh involving a rather awful animated doll, but something again

391

from Paramount. It could have been a blueprint for what's happened at Grimond's. James Mason is Bill Pardoe. If I remember rightly, malevolent old Robert Preston is you, Tony. In that, of course, the boys do the killing. And that, Unmann, Wittering and Zigo, is exactly what Mr Graham has in mind for you tonight. You are all going to kill me. You've already shown me what a fine, ritualistic and symbolic send off I'll have – the carrying of the coffin across the quad. Where do you keep that, by the way? But your real problem tonight is ... how are you going to get me in it? The coffin was empty before. But a third killing ... boys, you really are chancing your arms.'

Ape and Splinter were standing next to Graham, their fists flexing, their faces set. But Ape was blinking and Splinter glancing nervously at Graham. Selwyn was still in his chair, face in his hands. Maxwell walked up to the pair. 'Which one of you bastards,' he asked, 'tried to drive a pencil into my brain in the rugger match the other day?'

There was a sudden thud and crash at the auditorium doors and the room was alive with uniformed police, thumping down the stairs to the stage. Graham tried to run, but there was no escape to left or right. Jacquie was alongside Maxwell who had dropped down to floor level again. He lifted his shapeless tweed hat from his coat and with it the mobile phone underneath.

'The hat, Ape,' he waved it at the boy. 'If you're going to frisk somebody – don't forget the hat.'

One by one the characters on the stage were cuffed to officers and led away. Cassandra, snarling and spitting, Selwyn in tears, Ape and Splinter bewildered and confused. Only Tony Graham stood tall, still in his mortar board, still in his gown.

'Brilliant timing, Woman Policeman,' Maxwell smiled, kissing her cheek. 'I guessed when you got my call and heard snatches of conversation, you'd realise something was wrong. Much later, though, and I'd have had to hack my way out with a copy of the *Times Educational Supplement*.'

'Thank Jeremy Tubbs,' she told him. 'And, indirectly, DCI West.'

'What?'

'Tubbs confessed to being involved in the death of Pardoe, working with that foul girl and Tony Graham to get him up to the roof. When he accidentally dropped the name Arbiters to you he panicked and ran, fearing what they'd do to him or you would find out. It took all of Tony Graham's persuasion apparently to get him back here, to the last place any of us would think of looking for him. West was about to get here with the cavalry when Henry's balloon went up on the paedophile tape.'

'But...'

'Max.' She held up his mobile phone and waved it, shaking her head. 'If you're going to do your super-sleuth bit, at least switch the bloody thing on!'

'You'll be on your way back, then, Henry?' Chief Superintendent Mason was sitting across the desk from Detective Chief Inspector Hall. 'Case closed.'

Hall nodded. 'Never much fun, is it?' he asked. 'One of your own?'

'No,' Mason shook his head. Instinctively, he glanced down to his right wrist and saw, just for a fleeting moment, the scar on Mark West's arm. The one caused by the bullet that was meant for him.

'And all this started with an anonymous tip-off about Grimond's?'

'And other things,' Mason sighed. 'Rumours, little changes in West's behaviour. It will all be in the final report. Andy Love was on to him, tracking him around Petersfield on his nightly wanderings. Course, with a bike, he couldn't do much.'

'So West killed Love to shut him up?'

Mason shrugged. 'Looks that way. He hasn't coughed yet, but he will. I thought Love's cover as Robinson was pretty good. Wonder how Mark sussed it.' He stood up, hand outstretched. 'I want to thank you, Henry,' he said. 'It's a lonely road you've travelled. I'm afraid I had to tell Mark a few fibs.'

'Oh?'

'He was getting persistent the other night, about you, I mean. I told him you'd been seconded from West Sussex because you were under suspicion there. That relaxed him, made him careless, maybe; I don't know. If you ever want a change of air, Henry, I could use a man like you here in Hampshire.'

Hall almost smiled. 'No you couldn't, David,' he said.

Mason *did* smile. 'You know what gets up my nose most about this stinking business?' he asked. 'When Mark West was going around on the prowl, picking up those kids, he had the gall to use my name. "Call me Dave". What a complete shit!'

Hall saw himself out.

Jacquie Carpenter took over George Sheffield's outer office late that night to complete the preliminary stages at least of the paperwork. She'd made the phone calls; DI Berman would be over at first light with half his team to co-ordinate things that end. Now that Mark West had been closed down there was no need to keep Grimond's as a no-go area. She'd let the Hampshire top brass deal with the Grimond's people. Didn't their Chief Constable get pissed regularly with their Chairman of Governors? The network would take over, rally round as it always did. No doubt some parents would accept Sir Arthur Wilkins' offer of waived fees. In time, the world would forget.

Peter Maxwell wandered by the lake in the wee, small hours. It was cold for spring and his breath smoked out. He felt chilled, numbed, vowing to himself to master the bewildering array of buttons on his mobile phone.

He didn't see her at first, the solid, dumpy shape in the cedars that lined the hill. Then she was walking towards him, in a hood and long trailing cloak like the Scottish widow in the telly advert.

'Janet.' He looked at her. 'Shouldn't you be in Northanger?'

'Northanger's lonely,' the girl said. 'Cassie's gone.'

'Yes,' Maxwell nodded, his hands in his pockets. 'Yes, I know. And I'm sorry.'

'Are you?' Janet asked him. 'Are you really? Mr

Robinson was sorry.'

'Mr Robinson?' Maxwell indulged her.

'He raped Cassandra.'

'What?'

'Down there. In the boat-house. I saw them together.' She was crying softly, the salt tears trickling into her mouth.

'Did you, Janet?' Maxwell was close to her now.

'I couldn't let him do that,' the girl sobbed. 'Defile her like that. She was mine.'

'Yes,' Maxwell said softly. 'Yes, of course. I see.'

'No, you don't!' Janet shrieked. 'None of you! Men! All you want to do is fuck us, pull us about. You don't love us. None of you. You don't know what love is.'

A shiver was running up Maxwell's spine as realization kicked in with all its gut-wrenching force. 'Is that why you killed him, Janet? Mr Robinson? Is that why you hit him with the oar?'

'It wasn't difficult,' she said, sniffing back the tears. 'He was always asking questions, sticking his nose in. So I told him something was going on. Something to do with Mr Pardoe. There were all kinds of rumours. He seemed interested in that. I said I had to see him down by the lake, by the boat-house, that I had evidence for him and I couldn't see him in school time. It was too dangerous. It had to be in the early hours, like it is now. I just took an oar from Northanger and waited down there, in the bushes. He didn't see me at all. I just hit him. Just the once. There was hardly a splash when he fell in. But it served him right. It showed him he couldn't do what he did to dear Cassie.'

'But he didn't, Janet,' Maxwell said.

'I saw them.'

'No, darling,' Maxwell was shaking his head. 'What you saw was Cassandra and John Selwyn.'

'No,' she was shaking her head too. 'No, it couldn't have been John. Oh, I knew John loved her too, like I do. But he wouldn't touch her. She wouldn't let him.'

'Janet...' Maxwell reached out a hand.

'You!' she hissed, her eyes rolling in the dim light. 'You wanted to do it to her as well, didn't you? Well, you can't. Not now.'

'Janet.' He let the hand fall. 'I don't know what will happen to Cassandra...'

'Neither do I,' the girl sobbed. 'But I know what will happen to you!'

The cloak fell away, suddenly revealing the girl in all her plump nakedness. But Peter Maxwell wasn't looking at her full breasts, or the curve of her thighs. He was looking at the knife coming at him through the air. He felt it bang and slice across his cheek, like the sabre cut of the schlager, felt the blood hot on his face. Then he'd caught the girl's hand and twisted it, pulling her towards him and wrenching the blade out of her grasp. There was no fight in Janet Boyce. She crumpled to the grass, her pale naked body convulsed in shuddering sobs. Maxwell put the knife in his pocket, wiped the blood from his face and knelt beside the crying child, wrapping her up in her cloak.

The first birds were stirring in the cedars. It was a new Grimond's day.

'Lights out in the dorm,' Maxwell whispered. 'All's well.'

Dr George Sheffield reversed his car carefully into the allocated space at the municipal tip. First he opened the boot in the early morning and threw his gown and mortar board into the skip marked 'General'. Then he opened the suitcase, the one with the tapes sent to him over many months by Mark West, snapped it shut again and locked it. Then that too sailed through the air to land in the rubbish where it belonged. He revved the engine and drove away.

Dierdre Lessing, Senior Mistress, was standing at the window in the staffroom of Leighford High again that Wednesday afternoon, just in time to see Peter Maxwell, his face neatly dressed from Casualty, walking up the steps to the front door.

'Good God,' she muttered. 'What's he done to himself now?' She reached for the yellow memo pad that was never very far from her person and made a note. 'Must ask Maxwell what on earth he hoped to accomplish in the private sector. Judging by the look of him, he must have been in way over his head. Met his match at last.'

The publishers hope that this book has given you enjoyable reading. Large Print Books are especially designed to be as easy to see and hold as possible. If you wish a complete list of our books please ask at your local library or write directly to:

Magna Large Print Books
Magna House, Long Preston,
Skipton, North Yorkshire.
BD23 4ND

This Large Print Book for the partially sighted, who cannot read normal print, is published under the auspices of

THE ULVERSCROFT FOUNDATION

THE ULVERSCROFT FOUNDATION

... we hope that you have enjoyed this Large Print Book. Please think for a moment about those people who have worse eyesight problems than you ... and are unable to even read or enjoy Large Print, without great difficulty.

You can help them by sending a donation, large or small to:

**The Ulverscroft Foundation,
1, The Green, Bradgate Road,
Anstey, Leicestershire, LE7 7FU,
England.**
or request a copy of our brochure for more details.

The Foundation will use all your help to assist those people who are handicapped by various sight problems and need special attention.

Thank you very much for your help.